JUST BEYOND™

MONSTROSITY

Published by

kaboom!™

More Books in the

JUST BEYOND™

Graphic Novel Series

THE SCARE SCHOOL

THE HORROR AT HAPPY LANDINGS

WELCOME TO BEAST ISLAND

MONSTROSITY

JUST BEYOND ™

MONSTROSITY

Written by
R.L. Stine

Illustrated by
Irene Flores
with additional inks by **Lea Caballero**

Colored by
Joana Lafuente

Lettered by
Mike Fiorentino

Cover by
Julian Totino Tedesco

Just Beyond created by
R.L. Stine

Designer
Chelsea Roberts

Editors
Sophie Philips-Roberts and Bryce Carlson

JUST BEYOND: MONSTROSITY, October 2021. Published by KaBOOM!, a division of Boom Entertainment, Inc. Just Beyond is ™ & © 2021 R.L. Stine. All rights reserved. KaBOOM!™ and the KaBOOM! logo are trademarks of Boom Entertainment, Inc., registered in various countries and categories. All characters, events, and institutions depicted herein are fictional. Any similarity between any of the names, characters, persons, events, and/or institutions in this publication to actual names, characters, and persons, whether living or dead, events, and/or institutions is unintended and purely coincidental. KaBOOM! does not read or accept unsolicited submissions of ideas, stories, or artwork.

BOOM! Studios, 5670 Wilshire Boulevard, Suite 400, Los Angeles, CA 90036-5679. Printed in China. First Printing.

ISBN: 978-1-68415-697-9, eISBN: 978-1-64668-241-6

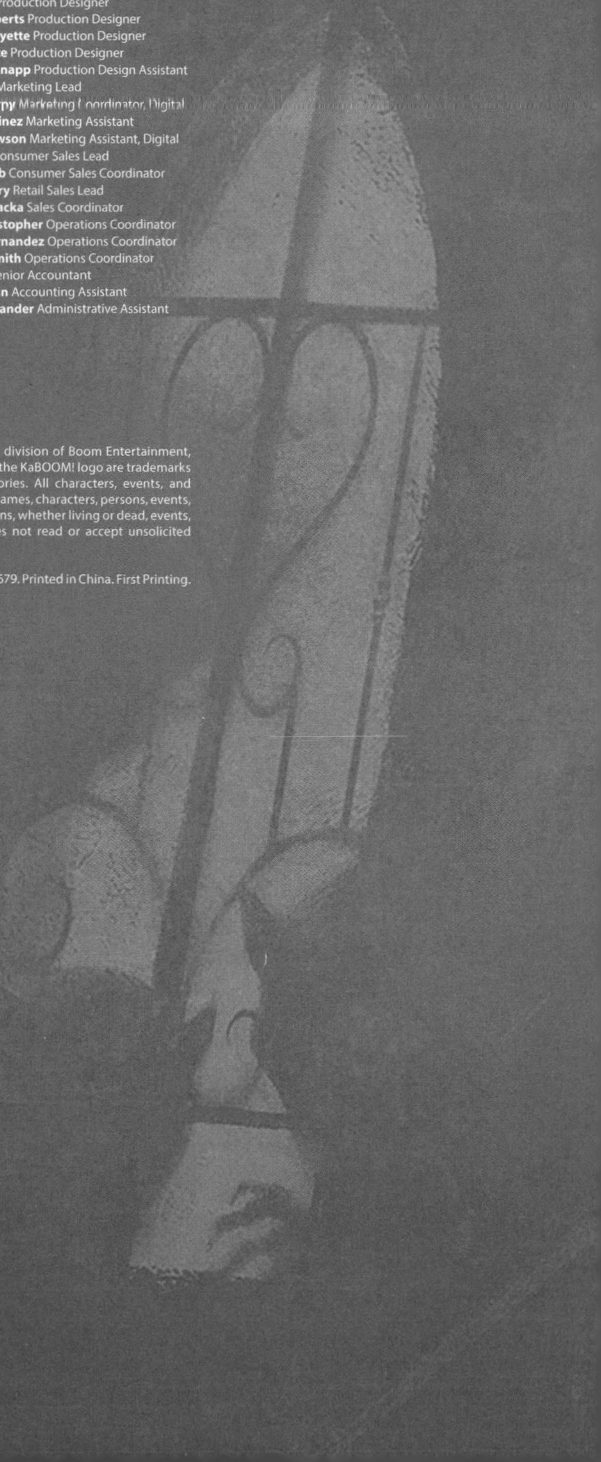

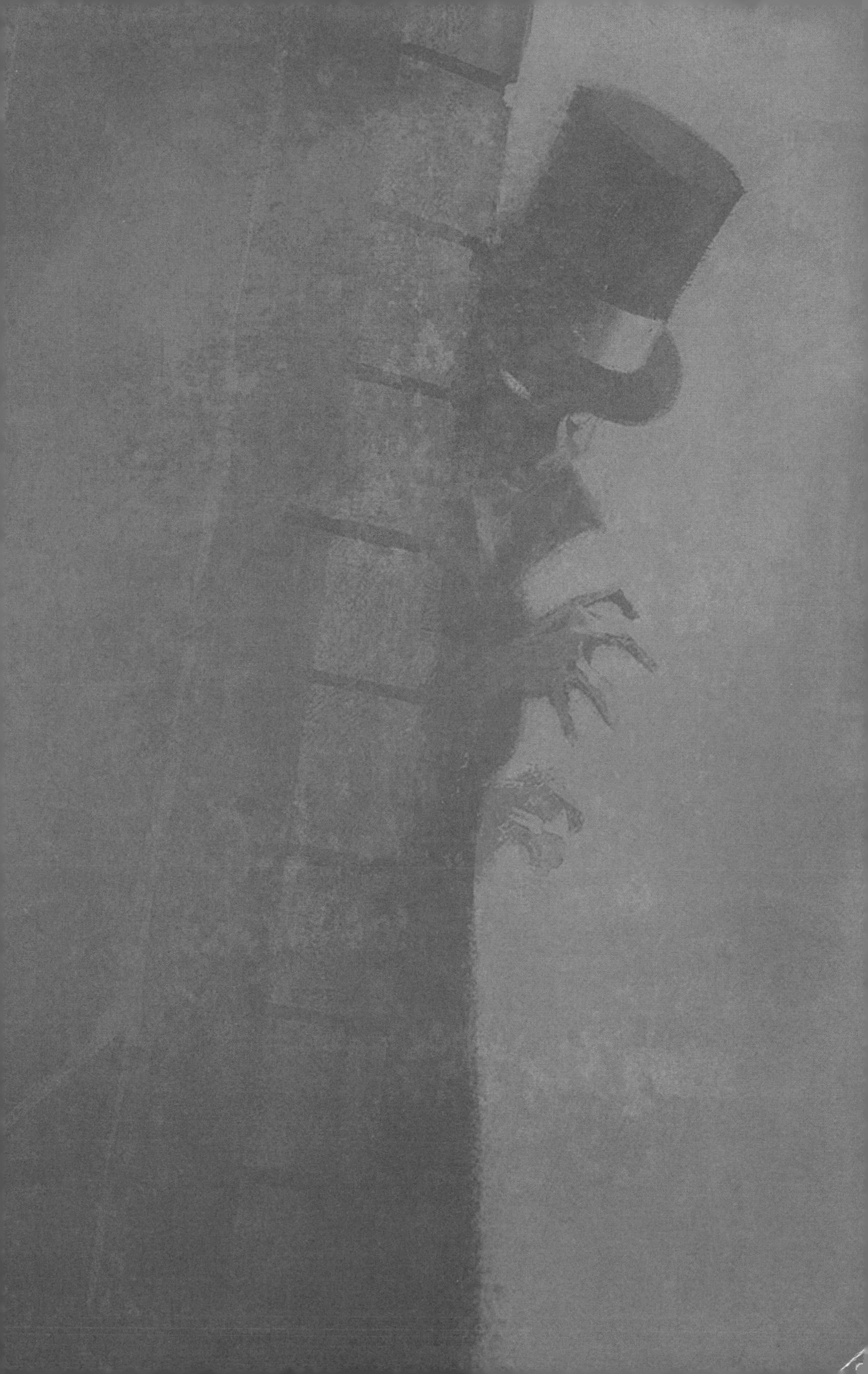

PART
ONE

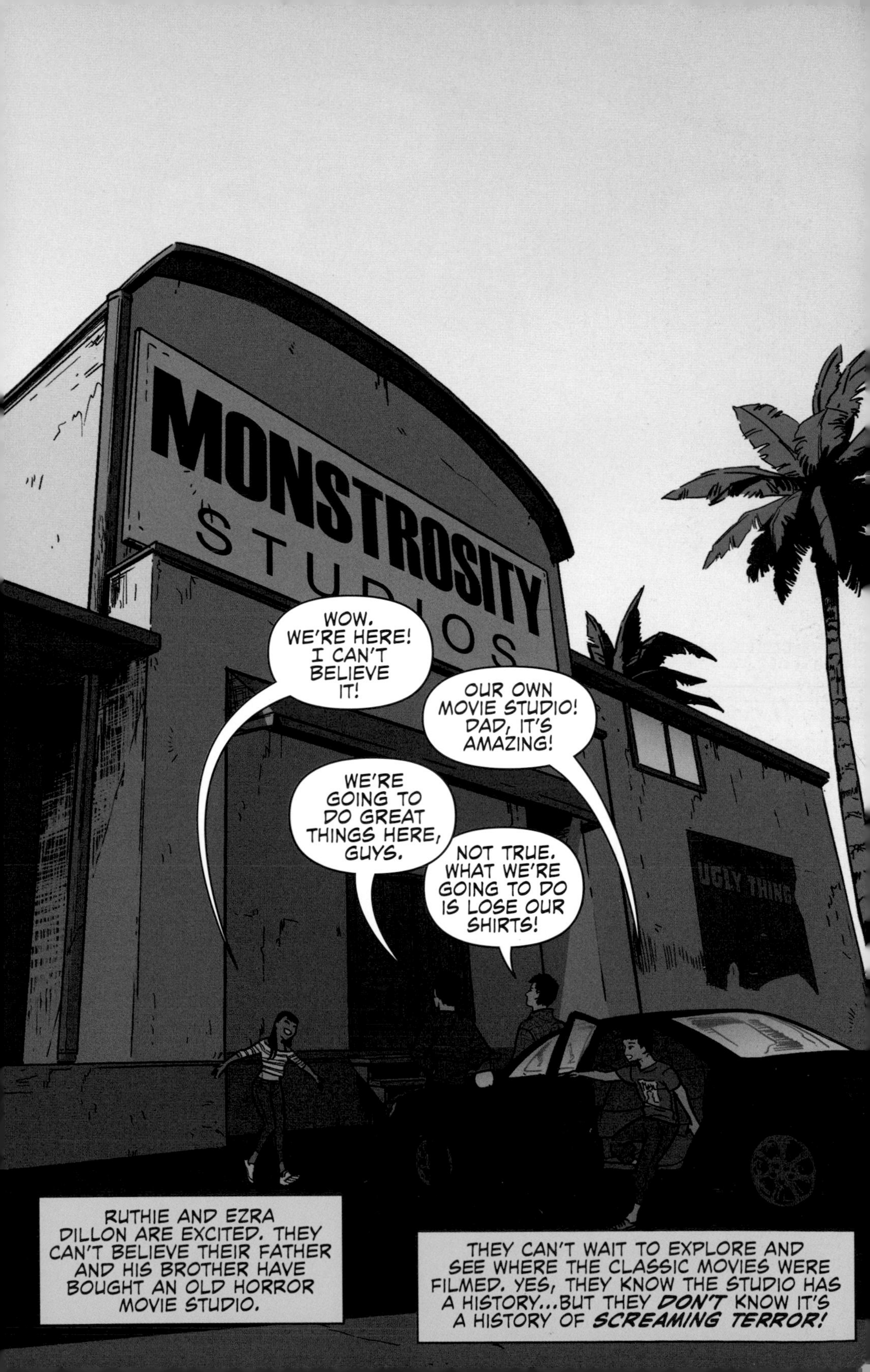
MONSTROSITY STUDIOS
WOW. WE'RE HERE! I CAN'T BELIEVE IT!
OUR OWN MOVIE STUDIO! DAD, IT'S AMAZING!
WE'RE GOING TO DO GREAT THINGS HERE, GUYS.
NOT TRUE. WHAT WE'RE GOING TO DO IS LOSE OUR SHIRTS!
RUTHIE AND EZRA DILLON ARE EXCITED. THEY CAN'T BELIEVE THEIR FATHER AND HIS BROTHER HAVE BOUGHT AN OLD HORROR MOVIE STUDIO.
THEY CAN'T WAIT TO EXPLORE AND SEE WHERE THE CLASSIC MOVIES WERE FILMED. YES, THEY KNOW THE STUDIO HAS A HISTORY...BUT THEY *DON'T* KNOW IT'S A HISTORY OF *SCREAMING TERROR!*

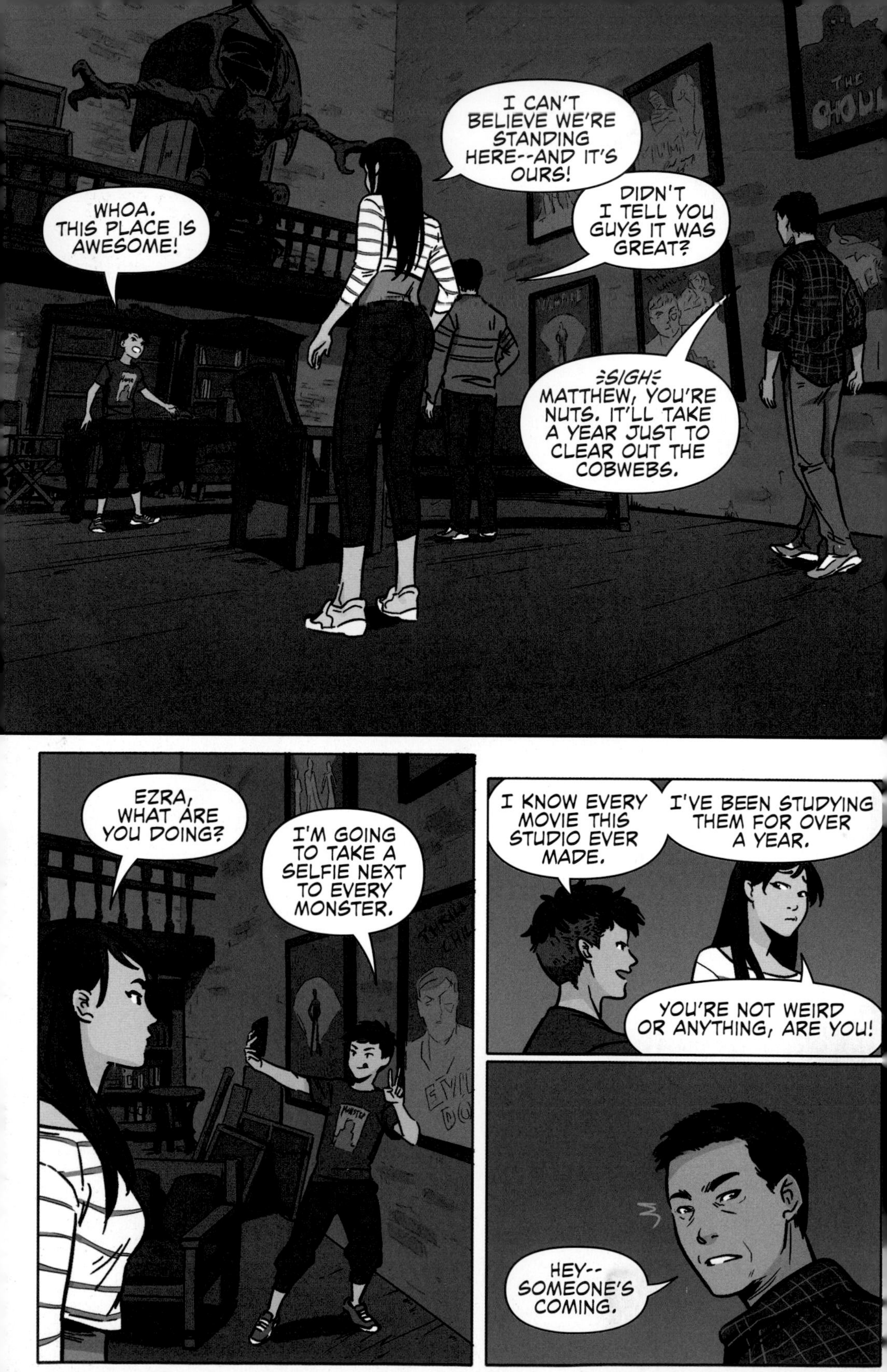
WHOA. THIS PLACE IS AWESOME!
I CAN'T BELIEVE WE'RE STANDING HERE--AND IT'S OURS!
DIDN'T I TELL YOU GUYS IT WAS GREAT?
SIGH MATTHEW, YOU'RE NUTS. IT'LL TAKE A YEAR JUST TO CLEAR OUT THE COBWEBS.
EZRA, WHAT ARE YOU DOING?
I'M GOING TO TAKE A SELFIE NEXT TO EVERY MONSTER.
I KNOW EVERY MOVIE THIS STUDIO EVER MADE.
I'VE BEEN STUDYING THEM FOR OVER A YEAR.
YOU'RE NOT WEIRD OR ANYTHING, ARE YOU!
HEY-- SOMEONE'S COMING.

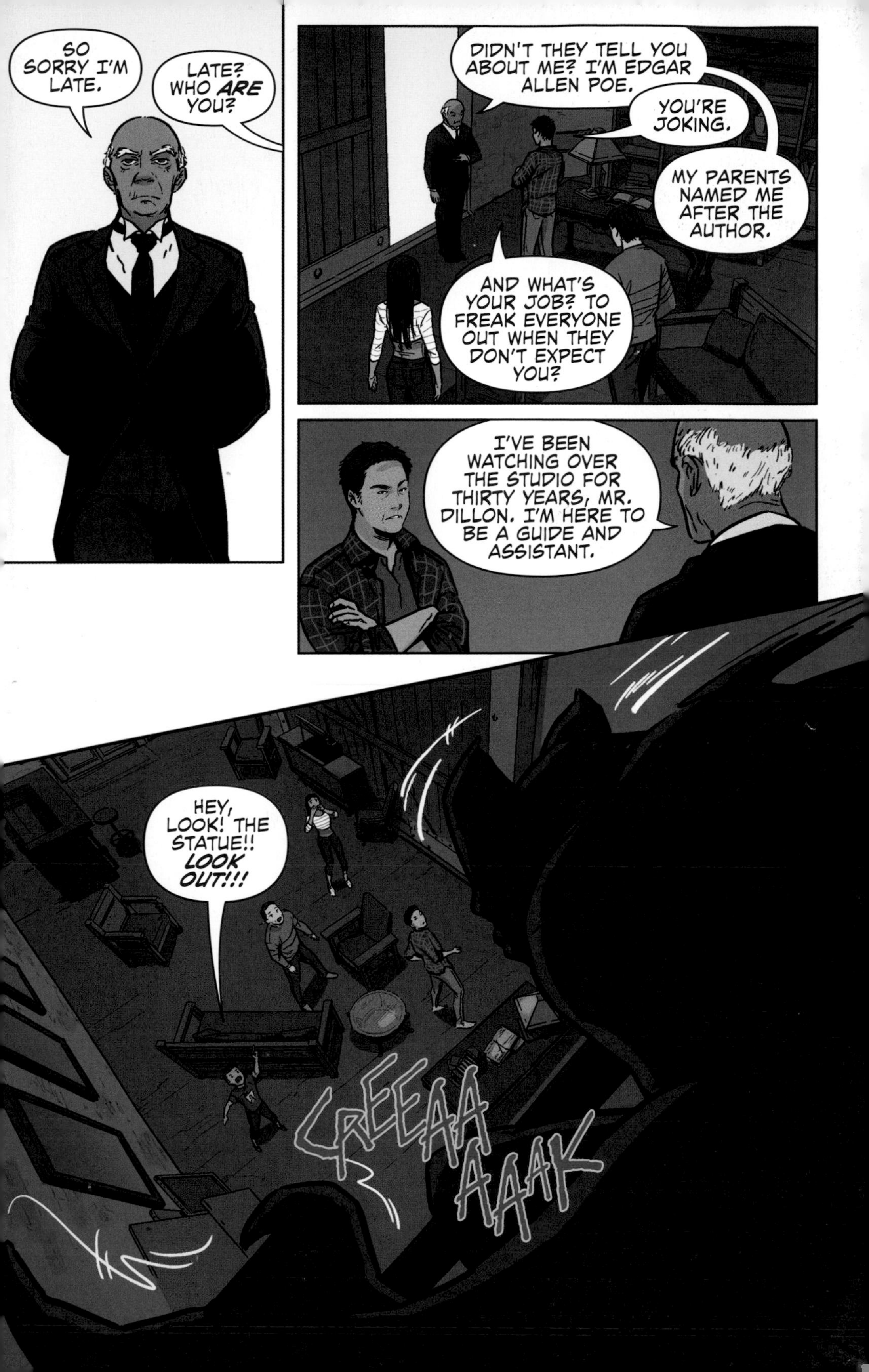
SO SORRY I'M LATE.
LATE? WHO **ARE** YOU?
DIDN'T THEY TELL YOU ABOUT ME? I'M EDGAR ALLEN POE.
YOU'RE JOKING.
MY PARENTS NAMED ME AFTER THE AUTHOR.
AND WHAT'S YOUR JOB? TO FREAK EVERYONE OUT WHEN THEY DON'T EXPECT YOU?
I'VE BEEN WATCHING OVER THE STUDIO FOR THIRTY YEARS, MR. DILLON. I'M HERE TO BE A GUIDE AND ASSISTANT.
HEY, LOOK! THE STATUE!! ***LOOK OUT!!!***
CREEAAAAAK

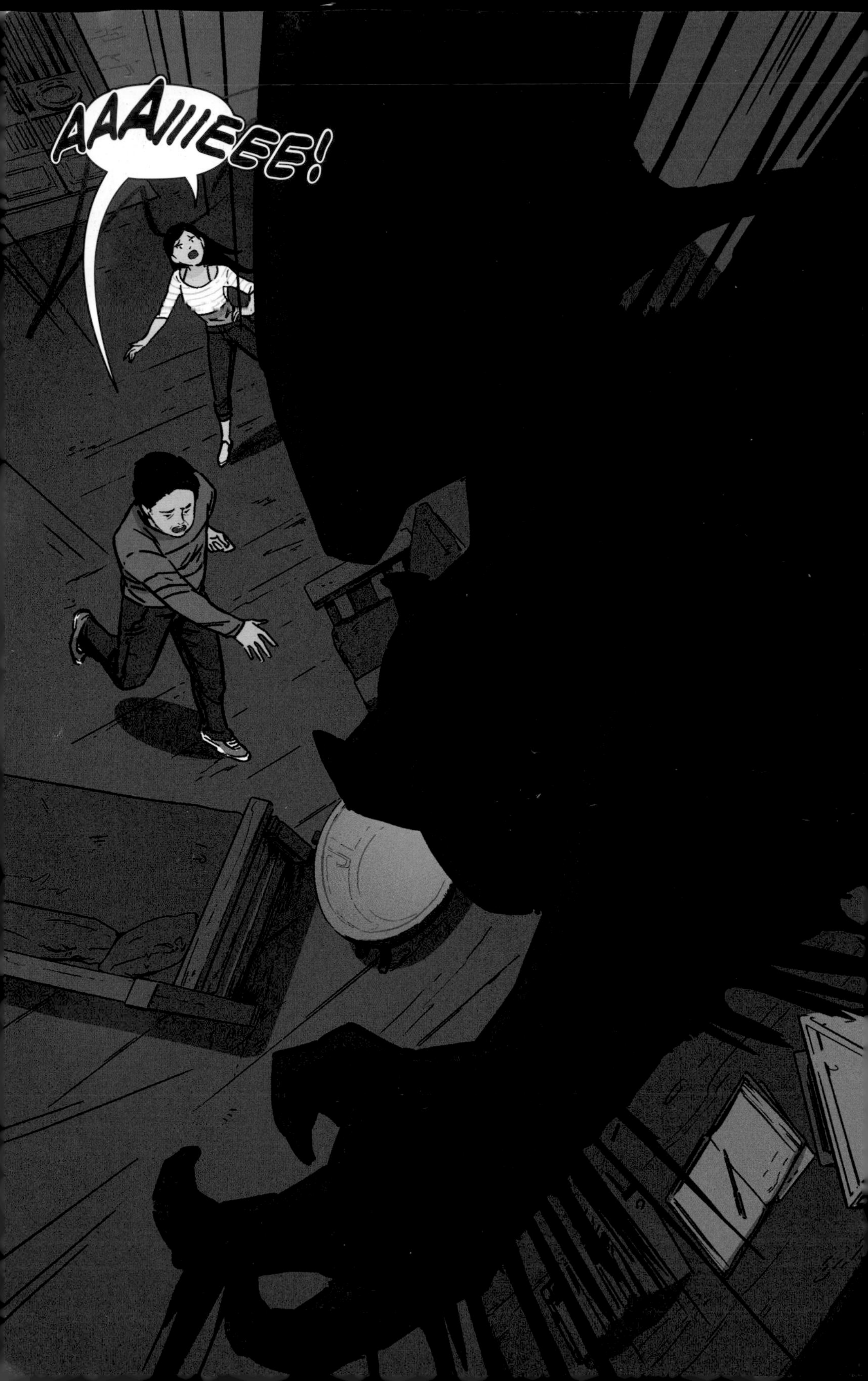
AAAIIIEEEE!

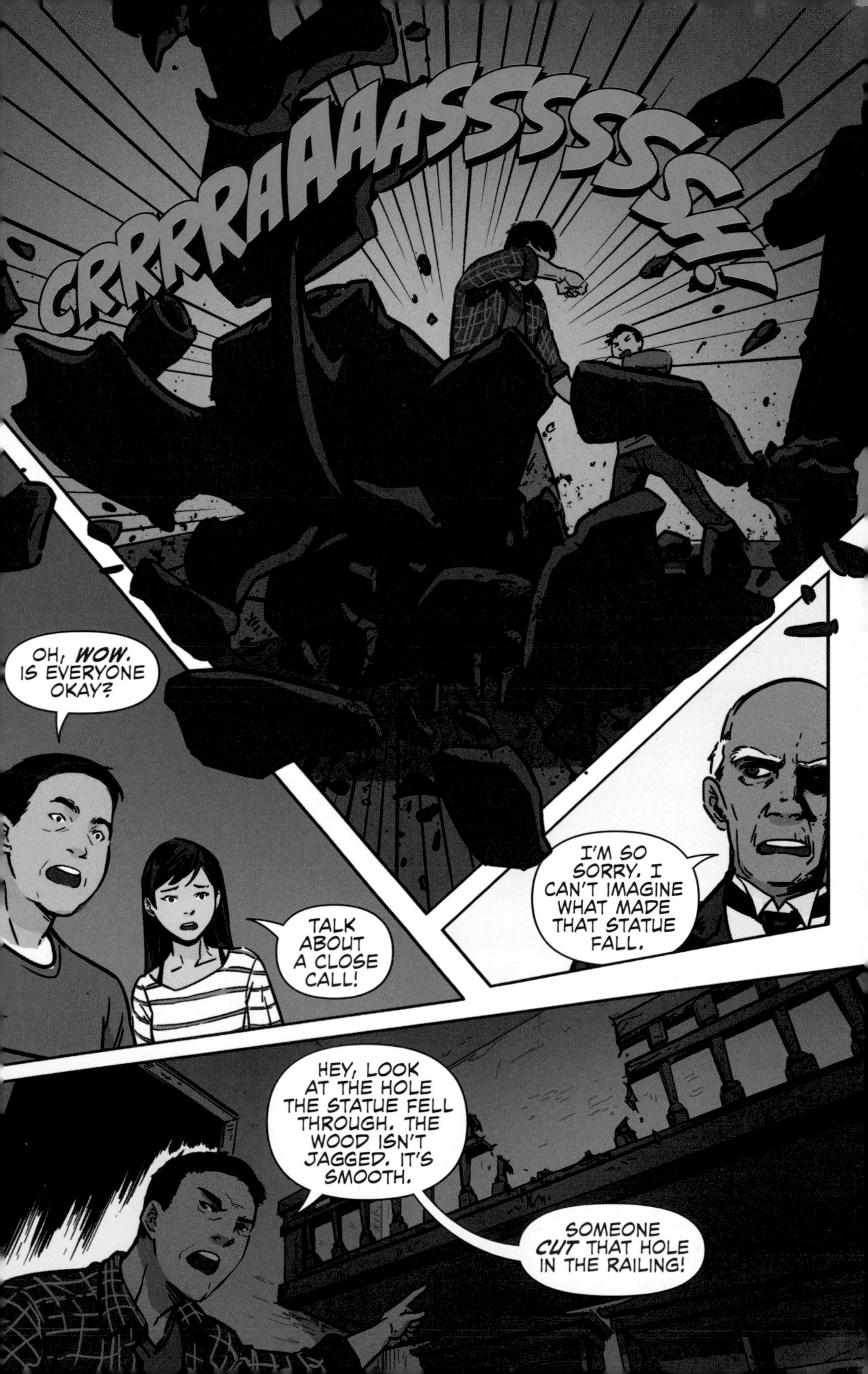
CRRRAAAASSSSSH!
OH, WOW. IS EVERYONE OKAY?
TALK ABOUT A CLOSE CALL!
I'M SO SORRY. I CAN'T IMAGINE WHAT MADE THAT STATUE FALL.
HEY, LOOK AT THE HOLE THE STATUE FELL THROUGH. THE WOOD ISN'T JAGGED. IT'S SMOOTH.
SOMEONE CUT THAT HOLE IN THE RAILING!

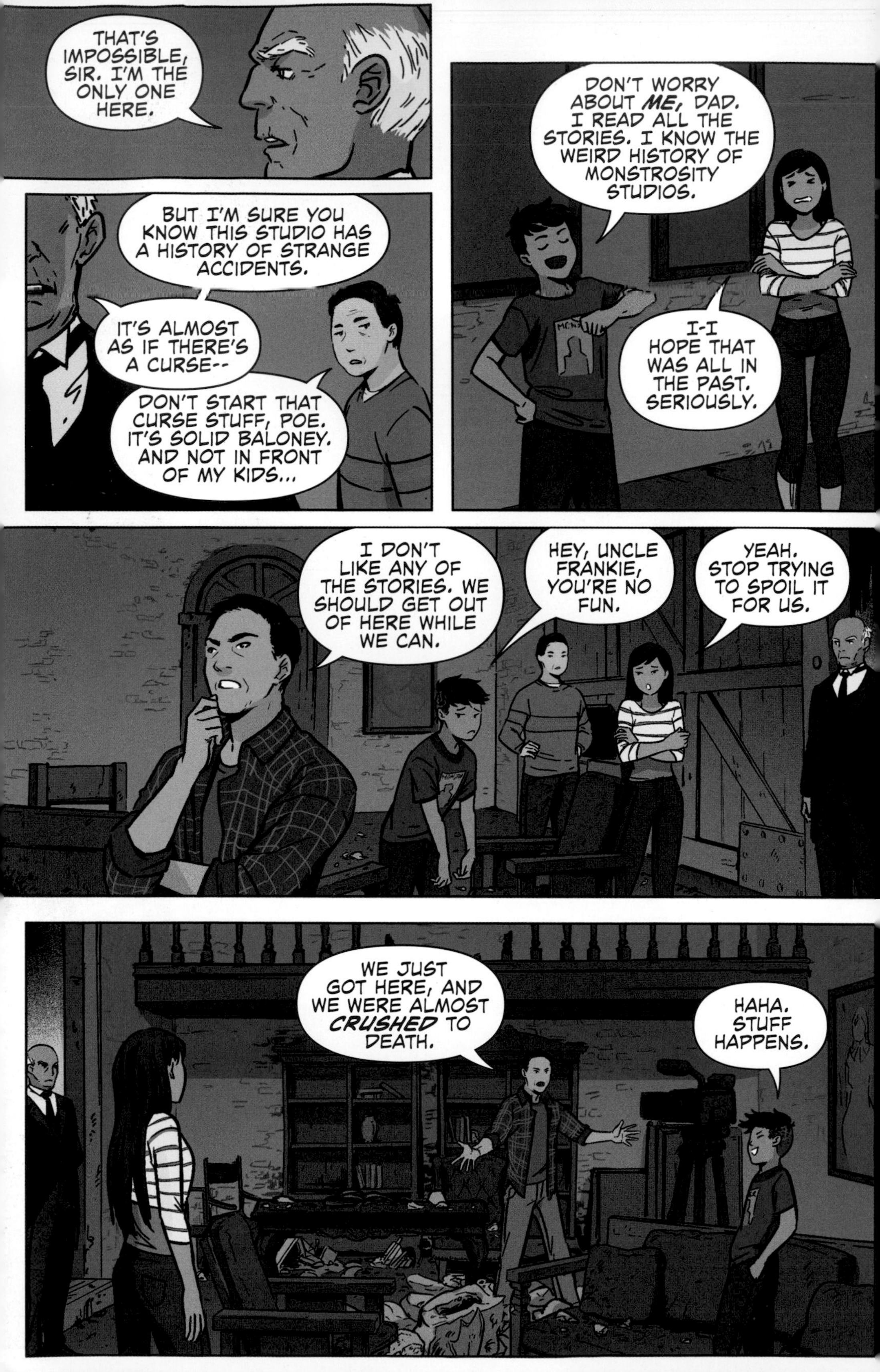
THAT'S IMPOSSIBLE, SIR. I'M THE ONLY ONE HERE.
BUT I'M SURE YOU KNOW THIS STUDIO HAS A HISTORY OF STRANGE ACCIDENTS.
IT'S ALMOST AS IF THERE'S A CURSE--
DON'T START THAT CURSE STUFF, POE. IT'S SOLID BALONEY. AND NOT IN FRONT OF MY KIDS...
DON'T WORRY ABOUT ME, DAD. I READ ALL THE STORIES. I KNOW THE WEIRD HISTORY OF MONSTROSITY STUDIOS.
I-I HOPE THAT WAS ALL IN THE PAST. SERIOUSLY.
I DON'T LIKE ANY OF THE STORIES. WE SHOULD GET OUT OF HERE WHILE WE CAN.
HEY, UNCLE FRANKIE, YOU'RE NO FUN.
YEAH. STOP TRYING TO SPOIL IT FOR US.
WE JUST GOT HERE, AND WE WERE ALMOST CRUSHED TO DEATH.
HAHA. STUFF HAPPENS.

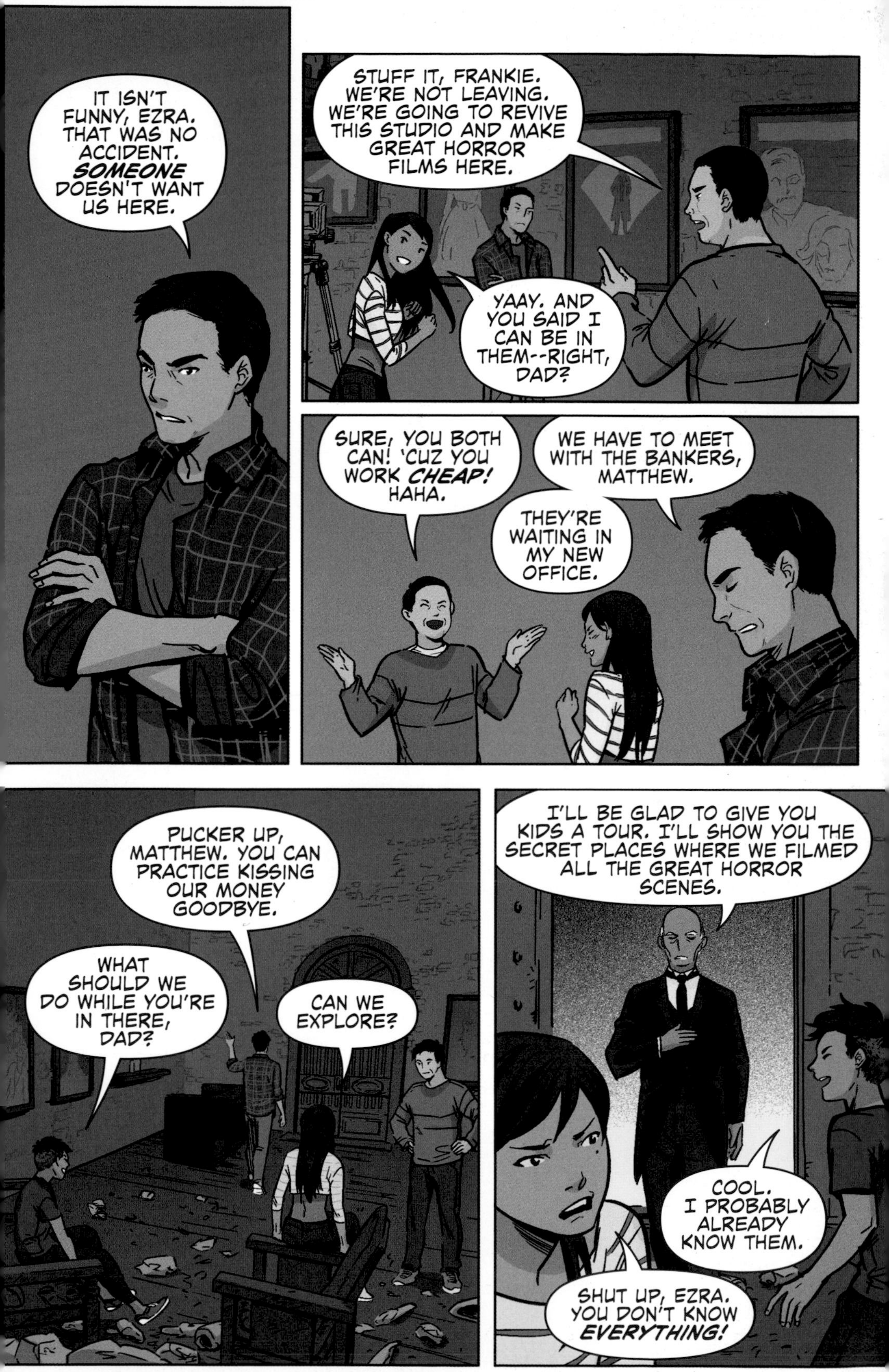
IT ISN'T FUNNY, EZRA. THAT WAS NO ACCIDENT. ***SOMEONE*** DOESN'T WANT US HERE.
STUFF IT, FRANKIE. WE'RE NOT LEAVING. WE'RE GOING TO REVIVE THIS STUDIO AND MAKE GREAT HORROR FILMS HERE.
YAAY. AND YOU SAID I CAN BE IN THEM--RIGHT, DAD?
SURE, YOU BOTH CAN! 'CUZ YOU WORK ***CHEAP!*** HAHA.
WE HAVE TO MEET WITH THE BANKERS, MATTHEW.
THEY'RE WAITING IN MY NEW OFFICE.
PUCKER UP, MATTHEW. YOU CAN PRACTICE KISSING OUR MONEY GOODBYE.
WHAT SHOULD WE DO WHILE YOU'RE IN THERE, DAD?
CAN WE EXPLORE?
I'LL BE GLAD TO GIVE YOU KIDS A TOUR. I'LL SHOW YOU THE SECRET PLACES WHERE WE FILMED ALL THE GREAT HORROR SCENES.
COOL. I PROBABLY ALREADY KNOW THEM.
SHUT UP, EZRA. YOU DON'T KNOW ***EVERYTHING!***

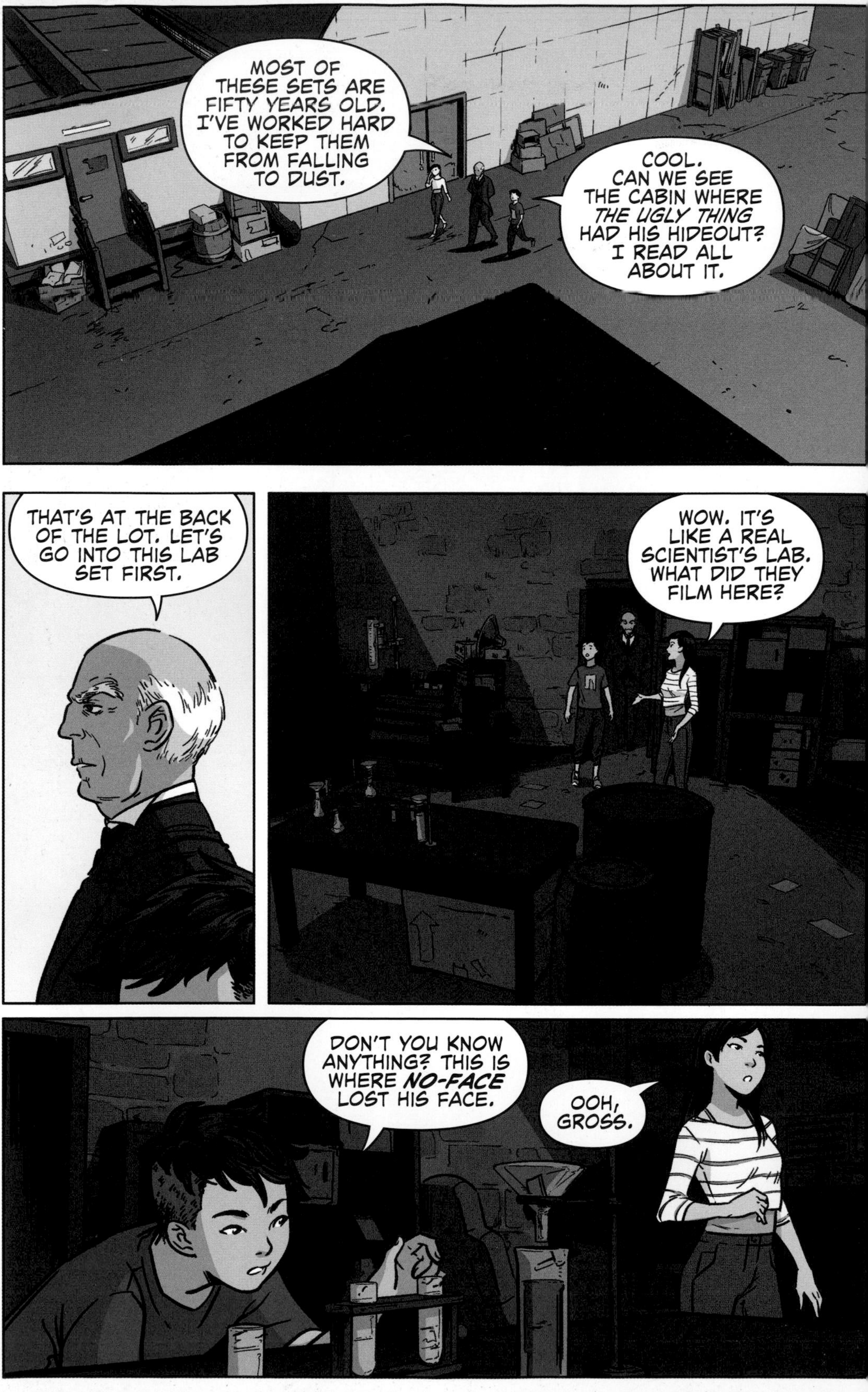
MOST OF THESE SETS ARE FIFTY YEARS OLD. I'VE WORKED HARD TO KEEP THEM FROM FALLING TO DUST.
COOL. CAN WE SEE THE CABIN WHERE *THE UGLY THING* HAD HIS HIDEOUT? I READ ALL ABOUT IT.
THAT'S AT THE BACK OF THE LOT. LET'S GO INTO THIS LAB SET FIRST.
WOW. IT'S LIKE A REAL SCIENTIST'S LAB. WHAT DID THEY FILM HERE?
DON'T YOU KNOW ANYTHING? THIS IS WHERE ***NO-FACE*** LOST HIS FACE.
OOH, GROSS.

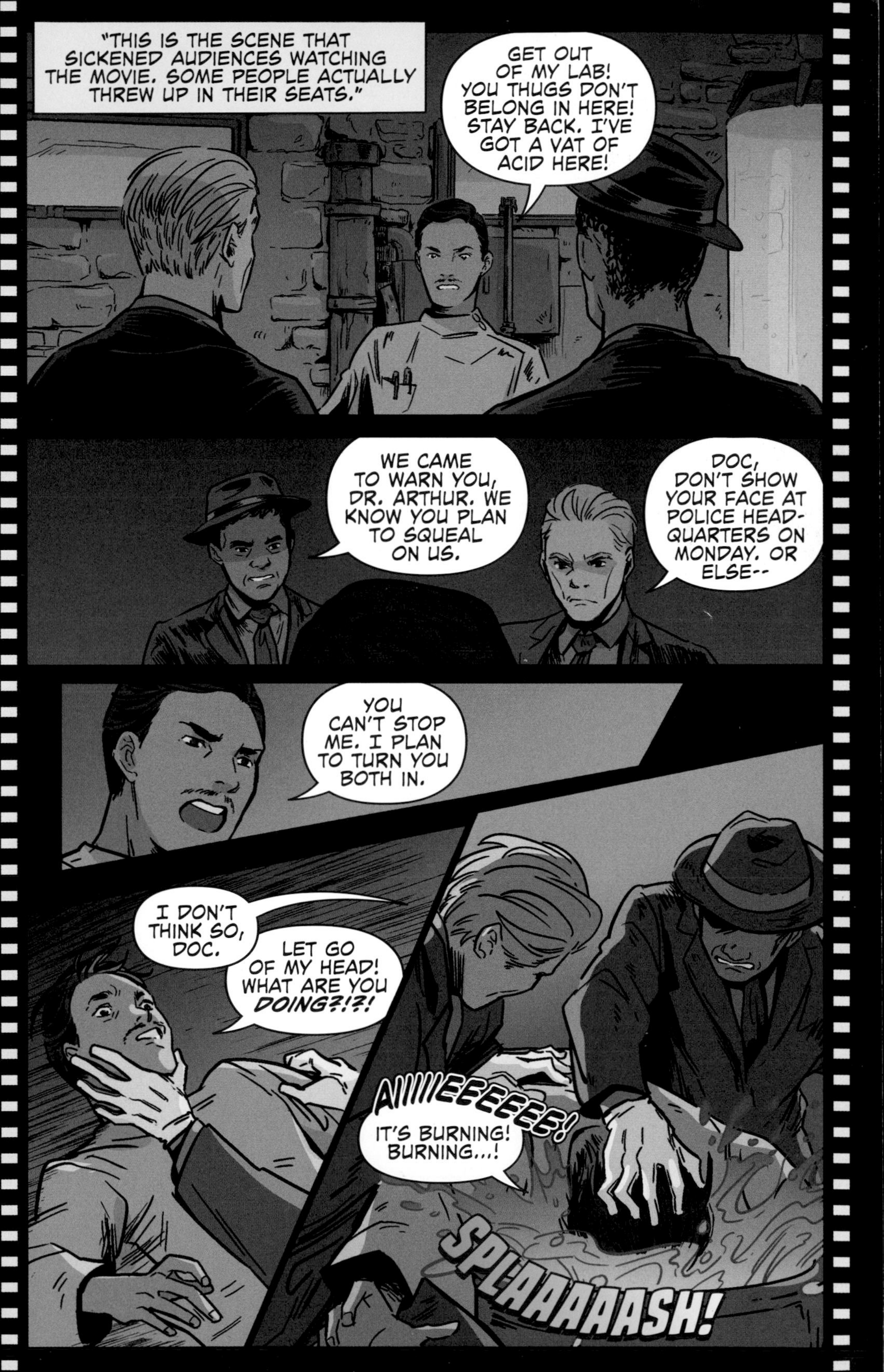
"THIS IS THE SCENE THAT SICKENED AUDIENCES WATCHING THE MOVIE. SOME PEOPLE ACTUALLY THREW UP IN THEIR SEATS."
GET OUT OF MY LAB! YOU THUGS DON'T BELONG IN HERE! STAY BACK. I'VE GOT A VAT OF ACID HERE!
WE CAME TO WARN YOU, DR. ARTHUR. WE KNOW YOU PLAN TO SQUEAL ON US.
DOC, DON'T SHOW YOUR FACE AT POLICE HEAD-QUARTERS ON MONDAY. OR ELSE--
YOU CAN'T STOP ME. I PLAN TO TURN YOU BOTH IN.
I DON'T THINK SO, DOC.
LET GO OF MY HEAD! WHAT ARE YOU *DOING?!?!*
AIIIIEEEEEEE! IT'S BURNING! BURNING...!
SPLAAAAAASH!

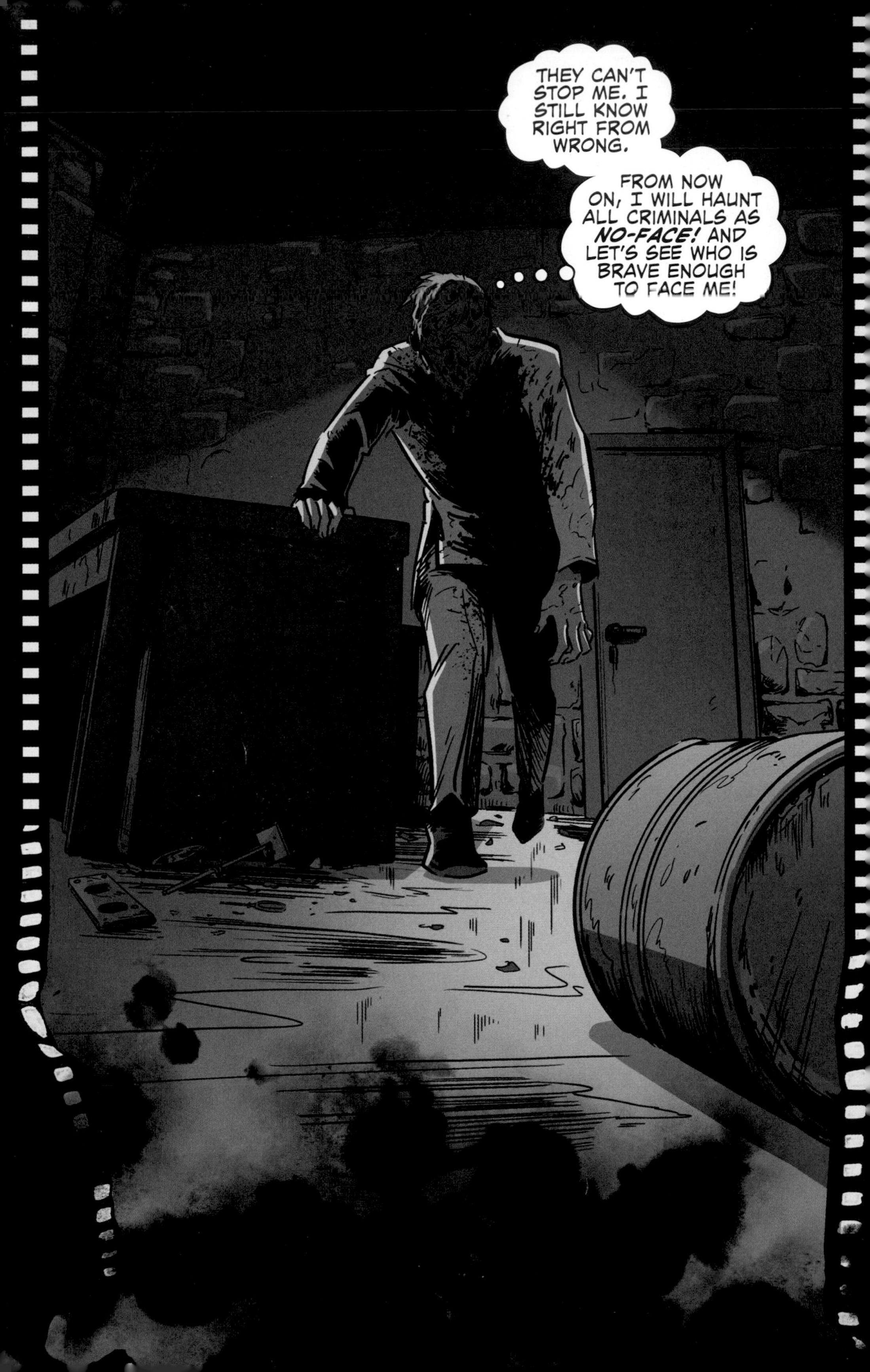
THEY CAN'T STOP ME. I STILL KNOW RIGHT FROM WRONG.
FROM NOW ON, I WILL HAUNT ALL CRIMINALS AS NO-FACE! AND LET'S SEE WHO IS BRAVE ENOUGH TO FACE ME!

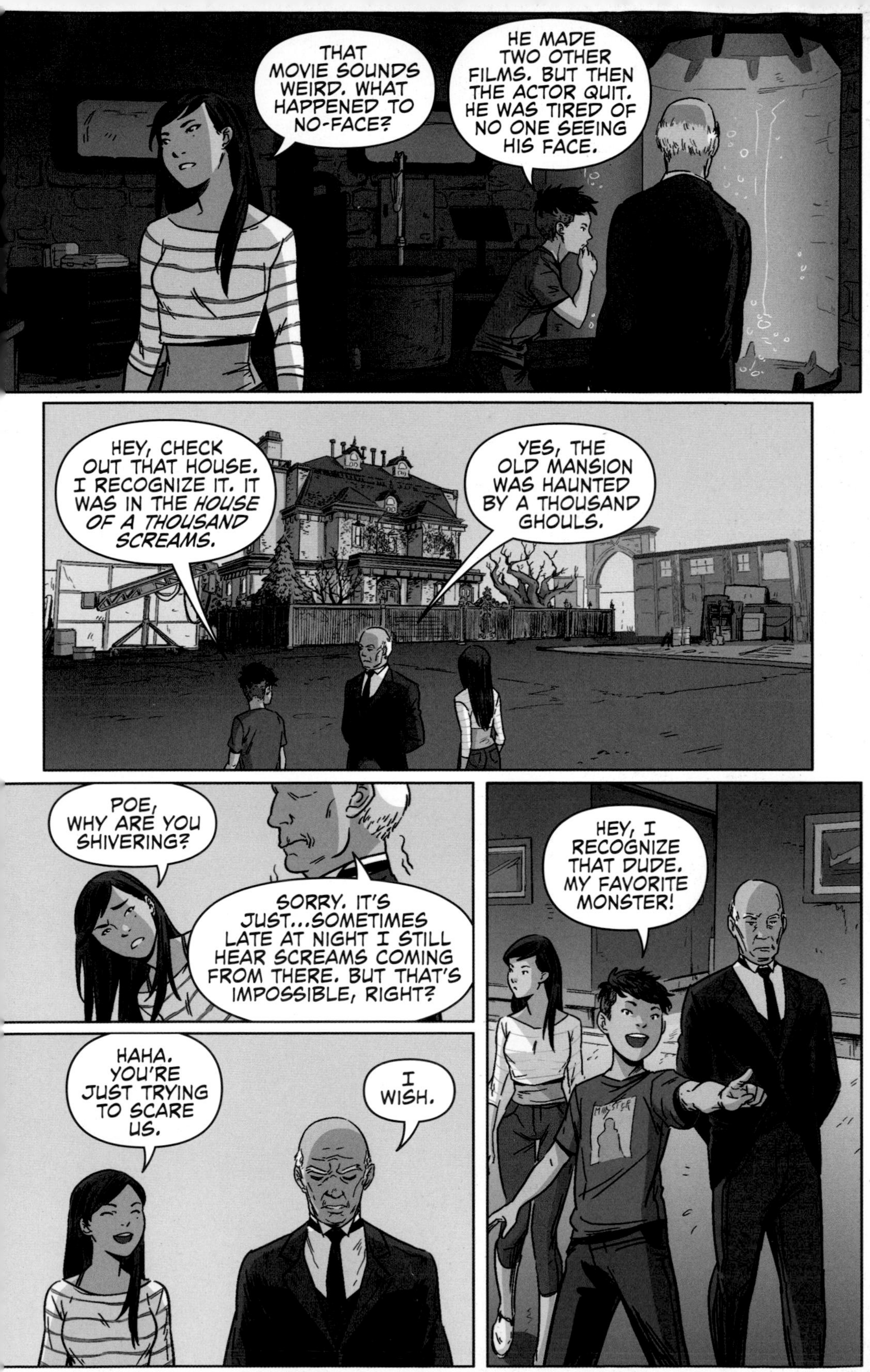
THAT MOVIE SOUNDS WEIRD. WHAT HAPPENED TO NO-FACE?
HE MADE TWO OTHER FILMS. BUT THEN THE ACTOR QUIT. HE WAS TIRED OF NO ONE SEEING HIS FACE.
HEY, CHECK OUT THAT HOUSE. I RECOGNIZE IT. IT WAS IN THE *HOUSE OF A THOUSAND SCREAMS*.
YES, THE OLD MANSION WAS HAUNTED BY A THOUSAND GHOULS.
POE, WHY ARE YOU SHIVERING?
SORRY. IT'S JUST...SOMETIMES LATE AT NIGHT I STILL HEAR SCREAMS COMING FROM THERE. BUT THAT'S IMPOSSIBLE, RIGHT?
HAHA. YOU'RE JUST TRYING TO SCARE US.
I WISH.
HEY, I RECOGNIZE THAT DUDE. MY FAVORITE MONSTER!
MONSTER

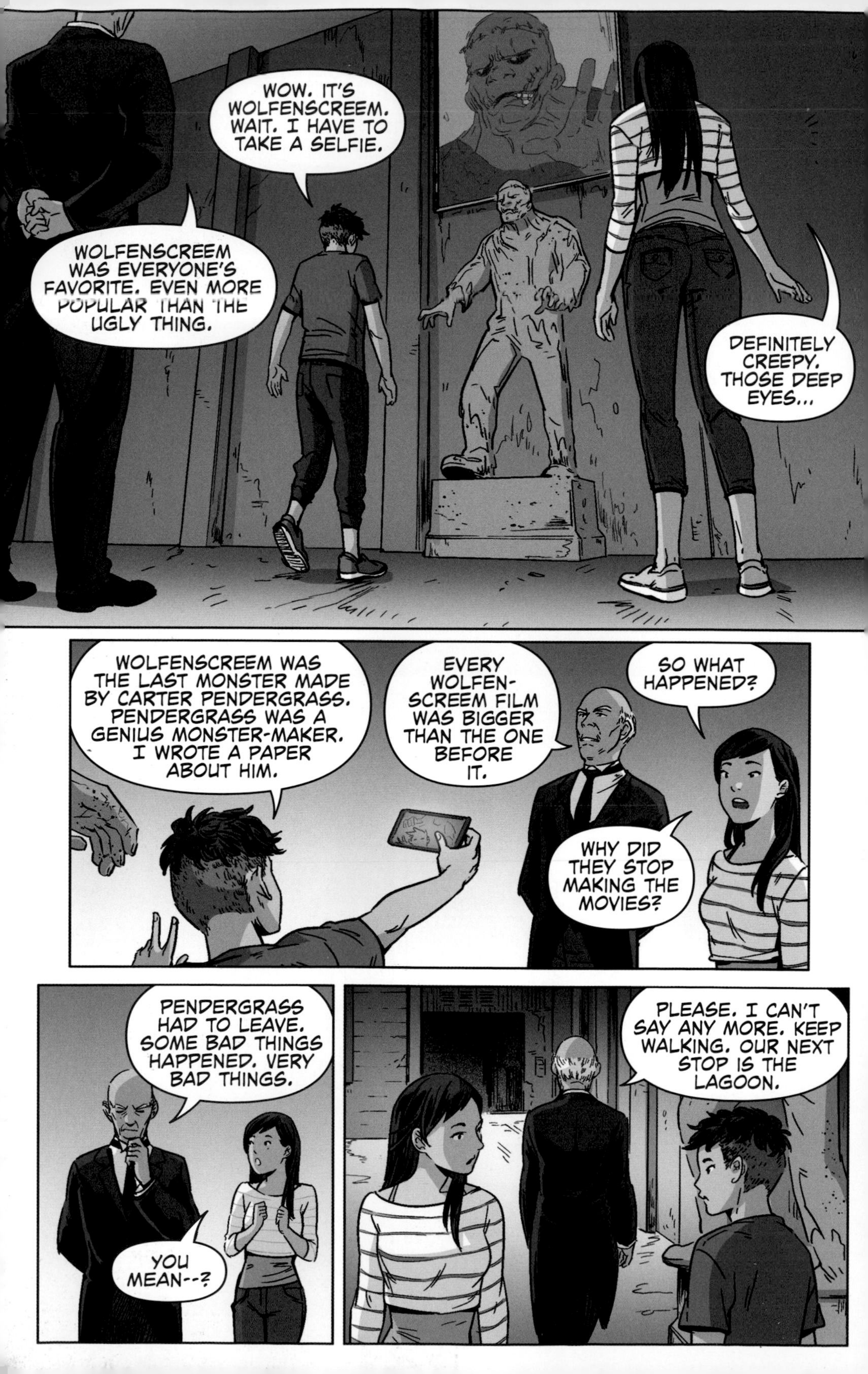
WOW. IT'S WOLFENSCREEM. WAIT. I HAVE TO TAKE A SELFIE.
WOLFENSCREEM WAS EVERYONE'S FAVORITE. EVEN MORE POPULAR THAN THE UGLY THING.
DEFINITELY CREEPY. THOSE DEEP EYES...
WOLFENSCREEM WAS THE LAST MONSTER MADE BY CARTER PENDERGRASS. PENDERGRASS WAS A GENIUS MONSTER-MAKER. I WROTE A PAPER ABOUT HIM.
EVERY WOLFEN-SCREEM FILM WAS BIGGER THAN THE ONE BEFORE IT.
SO WHAT HAPPENED?
WHY DID THEY STOP MAKING THE MOVIES?
PENDERGRASS HAD TO LEAVE. SOME BAD THINGS HAPPENED. VERY BAD THINGS.
YOU MEAN--?
PLEASE. I CAN'T SAY ANY MORE. KEEP WALKING. OUR NEXT STOP IS THE LAGOON.

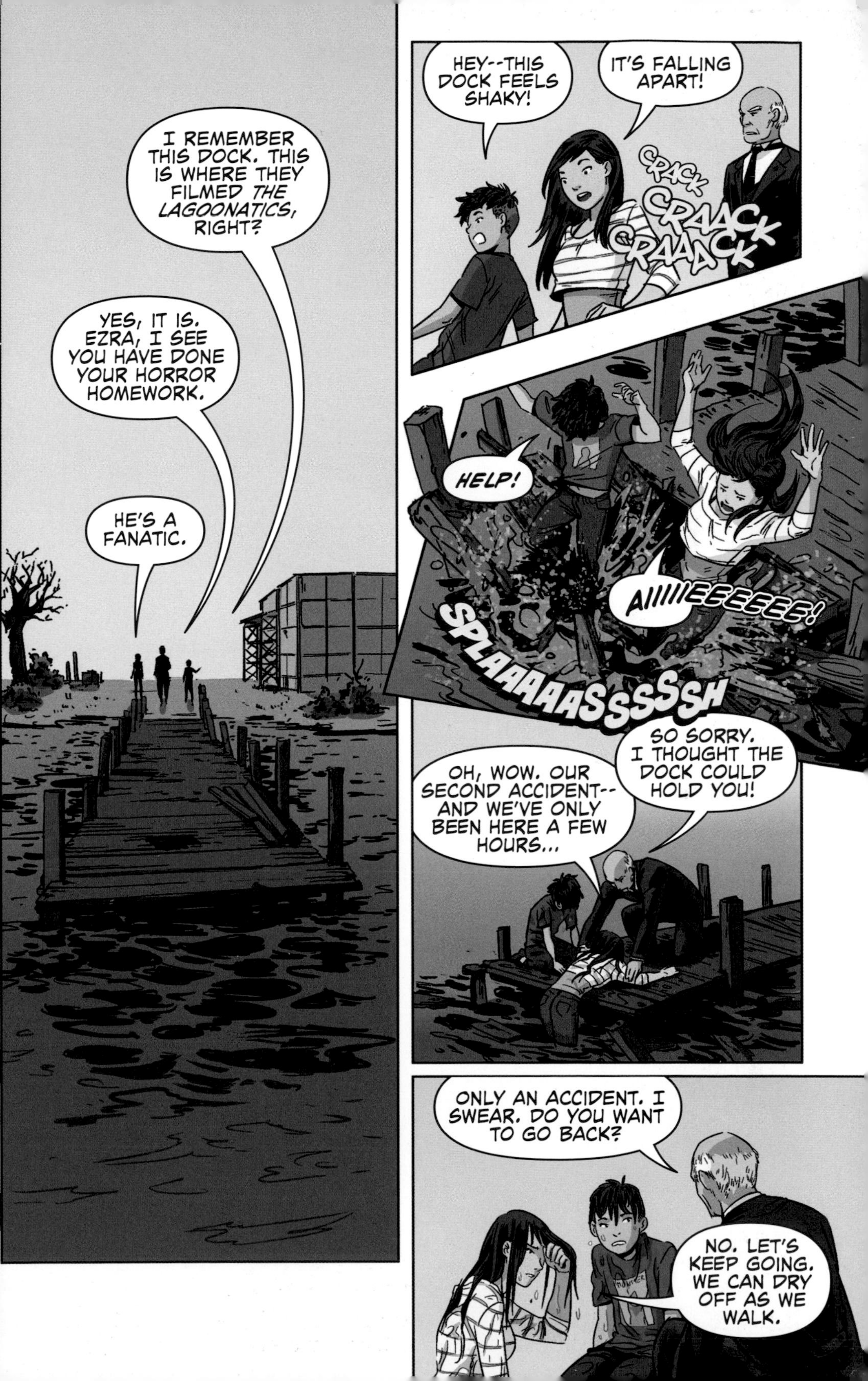
I REMEMBER THIS DOCK. THIS IS WHERE THEY FILMED *THE LAGOONATICS*, RIGHT?
YES, IT IS. EZRA, I SEE YOU HAVE DONE YOUR HORROR HOMEWORK.
HE'S A FANATIC.
HEY--THIS DOCK FEELS SHAKY!
IT'S FALLING APART!
CRACK
CRAAACK
CRAAACK
HELP!
AIIIIIEEEEEEE!
SPLAAAAAASSSSSH
OH, WOW. OUR SECOND ACCIDENT--AND WE'VE ONLY BEEN HERE A FEW HOURS...
SO SORRY. I THOUGHT THE DOCK COULD HOLD YOU!
ONLY AN ACCIDENT. I SWEAR. DO YOU WANT TO GO BACK?
NO. LET'S KEEP GOING. WE CAN DRY OFF AS WE WALK.

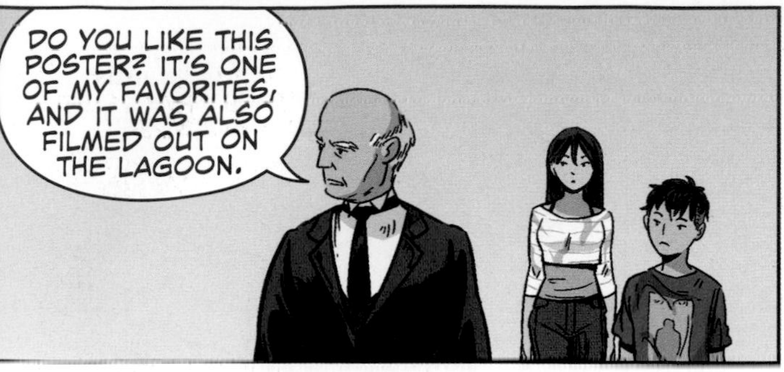
DO YOU LIKE THIS POSTER? IT'S ONE OF MY FAVORITES, AND IT WAS ALSO FILMED OUT ON THE LAGOON.

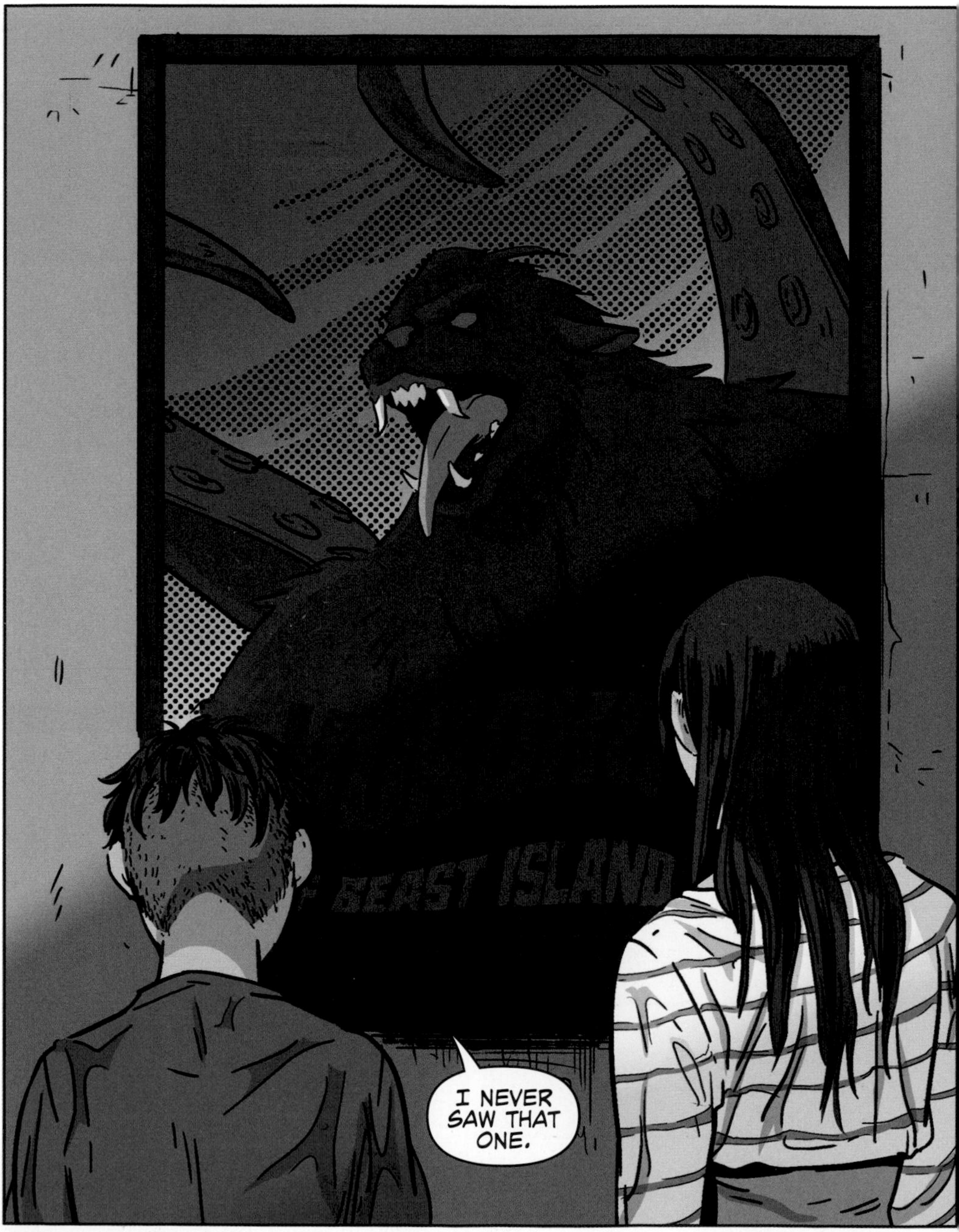
BEAST ISLAND
I NEVER SAW THAT ONE.

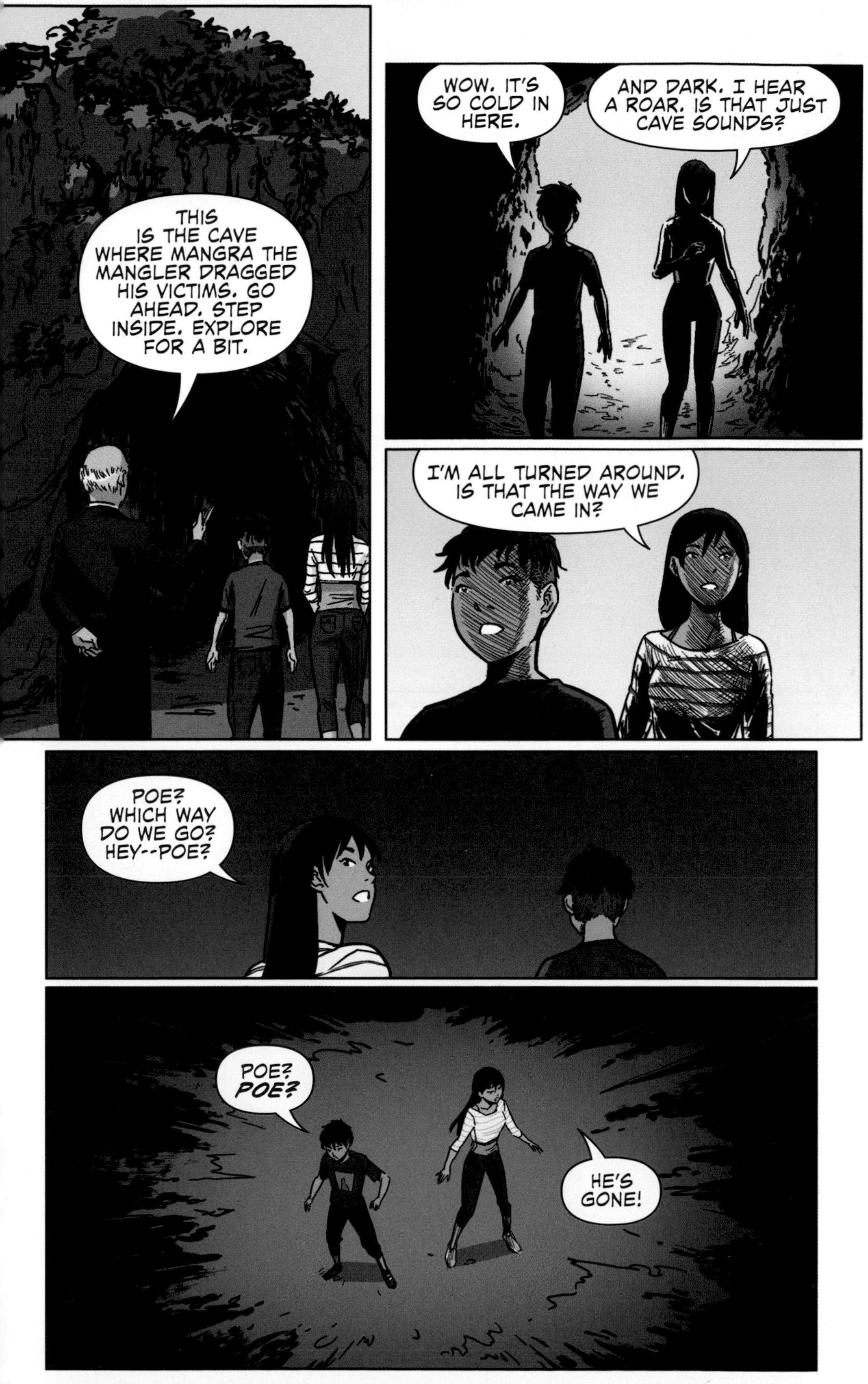
THIS IS THE CAVE WHERE MANGRA THE MANGLER DRAGGED HIS VICTIMS. GO AHEAD. STEP INSIDE. EXPLORE FOR A BIT.
WOW. IT'S SO COLD IN HERE.
AND DARK. I HEAR A ROAR. IS THAT JUST CAVE SOUNDS?
I'M ALL TURNED AROUND. IS THAT THE WAY WE CAME IN?
POE? WHICH WAY DO WE GO? HEY--POE?
POE? *POE?*
HE'S GONE!

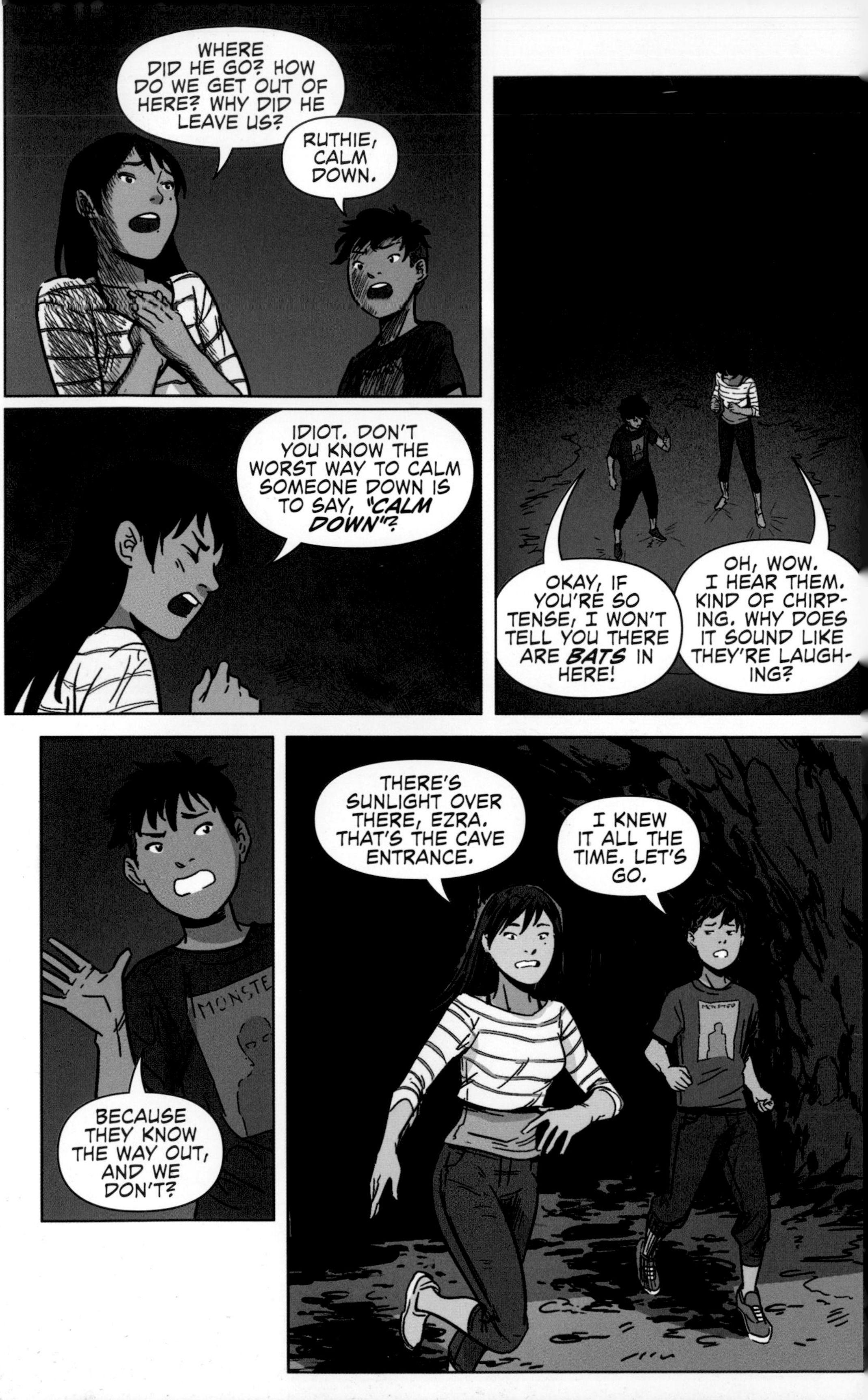
WHERE DID HE GO? HOW DO WE GET OUT OF HERE? WHY DID HE LEAVE US?
RUTHIE, CALM DOWN.
IDIOT. DON'T YOU KNOW THE WORST WAY TO CALM SOMEONE DOWN IS TO SAY, "CALM DOWN"?
OKAY, IF YOU'RE SO TENSE, I WON'T TELL YOU THERE ARE BATS IN HERE!
OH, WOW. I HEAR THEM. KIND OF CHIRP-ING. WHY DOES IT SOUND LIKE THEY'RE LAUGH-ING?
BECAUSE THEY KNOW THE WAY OUT, AND WE DON'T?
THERE'S SUNLIGHT OVER THERE, EZRA. THAT'S THE CAVE ENTRANCE.
I KNEW IT ALL THE TIME. LET'S GO.

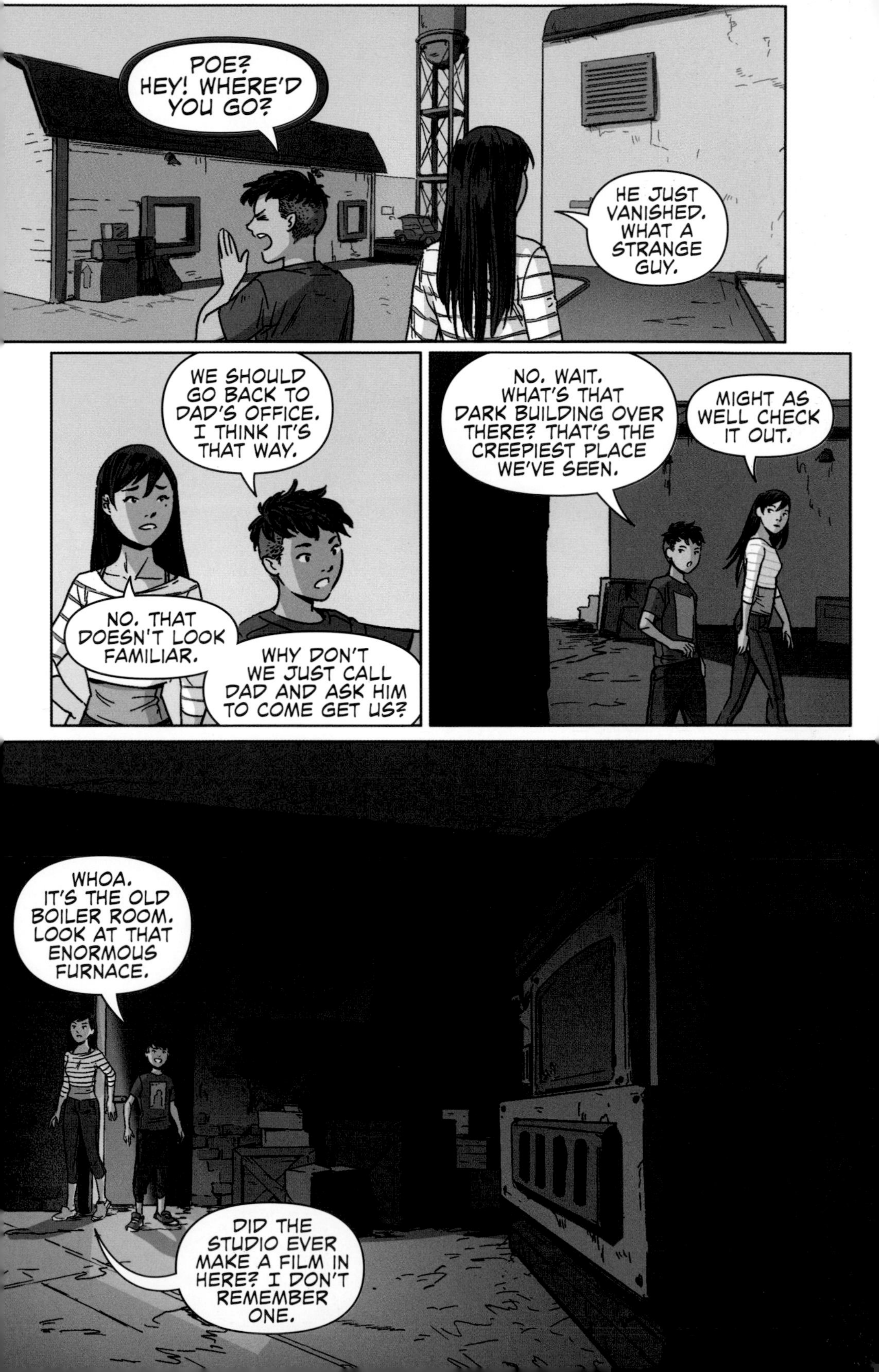
POE? HEY! WHERE'D YOU GO?
HE JUST VANISHED. WHAT A STRANGE GUY.
WE SHOULD GO BACK TO DAD'S OFFICE. I THINK IT'S THAT WAY.
NO. THAT DOESN'T LOOK FAMILIAR.
WHY DON'T WE JUST CALL DAD AND ASK HIM TO COME GET US?
NO. WAIT. WHAT'S THAT DARK BUILDING OVER THERE? THAT'S THE CREEPIEST PLACE WE'VE SEEN.
MIGHT AS WELL CHECK IT OUT.
WHOA. IT'S THE OLD BOILER ROOM. LOOK AT THAT ENORMOUS FURNACE.
DID THE STUDIO EVER MAKE A FILM IN HERE? I DON'T REMEMBER ONE.

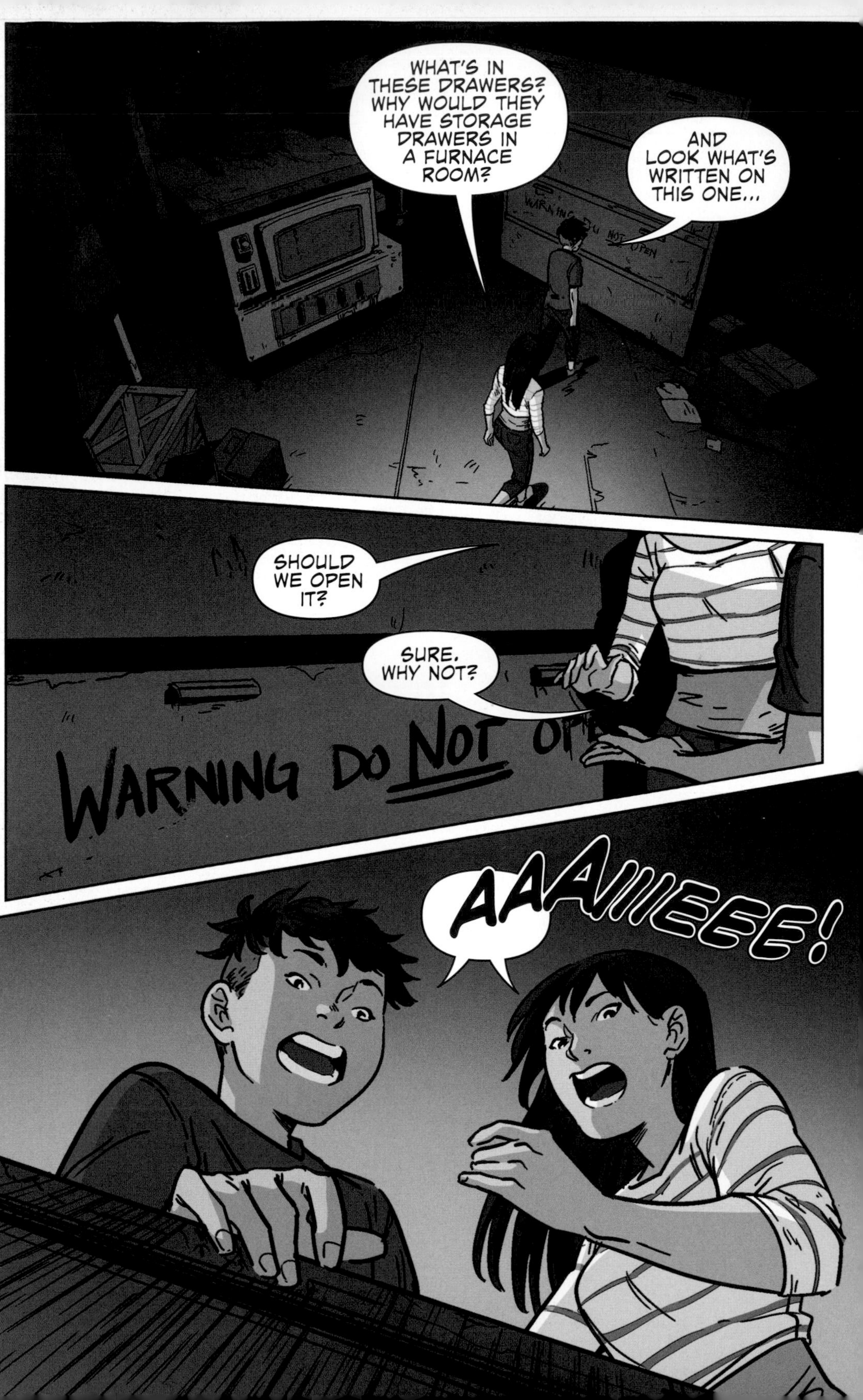
WHAT'S IN THESE DRAWERS? WHY WOULD THEY HAVE STORAGE DRAWERS IN A FURNACE ROOM?
AND LOOK WHAT'S WRITTEN ON THIS ONE...
SHOULD WE OPEN IT?
SURE. WHY NOT?
WARNING DO NOT
AAAIIIEEEE!

PART TWO

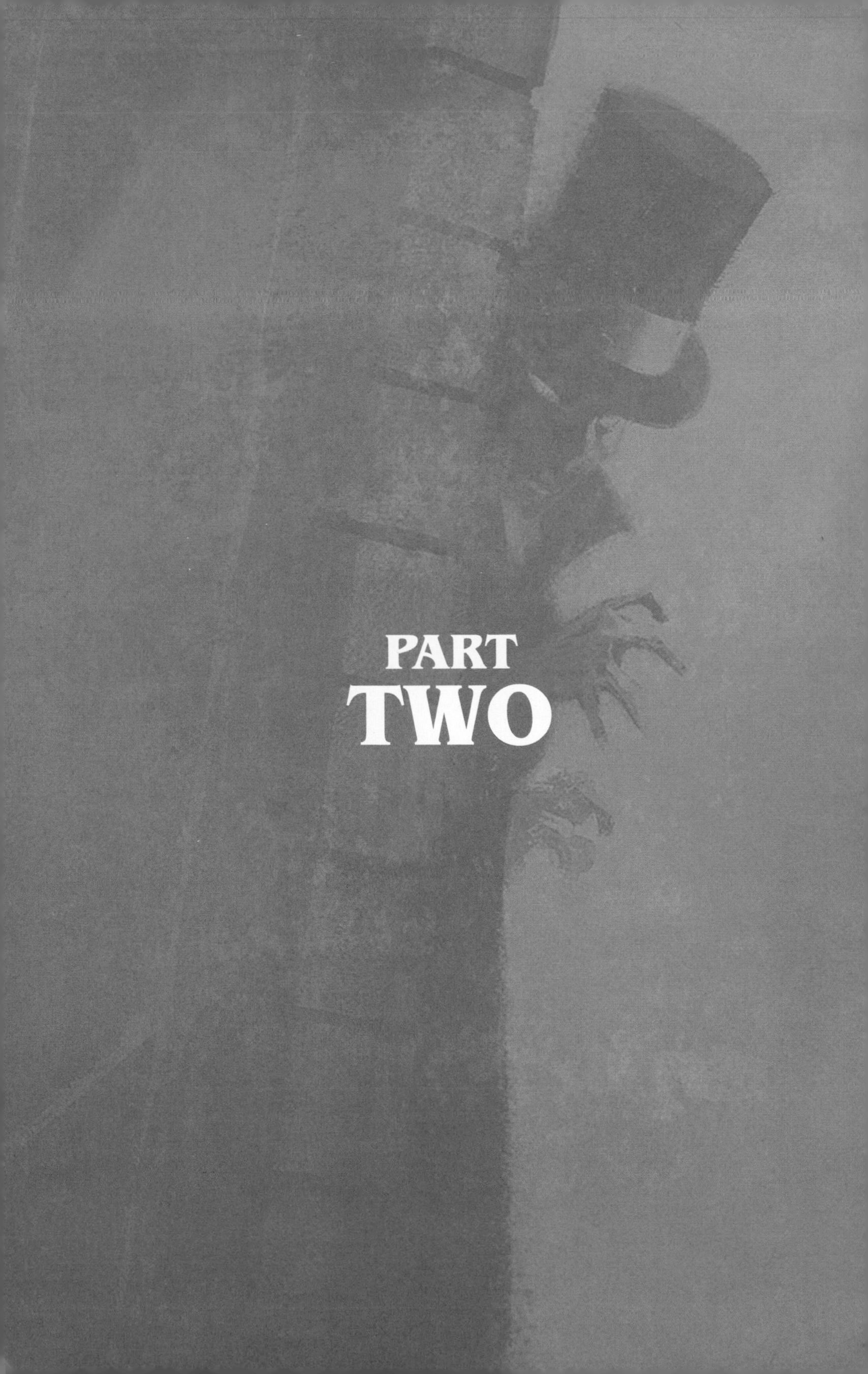

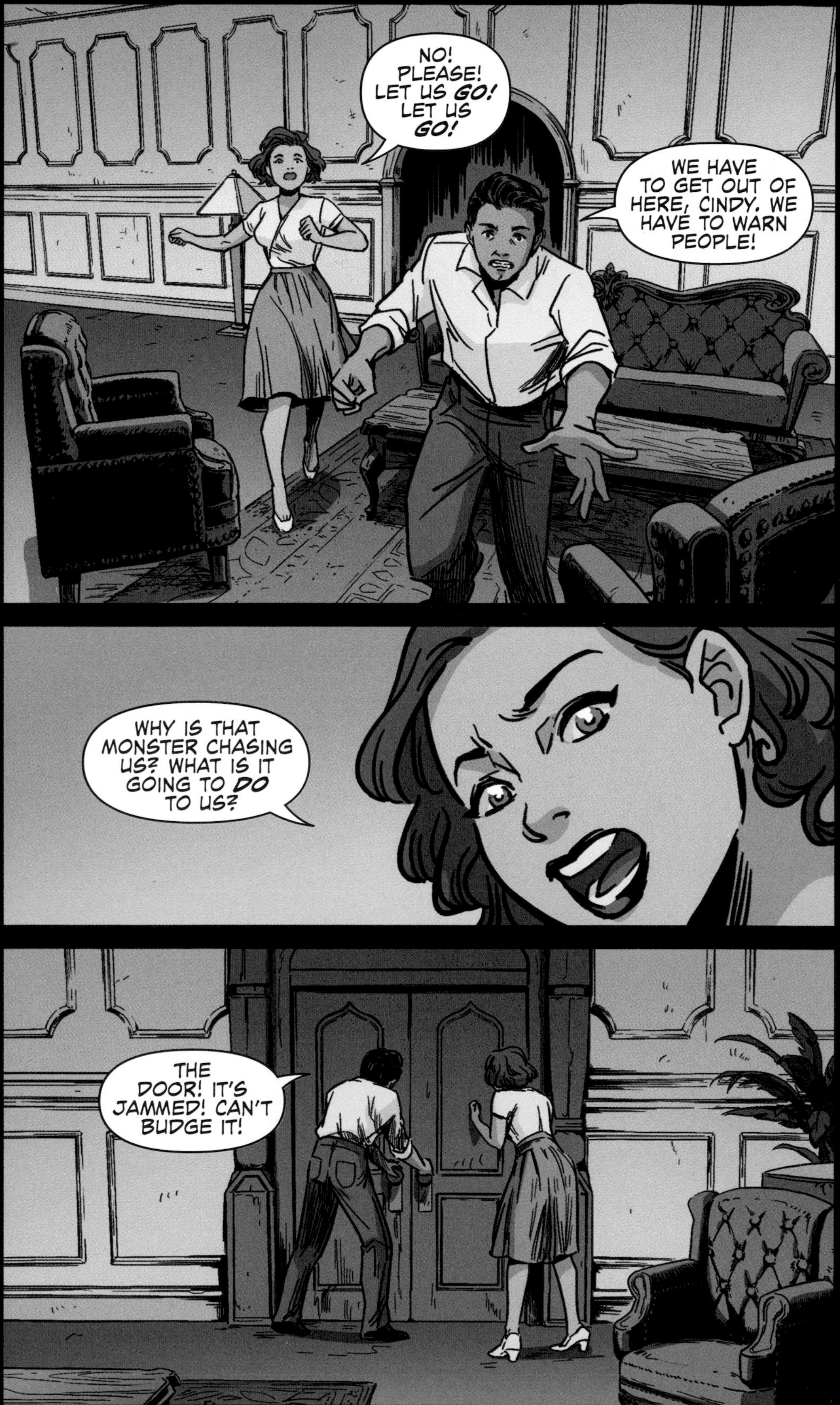
NO! PLEASE! LET US GO! LET US GO!
WE HAVE TO GET OUT OF HERE, CINDY. WE HAVE TO WARN PEOPLE!
WHY IS THAT MONSTER CHASING US? WHAT IS IT GOING TO DO TO US?
THE DOOR! IT'S JAMMED! CAN'T BUDGE IT!

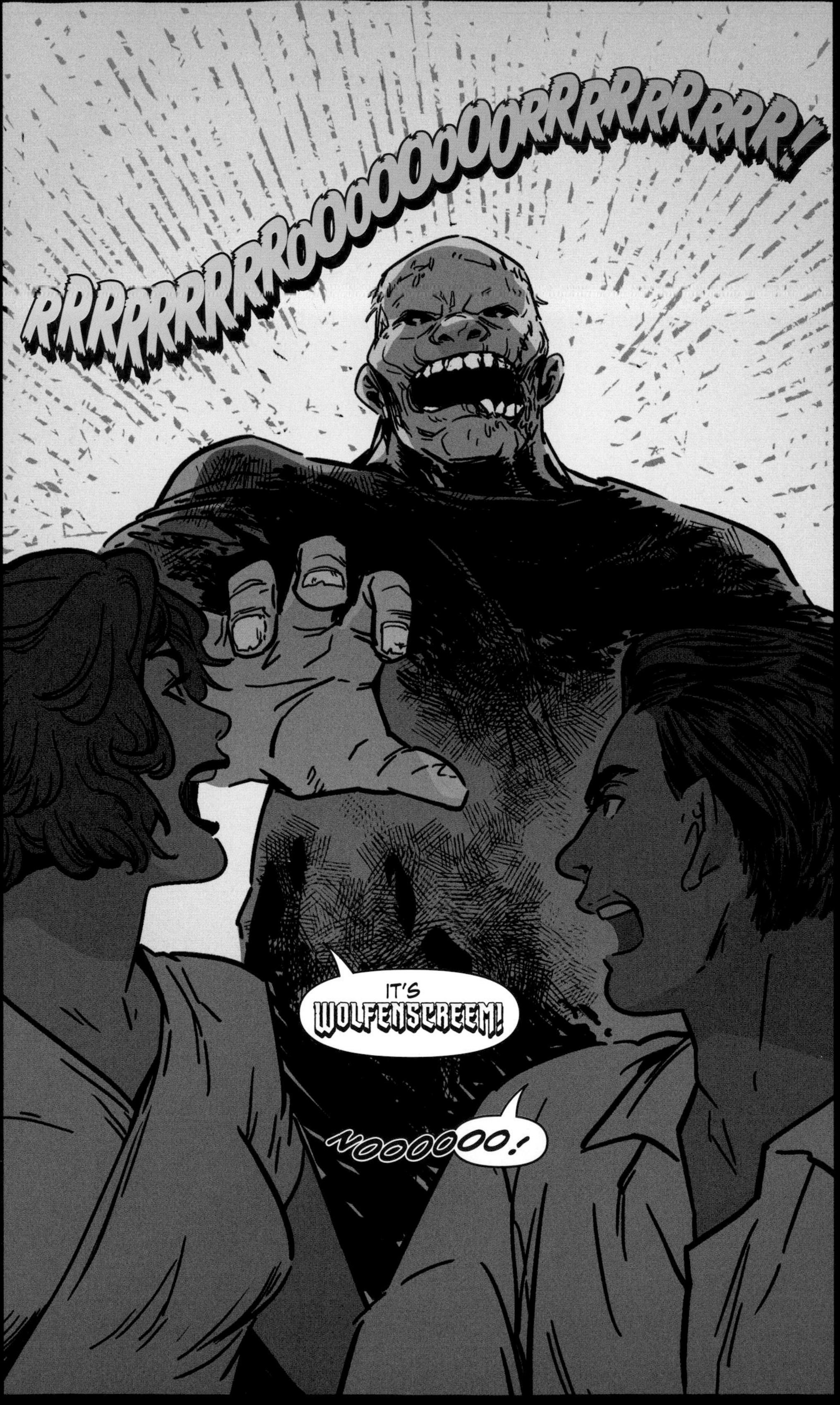
RRRRRRRRROOOOOOOOORRRRRRRRR!
IT'S WOLFENSCREEM!
NOOOOOOO!

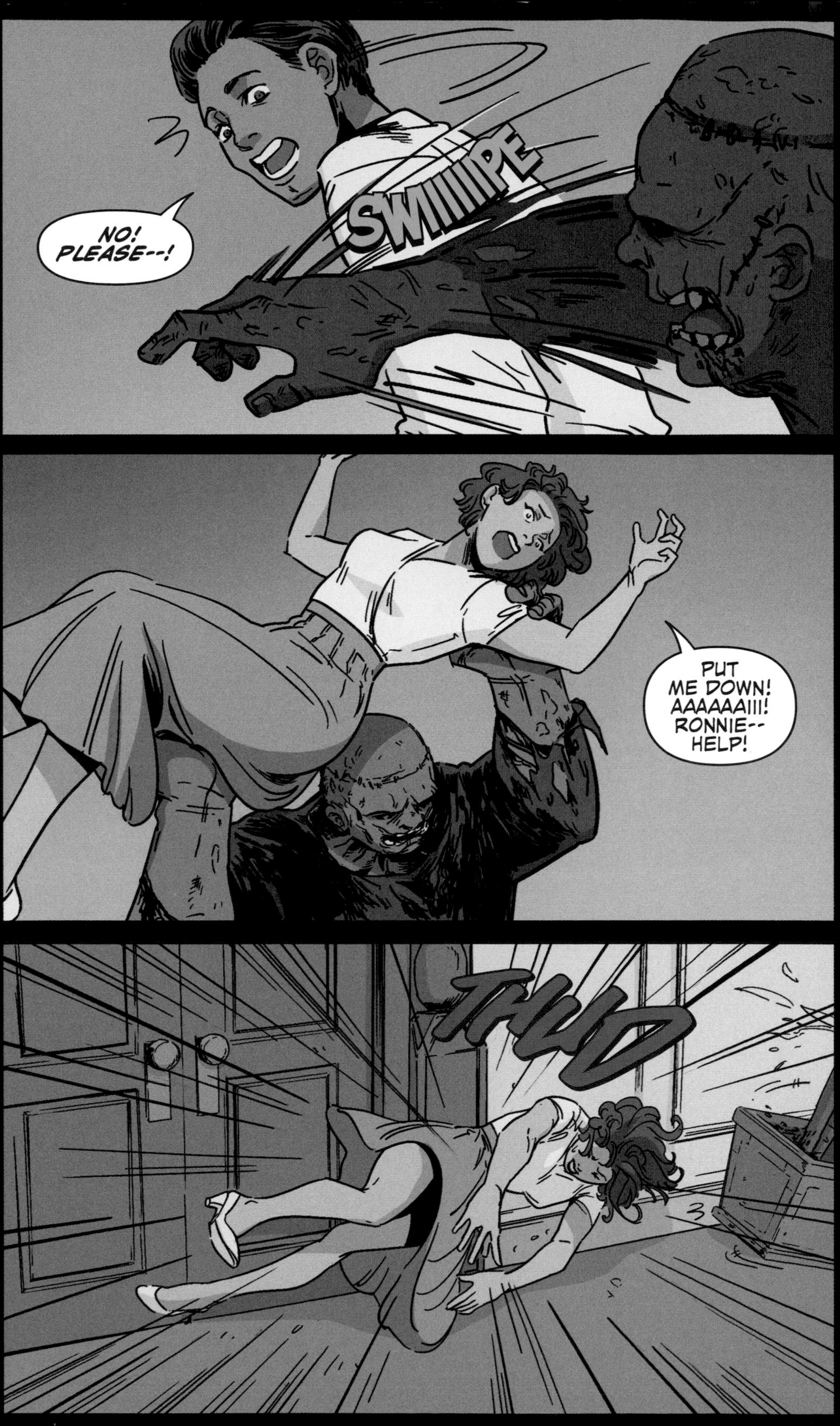
NO! PLEASE--!
SWIIIIIPE
PUT ME DOWN! AAAAAAIIII! RONNIE-- HELP!
THUD

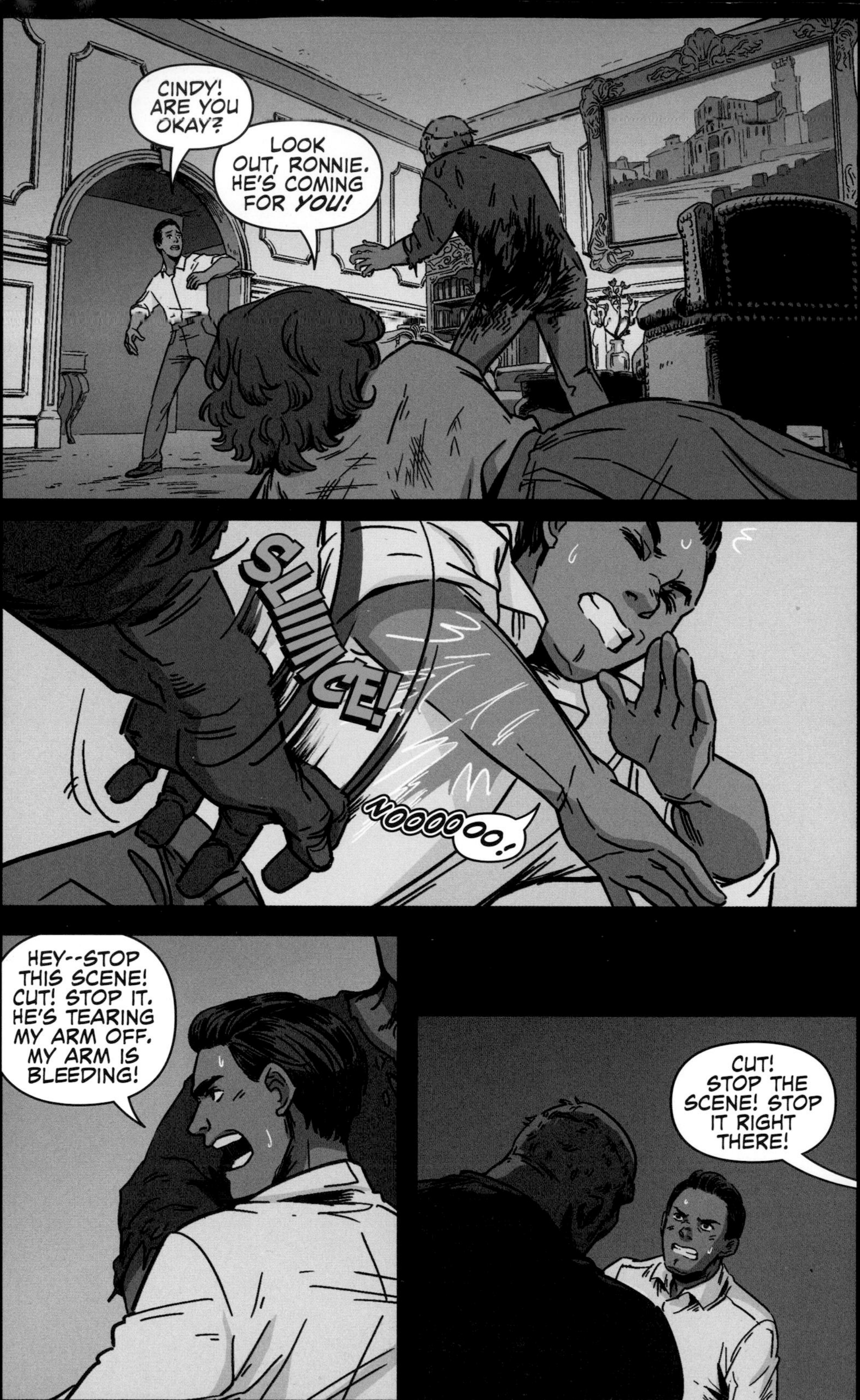
CINDY! ARE YOU OKAY?
LOOK OUT, RONNIE. HE'S COMING FOR YOU!
SLIIIIICE!
NOOOOOOO!
HEY--STOP THIS SCENE! CUT! STOP IT. HE'S TEARING MY ARM OFF. MY ARM IS BLEEDING!
CUT! STOP THE SCENE! STOP IT RIGHT THERE!

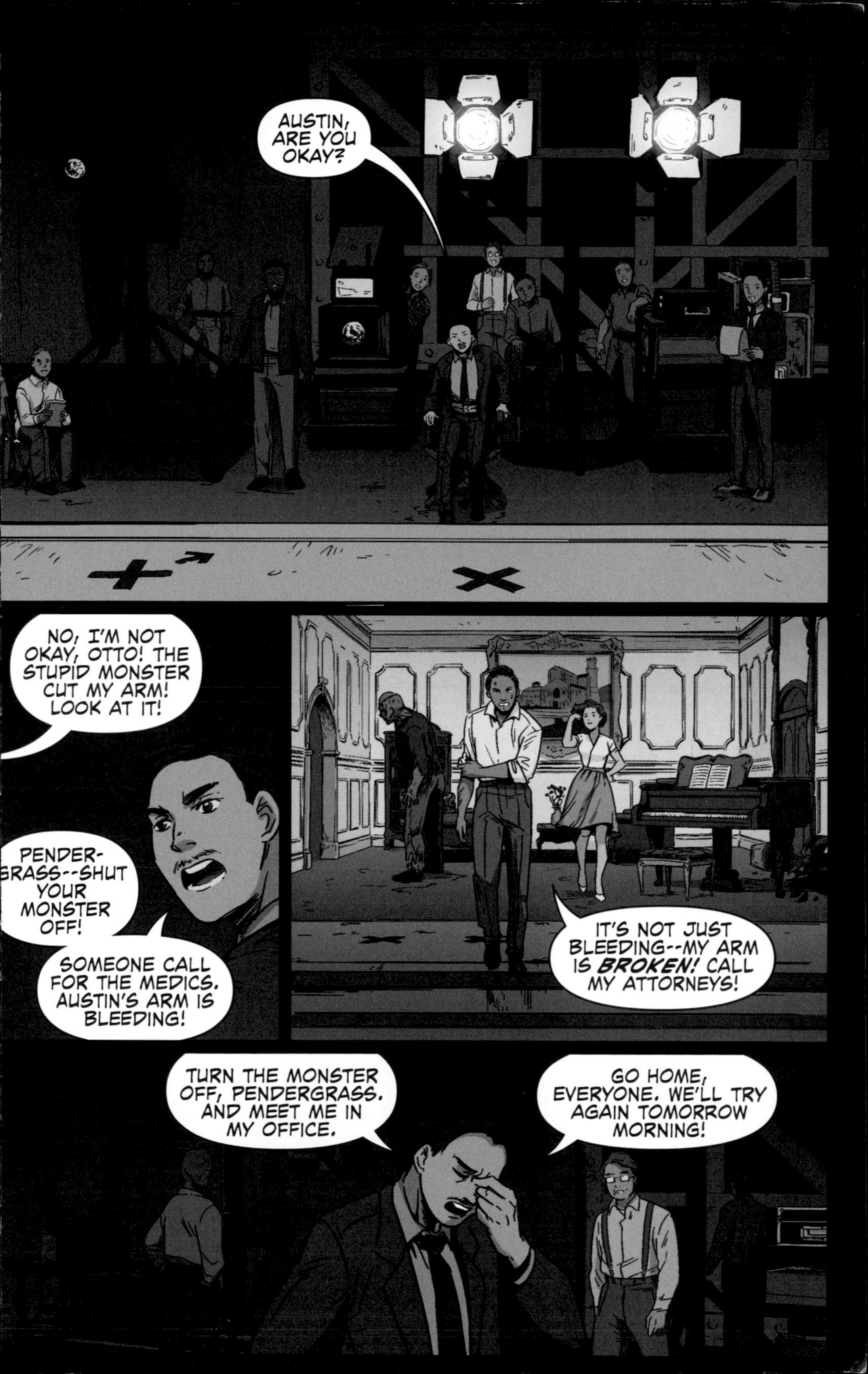
AUSTIN, ARE YOU OKAY?
NO, I'M NOT OKAY, OTTO! THE STUPID MONSTER CUT MY ARM! LOOK AT IT!
PENDER-GRASS--SHUT YOUR MONSTER OFF!
SOMEONE CALL FOR THE MEDICS. AUSTIN'S ARM IS BLEEDING!
IT'S NOT JUST BLEEDING--MY ARM IS ***BROKEN!*** CALL MY ATTORNEYS!
TURN THE MONSTER OFF, PENDERGRASS. AND MEET ME IN MY OFFICE.
GO HOME, EVERYONE. WE'LL TRY AGAIN TOMORROW MORNING!

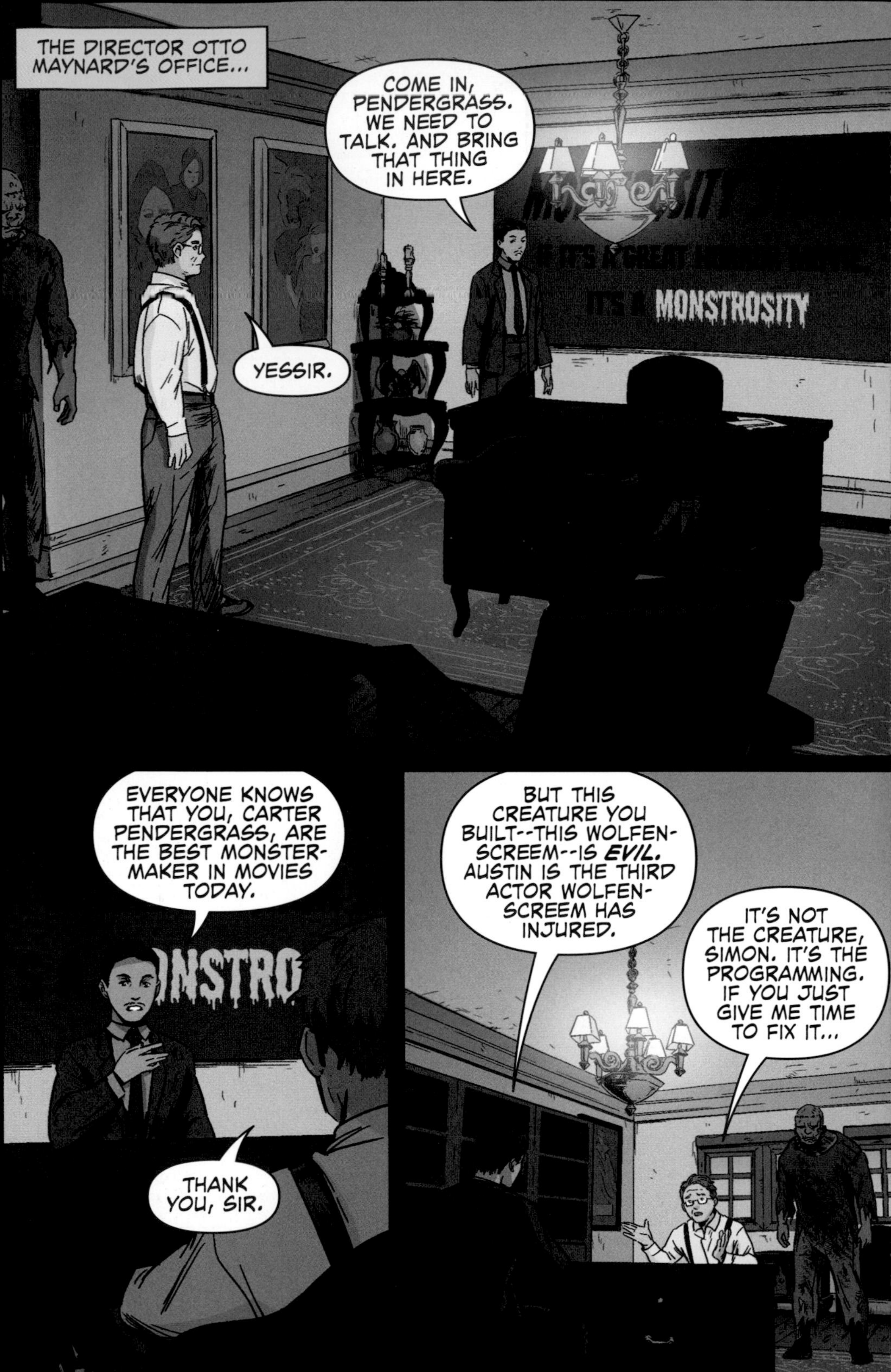

THE DIRECTOR OTTO MAYNARD'S OFFICE...
COME IN, PENDERGRASS. WE NEED TO TALK. AND BRING THAT THING IN HERE.
IT'S A MONSTROSITY
YESSIR.
EVERYONE KNOWS THAT YOU, CARTER PENDERGRASS, ARE THE BEST MONSTER-MAKER IN MOVIES TODAY.
THANK YOU, SIR.
BUT THIS CREATURE YOU BUILT--THIS WOLFEN-SCREEM--IS *EVIL.* AUSTIN IS THE THIRD ACTOR WOLFEN-SCREEM HAS INJURED.
IT'S NOT THE CREATURE, SIMON. IT'S THE PROGRAMMING. IF YOU JUST GIVE ME TIME TO FIX IT...

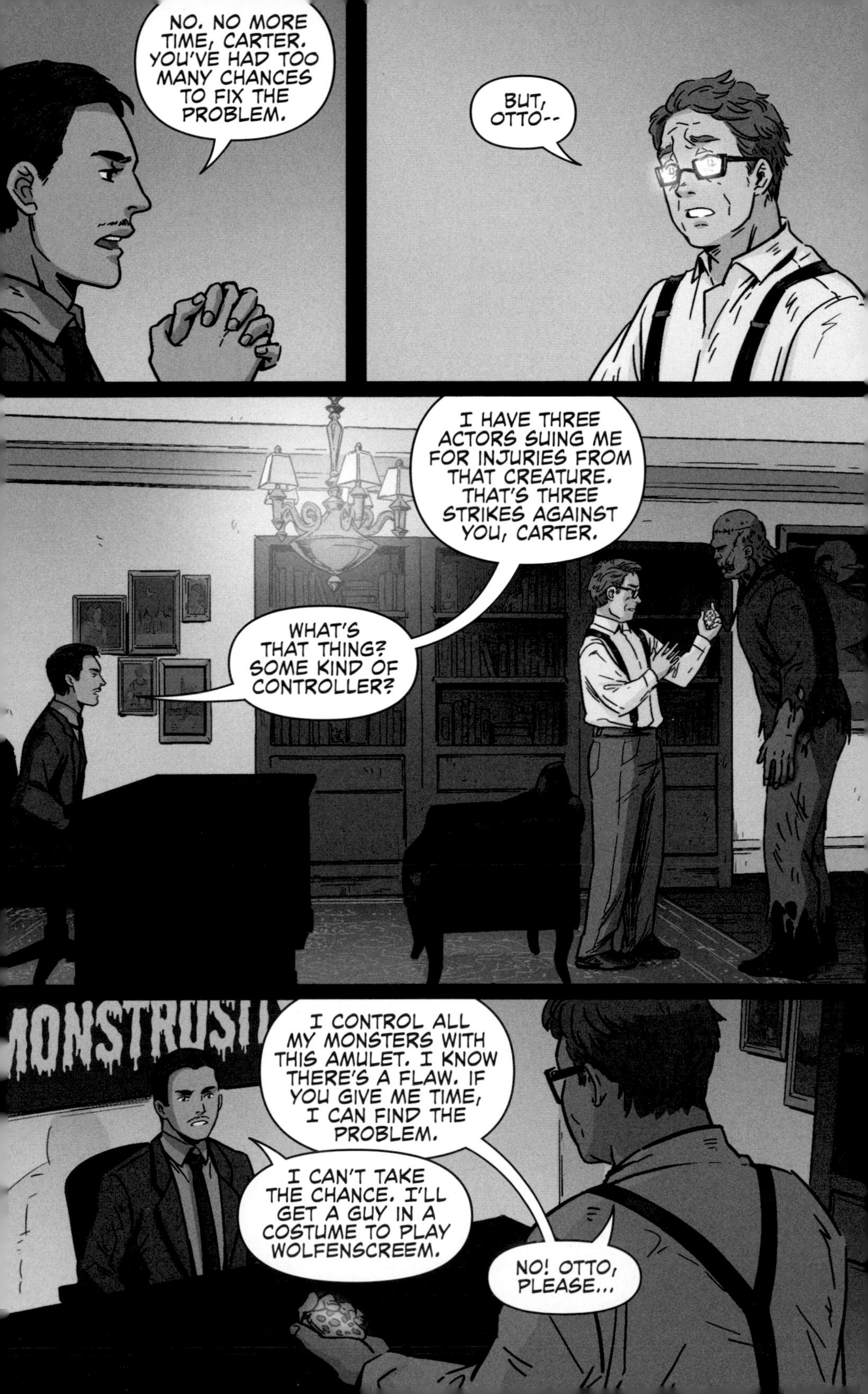
NO. NO MORE TIME, CARTER. YOU'VE HAD TOO MANY CHANCES TO FIX THE PROBLEM.
BUT, OTTO--
I HAVE THREE ACTORS SUING ME FOR INJURIES FROM THAT CREATURE. THAT'S THREE STRIKES AGAINST YOU, CARTER.
WHAT'S THAT THING? SOME KIND OF CONTROLLER?
MONSTROSI
I CONTROL ALL MY MONSTERS WITH THIS AMULET. I KNOW THERE'S A FLAW. IF YOU GIVE ME TIME, I CAN FIND THE PROBLEM.
I CAN'T TAKE THE CHANCE. I'LL GET A GUY IN A COSTUME TO PLAY WOLFENSCREEM.
NO! OTTO, PLEASE...

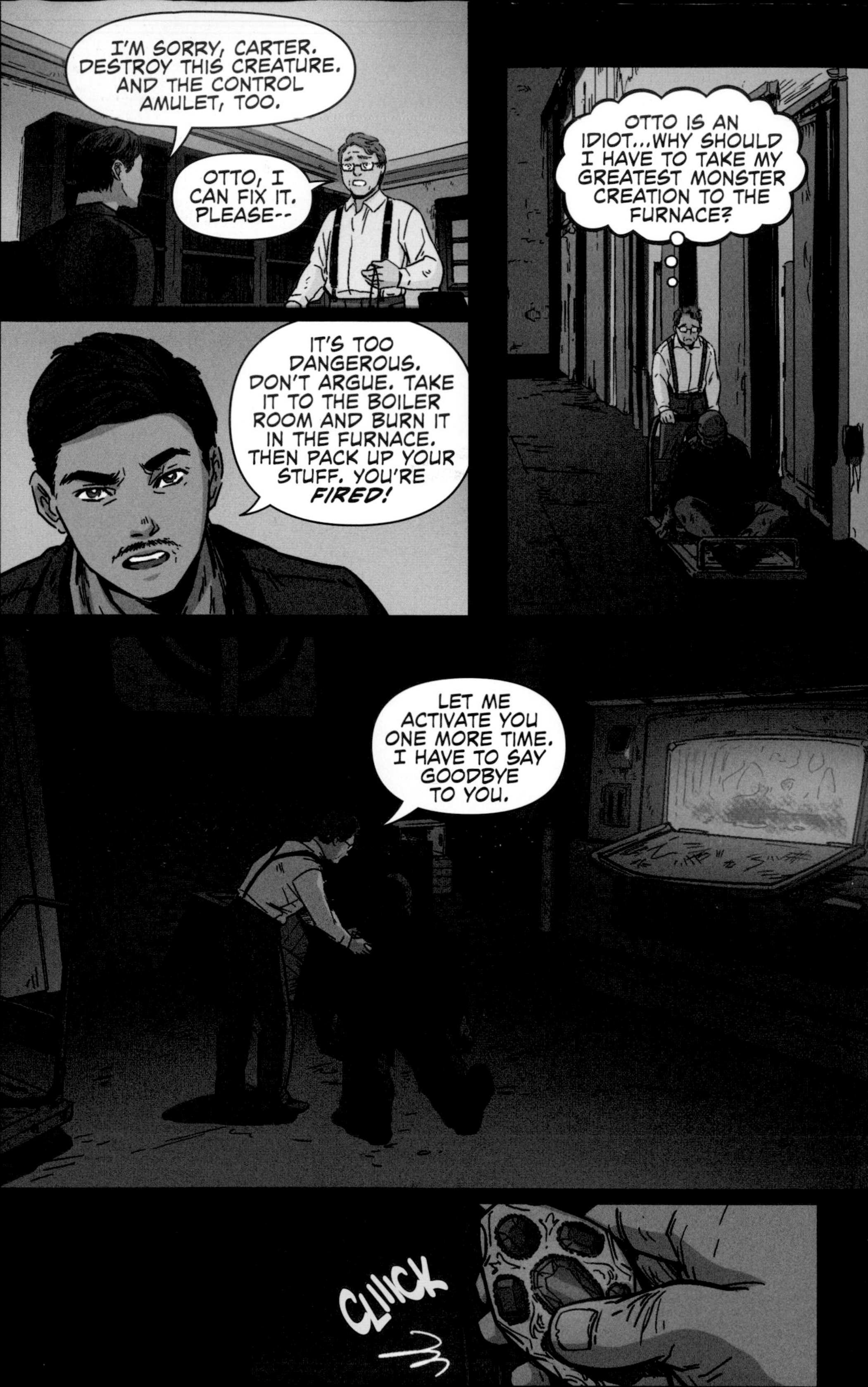
I'M SORRY, CARTER. DESTROY THIS CREATURE. AND THE CONTROL AMULET, TOO.
OTTO, I CAN FIX IT. PLEASE--
IT'S TOO DANGEROUS. DON'T ARGUE. TAKE IT TO THE BOILER ROOM AND BURN IT IN THE FURNACE. THEN PACK UP YOUR STUFF. YOU'RE *FIRED!*
OTTO IS AN IDIOT...WHY SHOULD I HAVE TO TAKE MY GREATEST MONSTER CREATION TO THE FURNACE?
LET ME ACTIVATE YOU ONE MORE TIME. I HAVE TO SAY GOODBYE TO YOU.
CLIICK

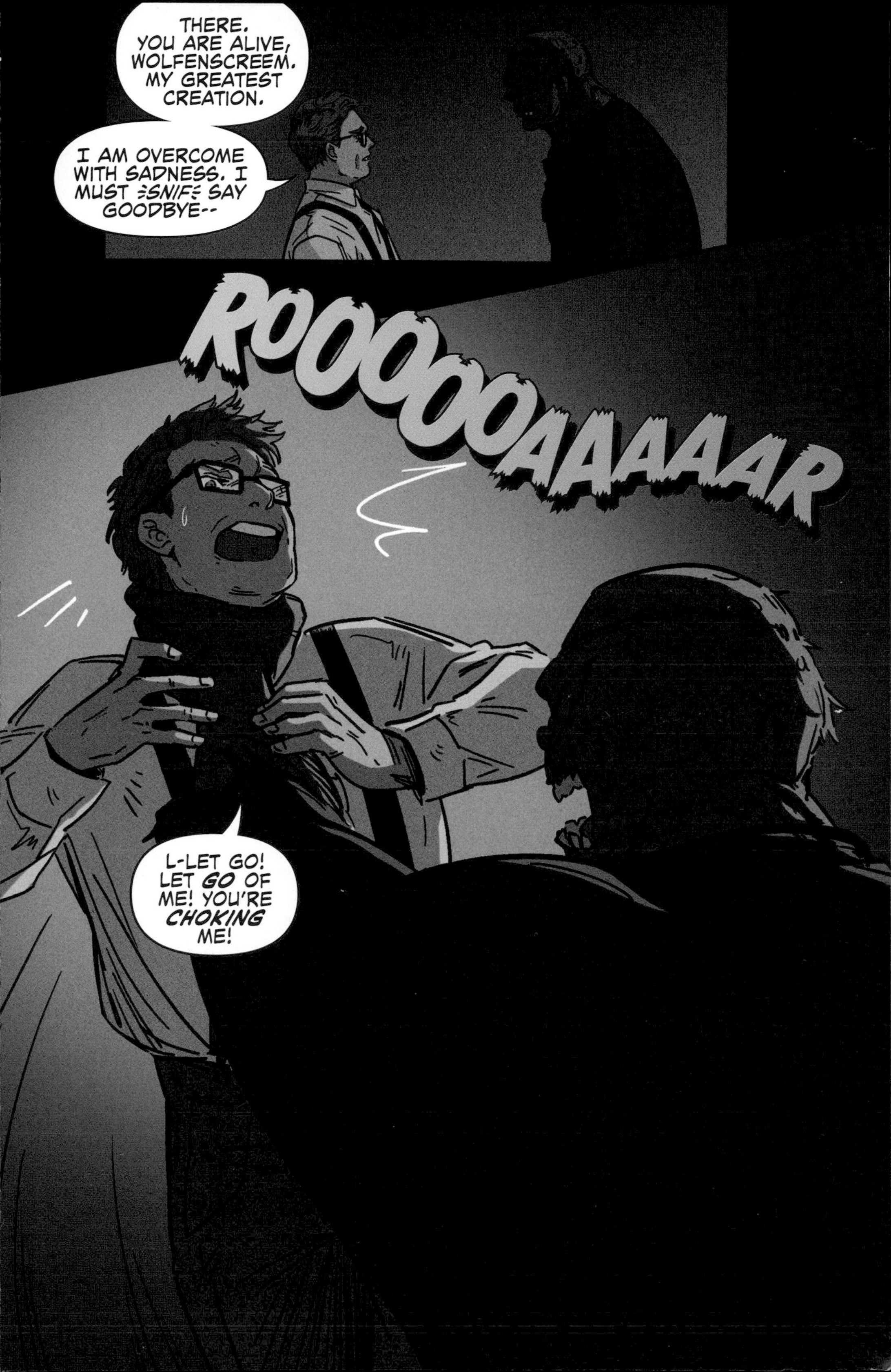
THERE. YOU ARE ALIVE, WOLFENSCREEM. MY GREATEST CREATION.
I AM OVERCOME WITH SADNESS. I MUST *SNIF* SAY GOODBYE--
ROOOOOOAAAAAR
L-LET GO! LET GO OF ME! YOU'RE CHOKING ME!

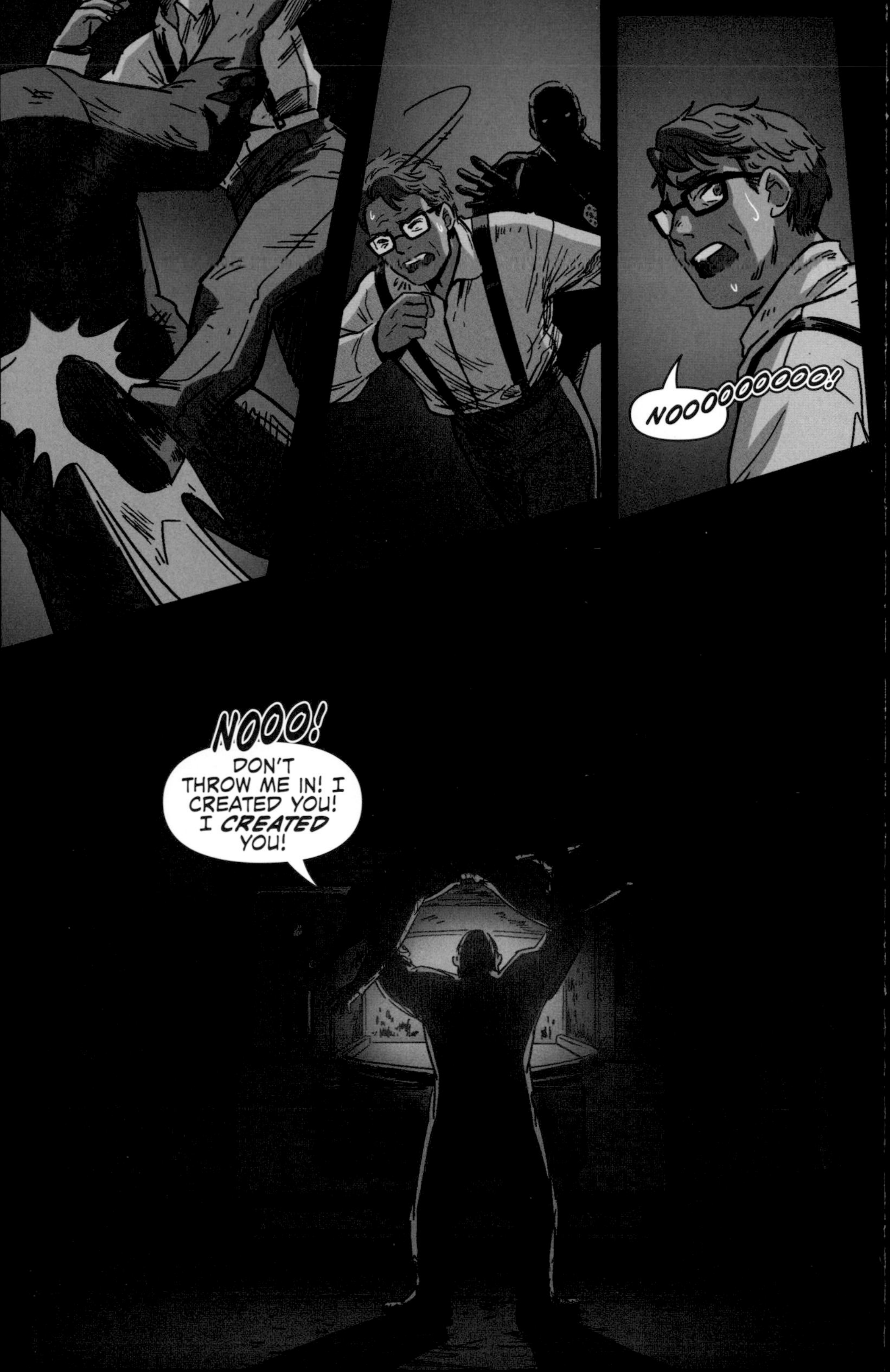
NOOOOOOOOOO!
NOOO! DON'T THROW ME IN! I CREATED YOU! I *CREATED* YOU!

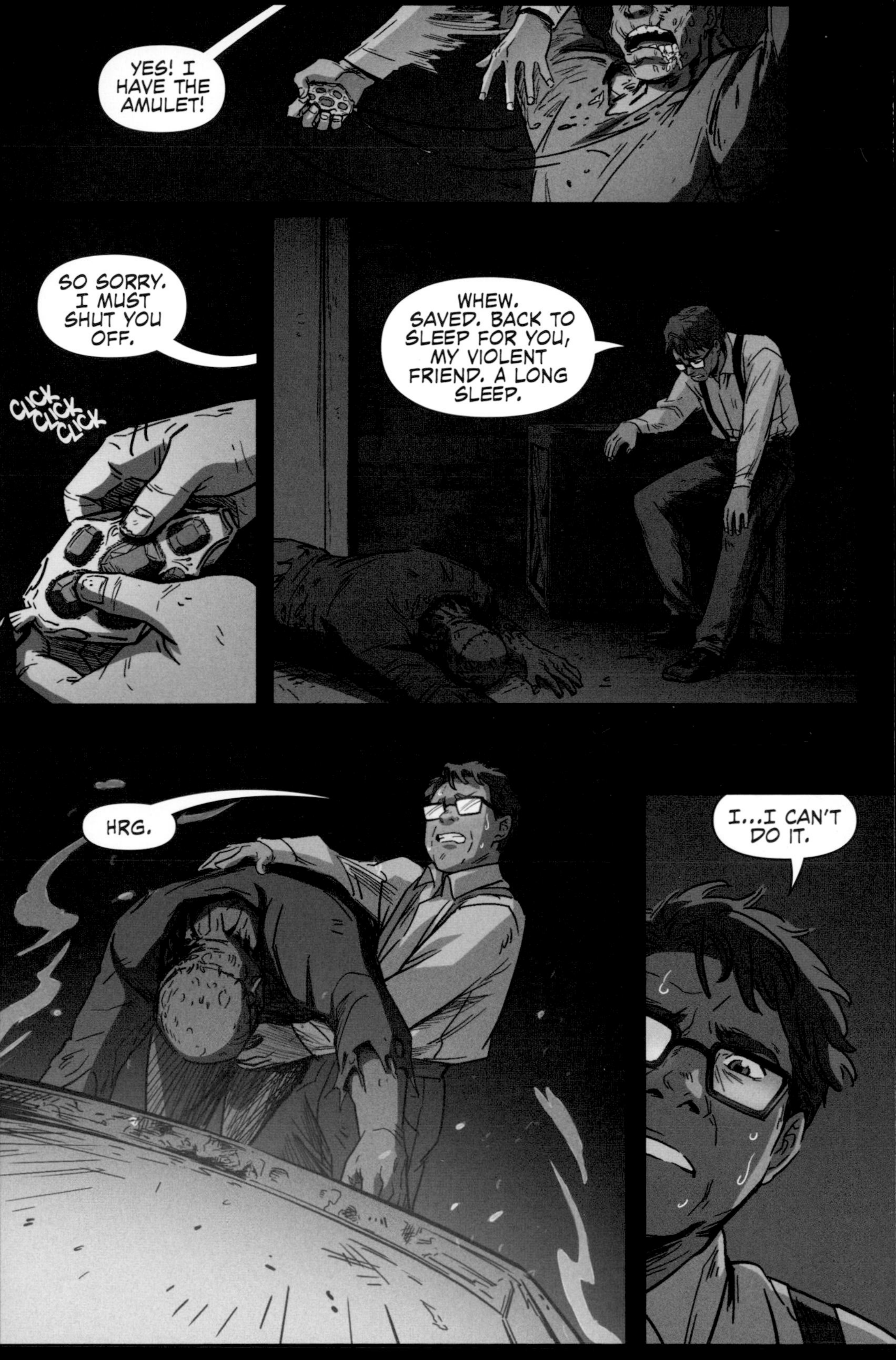
YES! I HAVE THE AMULET!
SO SORRY. I MUST SHUT YOU OFF.
CLICK CLICK CLICK
WHEW. SAVED. BACK TO SLEEP FOR YOU, MY VIOLENT FRIEND. A LONG SLEEP.
HRG.
I...I CAN'T DO IT.

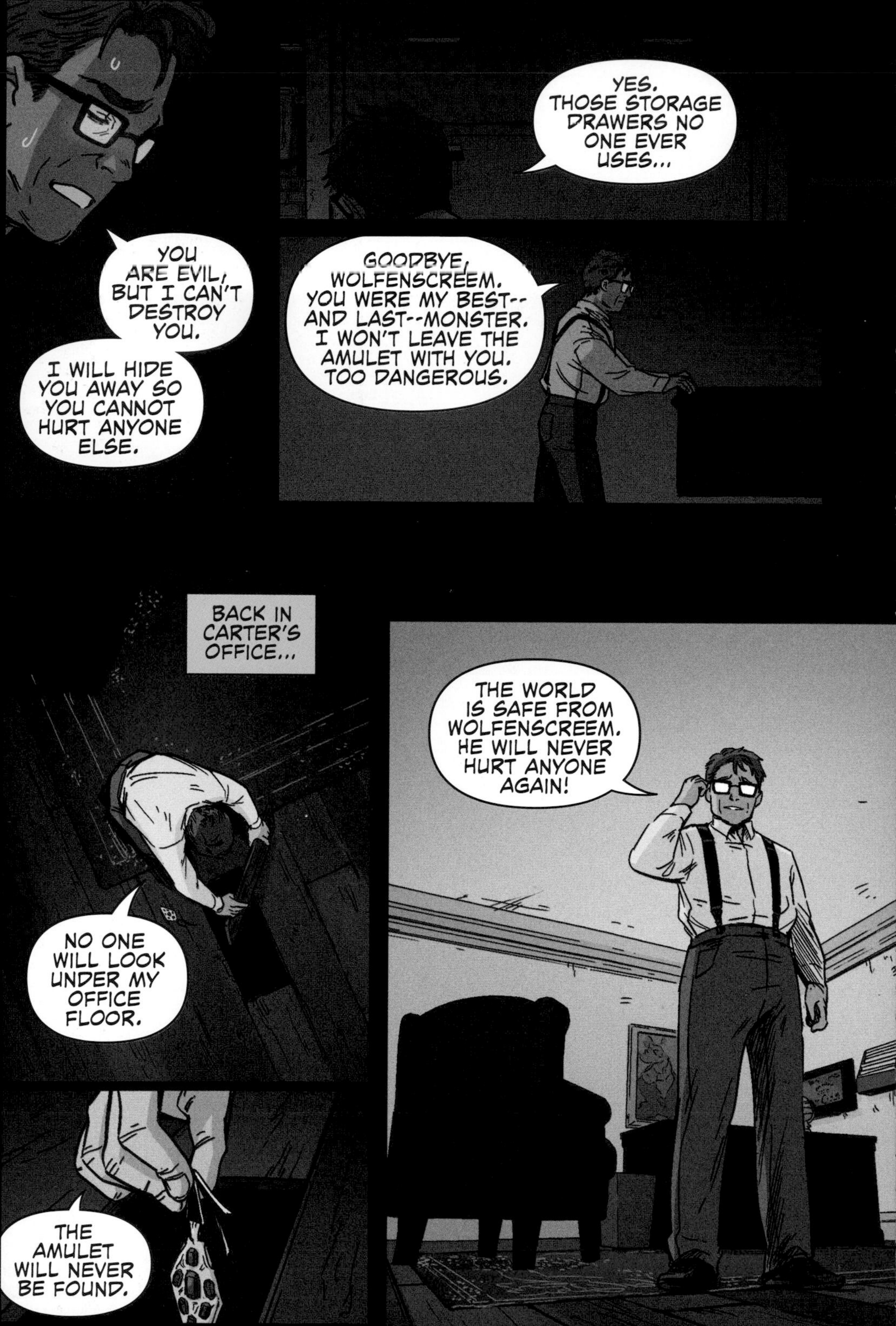

YES. THOSE STORAGE DRAWERS NO ONE EVER USES...
YOU ARE EVIL, BUT I CAN'T DESTROY YOU.
I WILL HIDE YOU AWAY SO YOU CANNOT HURT ANYONE ELSE.
GOODBYE, WOLFENSCREEM. YOU WERE MY BEST--AND LAST--MONSTER. I WON'T LEAVE THE AMULET WITH YOU. TOO DANGEROUS.
BACK IN CARTER'S OFFICE...
NO ONE WILL LOOK UNDER MY OFFICE FLOOR.
THE AMULET WILL NEVER BE FOUND.
THE WORLD IS SAFE FROM WOLFENSCREEM. HE WILL NEVER HURT ANYONE AGAIN!

PART THREE

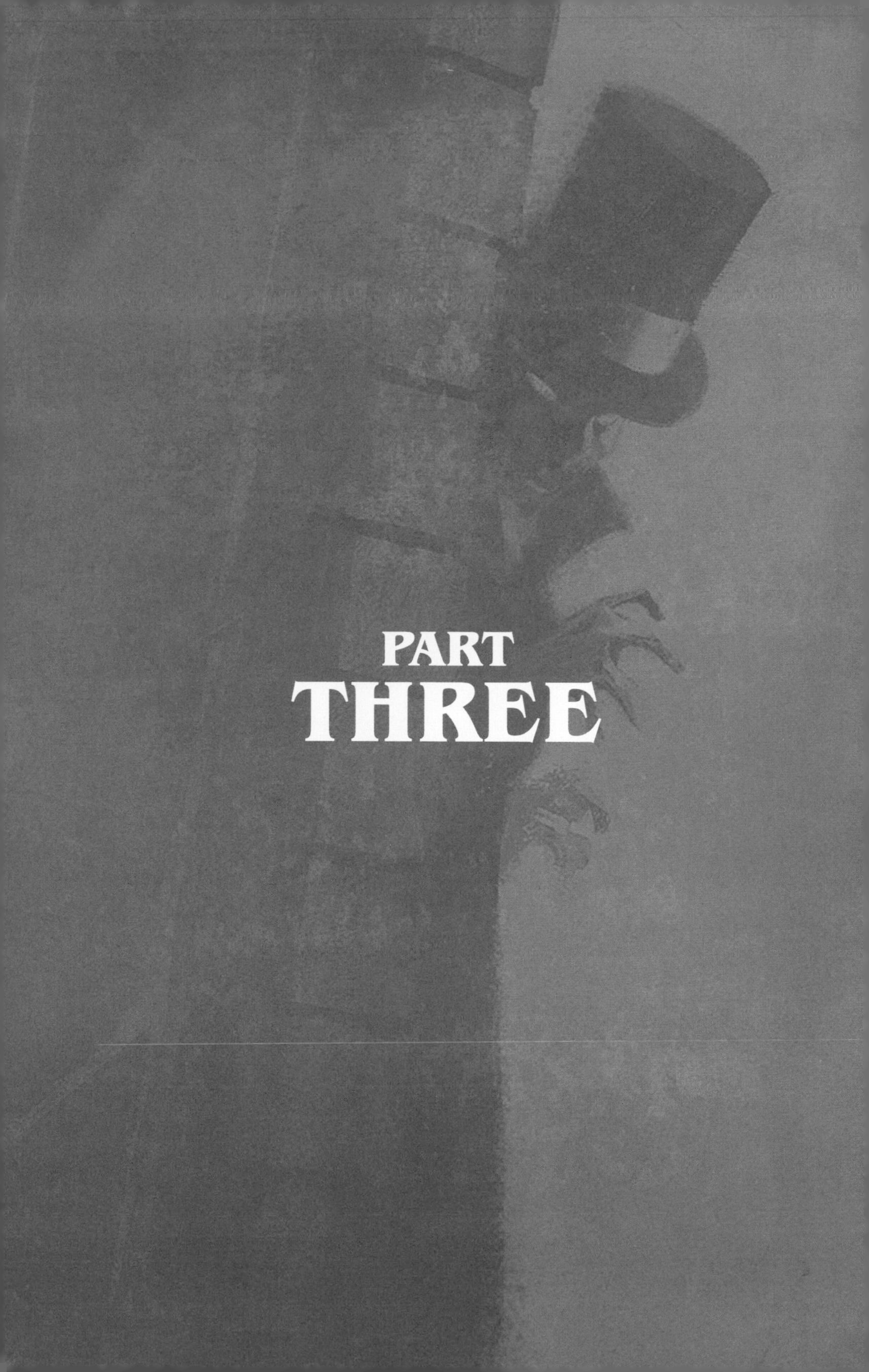

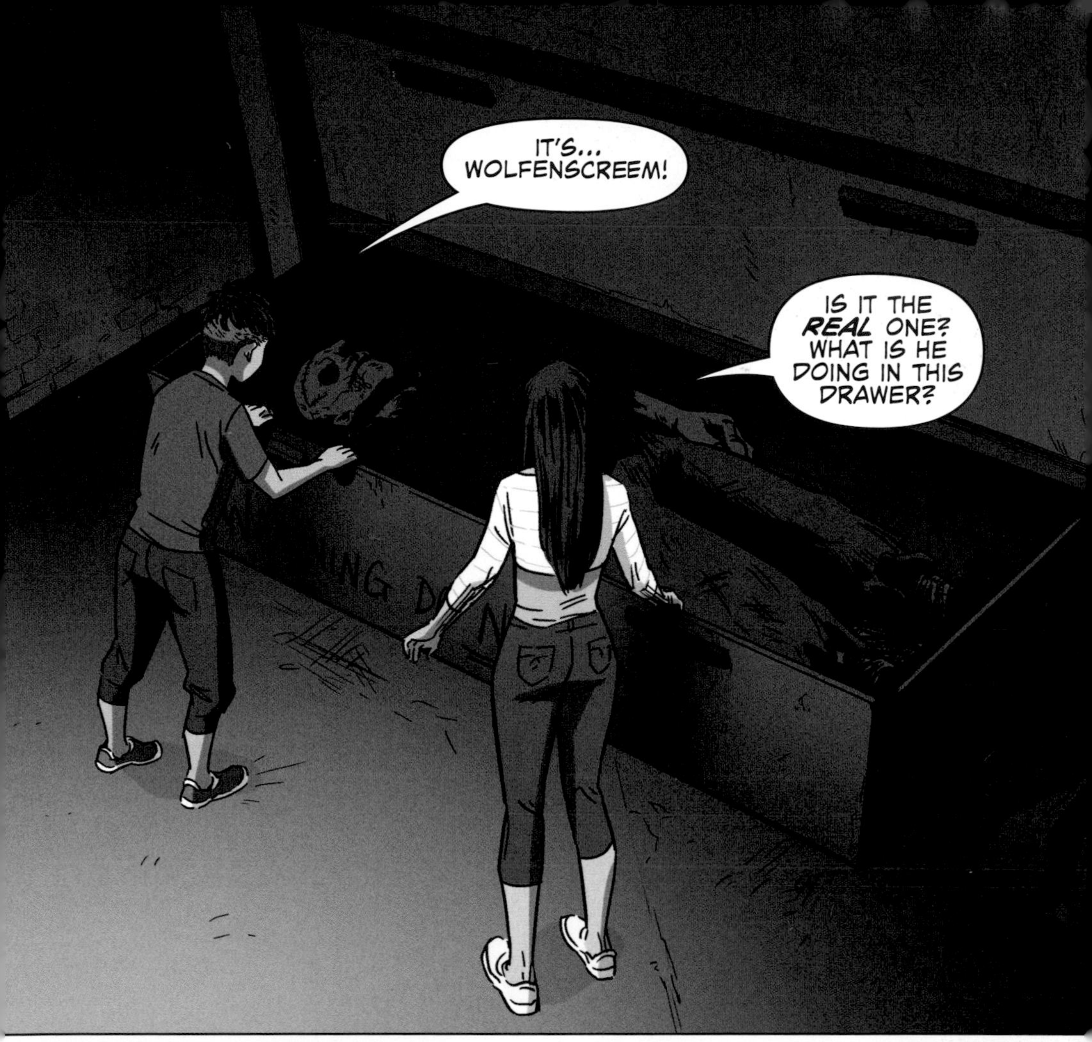
IT'S... WOLFENSCREEM!
IS IT THE ***REAL*** ONE? WHAT IS HE DOING IN THIS DRAWER?
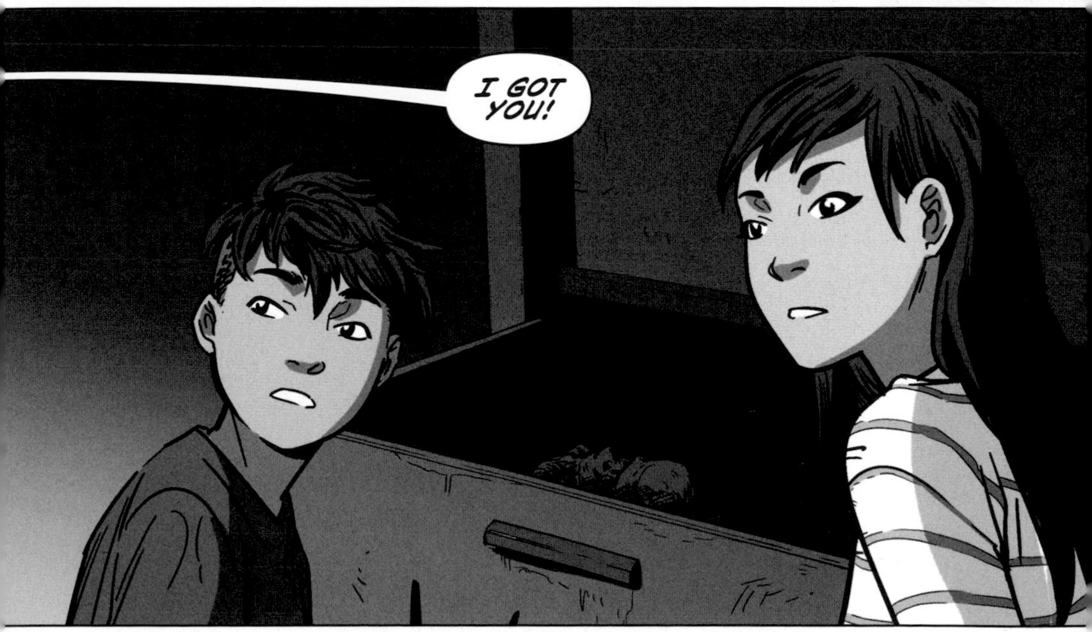
I GOT YOU!

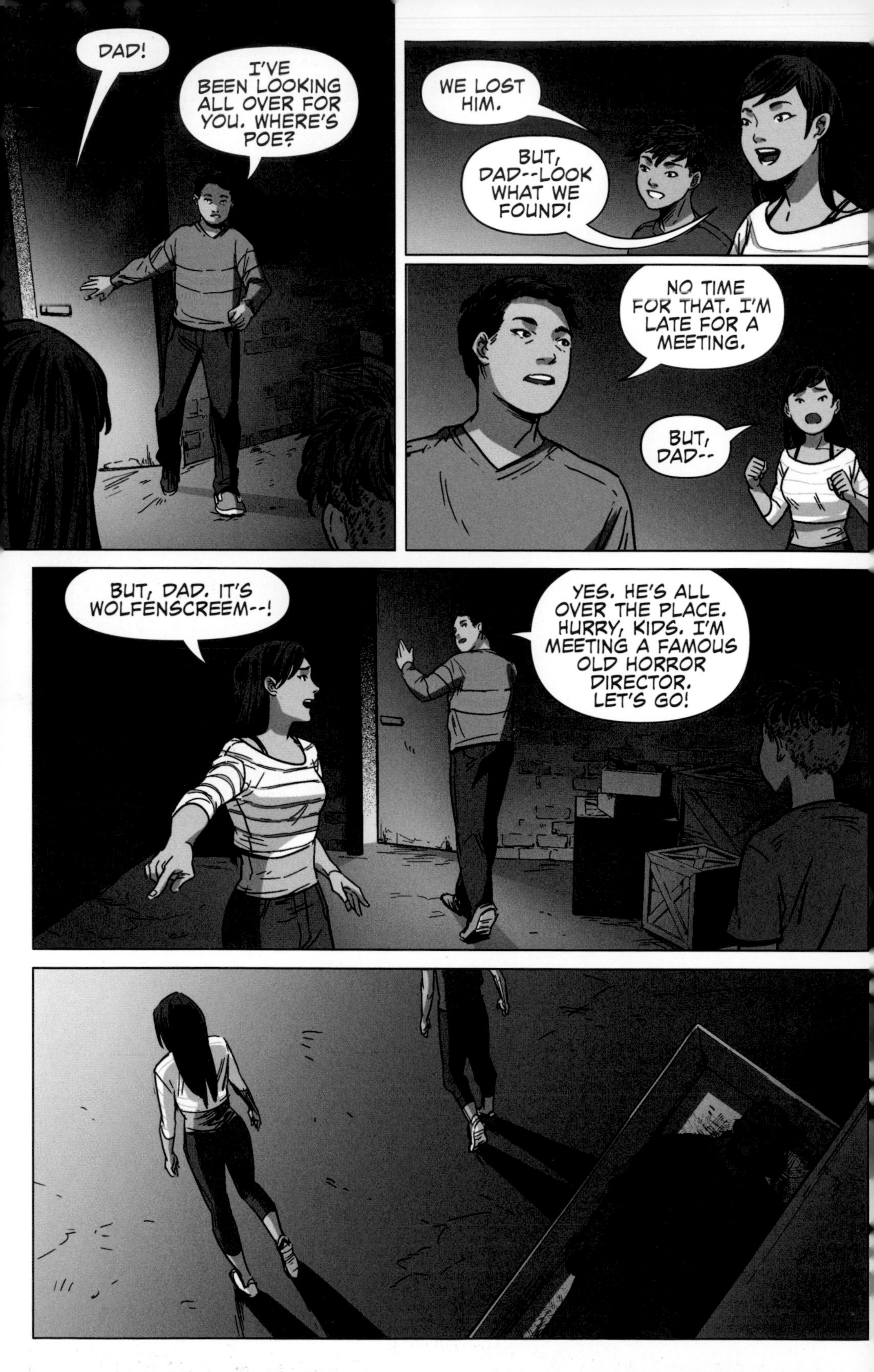
DAD!
I'VE BEEN LOOKING ALL OVER FOR YOU. WHERE'S POE?
WE LOST HIM.
BUT, DAD--LOOK WHAT WE FOUND!
NO TIME FOR THAT. I'M LATE FOR A MEETING.
BUT, DAD--
BUT, DAD. IT'S WOLFENSCREEM--!
YES. HE'S ALL OVER THE PLACE. HURRY, KIDS. I'M MEETING A FAMOUS OLD HORROR DIRECTOR. LET'S GO!

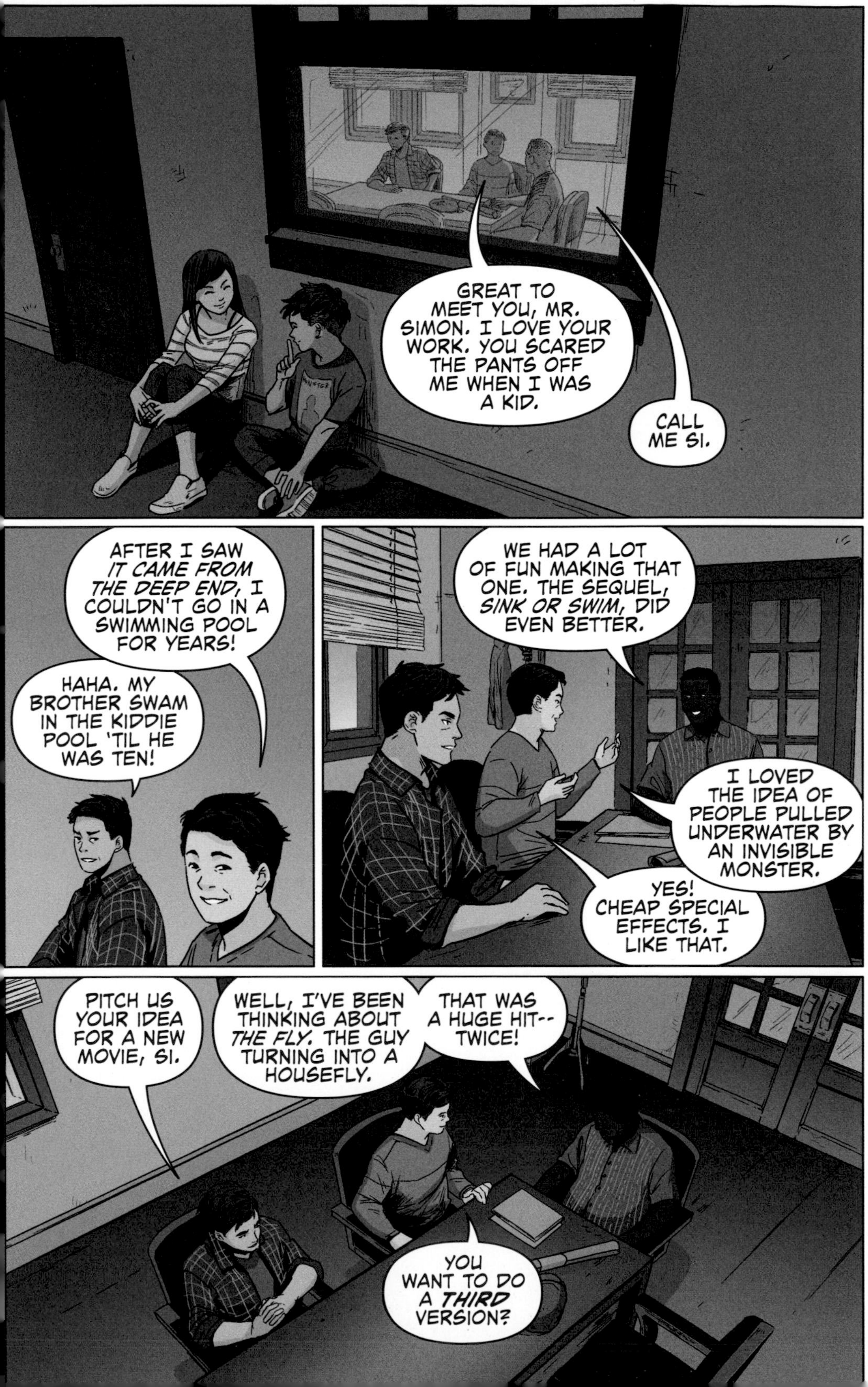
GREAT TO MEET YOU, MR. SIMON. I LOVE YOUR WORK. YOU SCARED THE PANTS OFF ME WHEN I WAS A KID.
CALL ME SI.
AFTER I SAW *IT CAME FROM THE DEEP END*, I COULDN'T GO IN A SWIMMING POOL FOR YEARS!
HAHA. MY BROTHER SWAM IN THE KIDDIE POOL 'TIL HE WAS TEN!
WE HAD A LOT OF FUN MAKING THAT ONE. THE SEQUEL, *SINK OR SWIM*, DID EVEN BETTER.
I LOVED THE IDEA OF PEOPLE PULLED UNDERWATER BY AN INVISIBLE MONSTER.
YES! CHEAP SPECIAL EFFECTS. I LIKE THAT.
PITCH US YOUR IDEA FOR A NEW MOVIE, SI.
WELL, I'VE BEEN THINKING ABOUT *THE FLY*. THE GUY TURNING INTO A HOUSEFLY.
THAT WAS A HUGE HIT-- TWICE!
YOU WANT TO DO A ***THIRD*** VERSION?

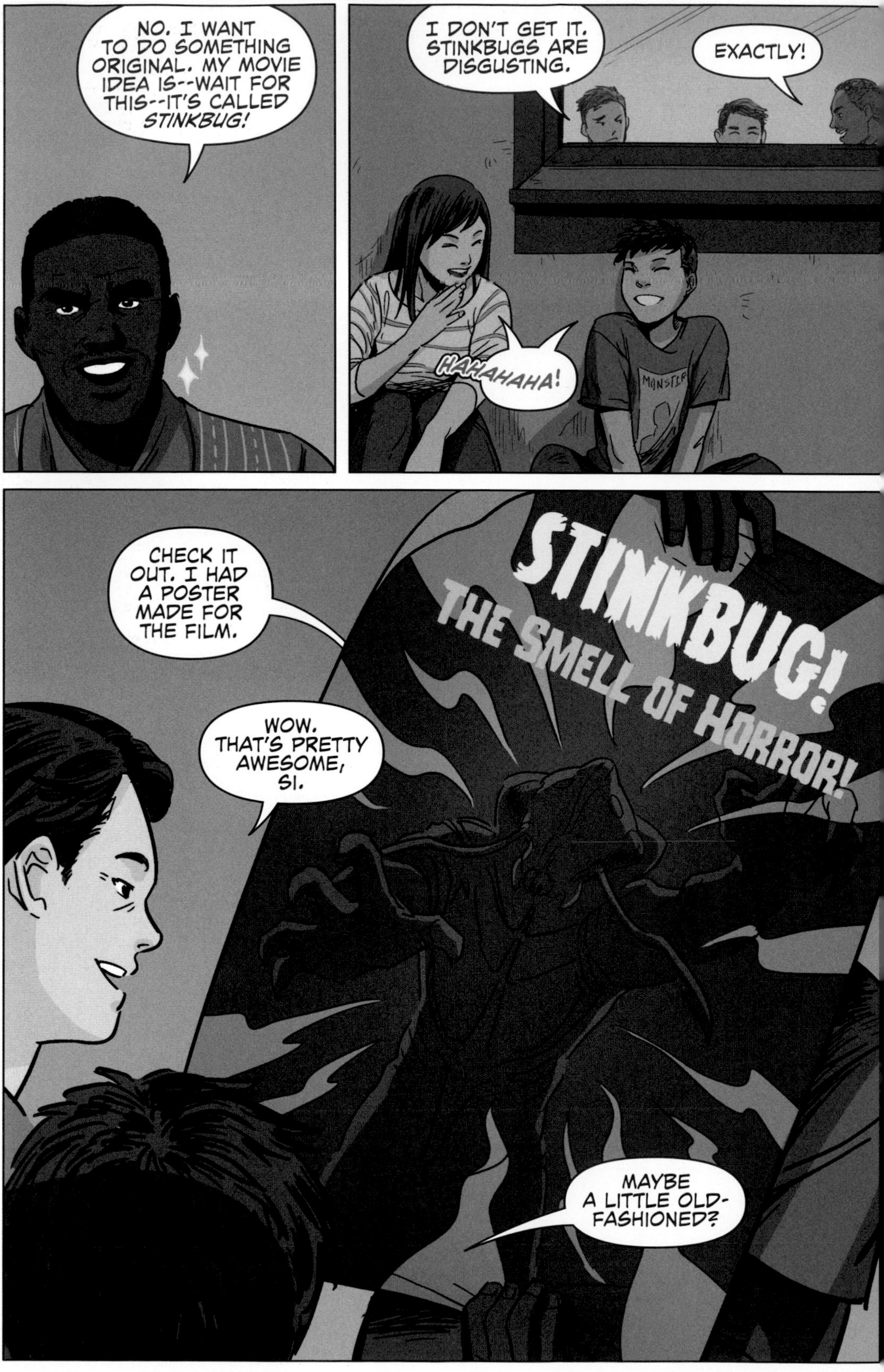
NO. I WANT TO DO SOMETHING ORIGINAL. MY MOVIE IDEA IS--WAIT FOR THIS--IT'S CALLED *STINKBUG!*
I DON'T GET IT. STINKBUGS ARE DISGUSTING.
EXACTLY!
HAHAHAHA!
MONSTER
CHECK IT OUT. I HAD A POSTER MADE FOR THE FILM.
STINKBUG! THE SMELL OF HORROR!
WOW. THAT'S PRETTY AWESOME, SI.
MAYBE A LITTLE OLD-FASHIONED?

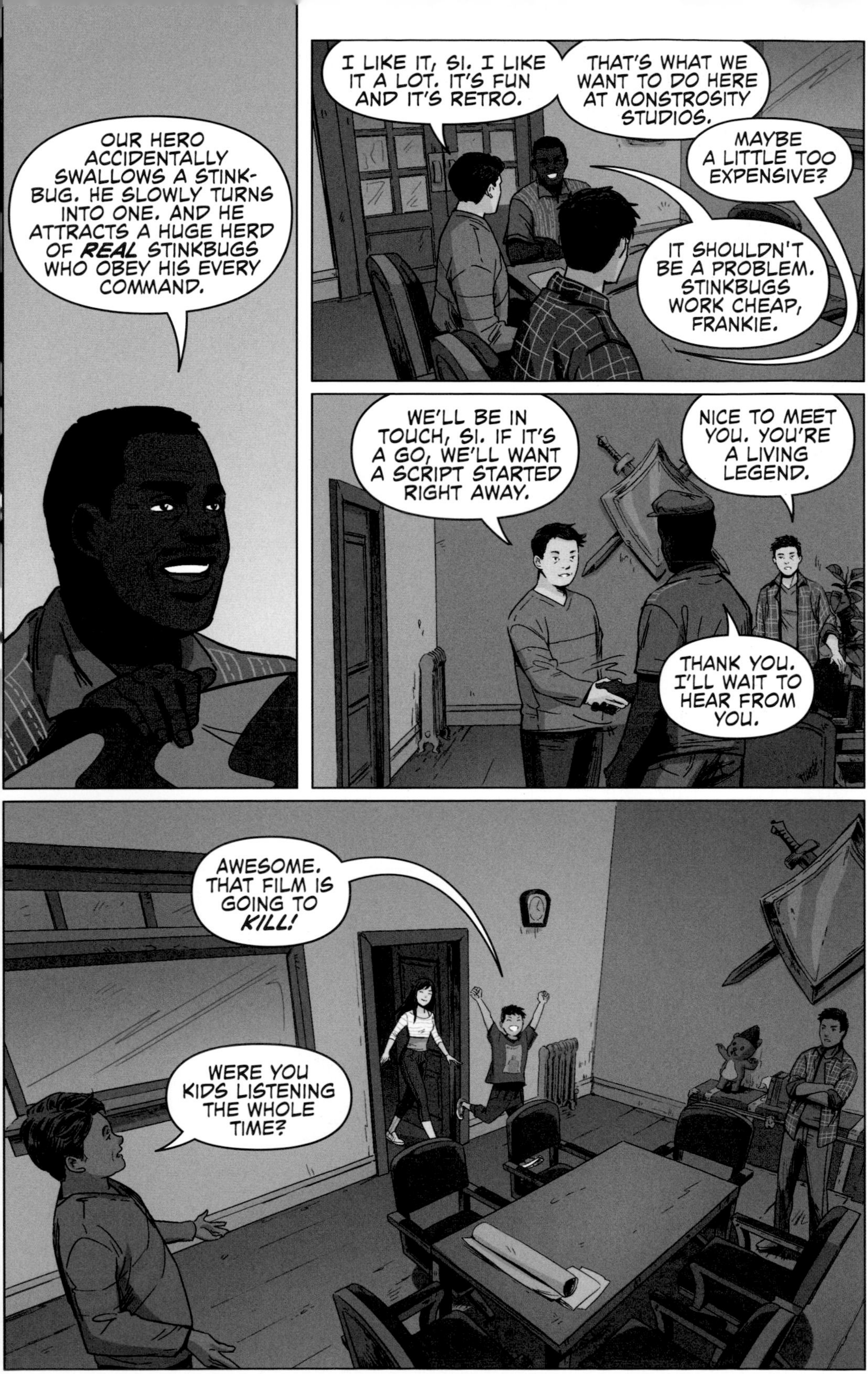
OUR HERO ACCIDENTALLY SWALLOWS A STINK-BUG. HE SLOWLY TURNS INTO ONE. AND HE ATTRACTS A HUGE HERD OF *REAL* STINKBUGS WHO OBEY HIS EVERY COMMAND.
I LIKE IT, SI. I LIKE IT A LOT. IT'S FUN AND IT'S RETRO.
THAT'S WHAT WE WANT TO DO HERE AT MONSTROSITY STUDIOS.
MAYBE A LITTLE TOO EXPENSIVE?
IT SHOULDN'T BE A PROBLEM. STINKBUGS WORK CHEAP, FRANKIE.
WE'LL BE IN TOUCH, SI. IF IT'S A GO, WE'LL WANT A SCRIPT STARTED RIGHT AWAY.
NICE TO MEET YOU. YOU'RE A LIVING LEGEND.
THANK YOU. I'LL WAIT TO HEAR FROM YOU.
AWESOME. THAT FILM IS GOING TO *KILL!*
WERE YOU KIDS LISTENING THE WHOLE TIME?

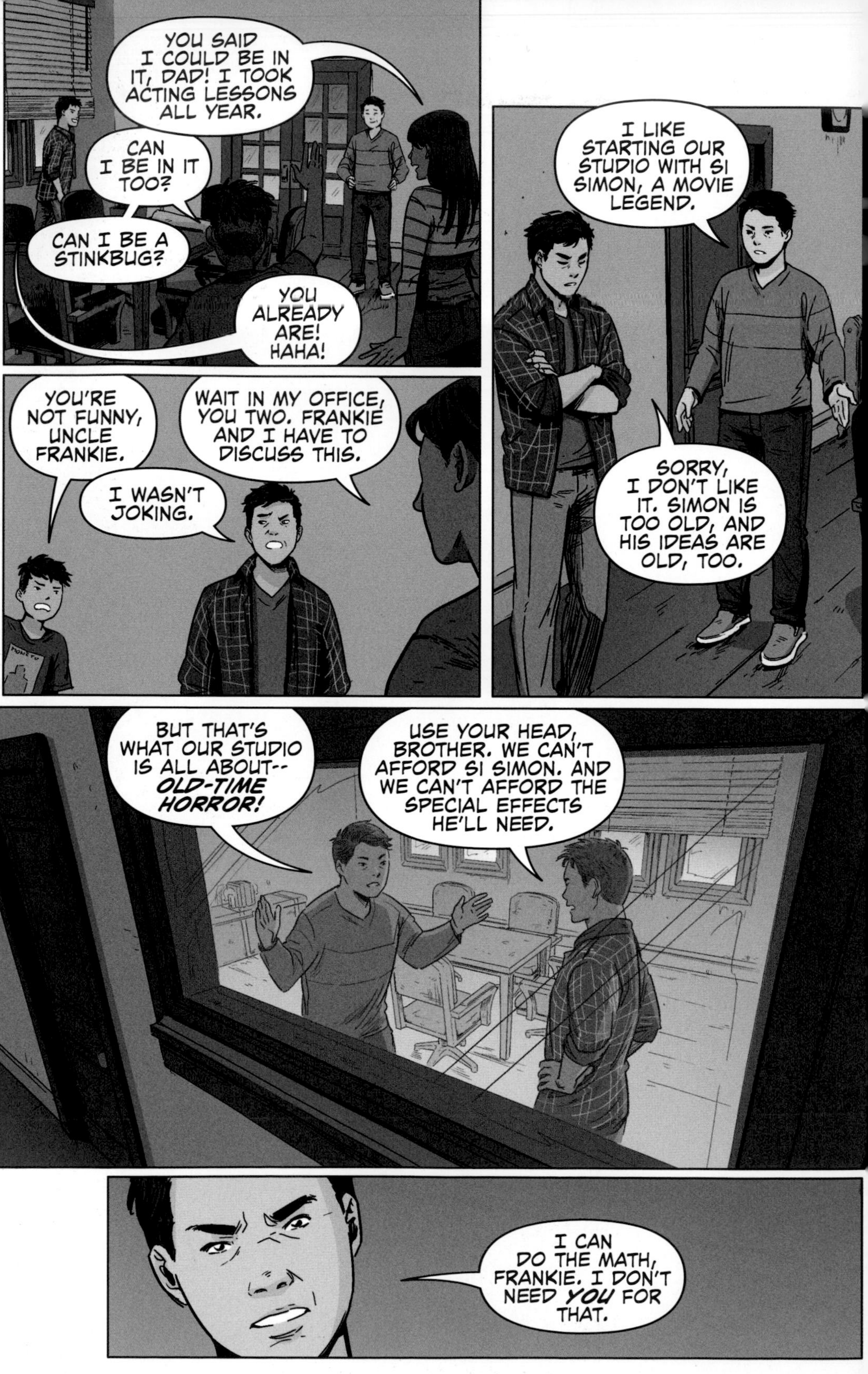
YOU SAID I COULD BE IN IT, DAD! I TOOK ACTING LESSONS ALL YEAR.
CAN I BE IN IT TOO?
CAN I BE A STINKBUG?
YOU ALREADY ARE! HAHA!
YOU'RE NOT FUNNY, UNCLE FRANKIE.
I WASN'T JOKING.
WAIT IN MY OFFICE, YOU TWO. FRANKIE AND I HAVE TO DISCUSS THIS.
I LIKE STARTING OUR STUDIO WITH SI SIMON, A MOVIE LEGEND.
SORRY, I DON'T LIKE IT. SIMON IS TOO OLD, AND HIS IDEAS ARE OLD, TOO.
BUT THAT'S WHAT OUR STUDIO IS ALL ABOUT-- *OLD-TIME HORROR!*
USE YOUR HEAD, BROTHER. WE CAN'T AFFORD SI SIMON. AND WE CAN'T AFFORD THE SPECIAL EFFECTS HE'LL NEED.
I CAN DO THE MATH, FRANKIE. I DON'T NEED *YOU* FOR THAT.

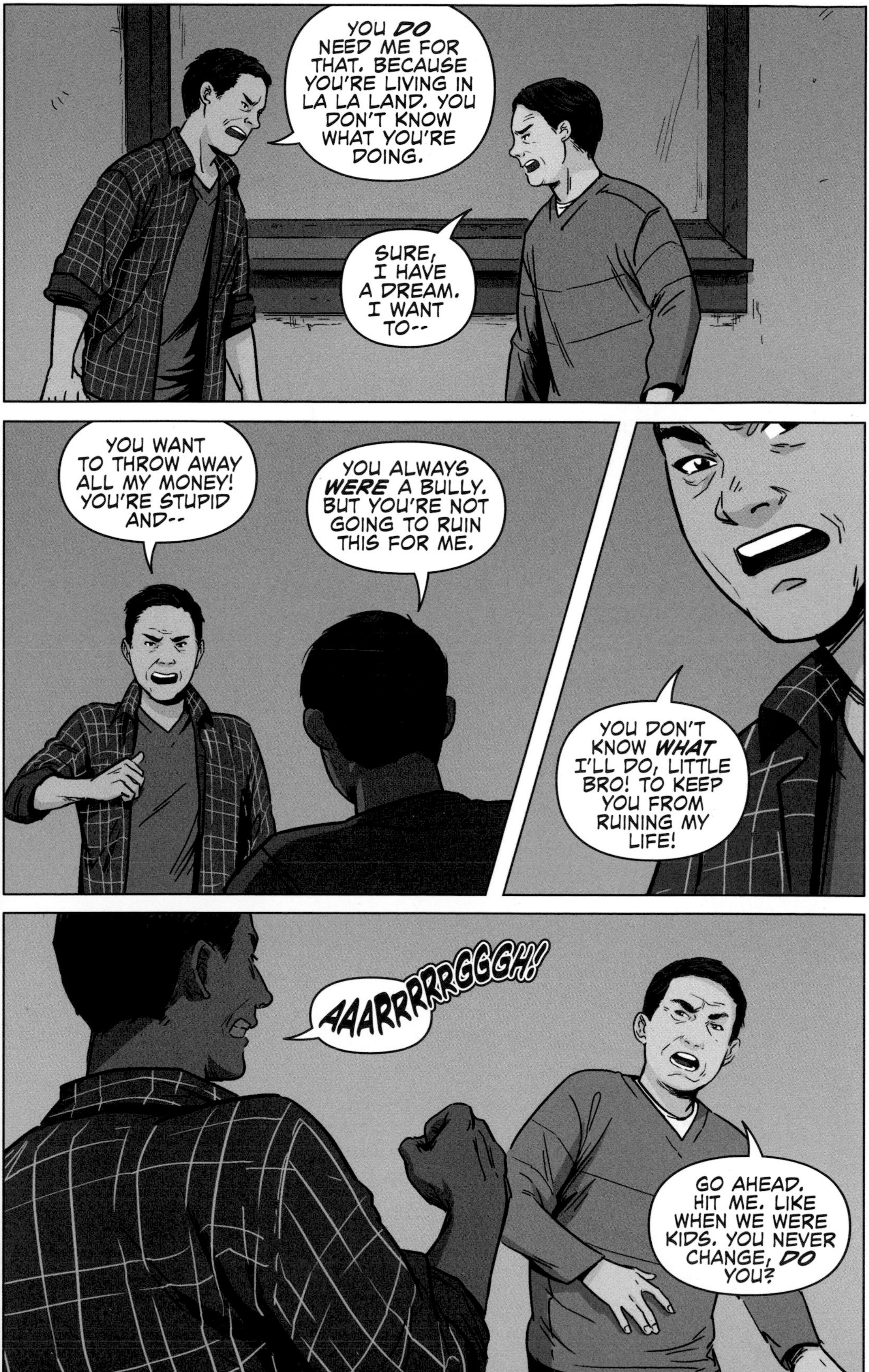
YOU *DO* NEED ME FOR THAT. BECAUSE YOU'RE LIVING IN LA LA LAND. YOU DON'T KNOW WHAT YOU'RE DOING.
SURE, I HAVE A DREAM. I WANT TO--
YOU WANT TO THROW AWAY ALL MY MONEY! YOU'RE STUPID AND--
YOU ALWAYS *WERE* A BULLY. BUT YOU'RE NOT GOING TO RUIN THIS FOR ME.
YOU DON'T KNOW *WHAT* I'LL DO, LITTLE BRO! TO KEEP YOU FROM RUINING MY LIFE!
AAARRRRRGGGH!
GO AHEAD. HIT ME. LIKE WHEN WE WERE KIDS. YOU NEVER CHANGE, *DO* YOU?

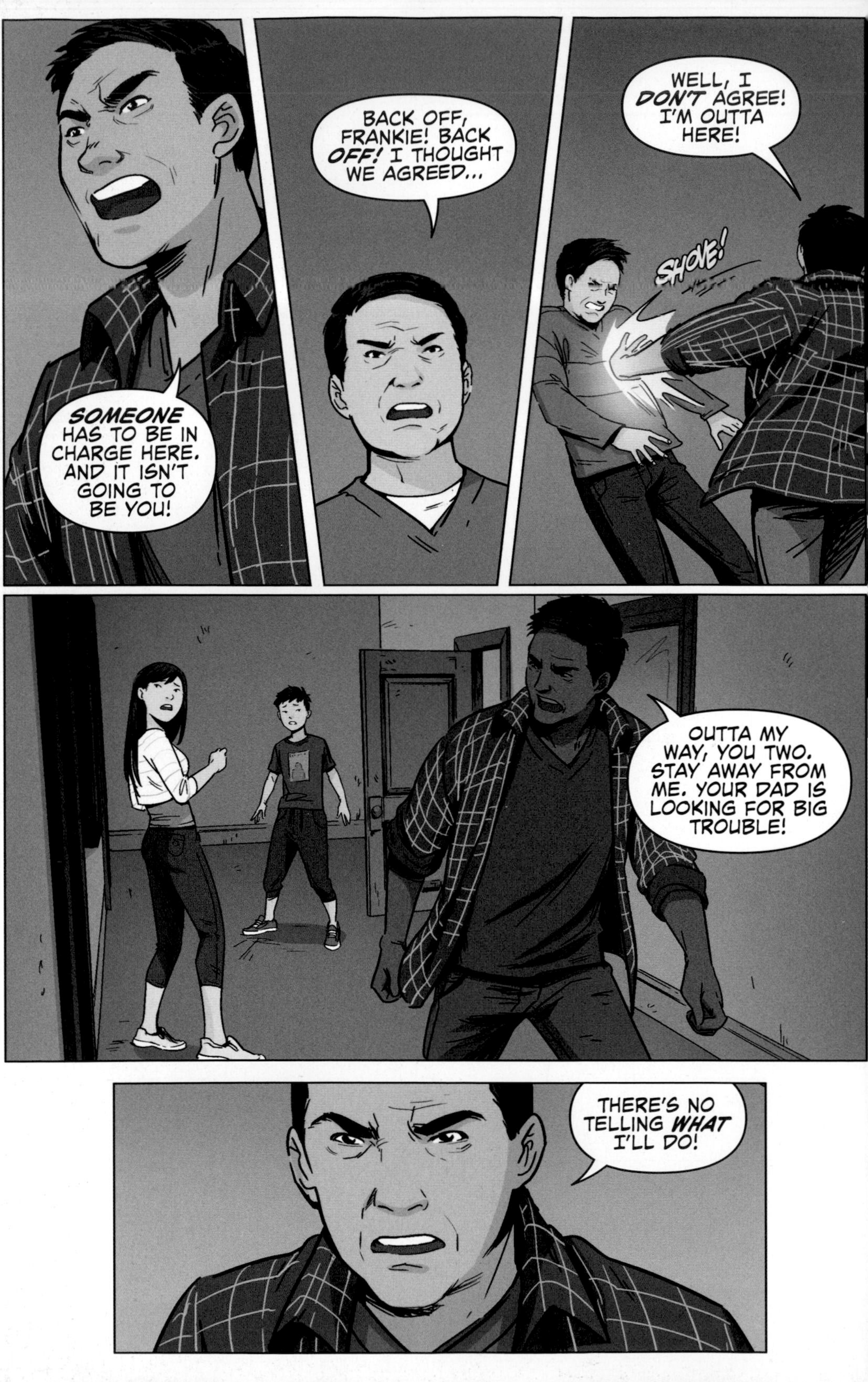
SOMEONE HAS TO BE IN CHARGE HERE. AND IT ISN'T GOING TO BE YOU!
BACK OFF, FRANKIE! BACK OFF! I THOUGHT WE AGREED...
WELL, I DON'T AGREE! I'M OUTTA HERE!
SHOVE!
OUTTA MY WAY, YOU TWO. STAY AWAY FROM ME. YOUR DAD IS LOOKING FOR BIG TROUBLE!
THERE'S NO TELLING WHAT I'LL DO!

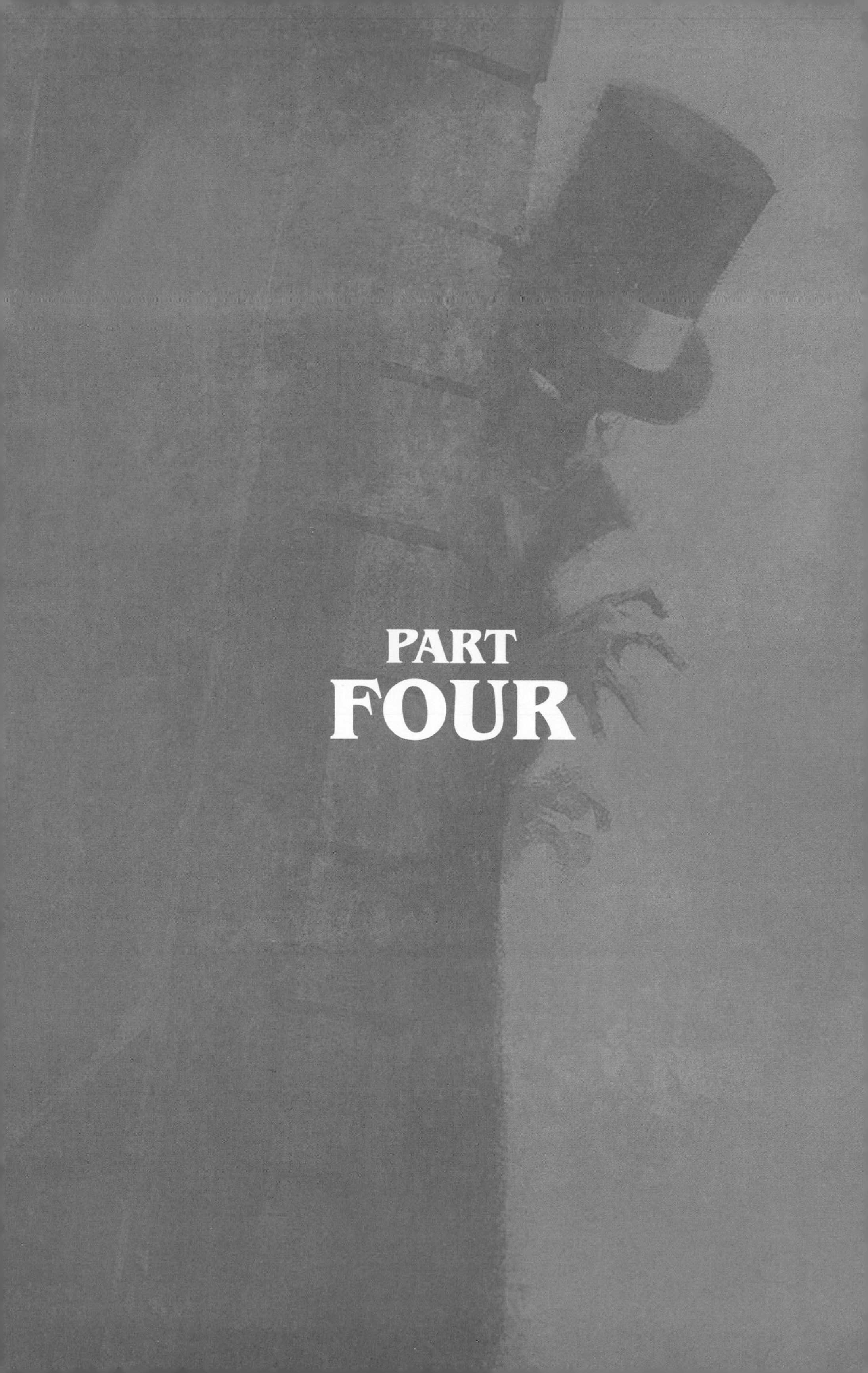

PART FOUR

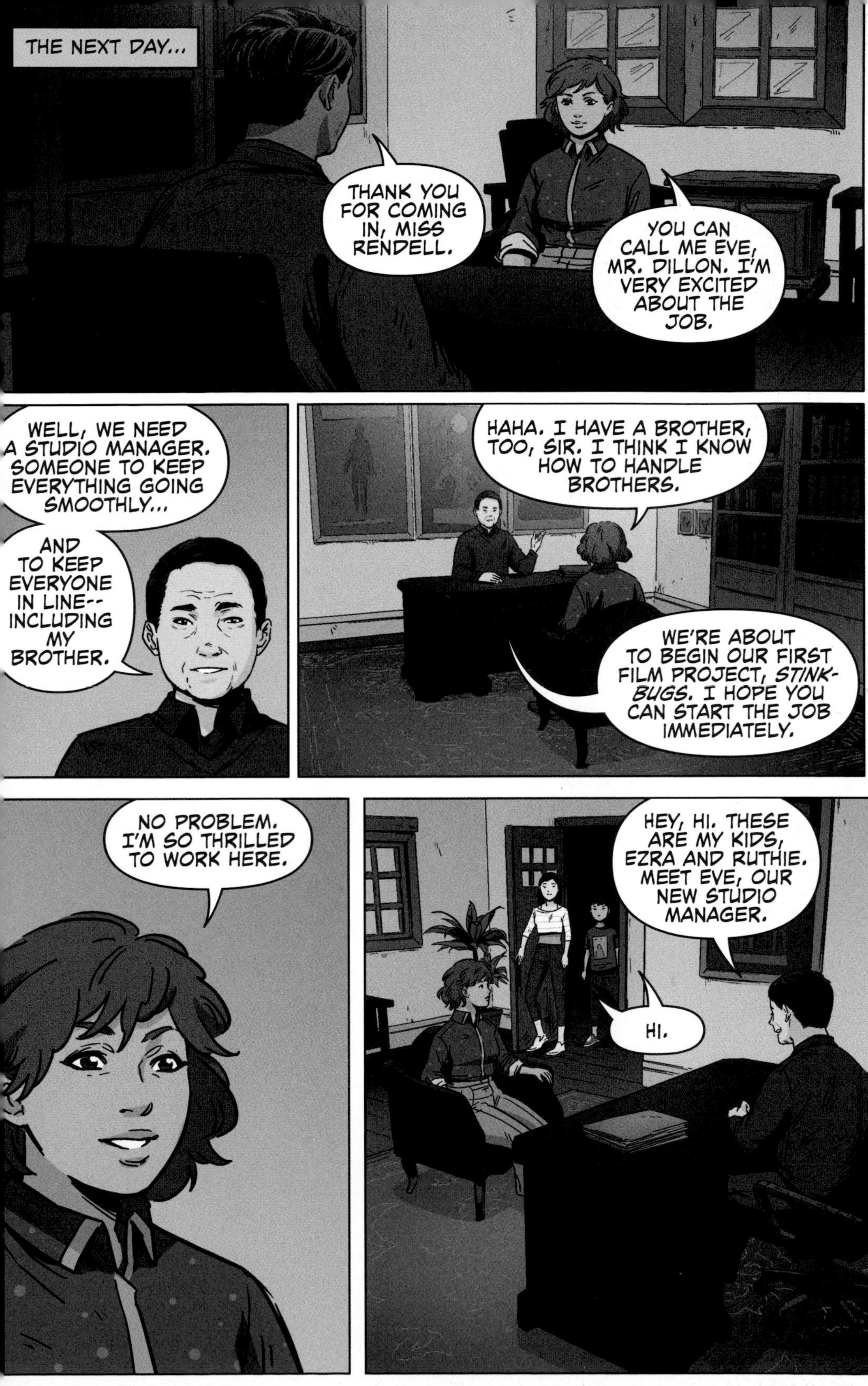

THE NEXT DAY...
THANK YOU FOR COMING IN, MISS RENDELL.
YOU CAN CALL ME EVE, MR. DILLON. I'M VERY EXCITED ABOUT THE JOB.
WELL, WE NEED A STUDIO MANAGER. SOMEONE TO KEEP EVERYTHING GOING SMOOTHLY...
AND TO KEEP EVERYONE IN LINE--INCLUDING MY BROTHER.
HAHA. I HAVE A BROTHER, TOO, SIR. I THINK I KNOW HOW TO HANDLE BROTHERS.
WE'RE ABOUT TO BEGIN OUR FIRST FILM PROJECT, *STINK-BUGS*. I HOPE YOU CAN START THE JOB IMMEDIATELY.
NO PROBLEM. I'M SO THRILLED TO WORK HERE.
HEY, HI. THESE ARE MY KIDS, EZRA AND RUTHIE. MEET EVE, OUR NEW STUDIO MANAGER.
HI.

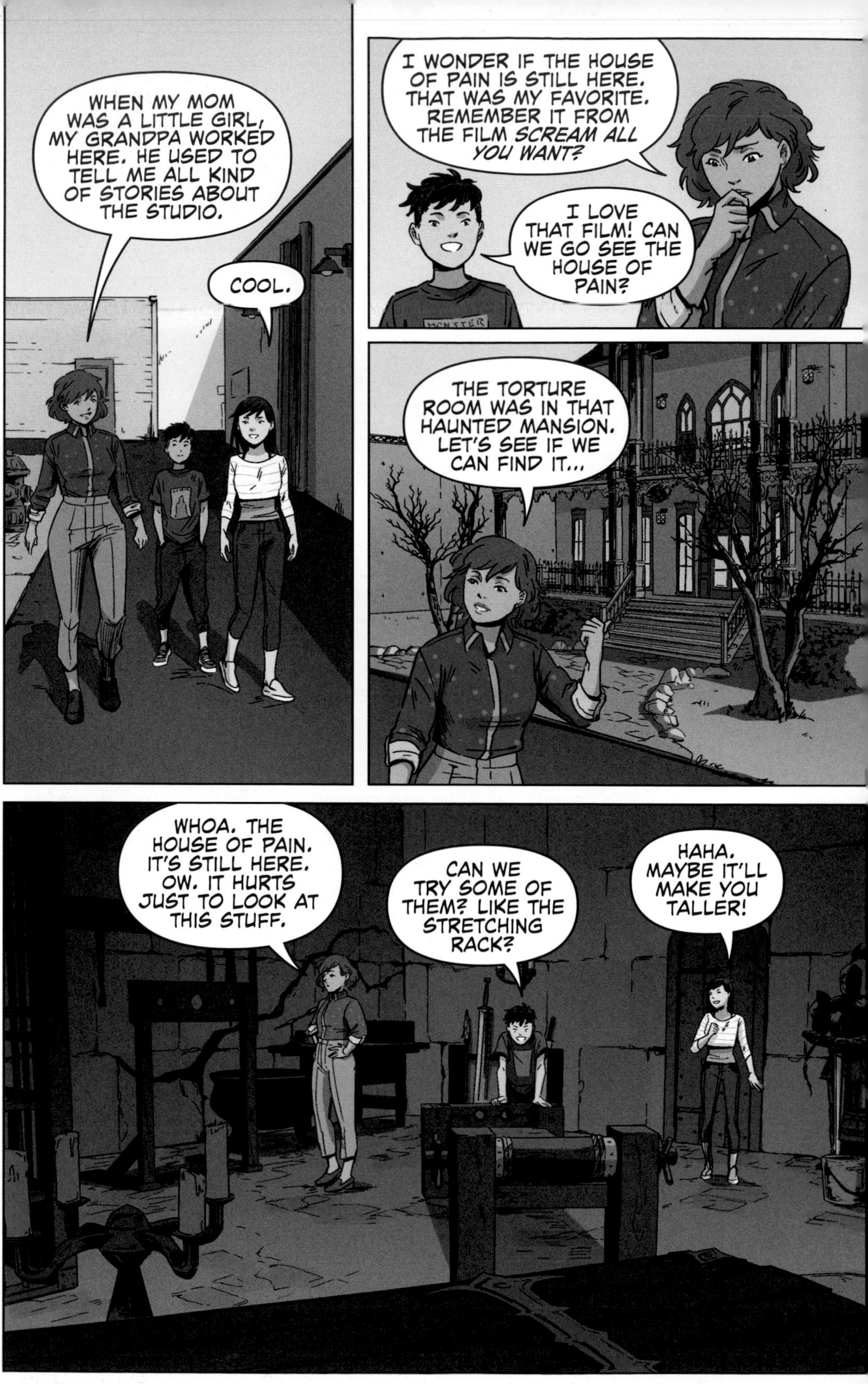
WHEN MY MOM WAS A LITTLE GIRL, MY GRANDPA WORKED HERE. HE USED TO TELL ME ALL KIND OF STORIES ABOUT THE STUDIO.
COOL.
I WONDER IF THE HOUSE OF PAIN IS STILL HERE. THAT WAS MY FAVORITE. REMEMBER IT FROM THE FILM *SCREAM ALL YOU WANT*?
I LOVE THAT FILM! CAN WE GO SEE THE HOUSE OF PAIN?
MONSTER
THE TORTURE ROOM WAS IN THAT HAUNTED MANSION. LET'S SEE IF WE CAN FIND IT...
WHOA. THE HOUSE OF PAIN. IT'S STILL HERE. OW. IT HURTS JUST TO LOOK AT THIS STUFF.
CAN WE TRY SOME OF THEM? LIKE THE STRETCHING RACK?
HAHA. MAYBE IT'LL MAKE YOU TALLER!

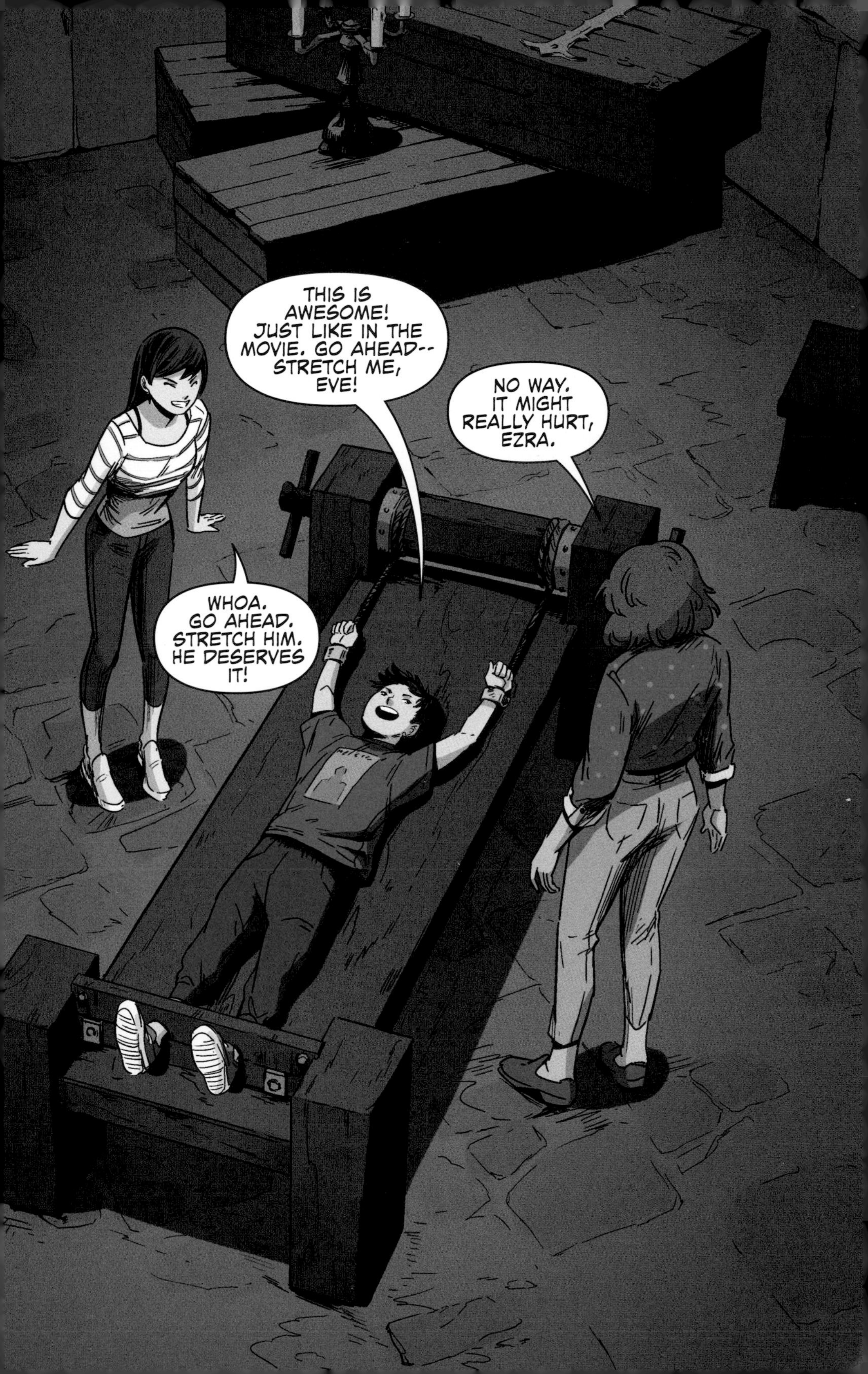
THIS IS AWESOME! JUST LIKE IN THE MOVIE. GO AHEAD-- STRETCH ME, EVE!
NO WAY. IT MIGHT REALLY HURT, EZRA.
WHOA. GO AHEAD. STRETCH HIM. HE DESERVES IT!

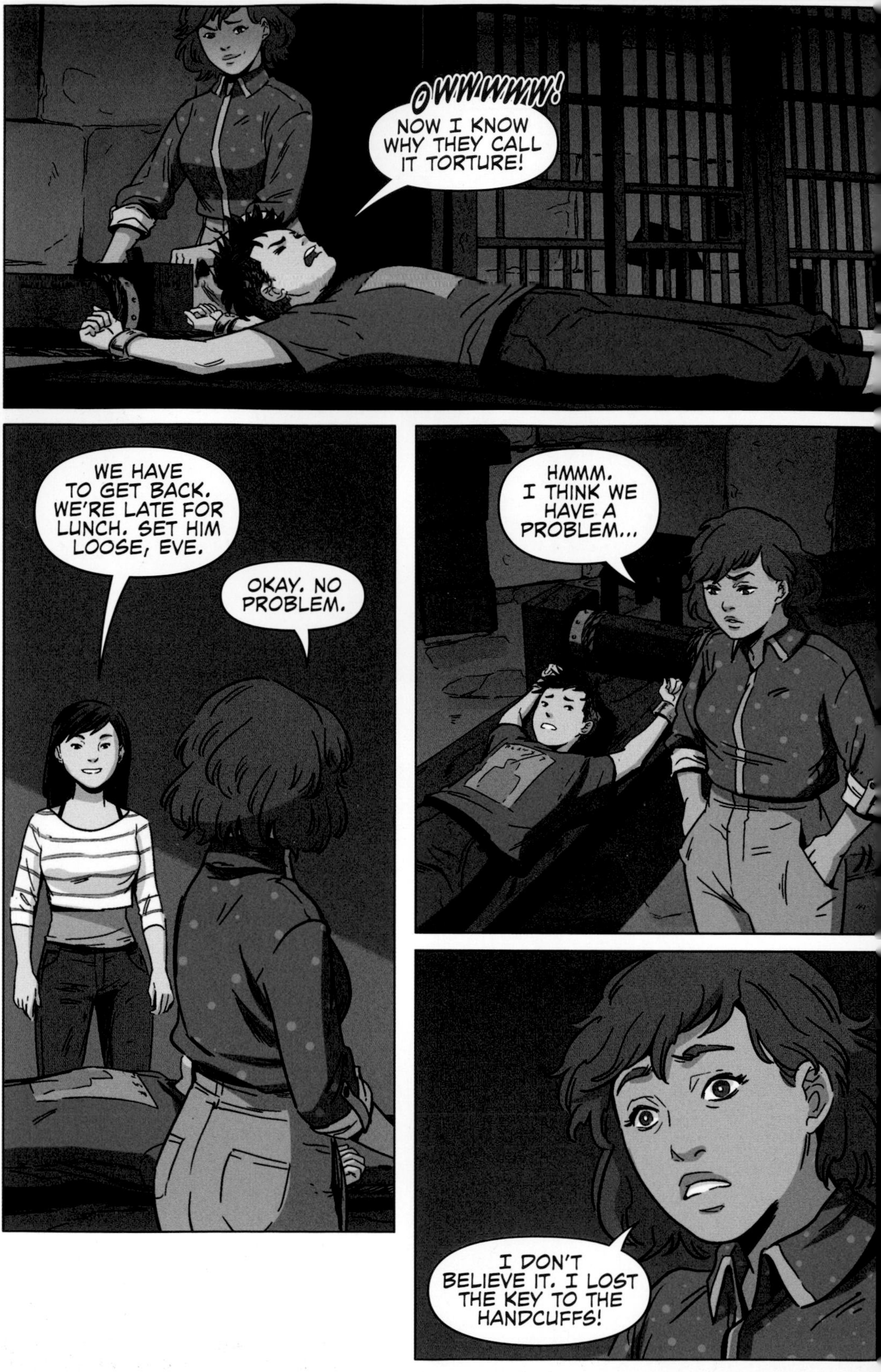
OWWWWWW!
NOW I KNOW WHY THEY CALL IT TORTURE!
WE HAVE TO GET BACK. WE'RE LATE FOR LUNCH. SET HIM LOOSE, EVE.
OKAY. NO PROBLEM.
HMMM. I THINK WE HAVE A PROBLEM...
I DON'T BELIEVE IT. I LOST THE KEY TO THE HANDCUFFS!

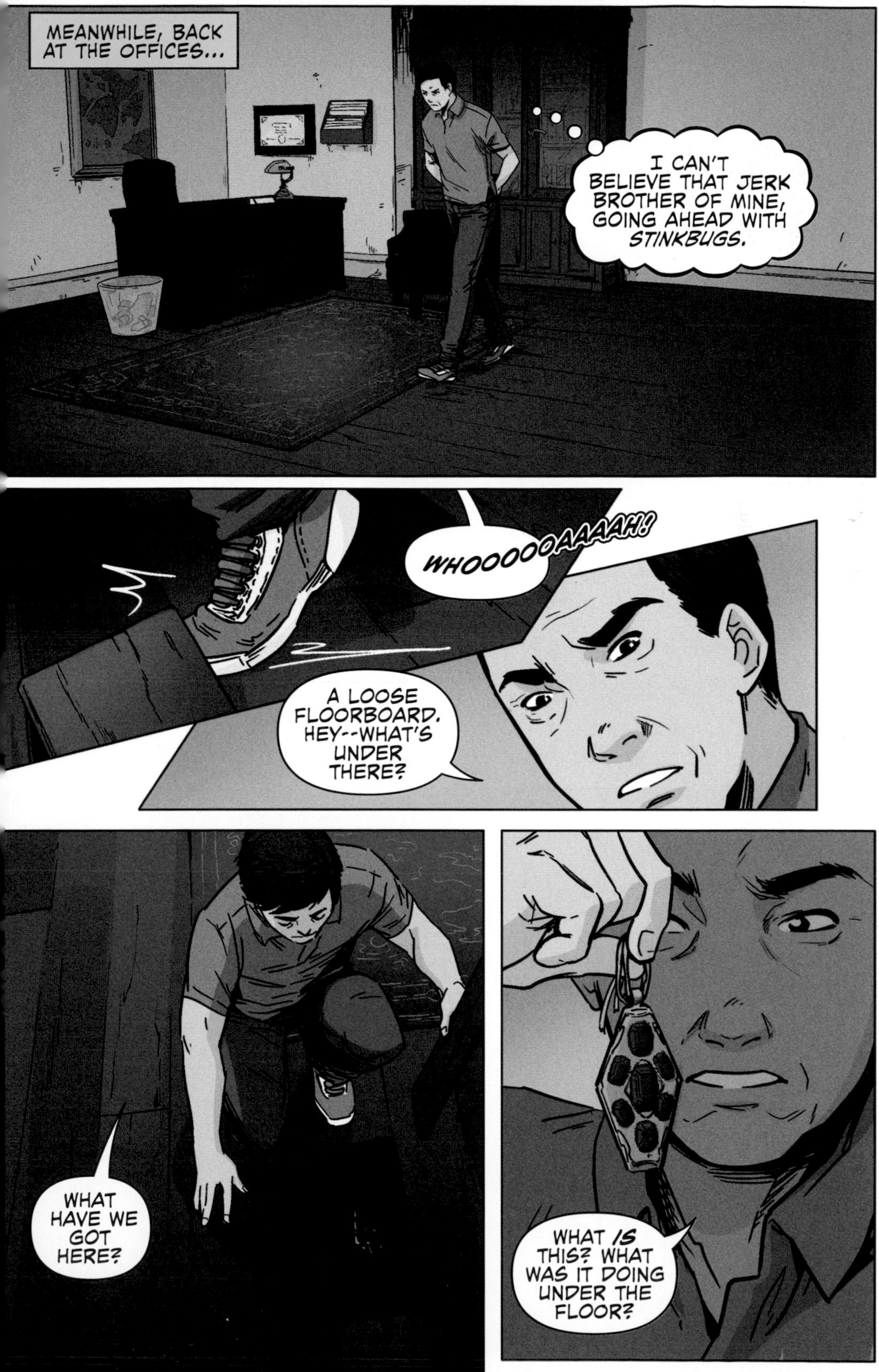
MEANWHILE, BACK AT THE OFFICES...
I CAN'T BELIEVE THAT JERK BROTHER OF MINE, GOING AHEAD WITH STINKBUGS.
WHOOOOOOAAAAH!
A LOOSE FLOORBOARD. HEY--WHAT'S UNDER THERE?
WHAT HAVE WE GOT HERE?
WHAT IS THIS? WHAT WAS IT DOING UNDER THE FLOOR?

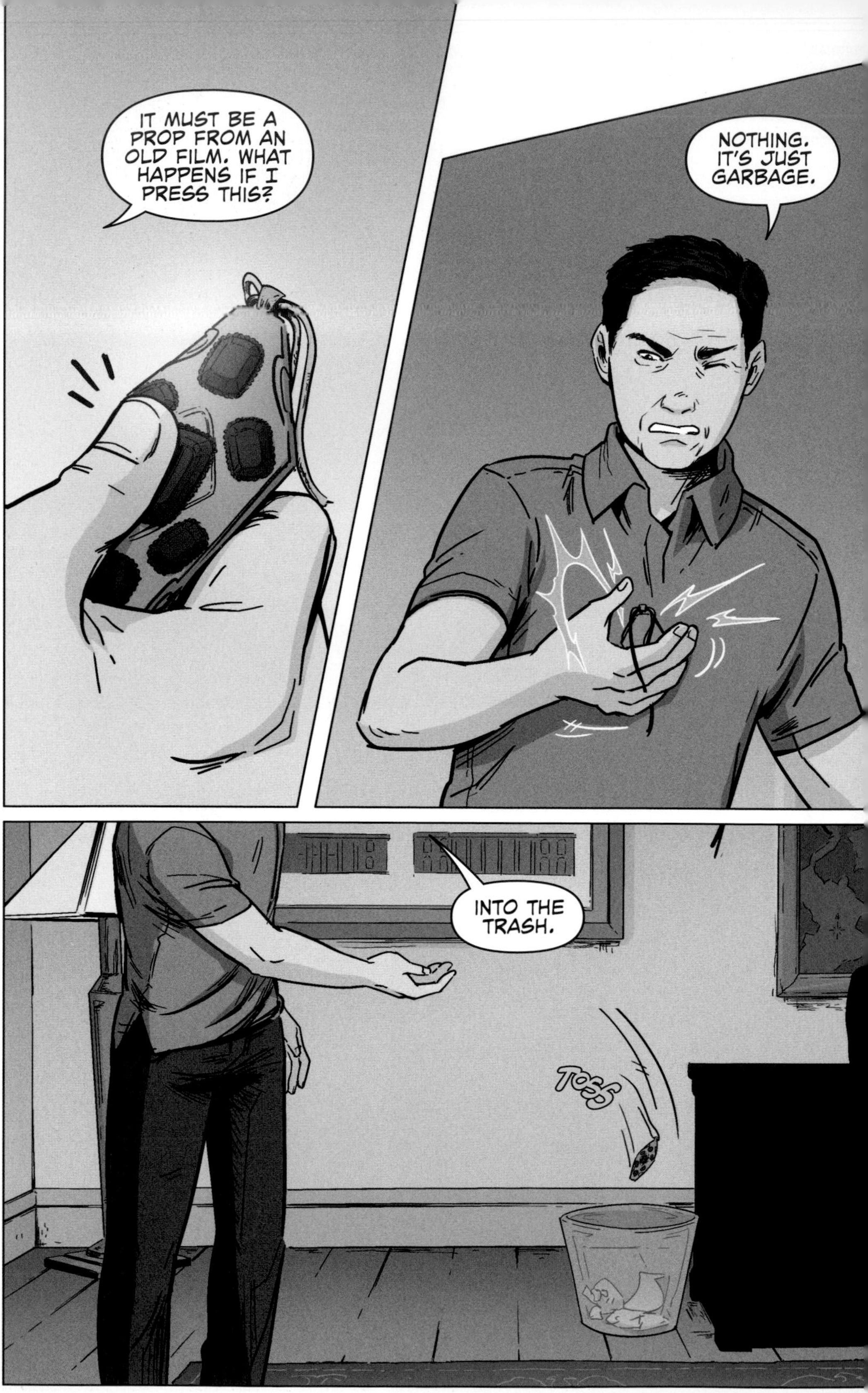
IT MUST BE A PROP FROM AN OLD FILM. WHAT HAPPENS IF I PRESS THIS?
NOTHING. IT'S JUST GARBAGE.
INTO THE TRASH.
TOSS

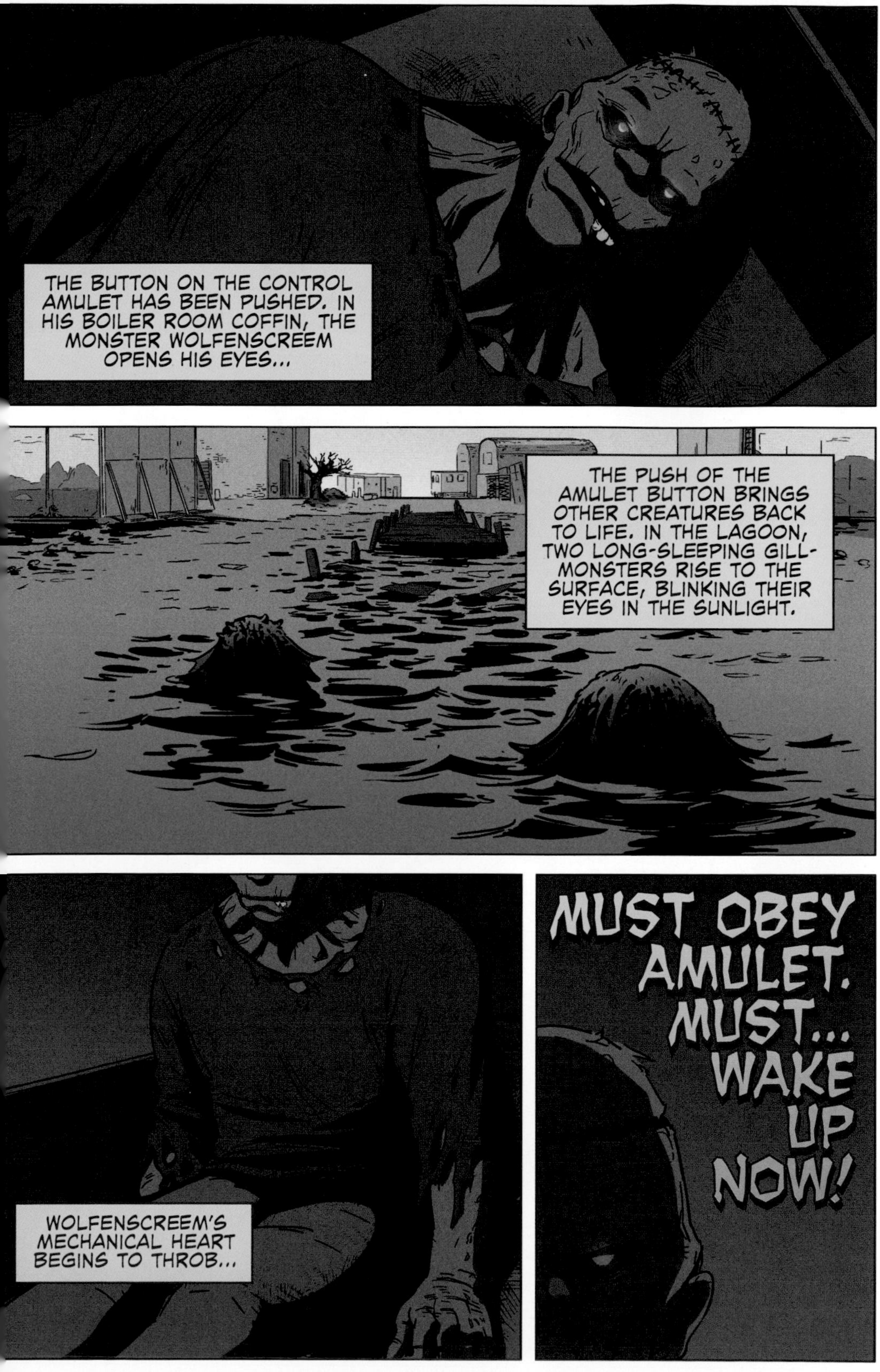
THE BUTTON ON THE CONTROL AMULET HAS BEEN PUSHED. IN HIS BOILER ROOM COFFIN, THE MONSTER WOLFENSCREEM OPENS HIS EYES...
THE PUSH OF THE AMULET BUTTON BRINGS OTHER CREATURES BACK TO LIFE. IN THE LAGOON, TWO LONG-SLEEPING GILL-MONSTERS RISE TO THE SURFACE, BLINKING THEIR EYES IN THE SUNLIGHT.
WOLFENSCREEM'S MECHANICAL HEART BEGINS TO THROB...
MUST OBEY AMULET. MUST... WAKE UP NOW!

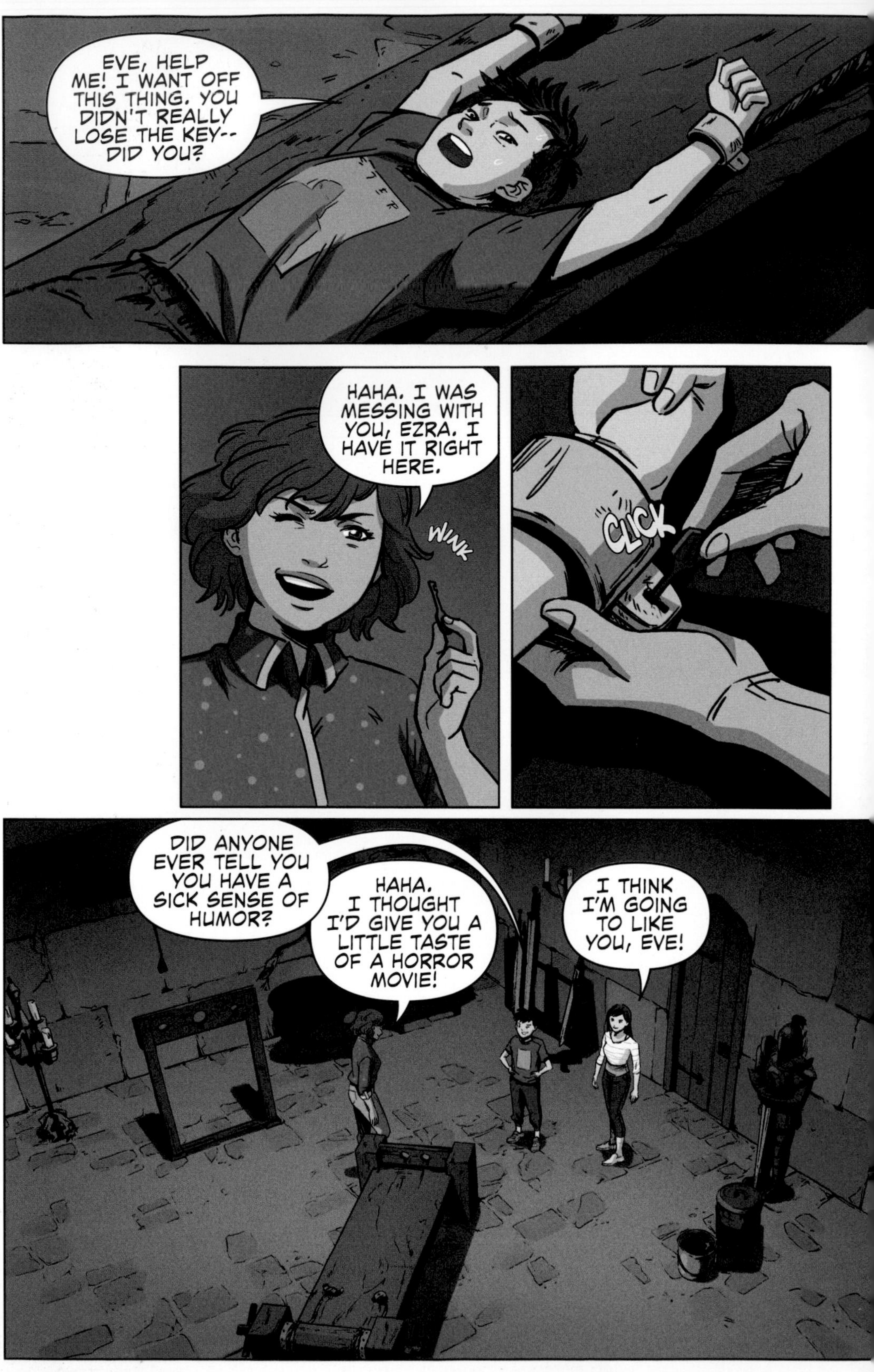
EVE, HELP ME! I WANT OFF THIS THING. YOU DIDN'T REALLY LOSE THE KEY-- DID YOU?
HAHA. I WAS MESSING WITH YOU, EZRA. I HAVE IT RIGHT HERE.
WINK
CLICK
DID ANYONE EVER TELL YOU YOU HAVE A SICK SENSE OF HUMOR?
HAHA. I THOUGHT I'D GIVE YOU A LITTLE TASTE OF A HORROR MOVIE!
I THINK I'M GOING TO LIKE YOU, EVE!

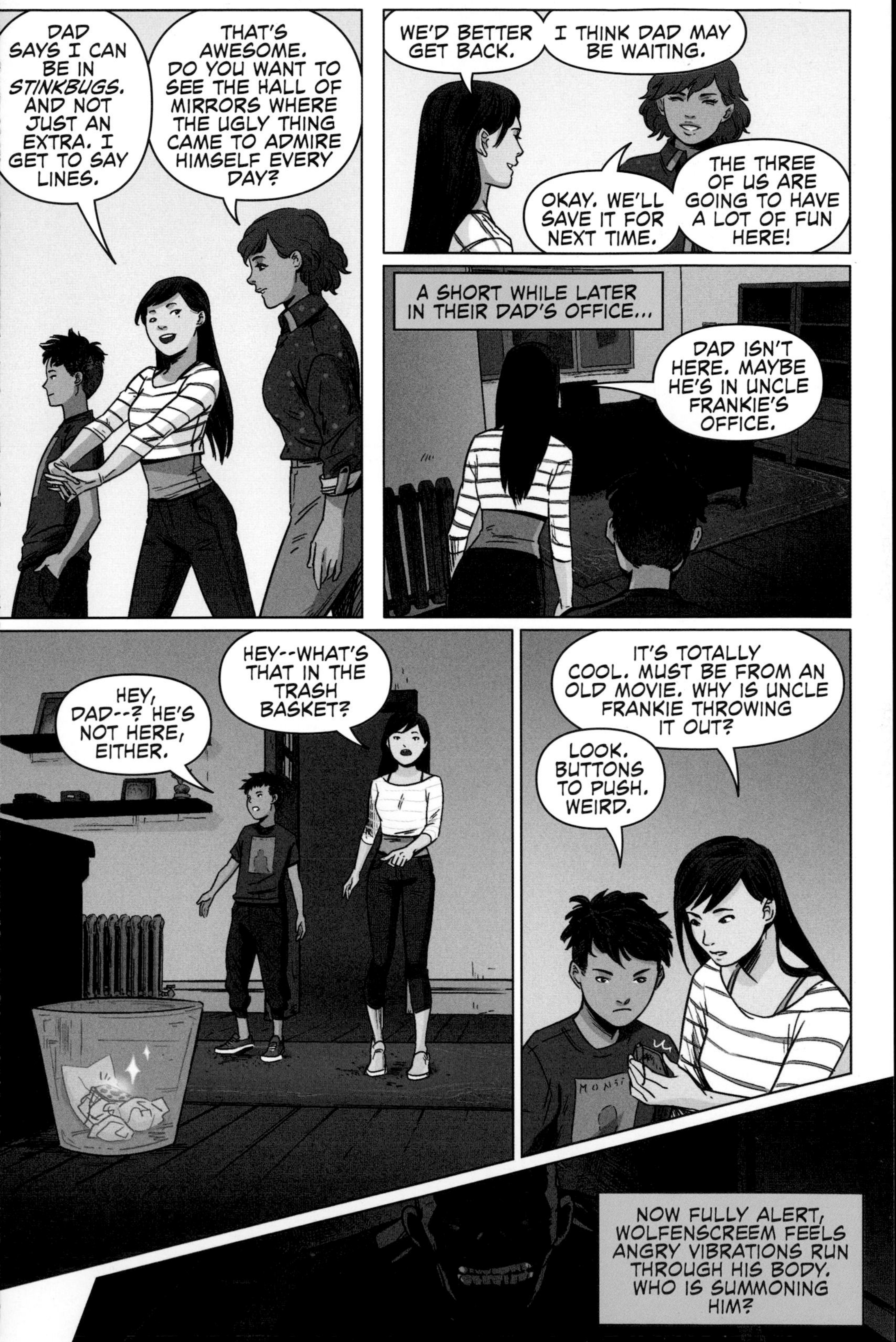
DAD SAYS I CAN BE IN *STINKBUGS*. AND NOT JUST AN EXTRA. I GET TO SAY LINES.
THAT'S AWESOME. DO YOU WANT TO SEE THE HALL OF MIRRORS WHERE THE UGLY THING CAME TO ADMIRE HIMSELF EVERY DAY?
WE'D BETTER GET BACK.
I THINK DAD MAY BE WAITING.
OKAY. WE'LL SAVE IT FOR NEXT TIME.
THE THREE OF US ARE GOING TO HAVE A LOT OF FUN HERE!
A SHORT WHILE LATER IN THEIR DAD'S OFFICE...
DAD ISN'T HERE. MAYBE HE'S IN UNCLE FRANKIE'S OFFICE.
HEY, DAD--? HE'S NOT HERE, EITHER.
HEY--WHAT'S THAT IN THE TRASH BASKET?
IT'S TOTALLY COOL. MUST BE FROM AN OLD MOVIE. WHY IS UNCLE FRANKIE THROWING IT OUT?
LOOK. BUTTONS TO PUSH. WEIRD.
NOW FULLY ALERT, WOLFENSCREEM FEELS ANGRY VIBRATIONS RUN THROUGH HIS BODY. WHO IS SUMMONING HIM?

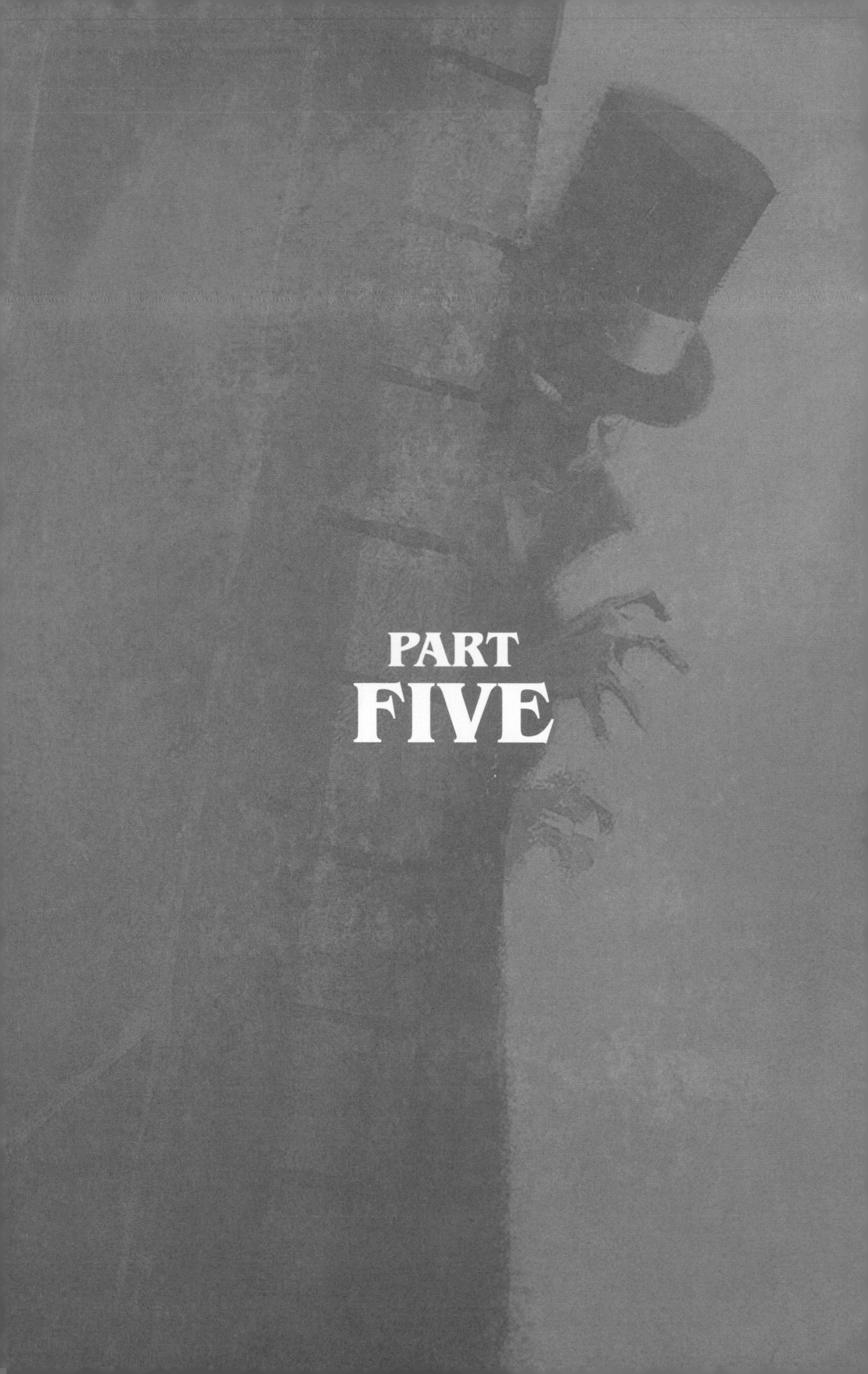

PART FIVE

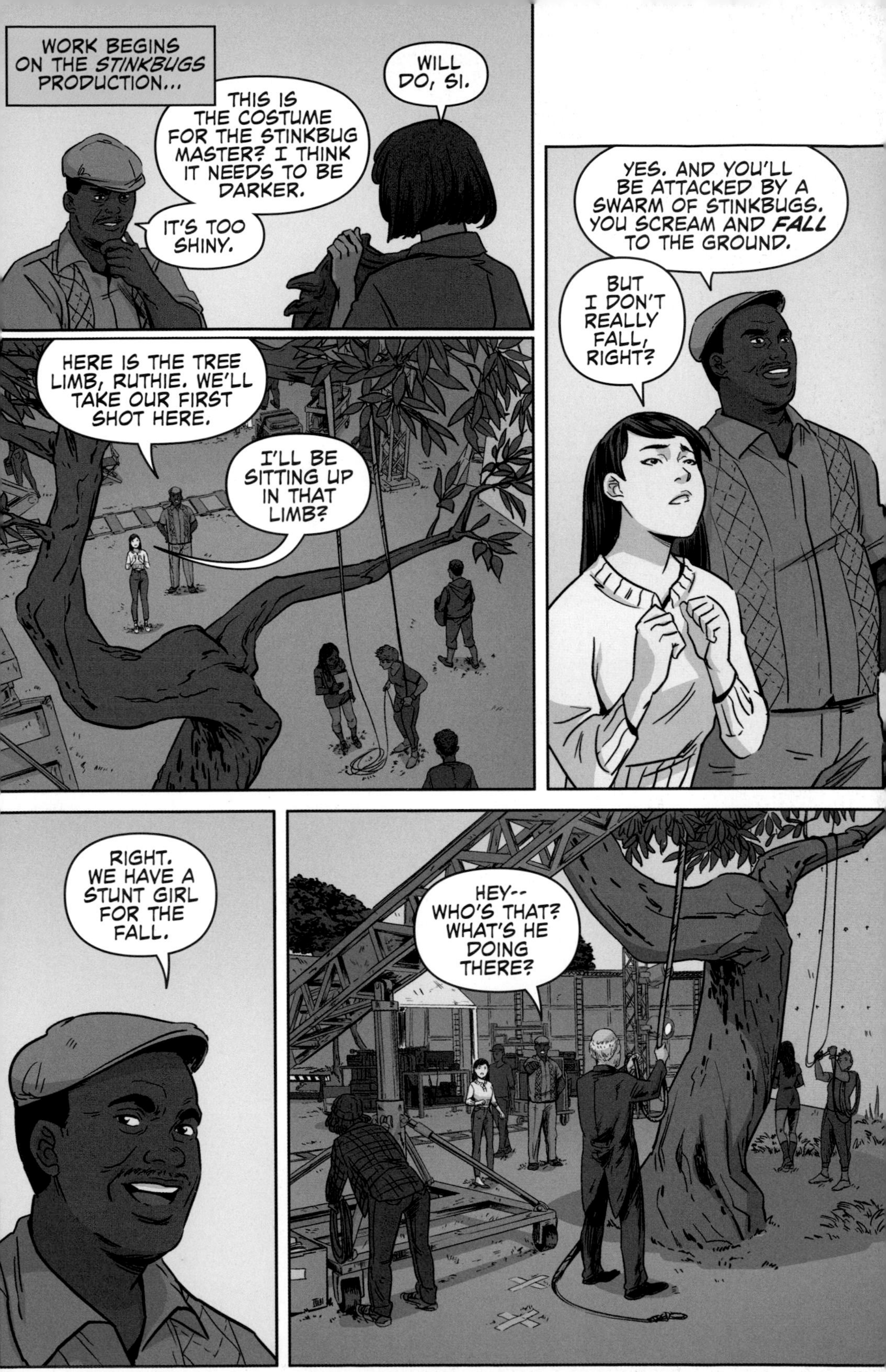
WORK BEGINS ON THE *STINKBUGS* PRODUCTION...
THIS IS THE COSTUME FOR THE STINKBUG MASTER? I THINK IT NEEDS TO BE DARKER.
IT'S TOO SHINY.
WILL DO, SI.
HERE IS THE TREE LIMB, RUTHIE. WE'LL TAKE OUR FIRST SHOT HERE.
I'LL BE SITTING UP IN THAT LIMB?
YES. AND YOU'LL BE ATTACKED BY A SWARM OF STINKBUGS. YOU SCREAM AND **FALL** TO THE GROUND.
BUT I DON'T REALLY FALL, RIGHT?
RIGHT. WE HAVE A STUNT GIRL FOR THE FALL.
HEY-- WHO'S THAT? WHAT'S HE DOING THERE?

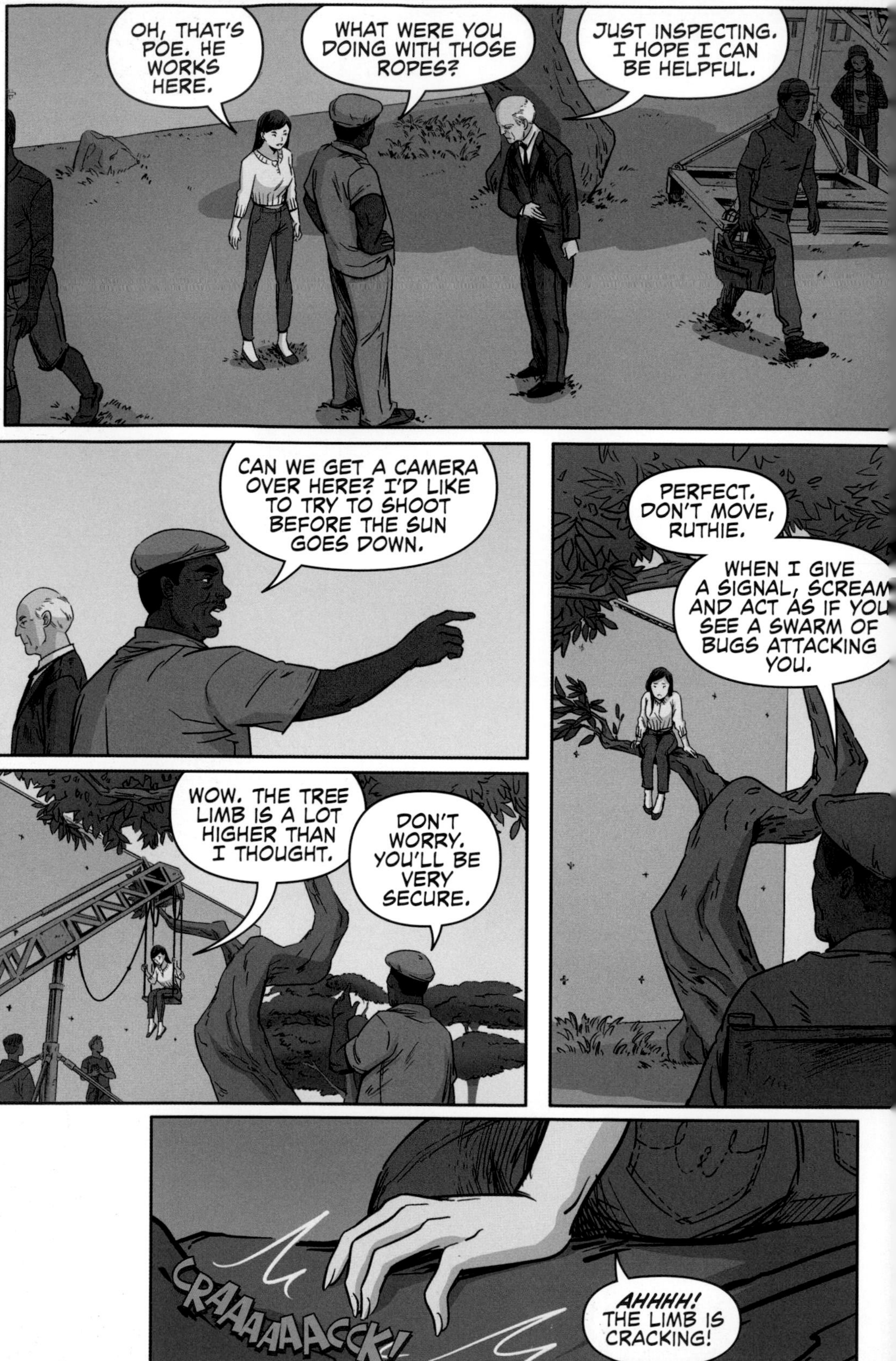
OH, THAT'S POE. HE WORKS HERE.
WHAT WERE YOU DOING WITH THOSE ROPES?
JUST INSPECTING. I HOPE I CAN BE HELPFUL.
CAN WE GET A CAMERA OVER HERE? I'D LIKE TO TRY TO SHOOT BEFORE THE SUN GOES DOWN.
WOW. THE TREE LIMB IS A LOT HIGHER THAN I THOUGHT.
DON'T WORRY. YOU'LL BE VERY SECURE.
PERFECT. DON'T MOVE, RUTHIE.
WHEN I GIVE A SIGNAL, SCREAM AND ACT AS IF YOU SEE A SWARM OF BUGS ATTACKING YOU.
CRAAAAAACCK!
AHHHH! THE LIMB IS CRACKING!

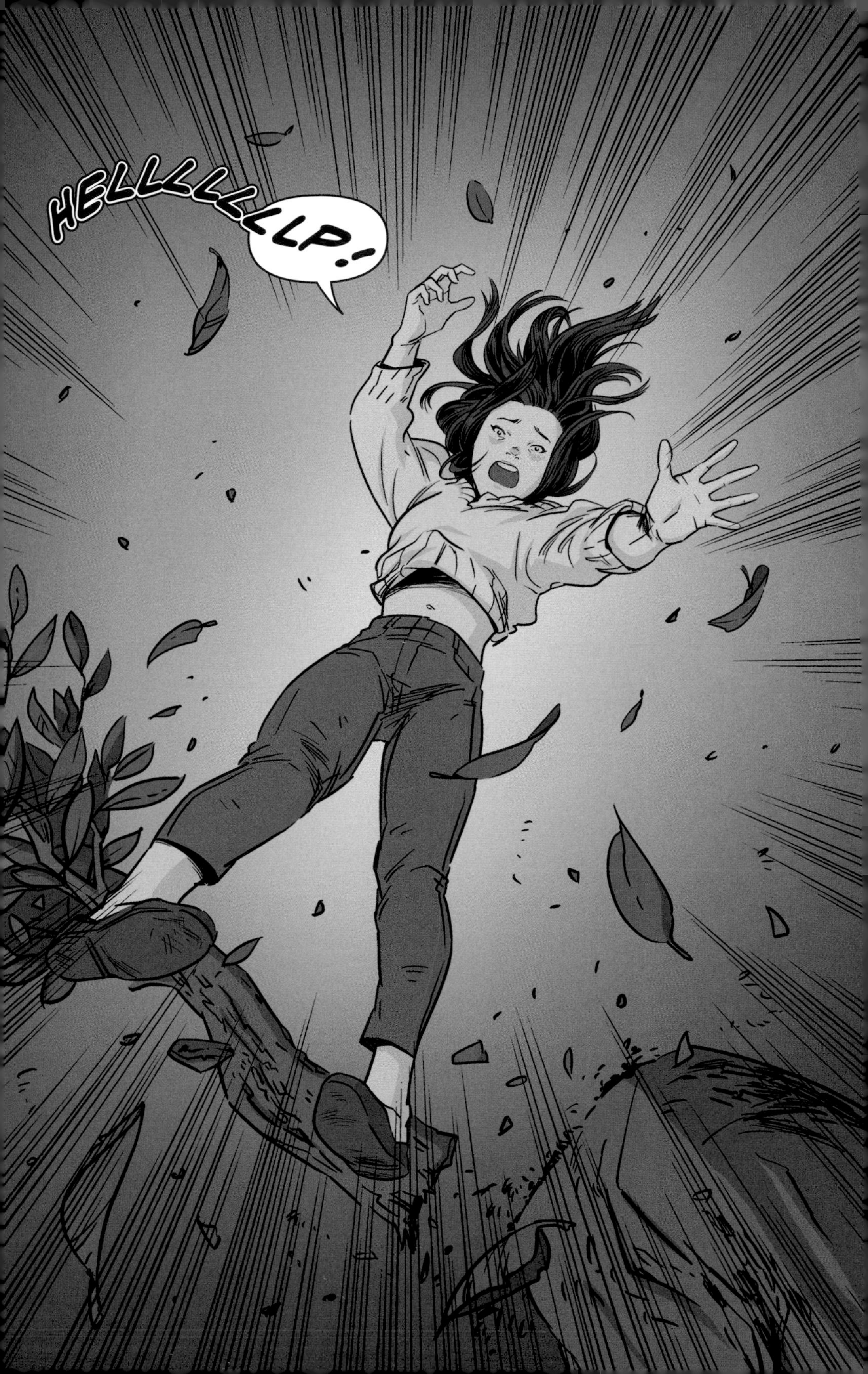
HELLLLLLLLP!

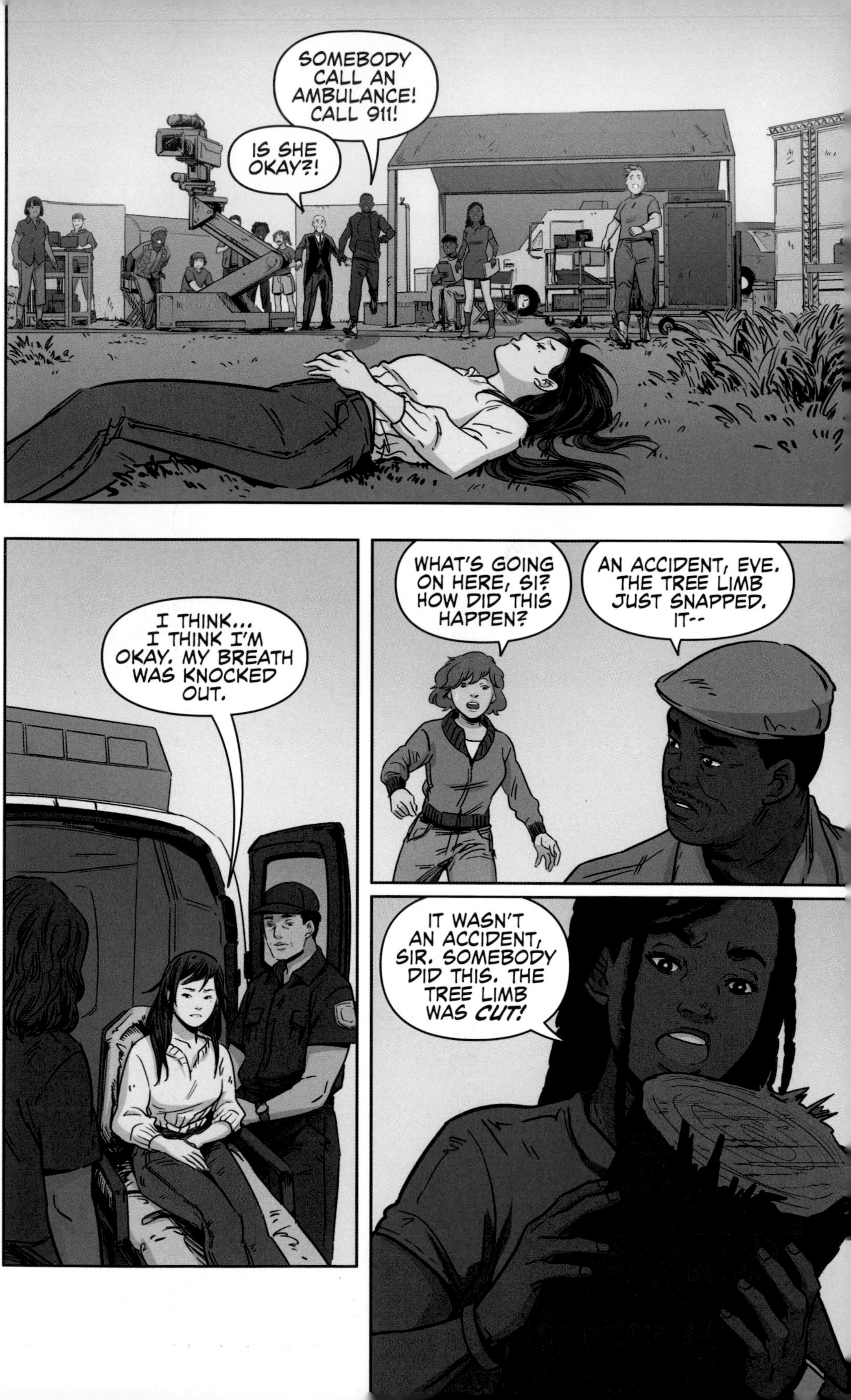
SOMEBODY CALL AN AMBULANCE! CALL 911!
IS SHE OKAY?!
I THINK... I THINK I'M OKAY. MY BREATH WAS KNOCKED OUT.
WHAT'S GOING ON HERE, SI? HOW DID THIS HAPPEN?
AN ACCIDENT, EVE. THE TREE LIMB JUST SNAPPED. IT--
IT WASN'T AN ACCIDENT, SIR. SOMEBODY DID THIS. THE TREE LIMB WAS *CUT!*

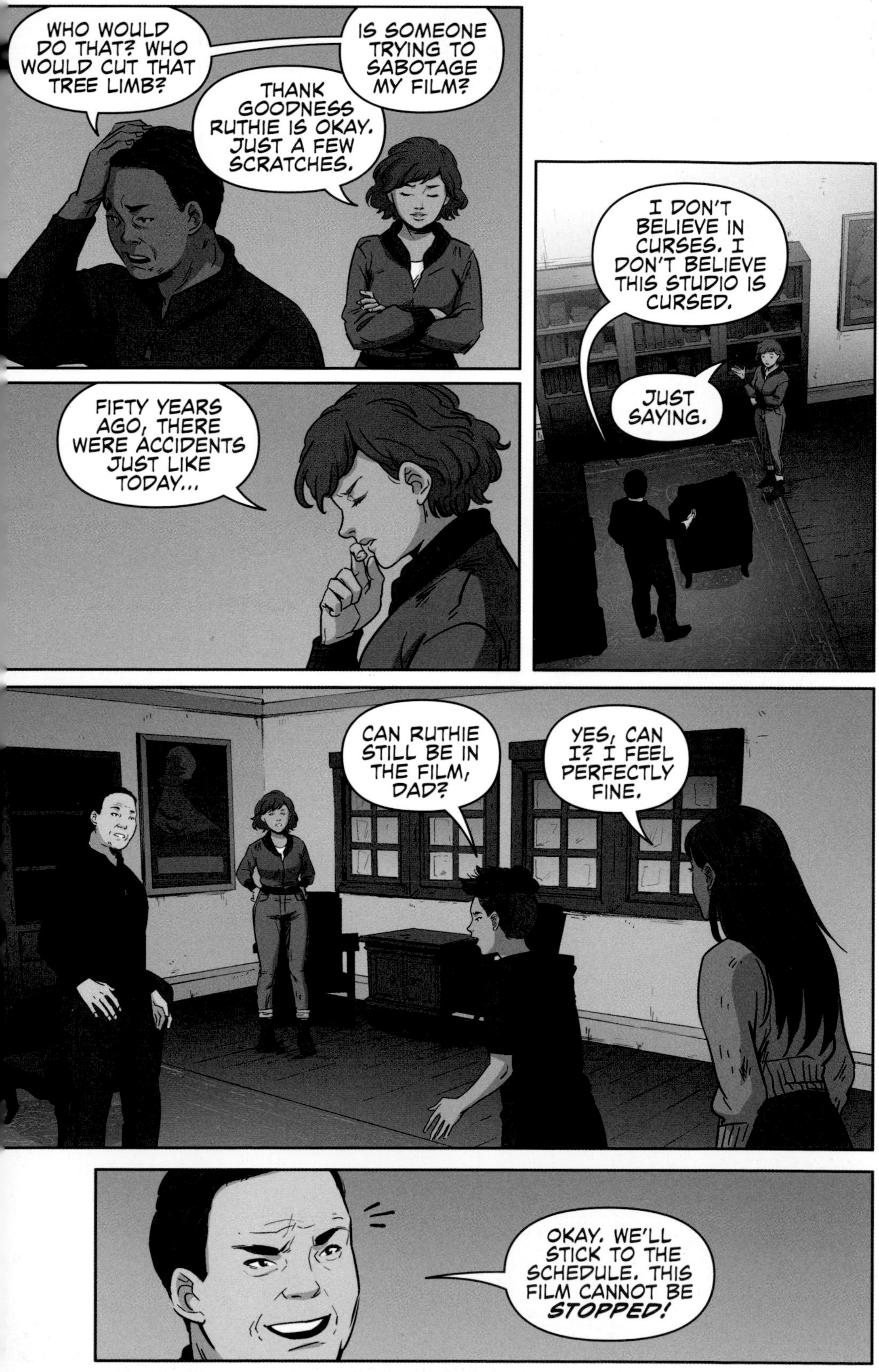
WHO WOULD DO THAT? WHO WOULD CUT THAT TREE LIMB?
IS SOMEONE TRYING TO SABOTAGE MY FILM?
THANK GOODNESS RUTHIE IS OKAY. JUST A FEW SCRATCHES.
FIFTY YEARS AGO, THERE WERE ACCIDENTS JUST LIKE TODAY...
I DON'T BELIEVE IN CURSES. I DON'T BELIEVE THIS STUDIO IS CURSED.
JUST SAYING.
CAN RUTHIE STILL BE IN THE FILM, DAD?
YES, CAN I? I FEEL PERFECTLY FINE.
OKAY. WE'LL STICK TO THE SCHEDULE. THIS FILM CANNOT BE *STOPPED!*

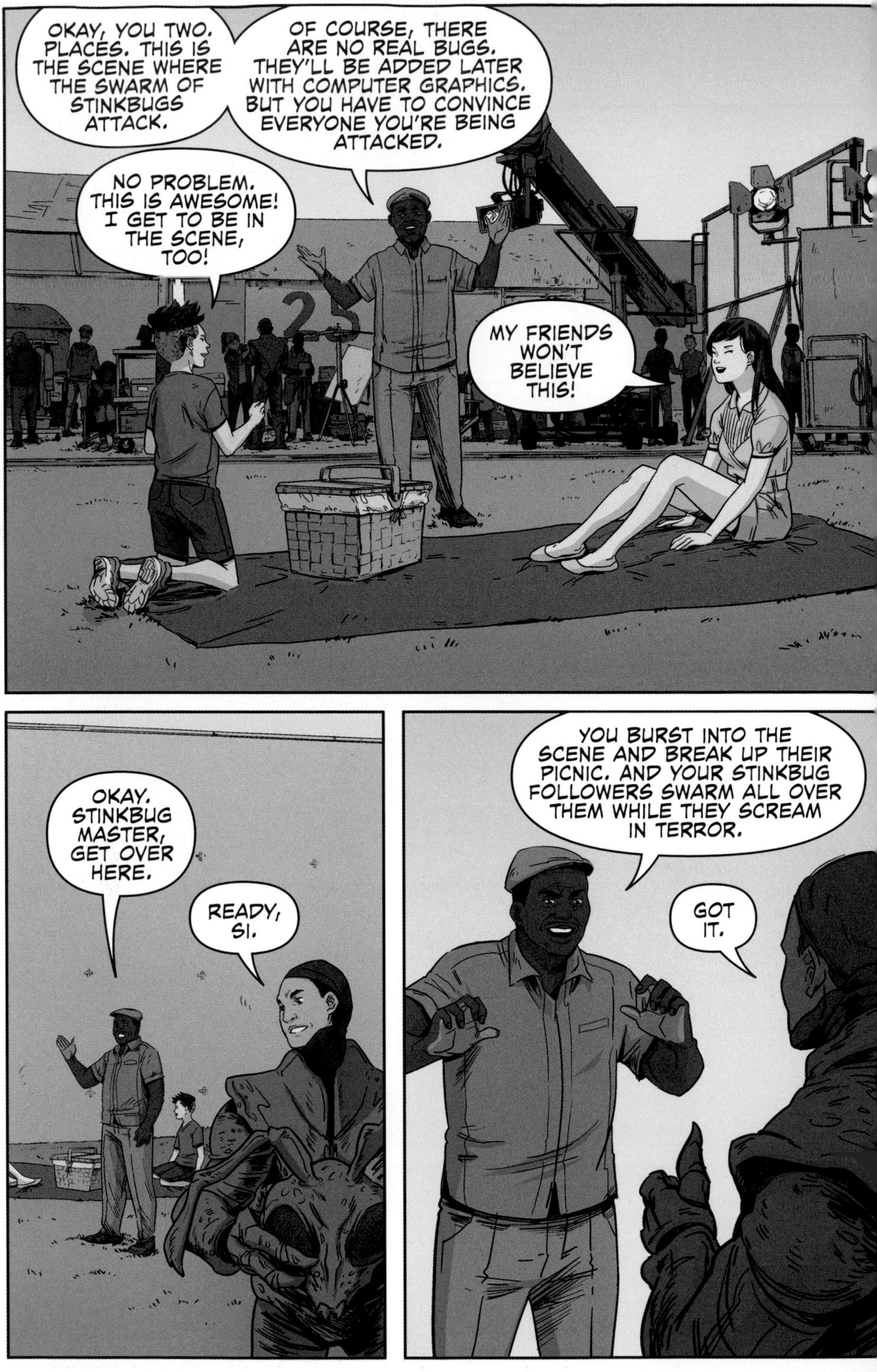
OKAY, YOU TWO. PLACES. THIS IS THE SCENE WHERE THE SWARM OF STINKBUGS ATTACK.
OF COURSE, THERE ARE NO REAL BUGS. THEY'LL BE ADDED LATER WITH COMPUTER GRAPHICS. BUT YOU HAVE TO CONVINCE EVERYONE YOU'RE BEING ATTACKED.
NO PROBLEM. THIS IS AWESOME! I GET TO BE IN THE SCENE, TOO!
MY FRIENDS WON'T BELIEVE THIS!
OKAY. STINKBUG MASTER, GET OVER HERE.
READY, SI.
YOU BURST INTO THE SCENE AND BREAK UP THEIR PICNIC. AND YOUR STINKBUG FOLLOWERS SWARM ALL OVER THEM WHILE THEY SCREAM IN TERROR.
GOT IT.

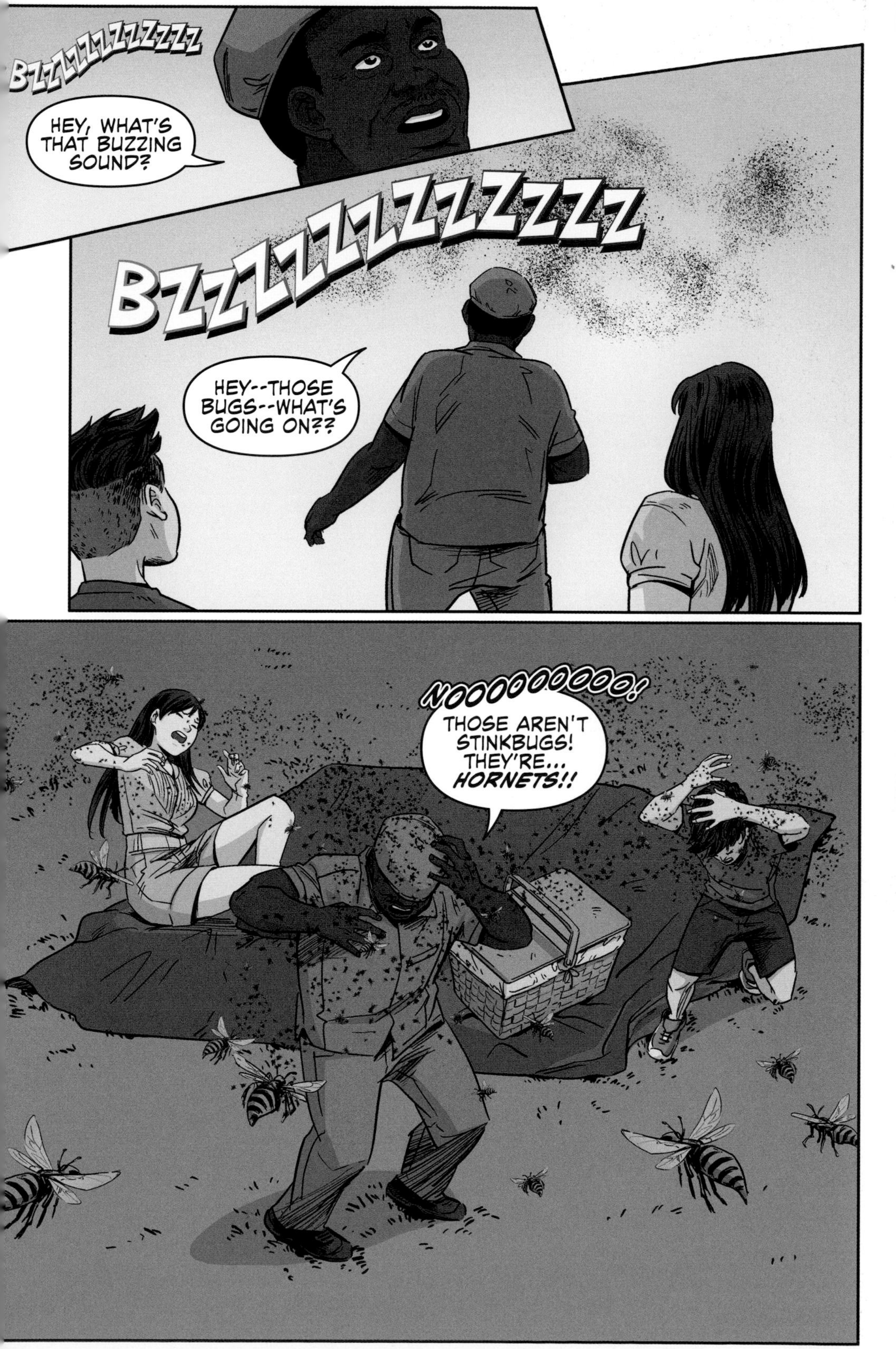
BZZZZZZZZZZZ
HEY, WHAT'S THAT BUZZING SOUND?
BZZZZZZZZZZZZZ
HEY--THOSE BUGS--WHAT'S GOING ON??
NOOOOOOOOOO!
THOSE AREN'T STINKBUGS! THEY'RE... *HORNETS!!*

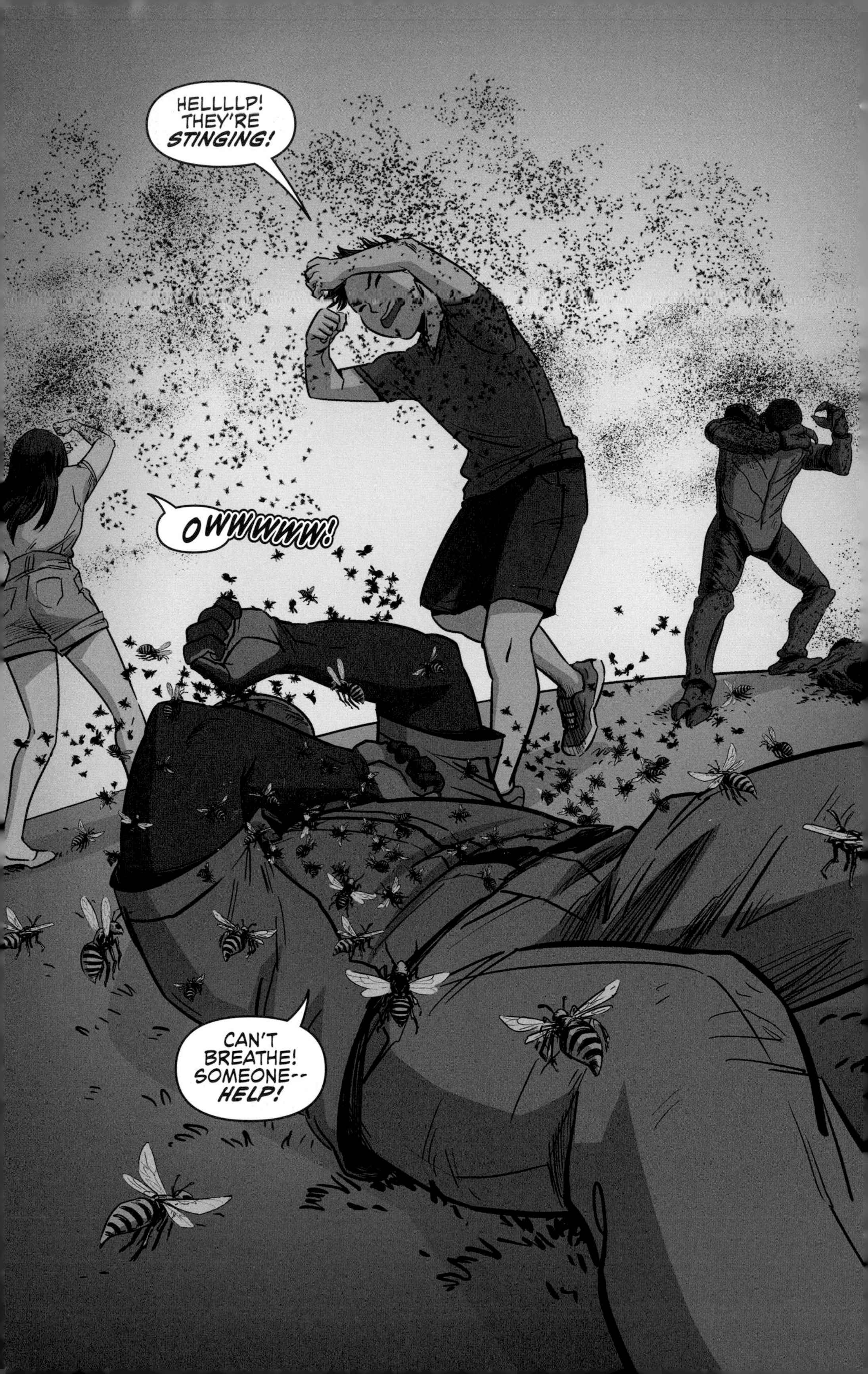
HELLLLP! THEY'RE *STINGING!*
OWWWWWW!
CAN'T BREATHE! SOMEONE-- *HELP!*

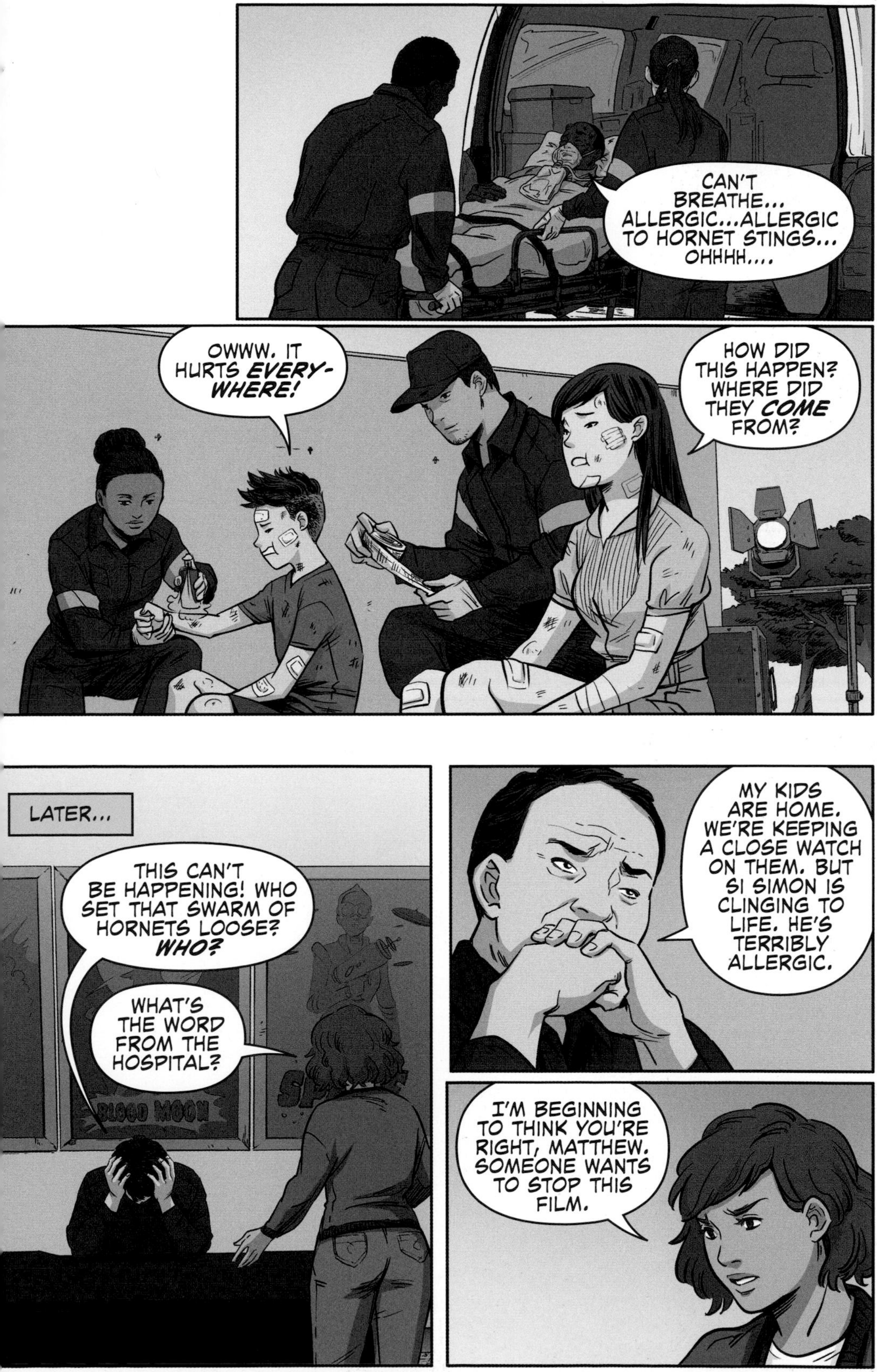

CAN'T BREATHE... ALLERGIC...ALLERGIC TO HORNET STINGS... OHHHH....
OWWW. IT HURTS *EVERY-WHERE!*
HOW DID THIS HAPPEN? WHERE DID THEY *COME* FROM?
LATER...
THIS CAN'T BE HAPPENING! WHO SET THAT SWARM OF HORNETS LOOSE? *WHO?*
WHAT'S THE WORD FROM THE HOSPITAL?
BLOOD MOON
MY KIDS ARE HOME. WE'RE KEEPING A CLOSE WATCH ON THEM. BUT SI SIMON IS CLINGING TO LIFE. HE'S TERRIBLY ALLERGIC.
I'M BEGINNING TO THINK YOU'RE RIGHT, MATTHEW. SOMEONE WANTS TO STOP THIS FILM.

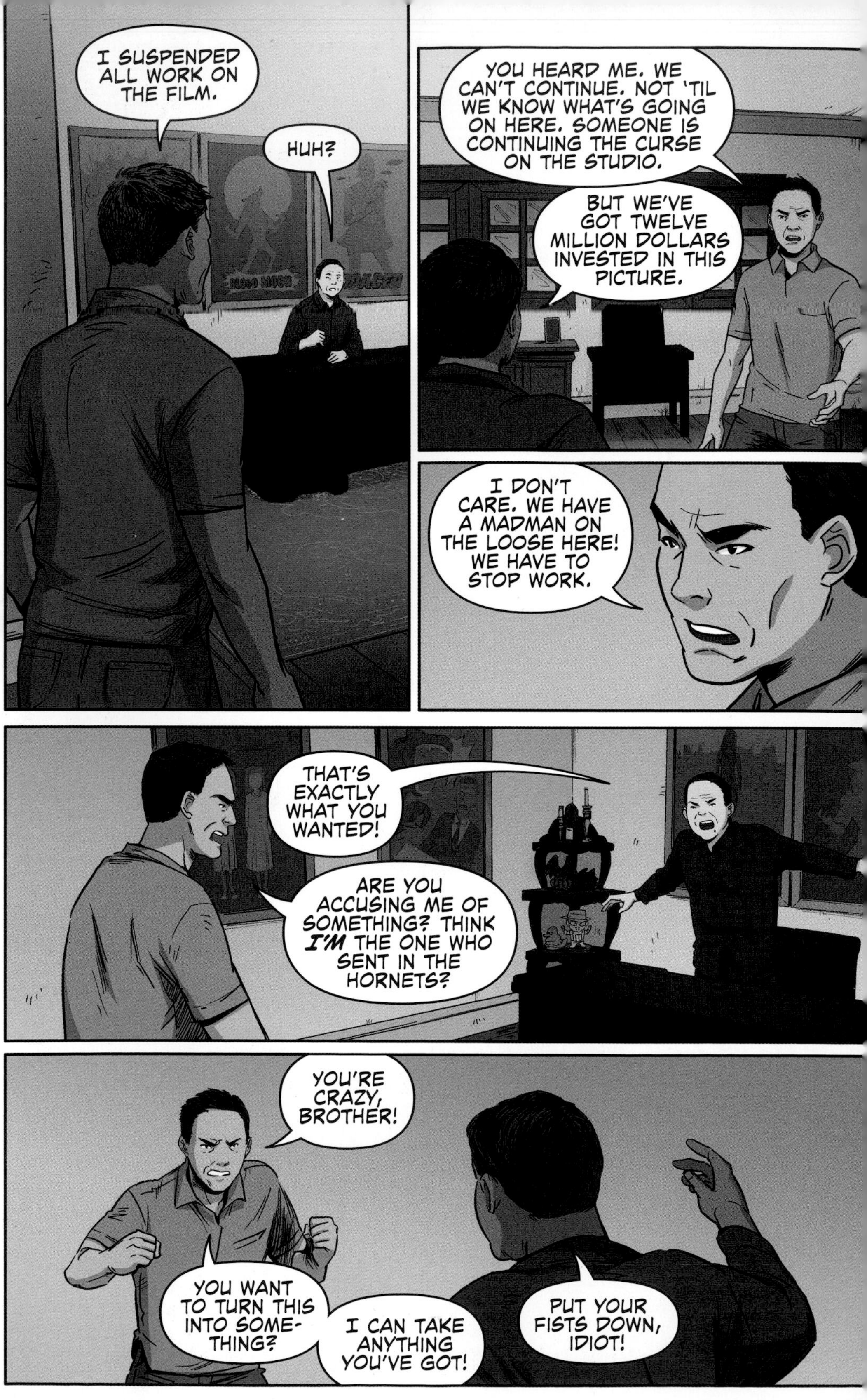
I SUSPENDED ALL WORK ON THE FILM.
HUH?
YOU HEARD ME. WE CAN'T CONTINUE. NOT 'TIL WE KNOW WHAT'S GOING ON HERE. SOMEONE IS CONTINUING THE CURSE ON THE STUDIO.
BUT WE'VE GOT TWELVE MILLION DOLLARS INVESTED IN THIS PICTURE.
I DON'T CARE. WE HAVE A MADMAN ON THE LOOSE HERE! WE HAVE TO STOP WORK.
THAT'S EXACTLY WHAT YOU WANTED!
ARE YOU ACCUSING ME OF SOMETHING? THINK *I'M* THE ONE WHO SENT IN THE HORNETS?
YOU'RE CRAZY, BROTHER!
YOU WANT TO TURN THIS INTO SOME-THING?
I CAN TAKE ANYTHING YOU'VE GOT!
PUT YOUR FISTS DOWN, IDIOT!

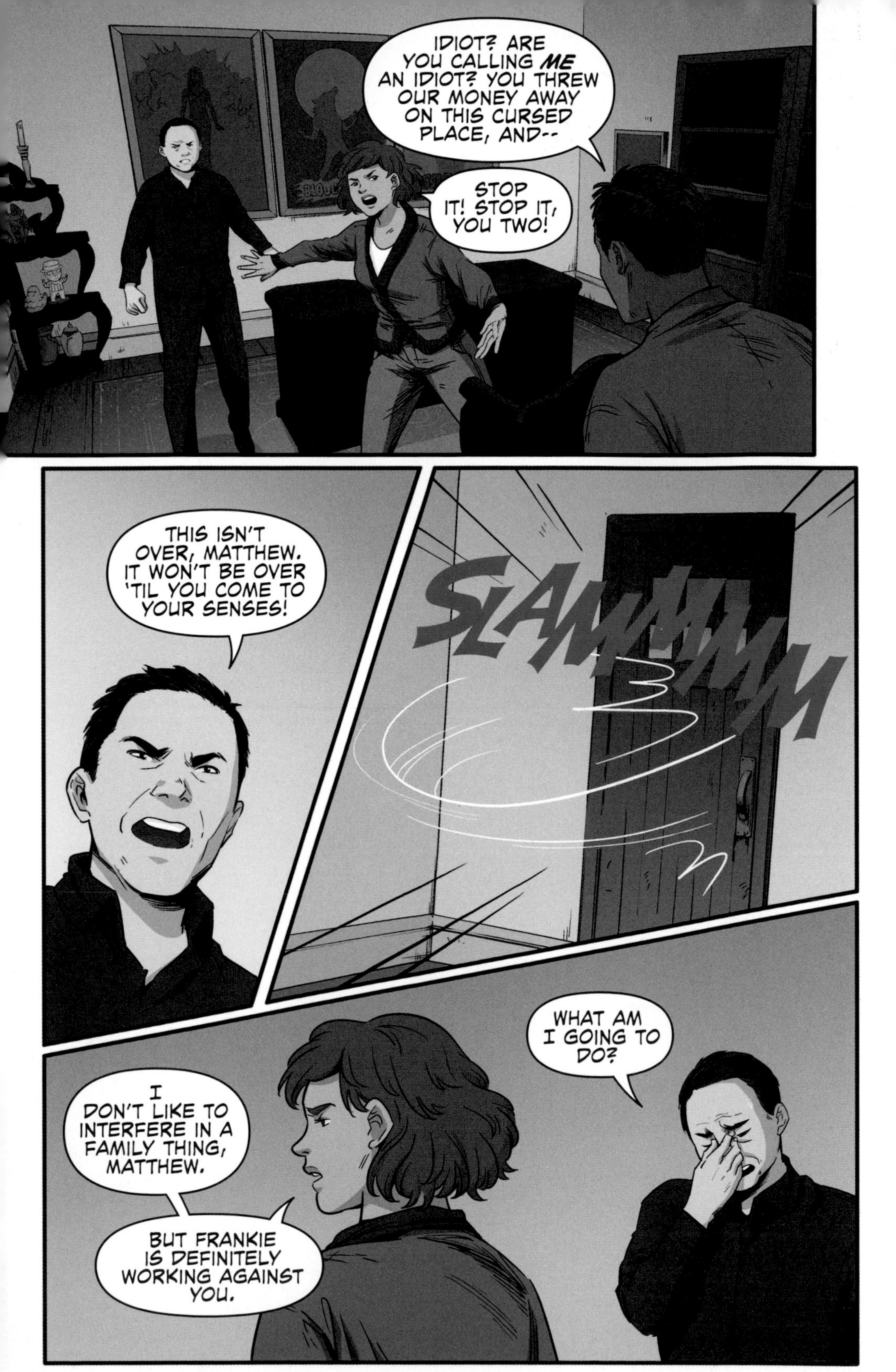
IDIOT? ARE YOU CALLING *ME* AN IDIOT? YOU THREW OUR MONEY AWAY ON THIS CURSED PLACE, AND--
STOP IT! STOP IT, YOU TWO!
THIS ISN'T OVER, MATTHEW. IT WON'T BE OVER 'TIL YOU COME TO YOUR SENSES!
SLAMMMMM
WHAT AM I GOING TO DO?
I DON'T LIKE TO INTERFERE IN A FAMILY THING, MATTHEW.
BUT FRANKIE IS DEFINITELY WORKING AGAINST YOU.

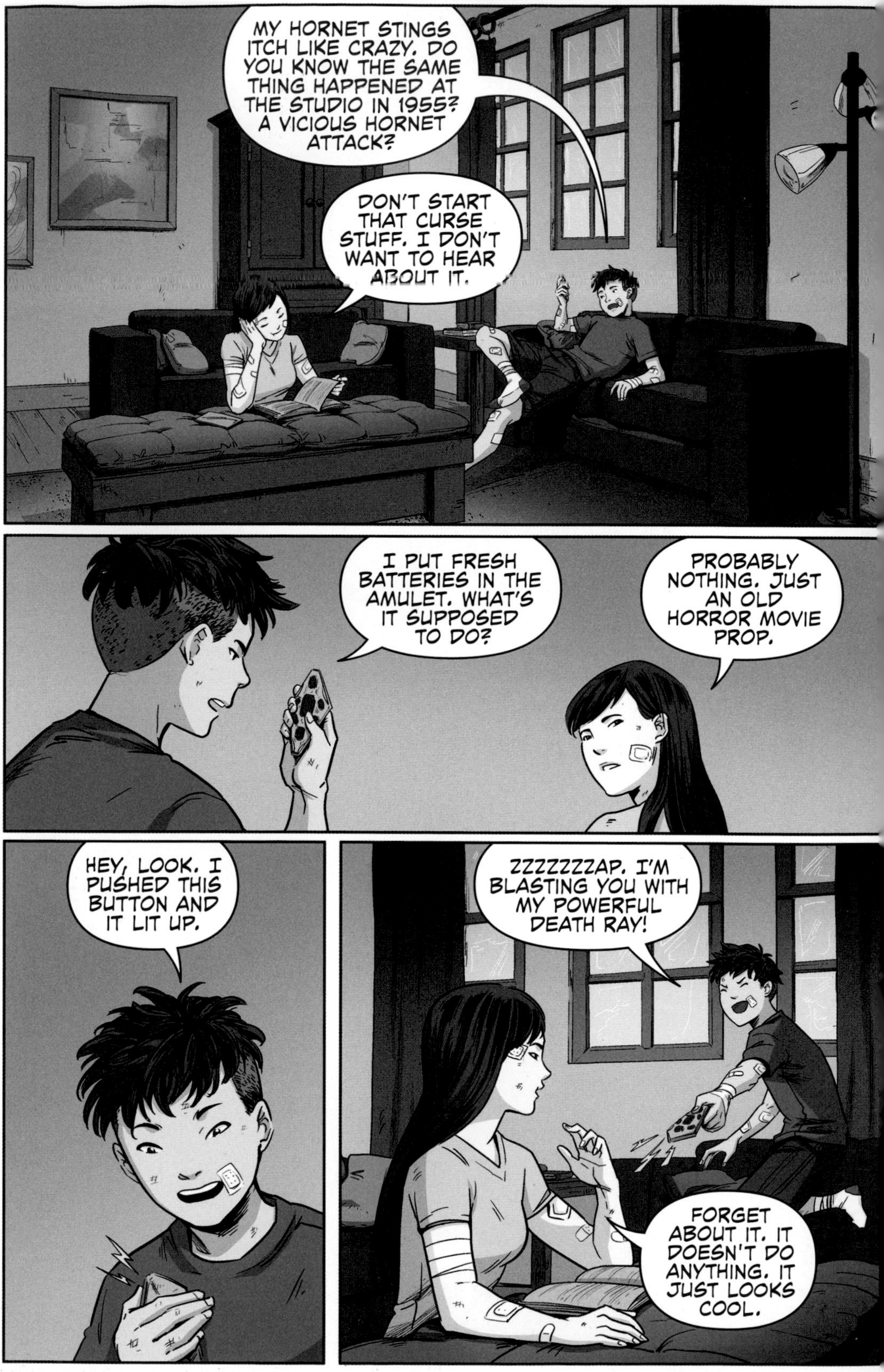
MY HORNET STINGS ITCH LIKE CRAZY. DO YOU KNOW THE SAME THING HAPPENED AT THE STUDIO IN 1955? A VICIOUS HORNET ATTACK?
DON'T START THAT CURSE STUFF. I DON'T WANT TO HEAR ABOUT IT.
I PUT FRESH BATTERIES IN THE AMULET. WHAT'S IT SUPPOSED TO DO?
PROBABLY NOTHING. JUST AN OLD HORROR MOVIE PROP.
HEY, LOOK. I PUSHED THIS BUTTON AND IT LIT UP.
ZZZZZZZAP. I'M BLASTING YOU WITH MY POWERFUL DEATH RAY!
FORGET ABOUT IT. IT DOESN'T DO ANYTHING. IT JUST LOOKS COOL.

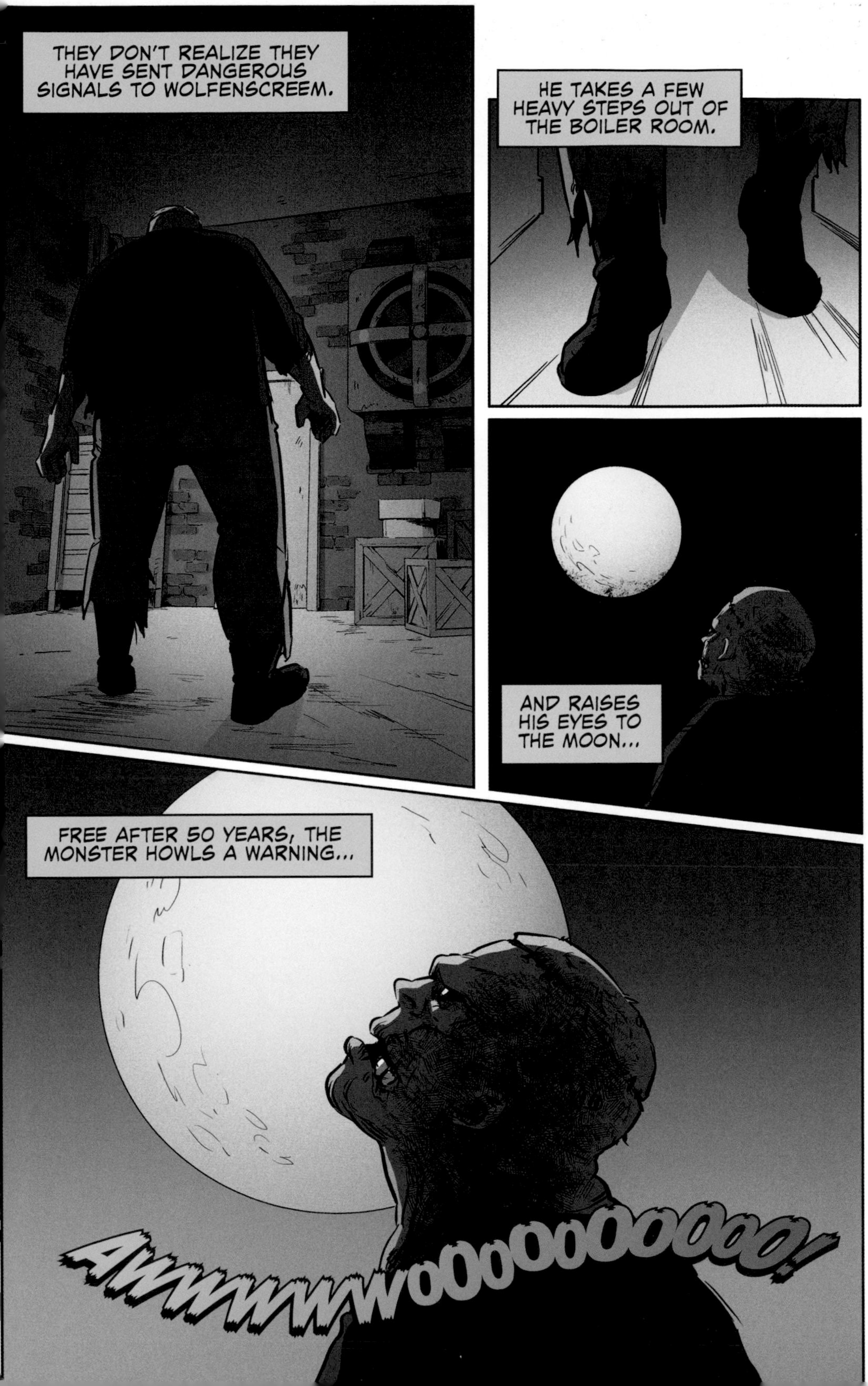
THEY DON'T REALIZE THEY HAVE SENT DANGEROUS SIGNALS TO WOLFENSCREEM.
HE TAKES A FEW HEAVY STEPS OUT OF THE BOILER ROOM.
AND RAISES HIS EYES TO THE MOON...
FREE AFTER 50 YEARS, THE MONSTER HOWLS A WARNING...
AWWWWOOOOOOOOOOO!

PART SIX

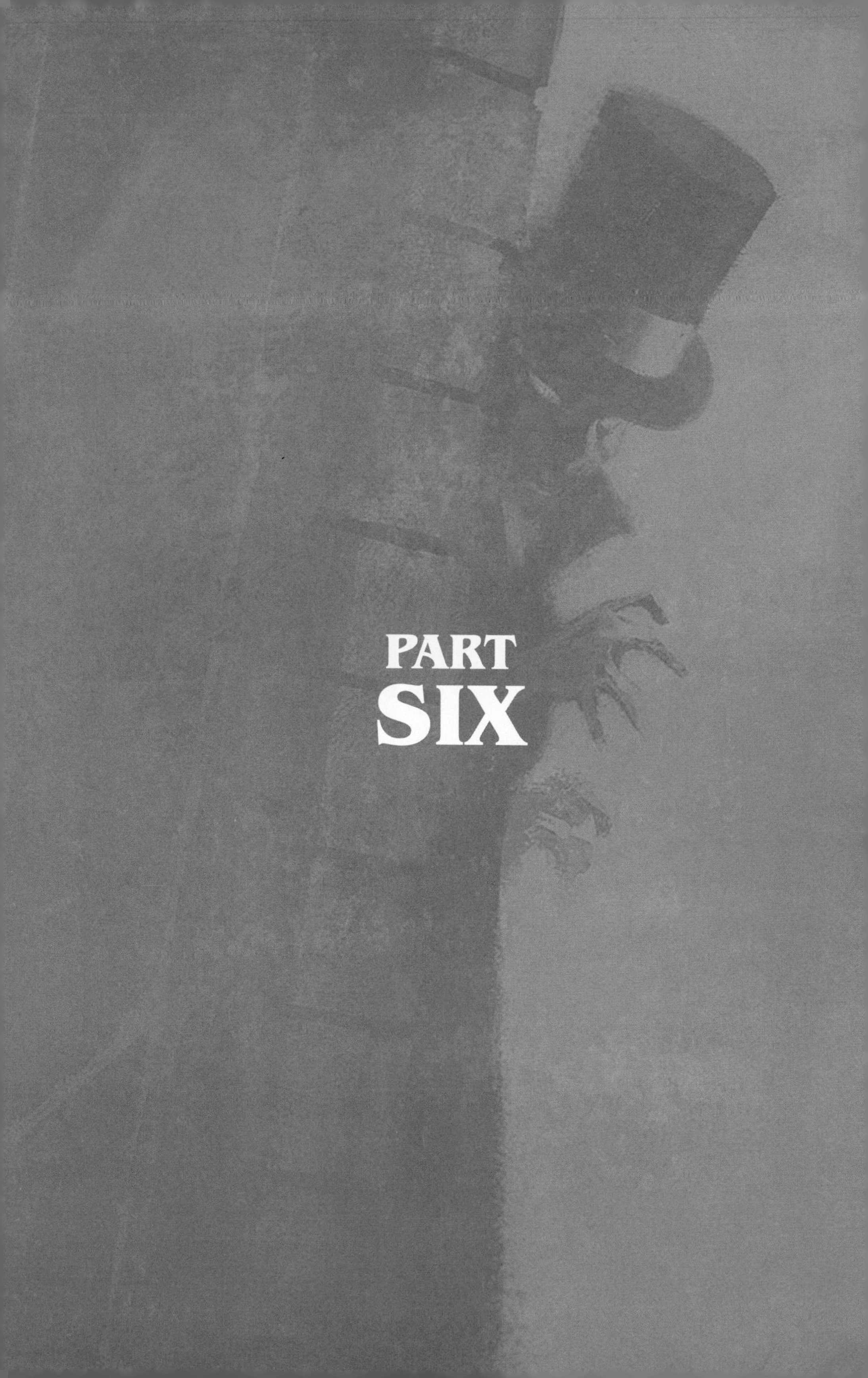

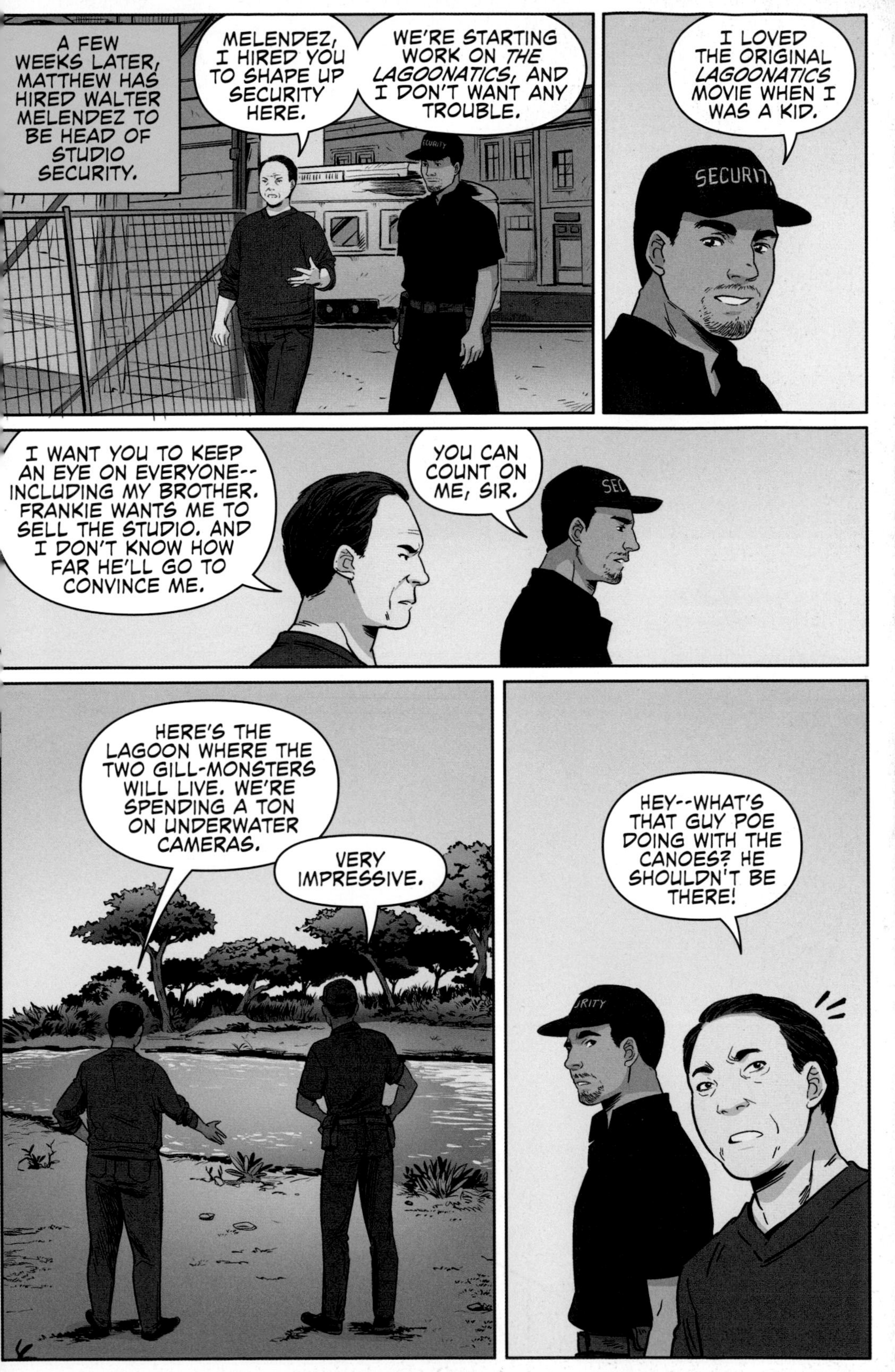
A FEW WEEKS LATER, MATTHEW HAS HIRED WALTER MELENDEZ TO BE HEAD OF STUDIO SECURITY.
MELENDEZ, I HIRED YOU TO SHAPE UP SECURITY HERE.
WE'RE STARTING WORK ON *THE LAGOONATICS*, AND I DON'T WANT ANY TROUBLE.
SECURITY
I LOVED THE ORIGINAL *LAGOONATICS* MOVIE WHEN I WAS A KID.
SECURITY
I WANT YOU TO KEEP AN EYE ON EVERYONE--INCLUDING MY BROTHER. FRANKIE WANTS ME TO SELL THE STUDIO. AND I DON'T KNOW HOW FAR HE'LL GO TO CONVINCE ME.
YOU CAN COUNT ON ME, SIR.
HERE'S THE LAGOON WHERE THE TWO GILL-MONSTERS WILL LIVE. WE'RE SPENDING A TON ON UNDERWATER CAMERAS.
VERY IMPRESSIVE.
HEY--WHAT'S THAT GUY POE DOING WITH THE CANOES? HE SHOULDN'T BE THERE!

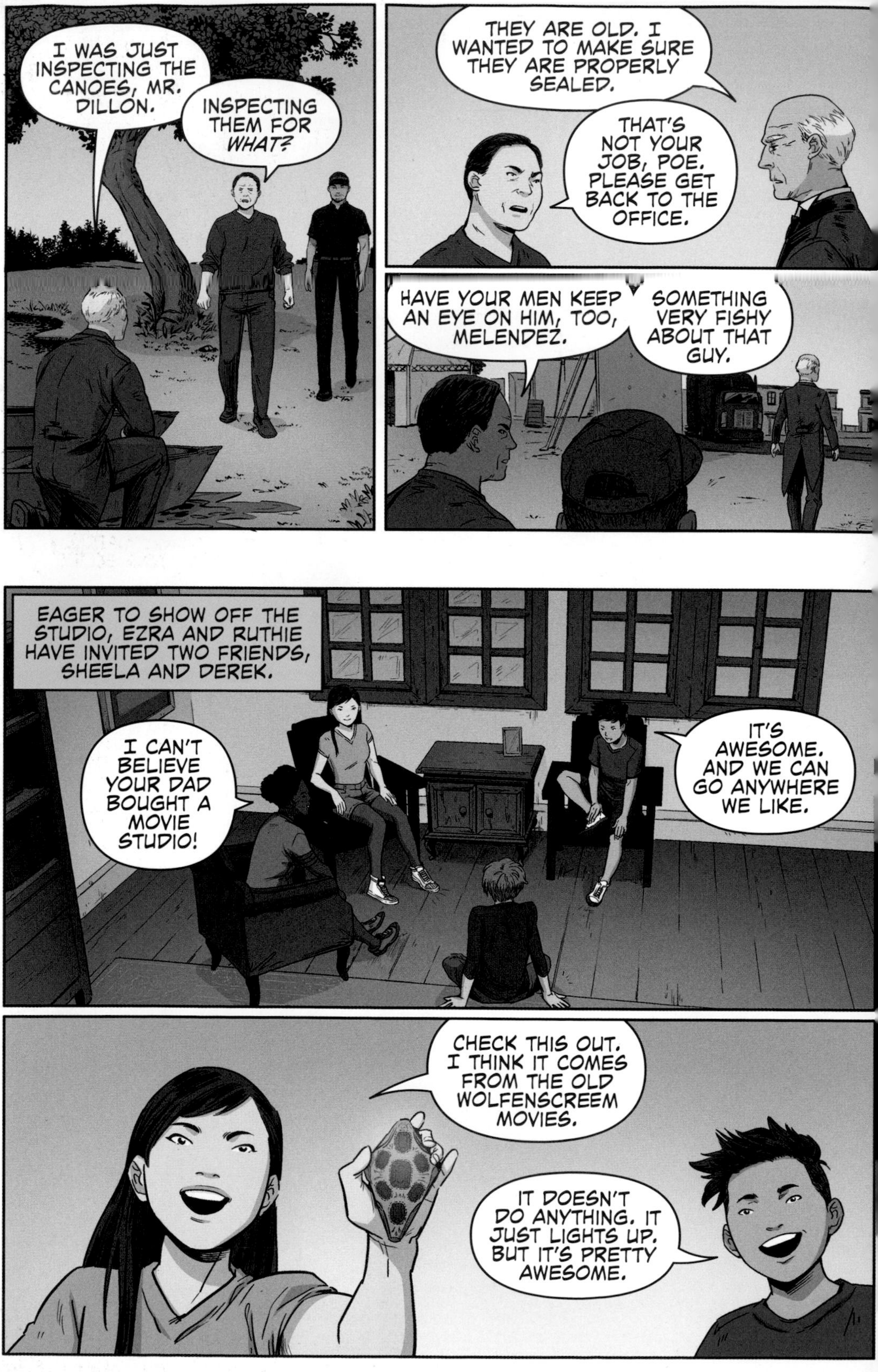
I WAS JUST INSPECTING THE CANOES, MR. DILLON.
INSPECTING THEM FOR *WHAT?*
THEY ARE OLD. I WANTED TO MAKE SURE THEY ARE PROPERLY SEALED.
THAT'S NOT YOUR JOB, POE. PLEASE GET BACK TO THE OFFICE.
HAVE YOUR MEN KEEP AN EYE ON HIM, TOO, MELENDEZ.
SOMETHING VERY FISHY ABOUT THAT GUY.
EAGER TO SHOW OFF THE STUDIO, EZRA AND RUTHIE HAVE INVITED TWO FRIENDS, SHEELA AND DEREK.
I CAN'T BELIEVE YOUR DAD BOUGHT A MOVIE STUDIO!
IT'S AWESOME. AND WE CAN GO ANYWHERE WE LIKE.
CHECK THIS OUT. I THINK IT COMES FROM THE OLD WOLFENSCREEM MOVIES.
IT DOESN'T DO ANYTHING. IT JUST LIGHTS UP. BUT IT'S PRETTY AWESOME.

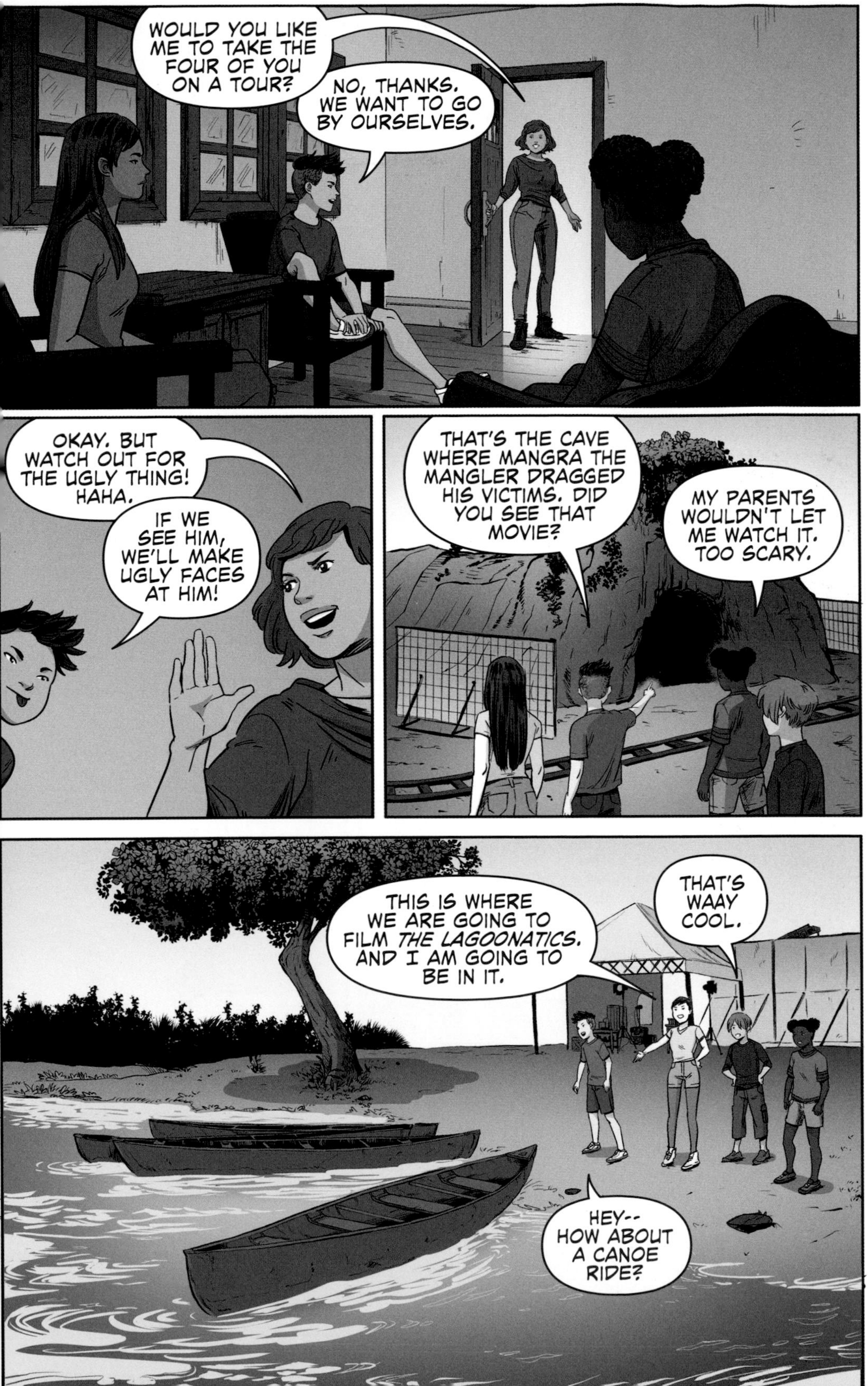

WOULD YOU LIKE ME TO TAKE THE FOUR OF YOU ON A TOUR?
NO, THANKS. WE WANT TO GO BY OURSELVES.
OKAY. BUT WATCH OUT FOR THE UGLY THING! HAHA.
IF WE SEE HIM, WE'LL MAKE UGLY FACES AT HIM!
THAT'S THE CAVE WHERE MANGRA THE MANGLER DRAGGED HIS VICTIMS. DID YOU SEE THAT MOVIE?
MY PARENTS WOULDN'T LET ME WATCH IT. TOO SCARY.
THIS IS WHERE WE ARE GOING TO FILM *THE LAGOONATICS*. AND I AM GOING TO BE IN IT.
THAT'S WAAY COOL.
HEY-- HOW ABOUT A CANOE RIDE?

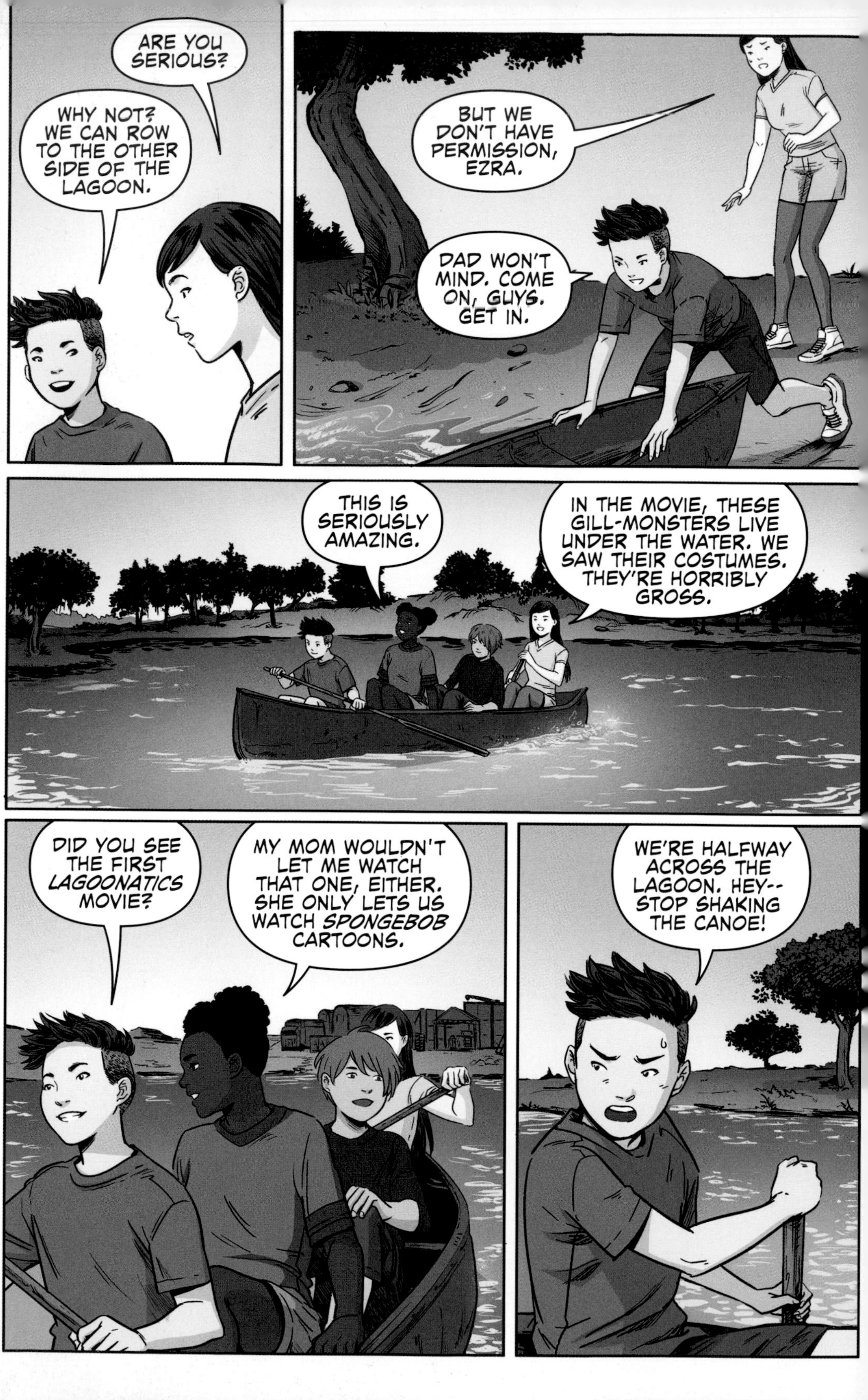

ARE YOU SERIOUS?
WHY NOT? WE CAN ROW TO THE OTHER SIDE OF THE LAGOON.
BUT WE DON'T HAVE PERMISSION, EZRA.
DAD WON'T MIND. COME ON, GUYS. GET IN.
THIS IS SERIOUSLY AMAZING.
IN THE MOVIE, THESE GILL-MONSTERS LIVE UNDER THE WATER. WE SAW THEIR COSTUMES. THEY'RE HORRIBLY GROSS.
DID YOU SEE THE FIRST *LAGOONATICS* MOVIE?
MY MOM WOULDN'T LET ME WATCH THAT ONE, EITHER. SHE ONLY LETS US WATCH *SPONGEBOB* CARTOONS.
WE'RE HALFWAY ACROSS THE LAGOON. HEY-- STOP SHAKING THE CANOE!

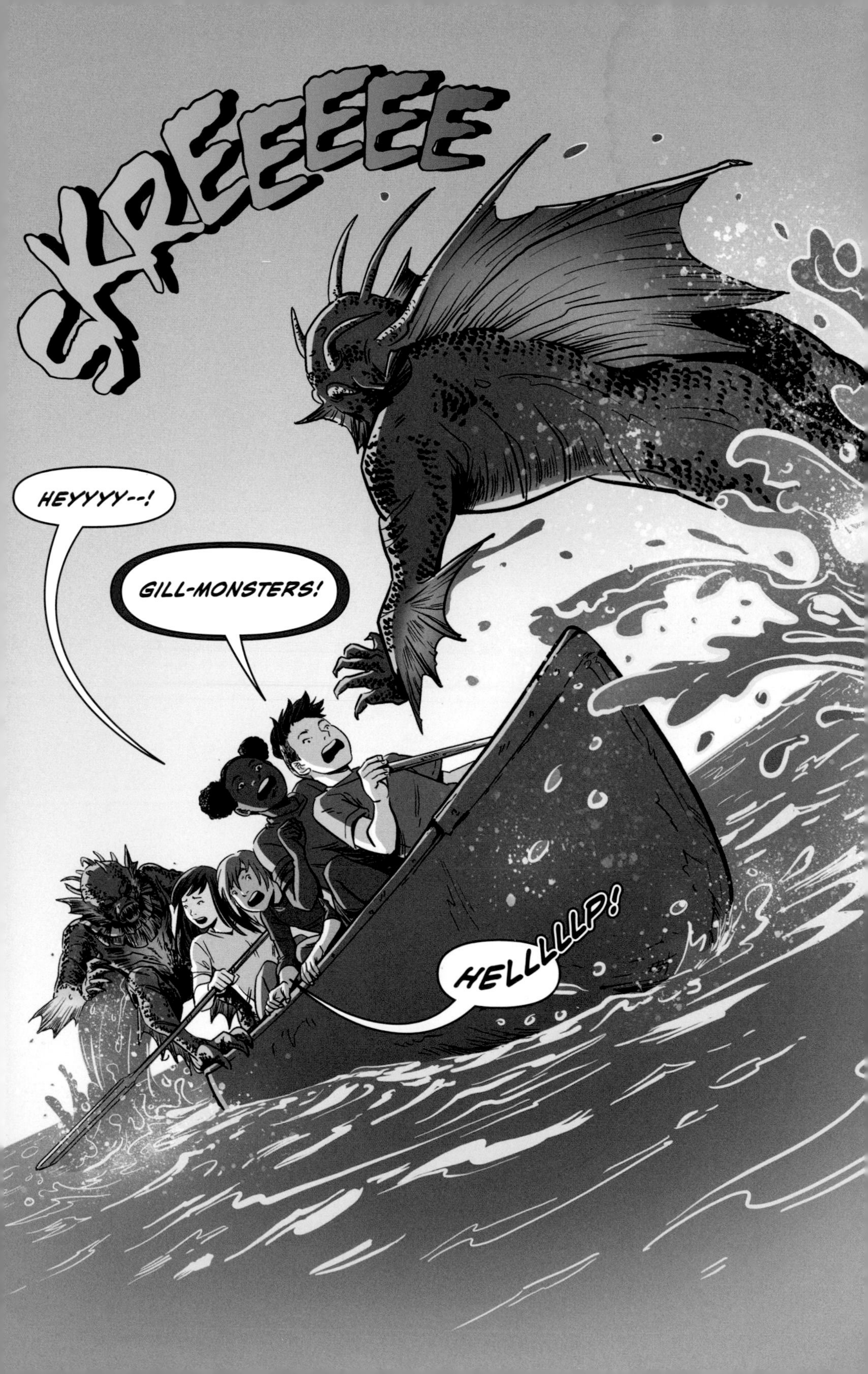
SKREEEEEE
HEYYYY--!
GILL-MONSTERS!
HELLLLLP!

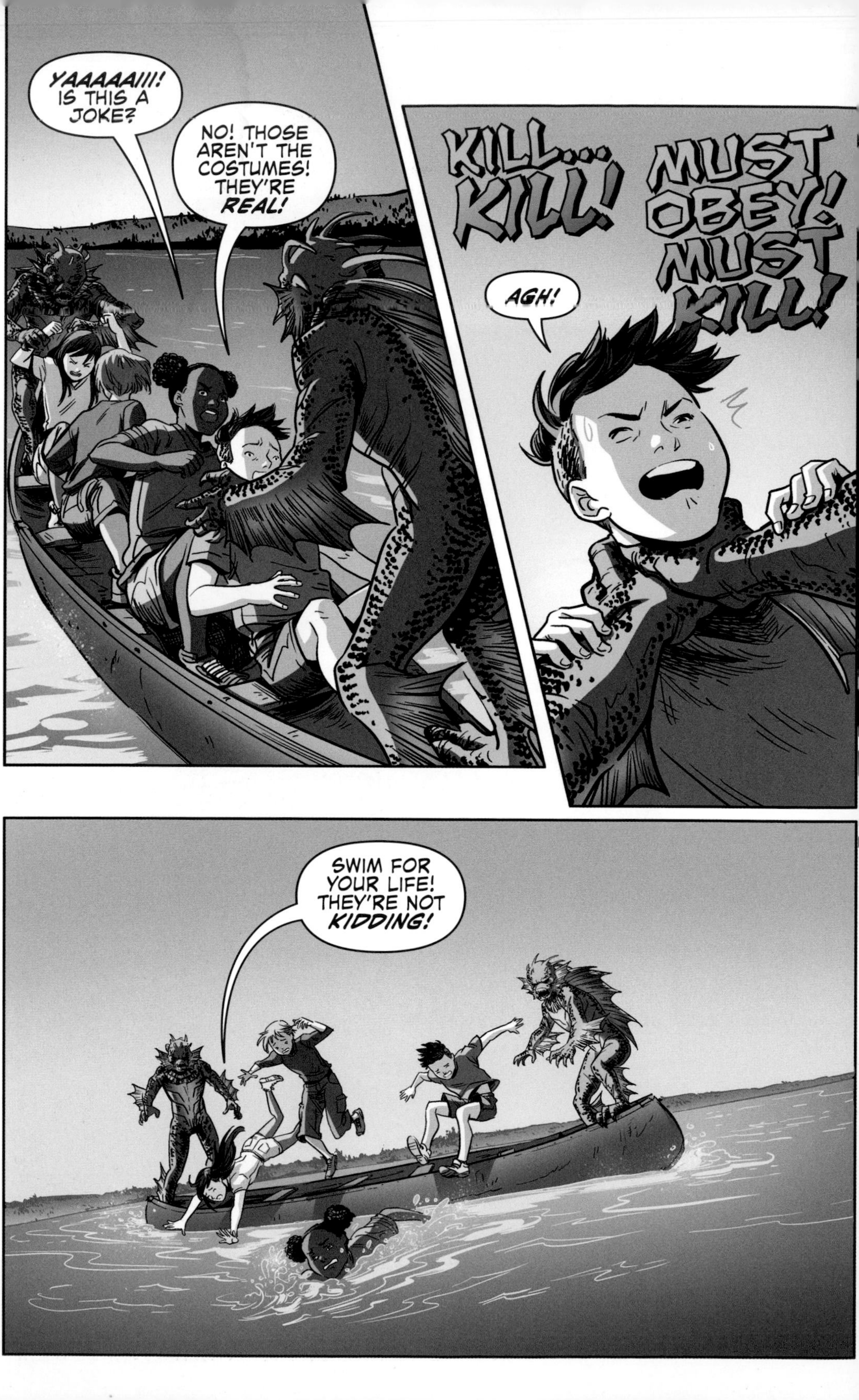
YAAAAAIII! IS THIS A JOKE?
NO! THOSE AREN'T THE COSTUMES! THEY'RE REAL!
KILL... KILL! MUST OBEY! MUST KILL!
AGH!
SWIM FOR YOUR LIFE! THEY'RE NOT KIDDING!

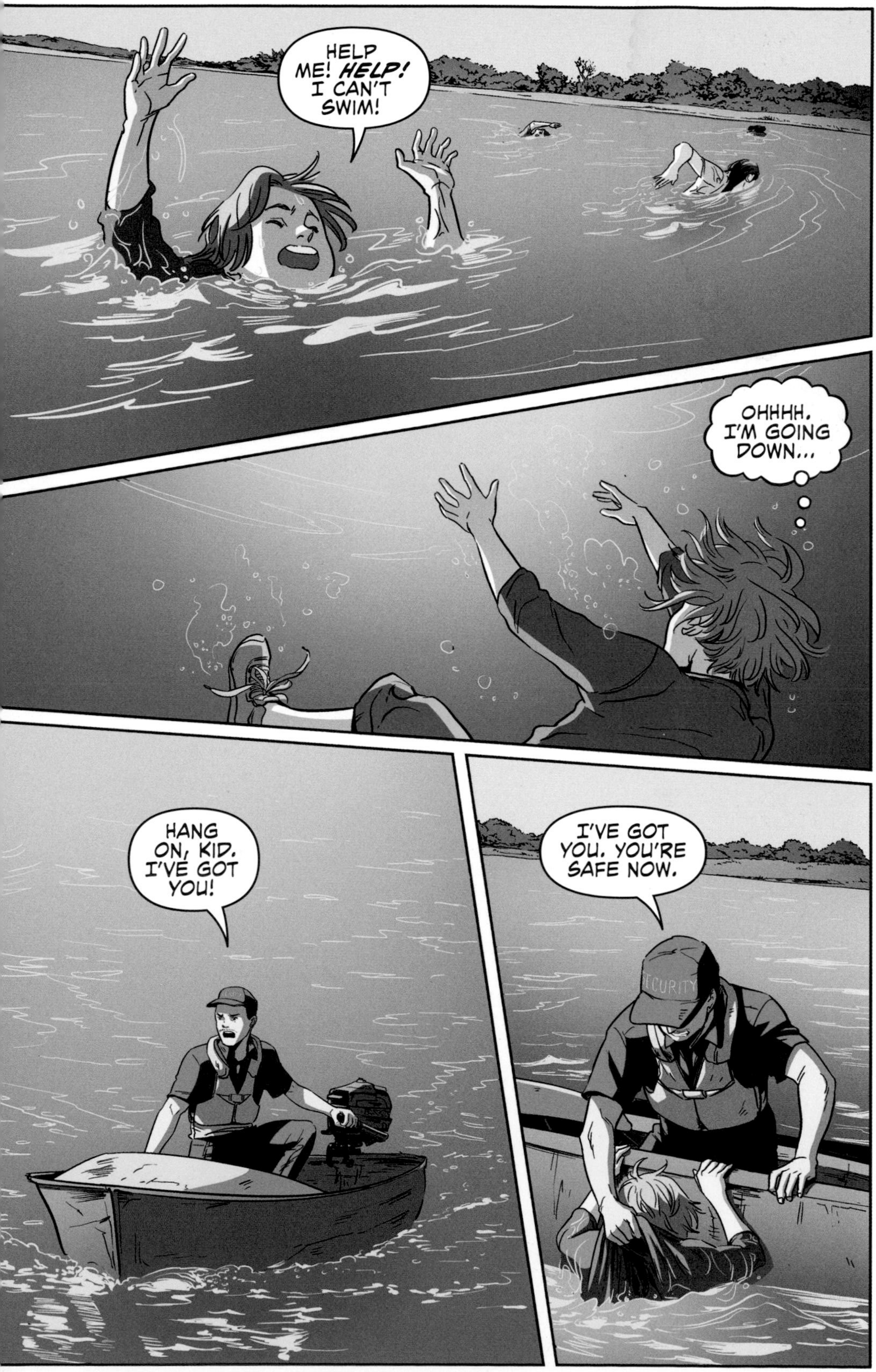
HELP ME! HELP! I CAN'T SWIM!
OHHHH. I'M GOING DOWN...
HANG ON, KID. I'VE GOT YOU!
SECURITY
I'VE GOT YOU. YOU'RE SAFE NOW.

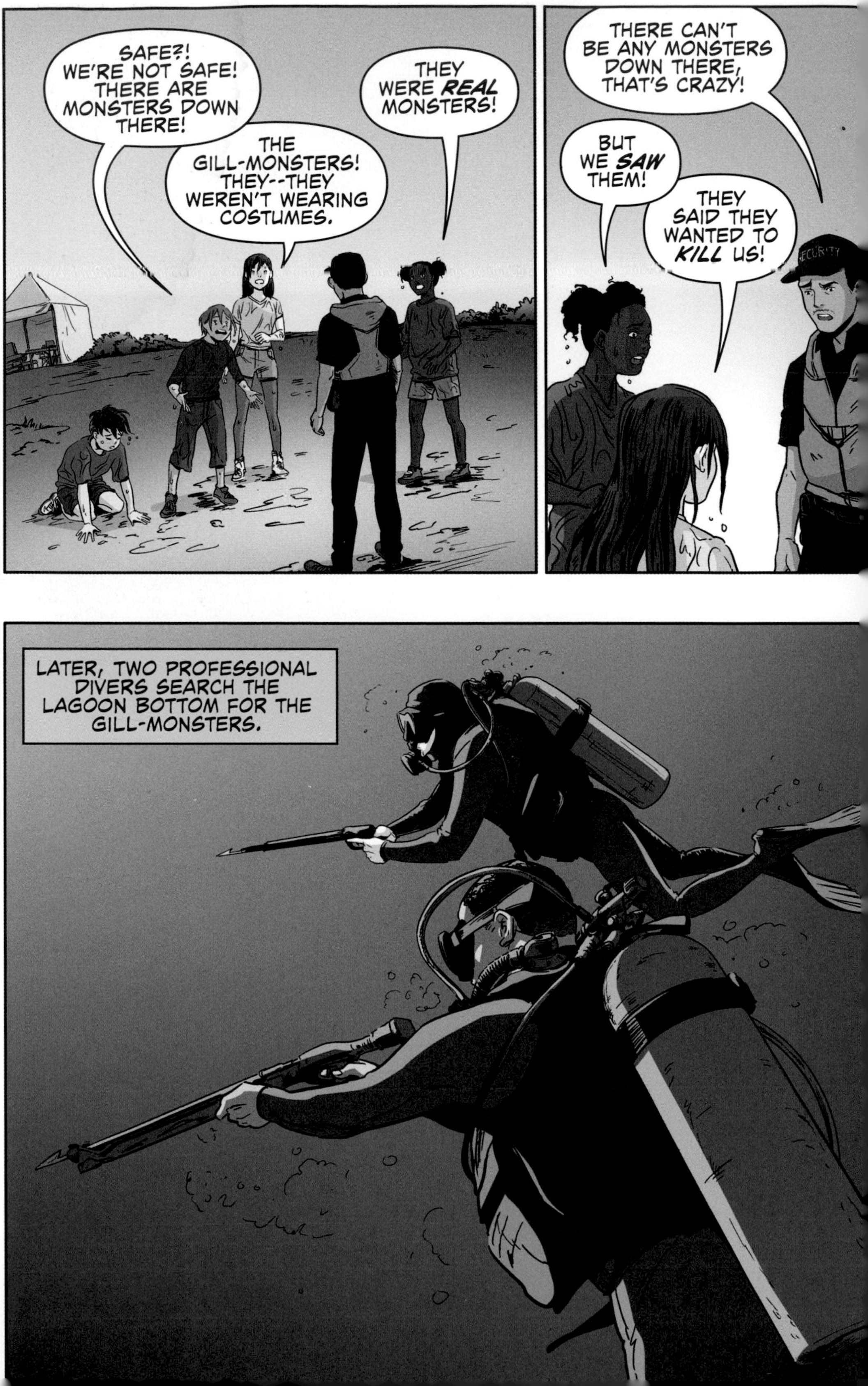

SAFE?! WE'RE NOT SAFE! THERE ARE MONSTERS DOWN THERE!
THE GILL-MONSTERS! THEY--THEY WEREN'T WEARING COSTUMES.
THEY WERE REAL MONSTERS!
THERE CAN'T BE ANY MONSTERS DOWN THERE, THAT'S CRAZY!
BUT WE SAW THEM!
THEY SAID THEY WANTED TO KILL US!
SECURITY
LATER, TWO PROFESSIONAL DIVERS SEARCH THE LAGOON BOTTOM FOR THE GILL-MONSTERS.

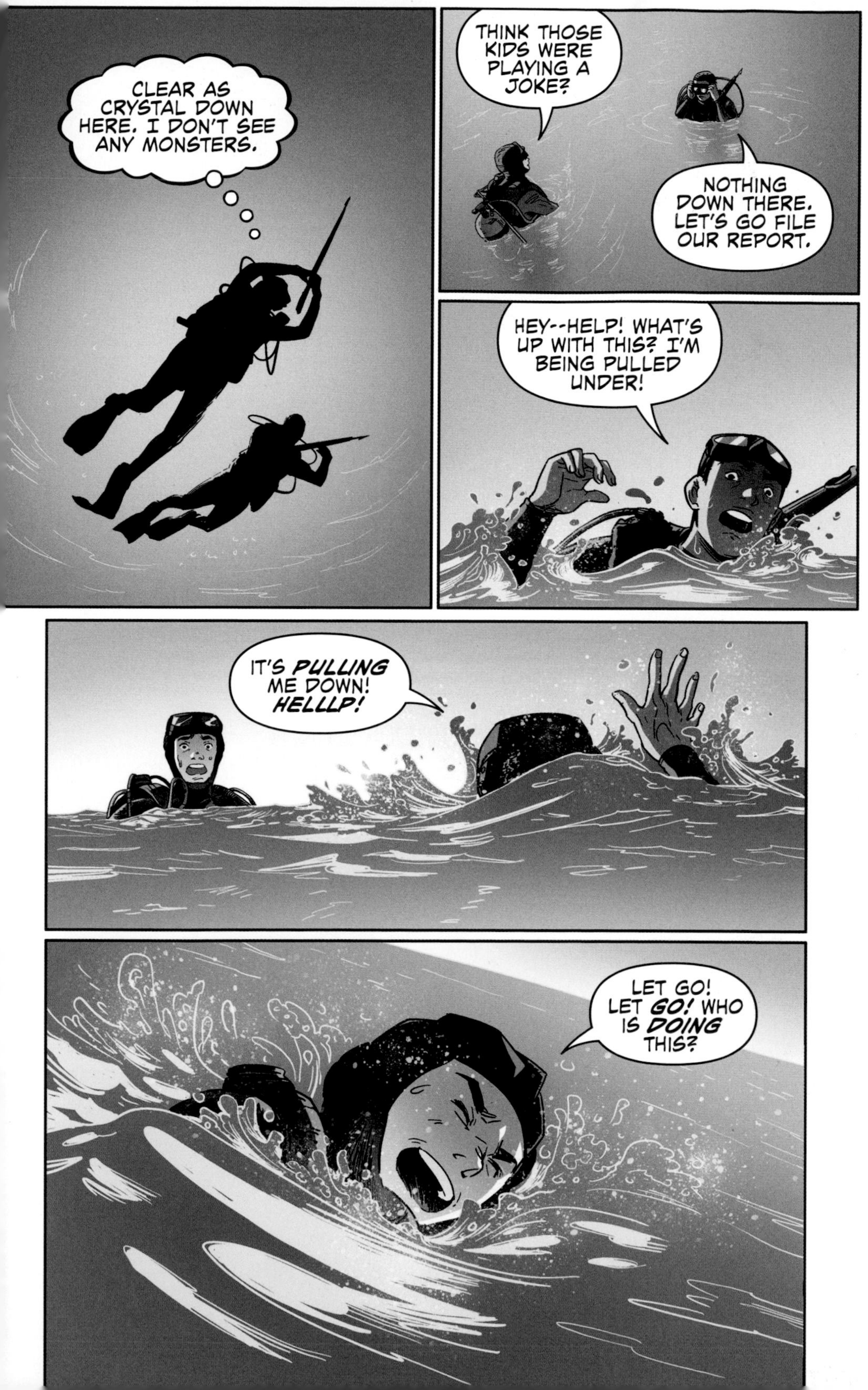
CLEAR AS CRYSTAL DOWN HERE. I DON'T SEE ANY MONSTERS.
THINK THOSE KIDS WERE PLAYING A JOKE?
NOTHING DOWN THERE. LET'S GO FILE OUR REPORT.
HEY--HELP! WHAT'S UP WITH THIS? I'M BEING PULLED UNDER!
IT'S PULLING ME DOWN! HELLLP!
LET GO! LET GO! WHO IS DOING THIS?

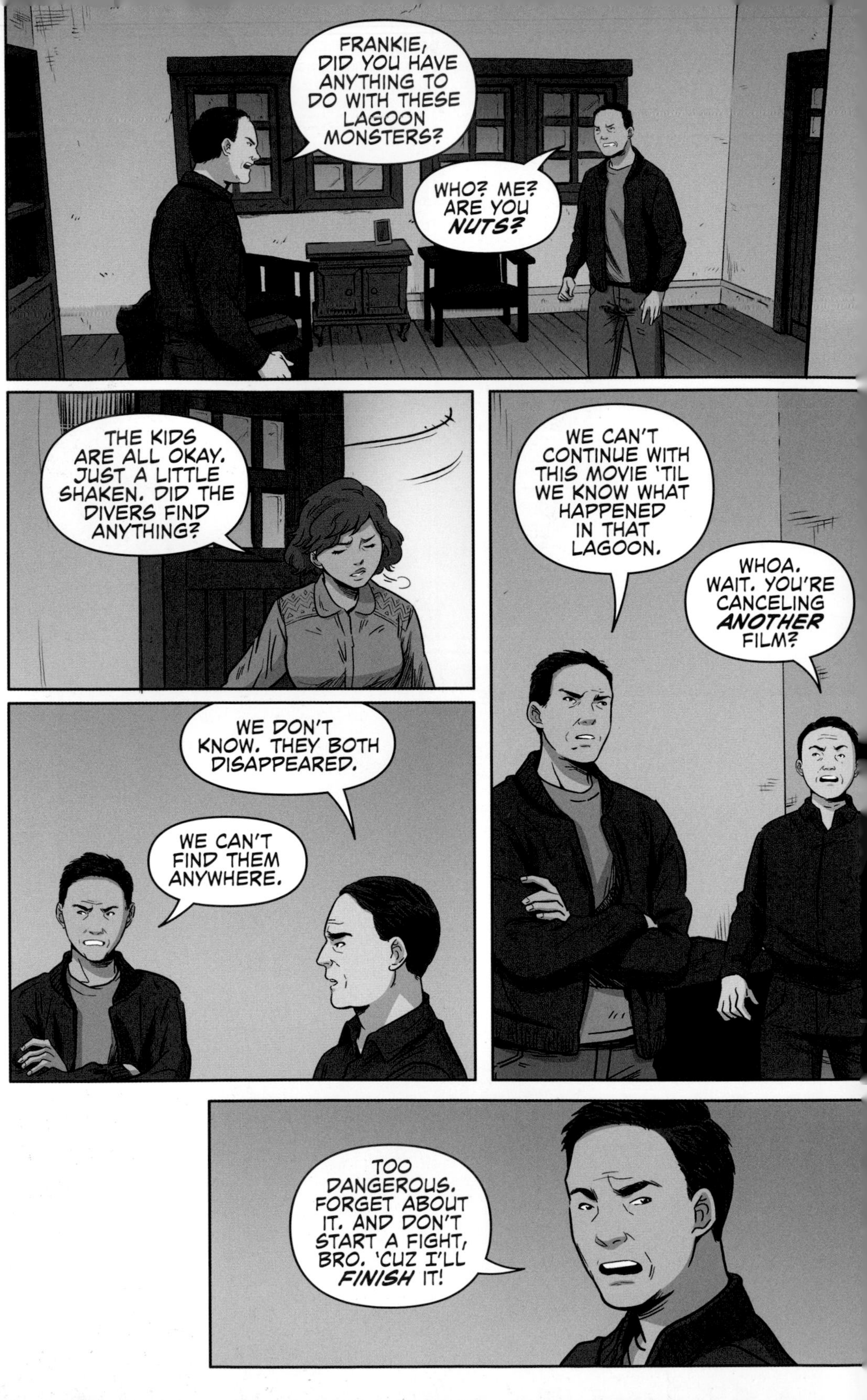
FRANKIE, DID YOU HAVE ANYTHING TO DO WITH THESE LAGOON MONSTERS?
WHO? ME? ARE YOU NUTS?
THE KIDS ARE ALL OKAY. JUST A LITTLE SHAKEN. DID THE DIVERS FIND ANYTHING?
WE DON'T KNOW. THEY BOTH DISAPPEARED.
WE CAN'T FIND THEM ANYWHERE.
WE CAN'T CONTINUE WITH THIS MOVIE 'TIL WE KNOW WHAT HAPPENED IN THAT LAGOON.
WHOA. WAIT. YOU'RE CANCELING ANOTHER FILM?
TOO DANGEROUS. FORGET ABOUT IT. AND DON'T START A FIGHT, BRO. 'CUZ I'LL FINISH IT!

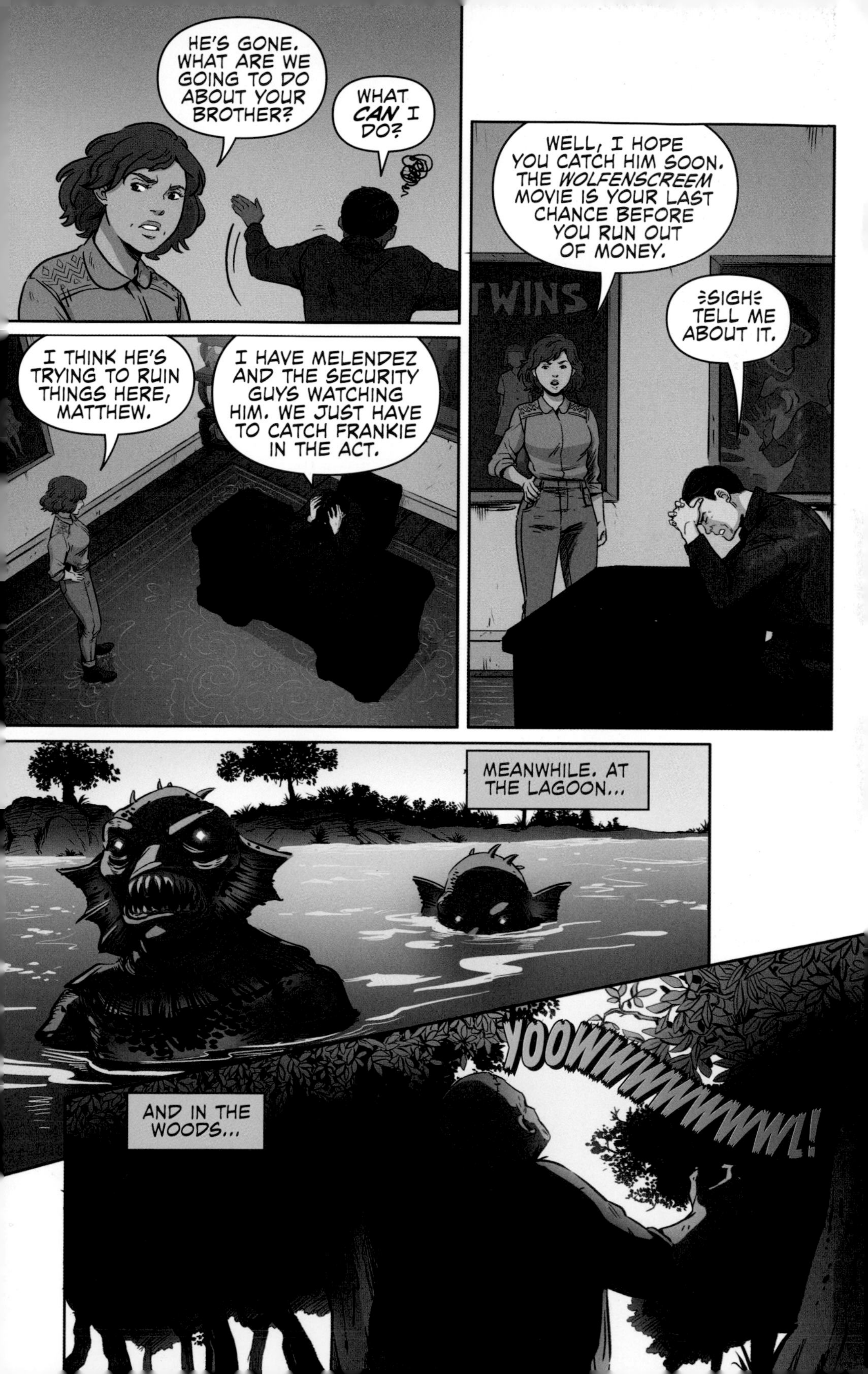
HE'S GONE. WHAT ARE WE GOING TO DO ABOUT YOUR BROTHER?
WHAT CAN I DO?
WELL, I HOPE YOU CATCH HIM SOON. THE WOLFENSCREEM MOVIE IS YOUR LAST CHANCE BEFORE YOU RUN OUT OF MONEY.
TWINS
SIGH TELL ME ABOUT IT.
I THINK HE'S TRYING TO RUIN THINGS HERE, MATTHEW.
I HAVE MELENDEZ AND THE SECURITY GUYS WATCHING HIM. WE JUST HAVE TO CATCH FRANKIE IN THE ACT.
MEANWHILE. AT THE LAGOON...
YOOWWWWWWWWL!
AND IN THE WOODS...

PART SEVEN

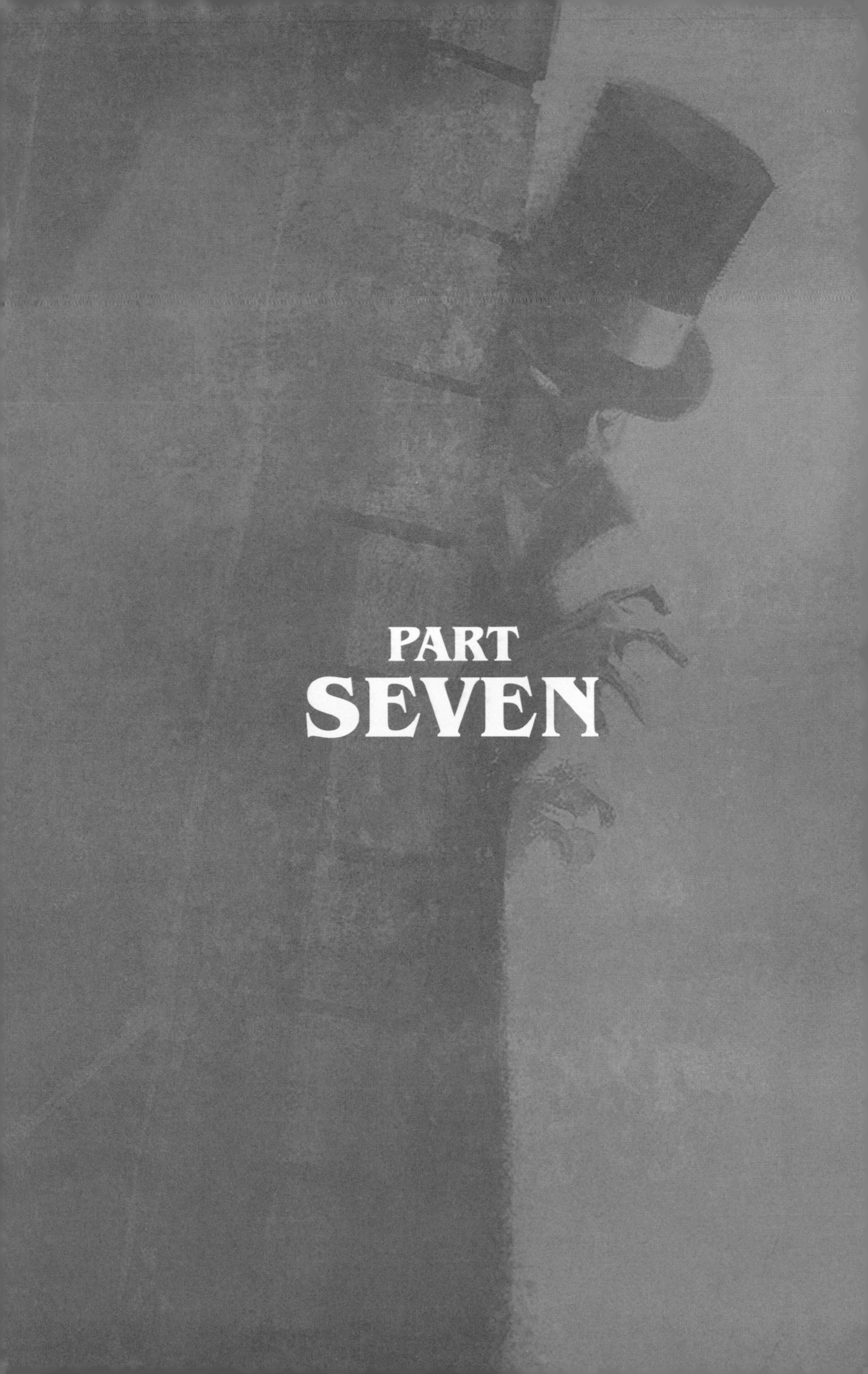

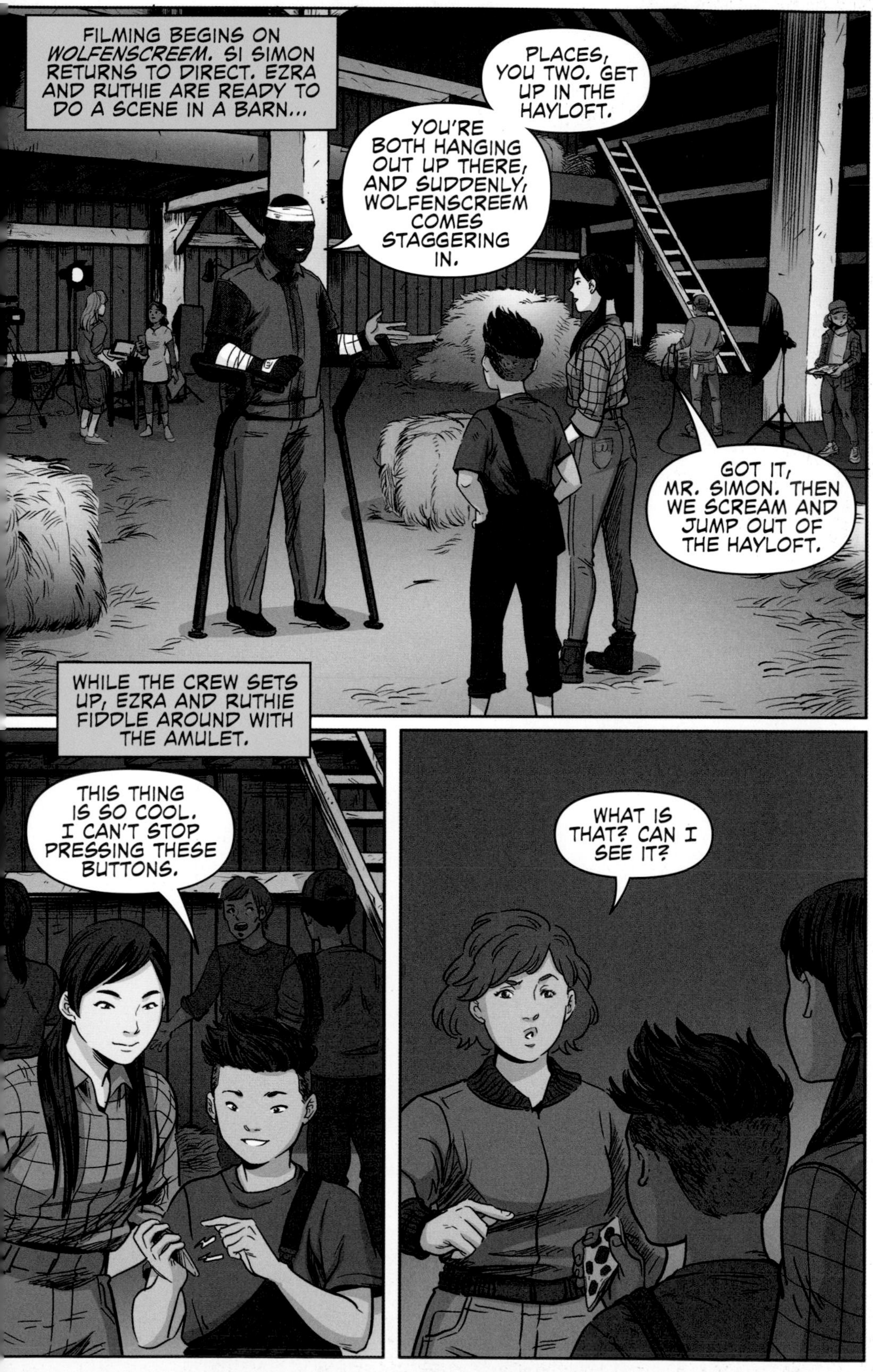
FILMING BEGINS ON *WOLFENSCREEM*. SI SIMON RETURNS TO DIRECT. EZRA AND RUTHIE ARE READY TO DO A SCENE IN A BARN...
PLACES, YOU TWO. GET UP IN THE HAYLOFT.
YOU'RE BOTH HANGING OUT UP THERE, AND SUDDENLY, WOLFENSCREEM COMES STAGGERING IN.
GOT IT, MR. SIMON. THEN WE SCREAM AND JUMP OUT OF THE HAYLOFT.
WHILE THE CREW SETS UP, EZRA AND RUTHIE FIDDLE AROUND WITH THE AMULET.
THIS THING IS SO COOL. I CAN'T STOP PRESSING THESE BUTTONS.
WHAT IS THAT? CAN I SEE IT?

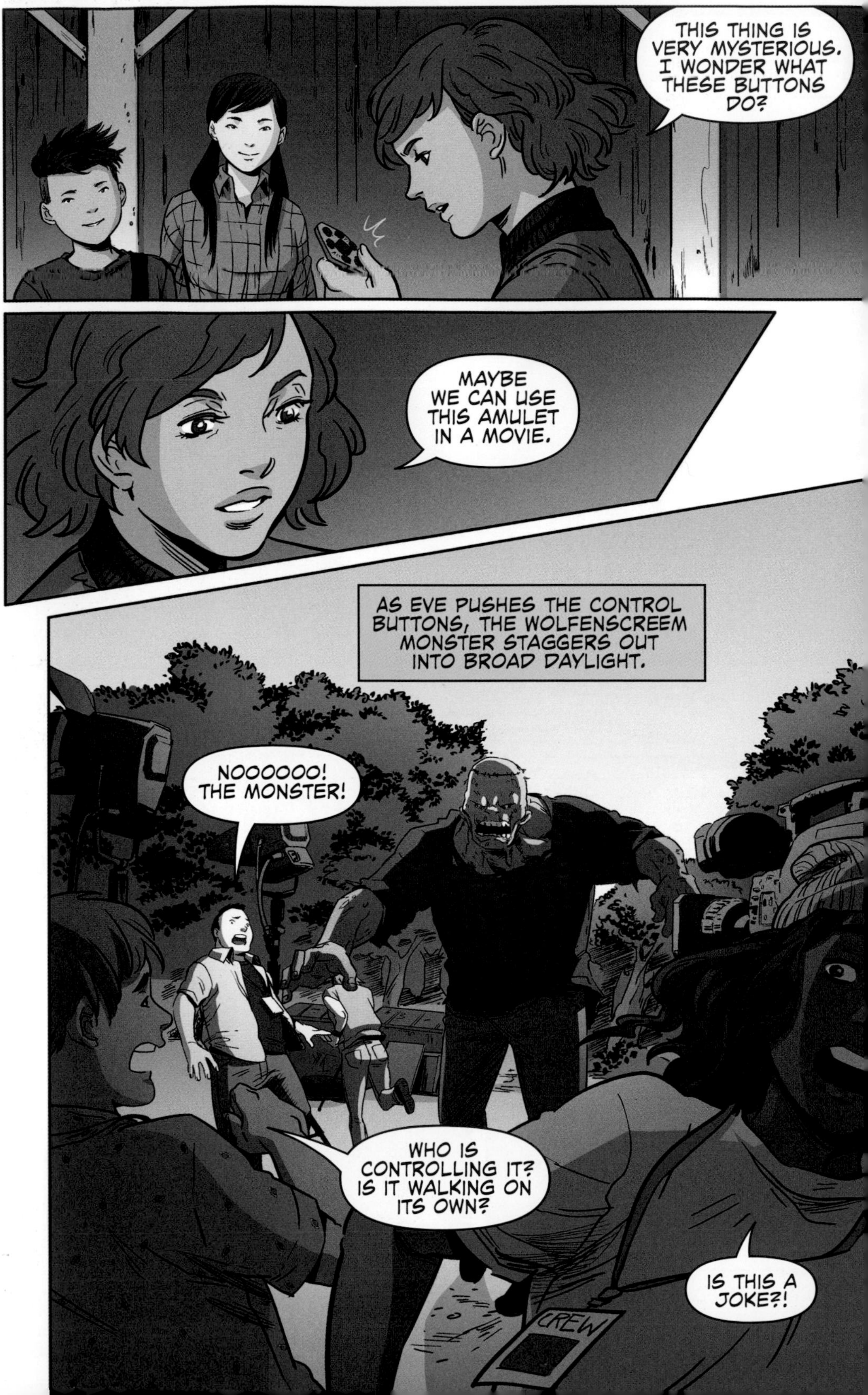
THIS THING IS VERY MYSTERIOUS. I WONDER WHAT THESE BUTTONS DO?
MAYBE WE CAN USE THIS AMULET IN A MOVIE.
AS EVE PUSHES THE CONTROL BUTTONS, THE WOLFENSCREEM MONSTER STAGGERS OUT INTO BROAD DAYLIGHT.
NOOOOOO! THE MONSTER!
WHO IS CONTROLLING IT? IS IT WALKING ON ITS OWN?
IS THIS A JOKE?!
CREW

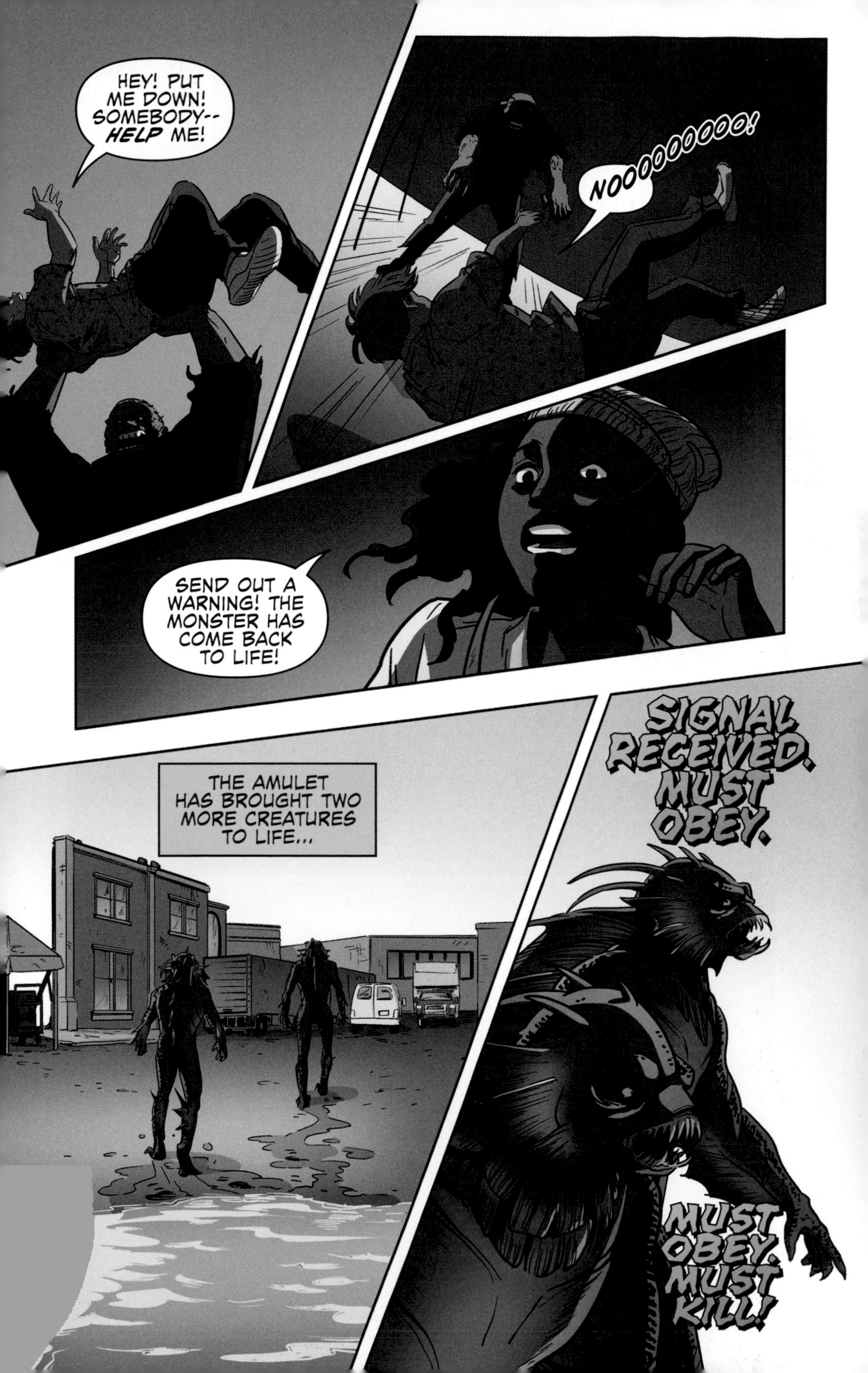
HEY! PUT ME DOWN! SOMEBODY-- HELP ME!
NOOOOOOOOOO!
SEND OUT A WARNING! THE MONSTER HAS COME BACK TO LIFE!
THE AMULET HAS BROUGHT TWO MORE CREATURES TO LIFE...
SIGNAL RECEIVED. MUST OBEY.
MUST OBEY. MUST KILL!

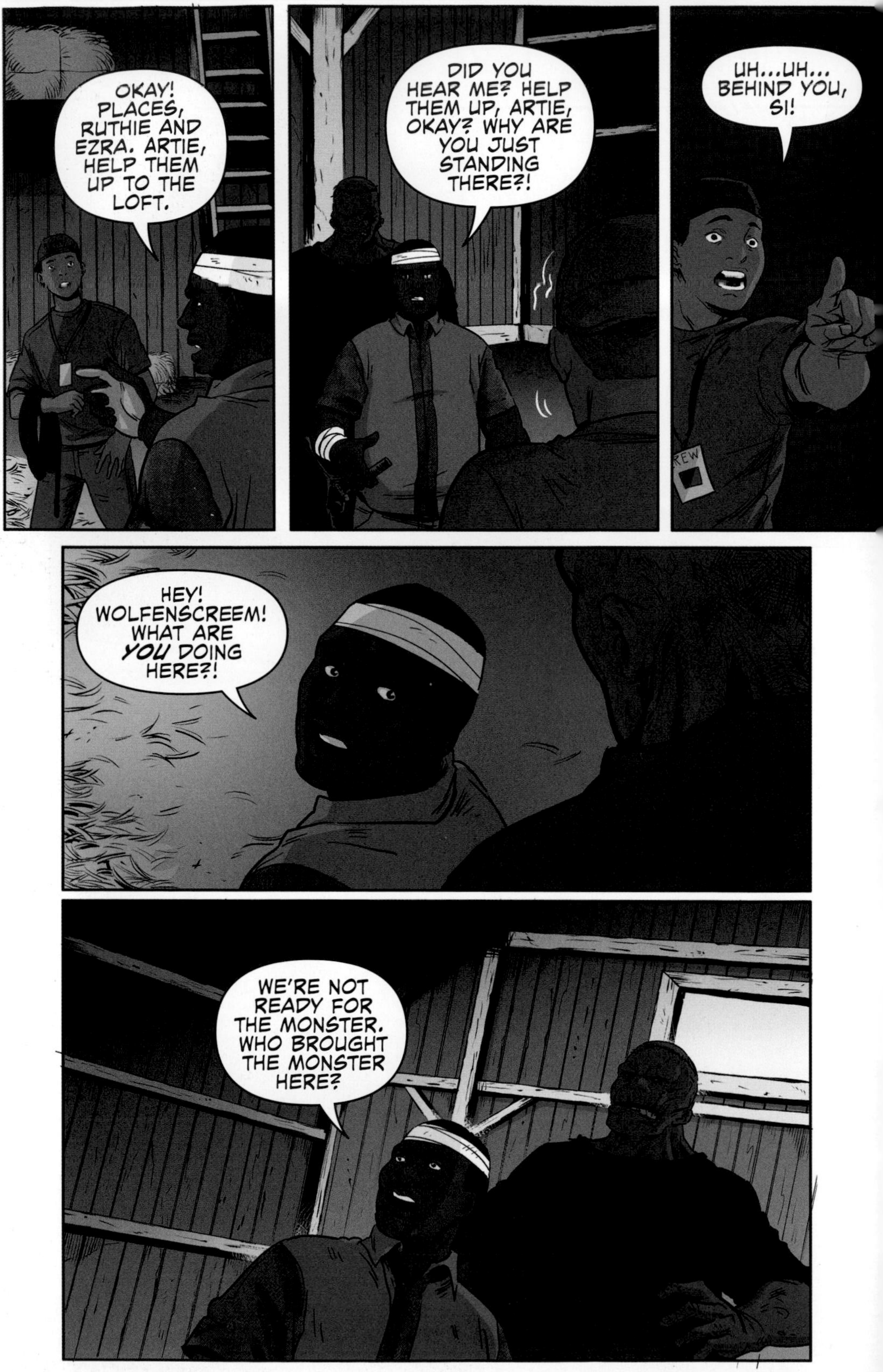
OKAY! PLACES, RUTHIE AND EZRA. ARTIE, HELP THEM UP TO THE LOFT.
DID YOU HEAR ME? HELP THEM UP, ARTIE, OKAY? WHY ARE YOU JUST STANDING THERE?!
UH...UH... BEHIND YOU, SI!
HEY! WOLFENSCREEM! WHAT ARE *YOU* DOING HERE?!
WE'RE NOT READY FOR THE MONSTER. WHO BROUGHT THE MONSTER HERE?

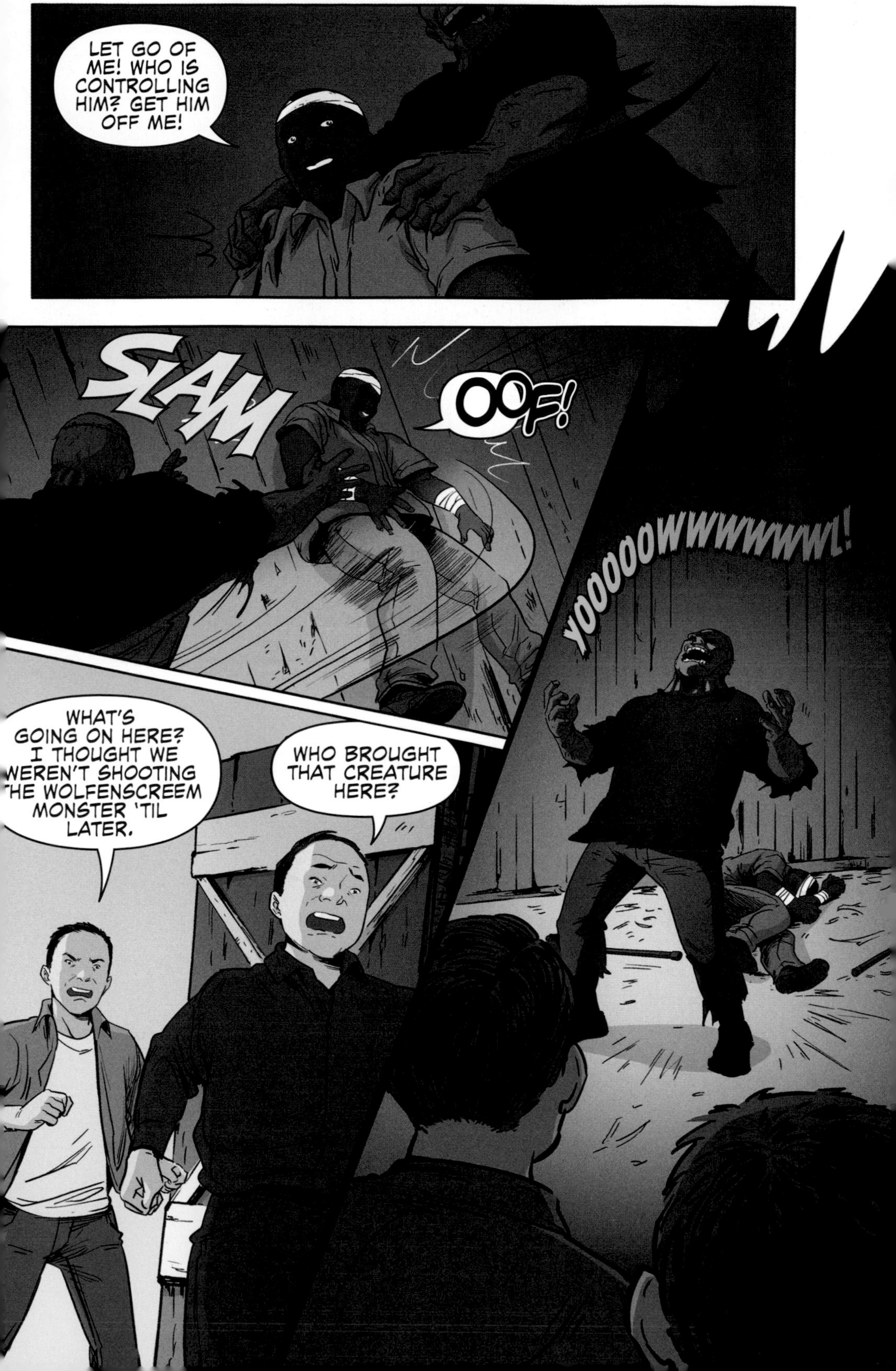
LET GO OF ME! WHO IS CONTROLLING HIM? GET HIM OFF ME!
SLAM
OOF!
YOOOOOWWWWWWL!
WHAT'S GOING ON HERE? I THOUGHT WE WEREN'T SHOOTING THE WOLFENSCREEM MONSTER 'TIL LATER.
WHO BROUGHT THAT CREATURE HERE?

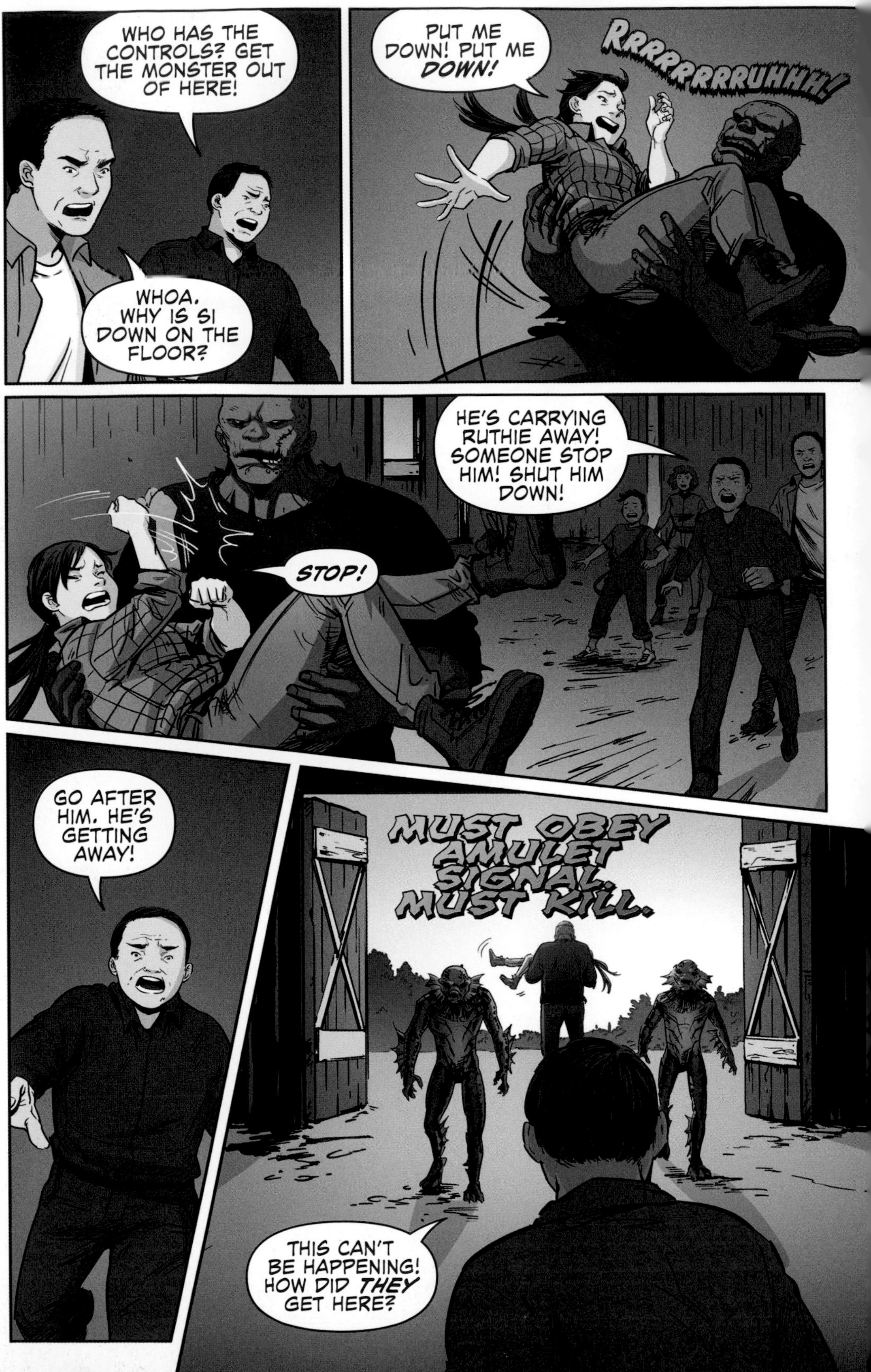
WHO HAS THE CONTROLS? GET THE MONSTER OUT OF HERE!
WHOA. WHY IS SI DOWN ON THE FLOOR?
PUT ME DOWN! PUT ME DOWN!
RRRRRRRRRUHHH!
HE'S CARRYING RUTHIE AWAY! SOMEONE STOP HIM! SHUT HIM DOWN!
STOP!
GO AFTER HIM. HE'S GETTING AWAY!
MUST OBEY AMULET SIGNAL. MUST KILL.
THIS CAN'T BE HAPPENING! HOW DID THEY GET HERE?

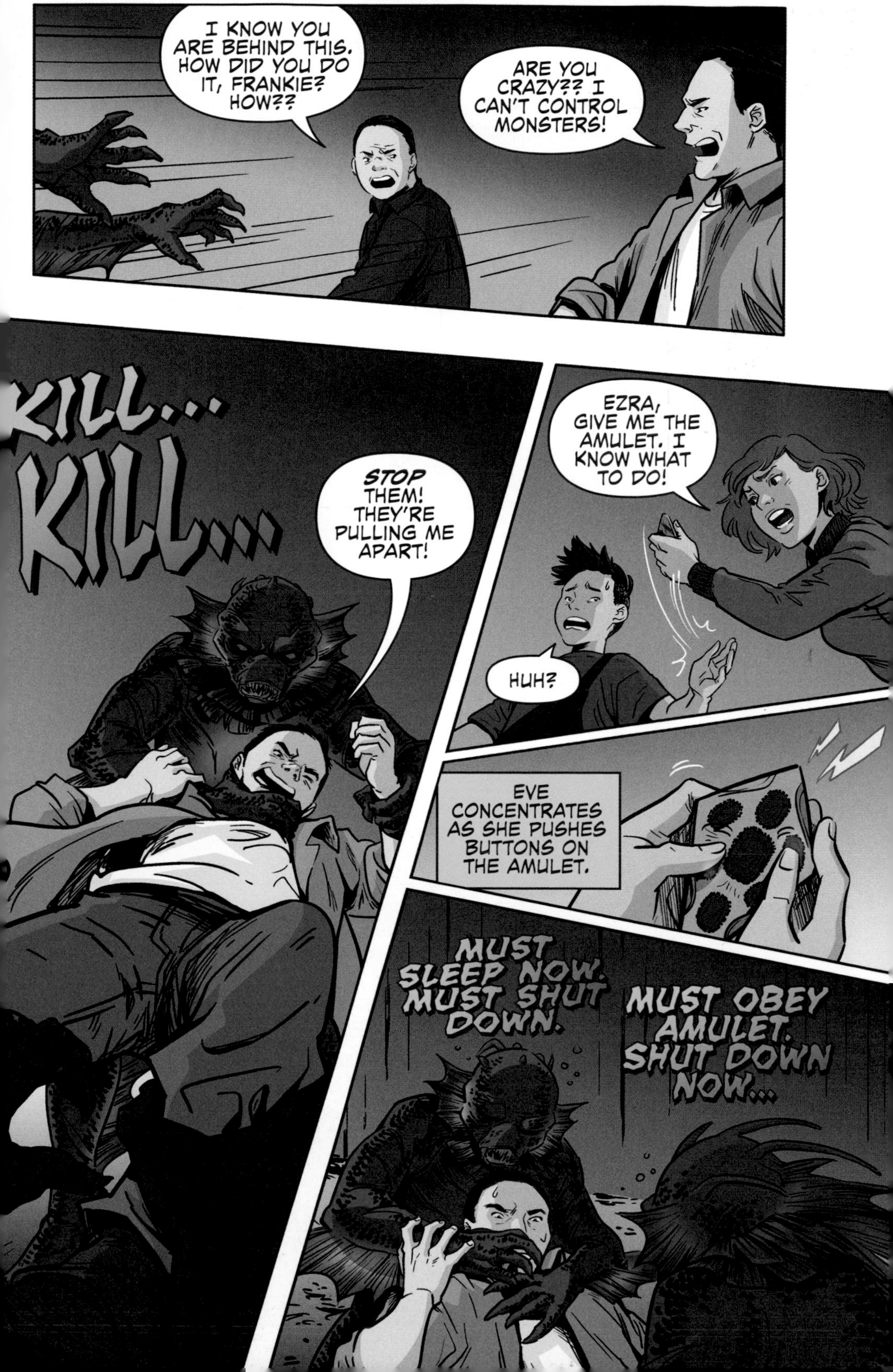
I KNOW YOU ARE BEHIND THIS. HOW DID YOU DO IT, FRANKIE? HOW??
ARE YOU CRAZY?? I CAN'T CONTROL MONSTERS!
KILL... KILL...
STOP THEM! THEY'RE PULLING ME APART!
EZRA, GIVE ME THE AMULET. I KNOW WHAT TO DO!
HUH?
EVE CONCENTRATES AS SHE PUSHES BUTTONS ON THE AMULET.
MUST SLEEP NOW. MUST SHUT DOWN.
MUST OBEY AMULET. SHUT DOWN NOW...

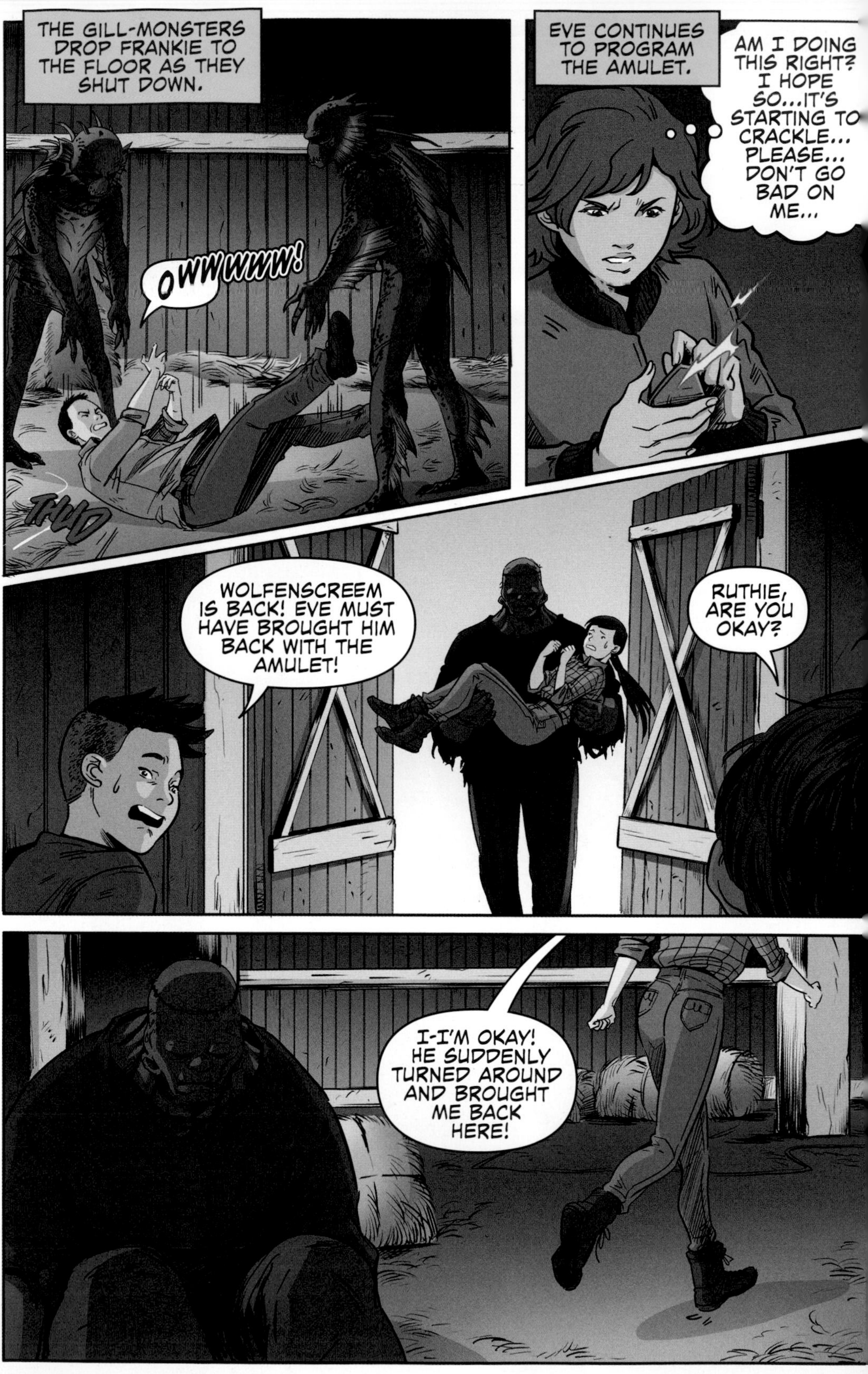
THE GILL-MONSTERS DROP FRANKIE TO THE FLOOR AS THEY SHUT DOWN.
OWWWWW!
THUD
EVE CONTINUES TO PROGRAM THE AMULET.
AM I DOING THIS RIGHT? I HOPE SO...IT'S STARTING TO CRACKLE... PLEASE... DON'T GO BAD ON ME...
WOLFENSCREEM IS BACK! EVE MUST HAVE BROUGHT HIM BACK WITH THE AMULET!
RUTHIE, ARE YOU OKAY?
I-I'M OKAY! HE SUDDENLY TURNED AROUND AND BROUGHT ME BACK HERE!

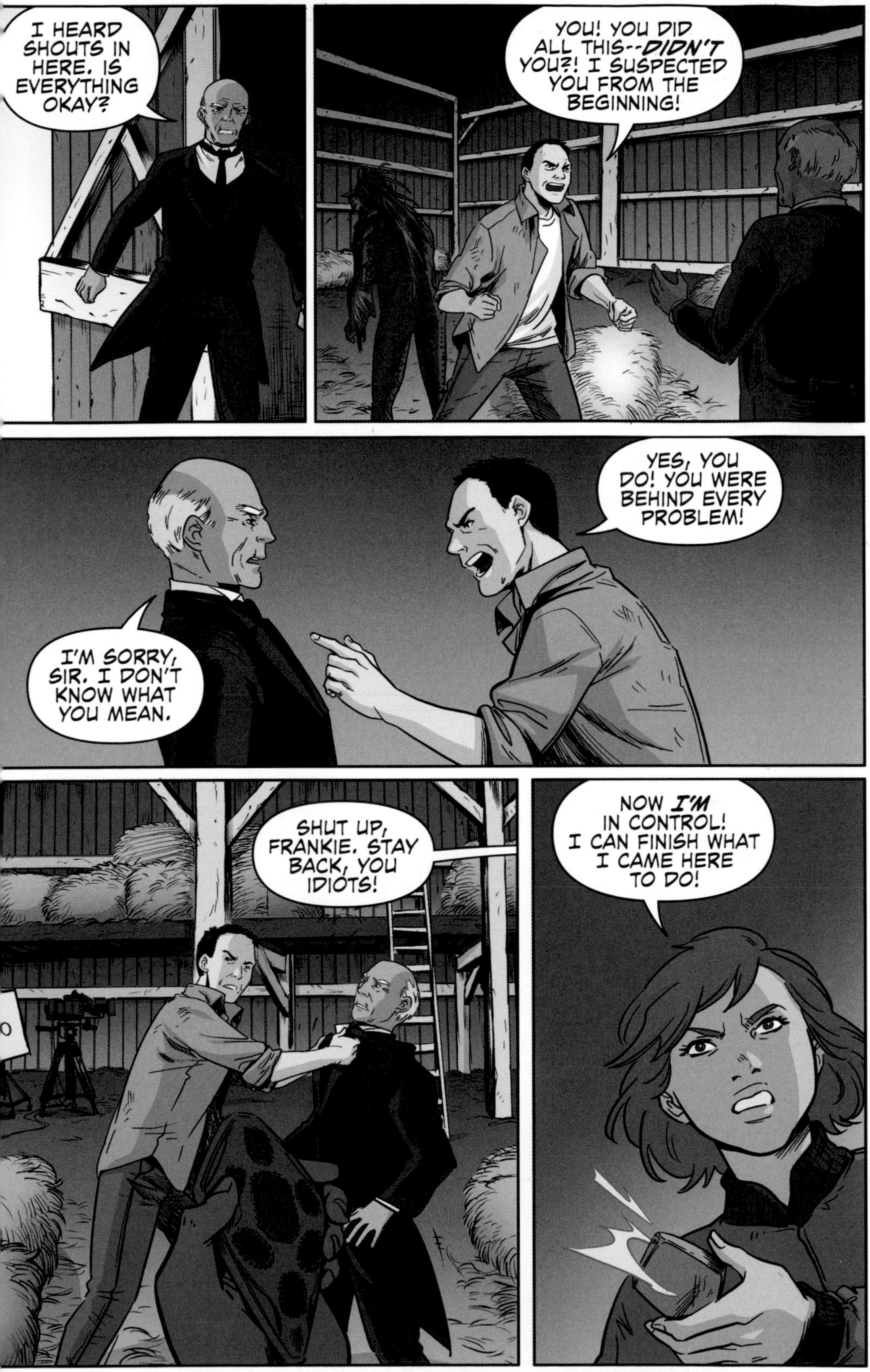
I HEARD SHOUTS IN HERE. IS EVERYTHING OKAY?
YOU! YOU DID ALL THIS--DIDN'T YOU?! I SUSPECTED YOU FROM THE BEGINNING!
I'M SORRY, SIR. I DON'T KNOW WHAT YOU MEAN.
YES, YOU DO! YOU WERE BEHIND EVERY PROBLEM!
SHUT UP, FRANKIE. STAY BACK, YOU IDIOTS!
NOW I'M IN CONTROL! I CAN FINISH WHAT I CAME HERE TO DO!

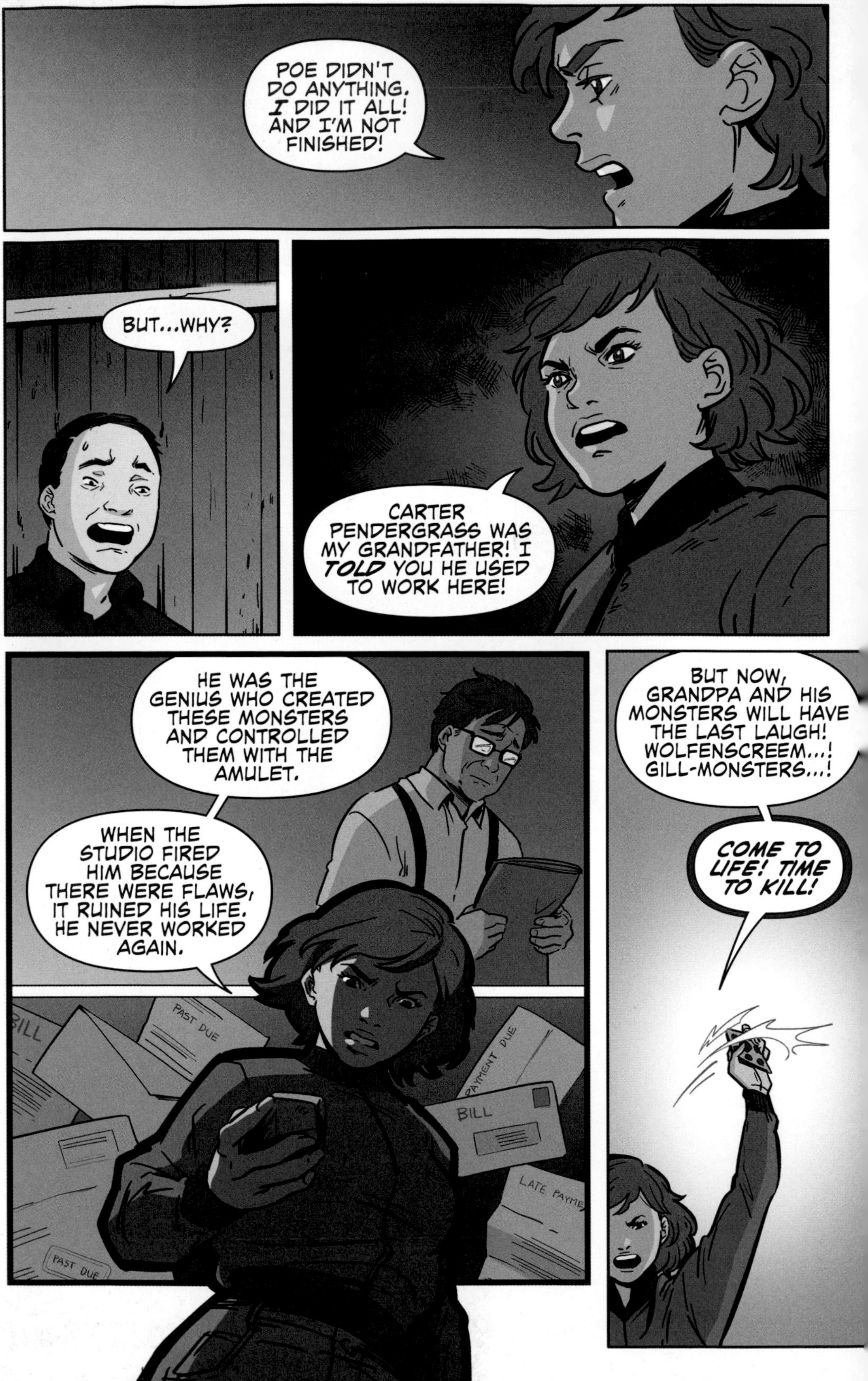
POE DIDN'T DO ANYTHING. *I* DID IT ALL! AND I'M NOT FINISHED!
BUT...WHY?
CARTER PENDERGRASS WAS MY GRANDFATHER! I *TOLD* YOU HE USED TO WORK HERE!
HE WAS THE GENIUS WHO CREATED THESE MONSTERS AND CONTROLLED THEM WITH THE AMULET.
WHEN THE STUDIO FIRED HIM BECAUSE THERE WERE FLAWS, IT RUINED HIS LIFE. HE NEVER WORKED AGAIN.
BILL
PAST DUE
PAYMENT DUE
BILL
LATE PAYME
PAST DUE
BUT NOW, GRANDPA AND HIS MONSTERS WILL HAVE THE LAST LAUGH! WOLFENSCREEM...! GILL-MONSTERS...!
COME TO LIFE! TIME TO KILL!

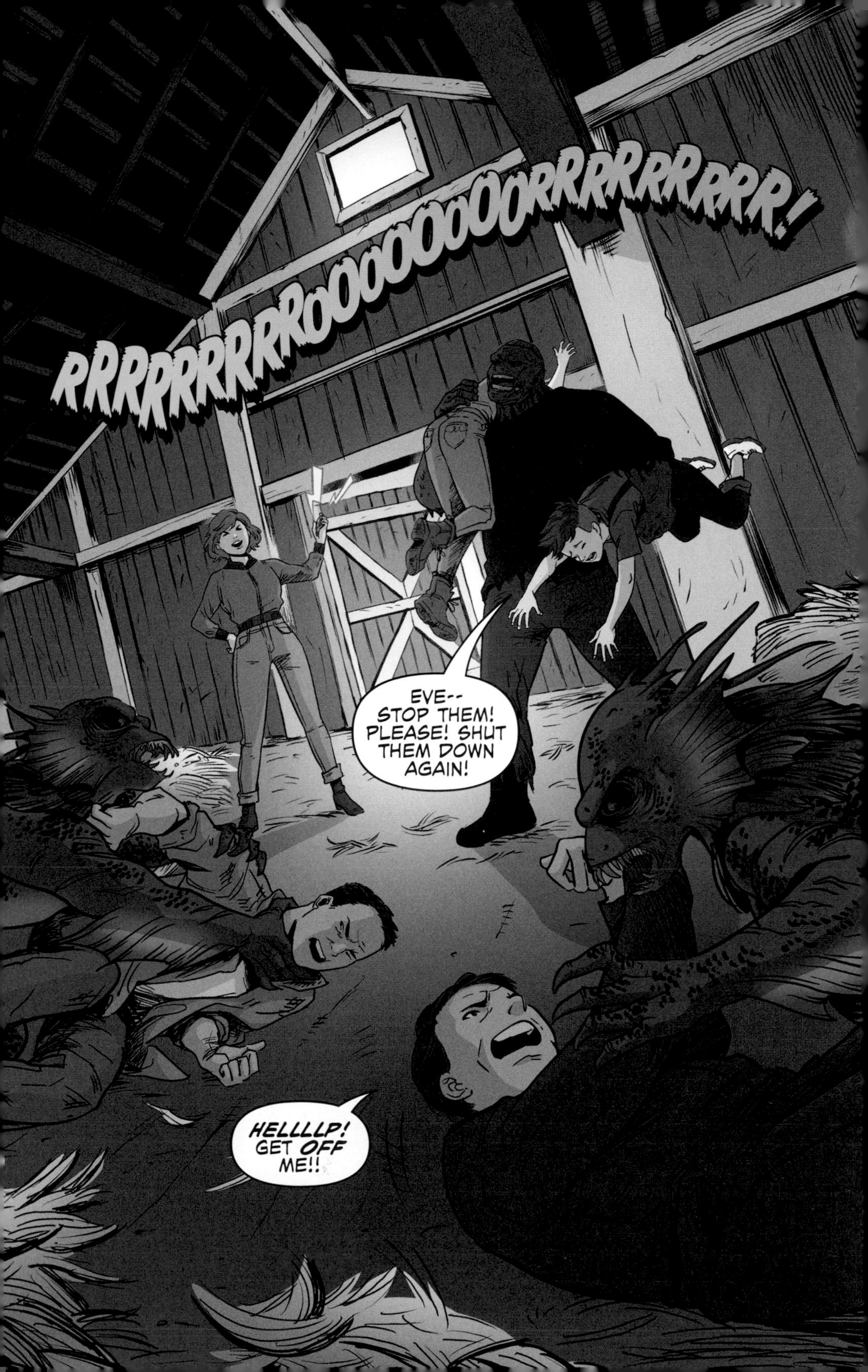
RRRRRRRRROOOOOOOOORRRRRRRRRR!
EVE-- STOP THEM! PLEASE! SHUT THEM DOWN AGAIN!
HELLLLP! GET OFF ME!!

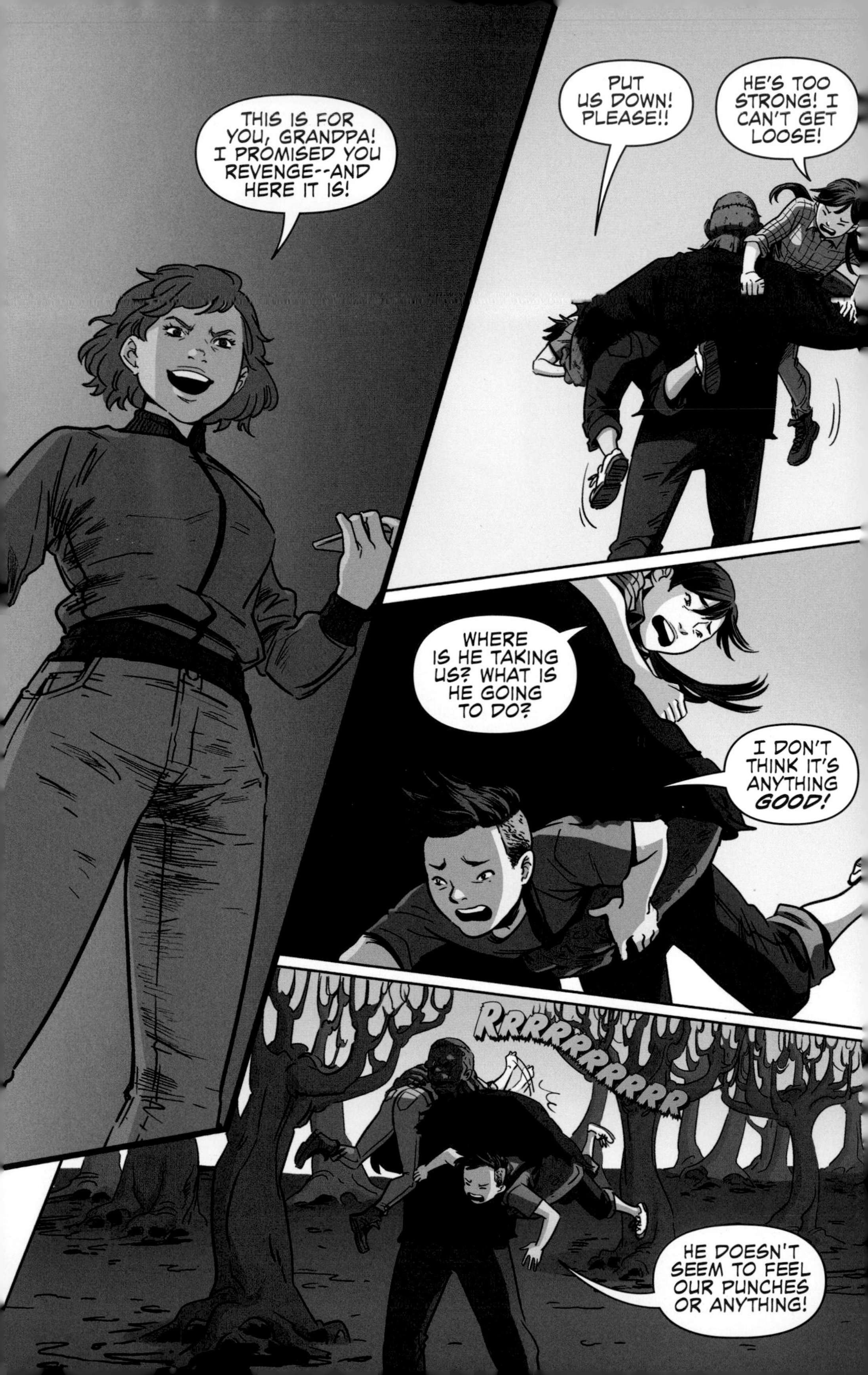
THIS IS FOR YOU, GRANDPA! I PROMISED YOU REVENGE--AND HERE IT IS!
PUT US DOWN! PLEASE!!
HE'S TOO STRONG! I CAN'T GET LOOSE!
WHERE IS HE TAKING US? WHAT IS HE GOING TO DO?
I DON'T THINK IT'S ANYTHING GOOD!
RRRRRRRRRRRR
HE DOESN'T SEEM TO FEEL OUR PUNCHES OR ANYTHING!

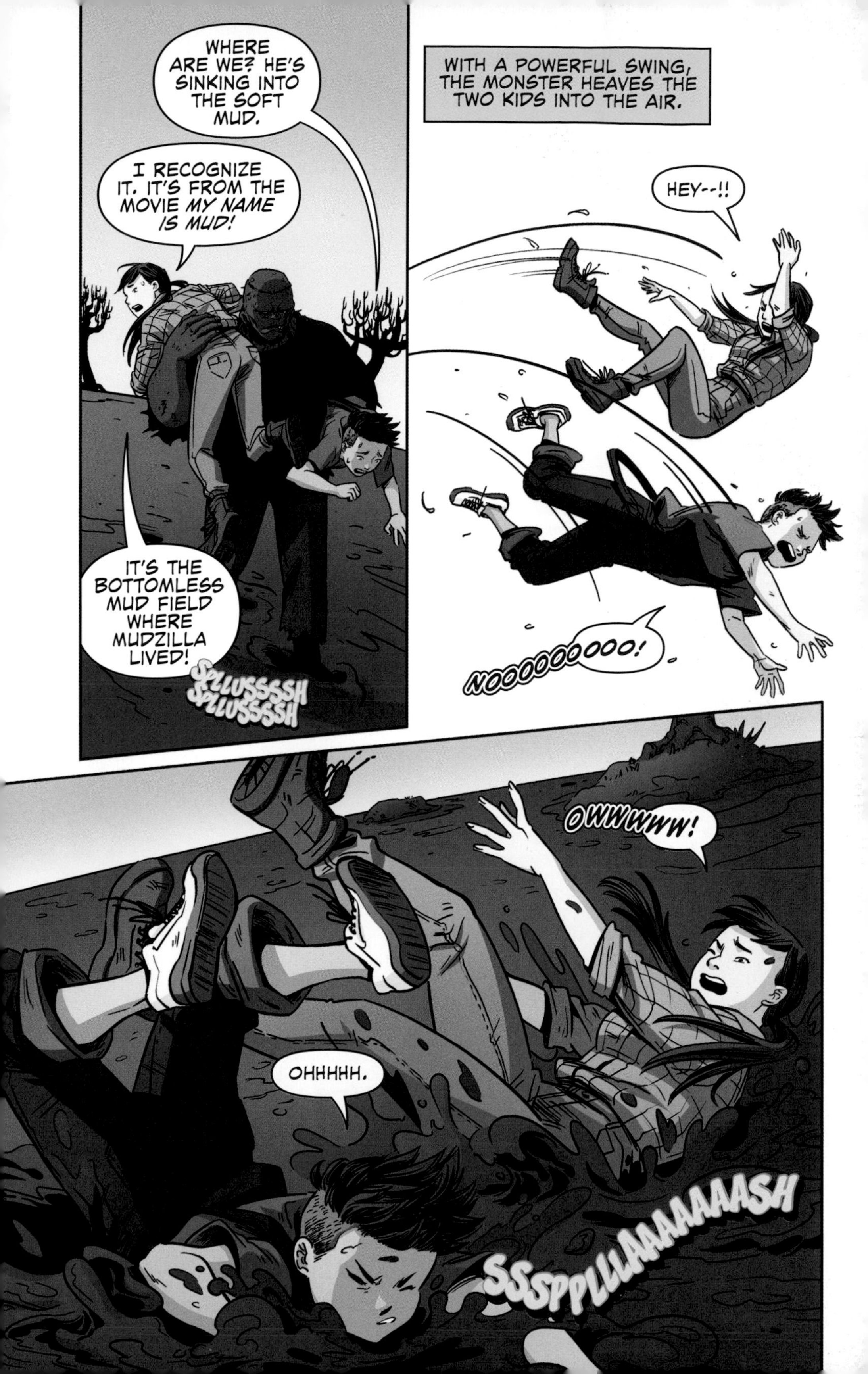
WHERE ARE WE? HE'S SINKING INTO THE SOFT MUD.
I RECOGNIZE IT. IT'S FROM THE MOVIE *MY NAME IS MUD!*
IT'S THE BOTTOMLESS MUD FIELD WHERE MUDZILLA LIVED!
SPLLUSSSSH SPLLUSSSSH
WITH A POWERFUL SWING, THE MONSTER HEAVES THE TWO KIDS INTO THE AIR.
HEY--!!
NOOOOOOOOOO!
OWWWWW!
OHHHHH.
SSSPPLLLAAAAAAASH

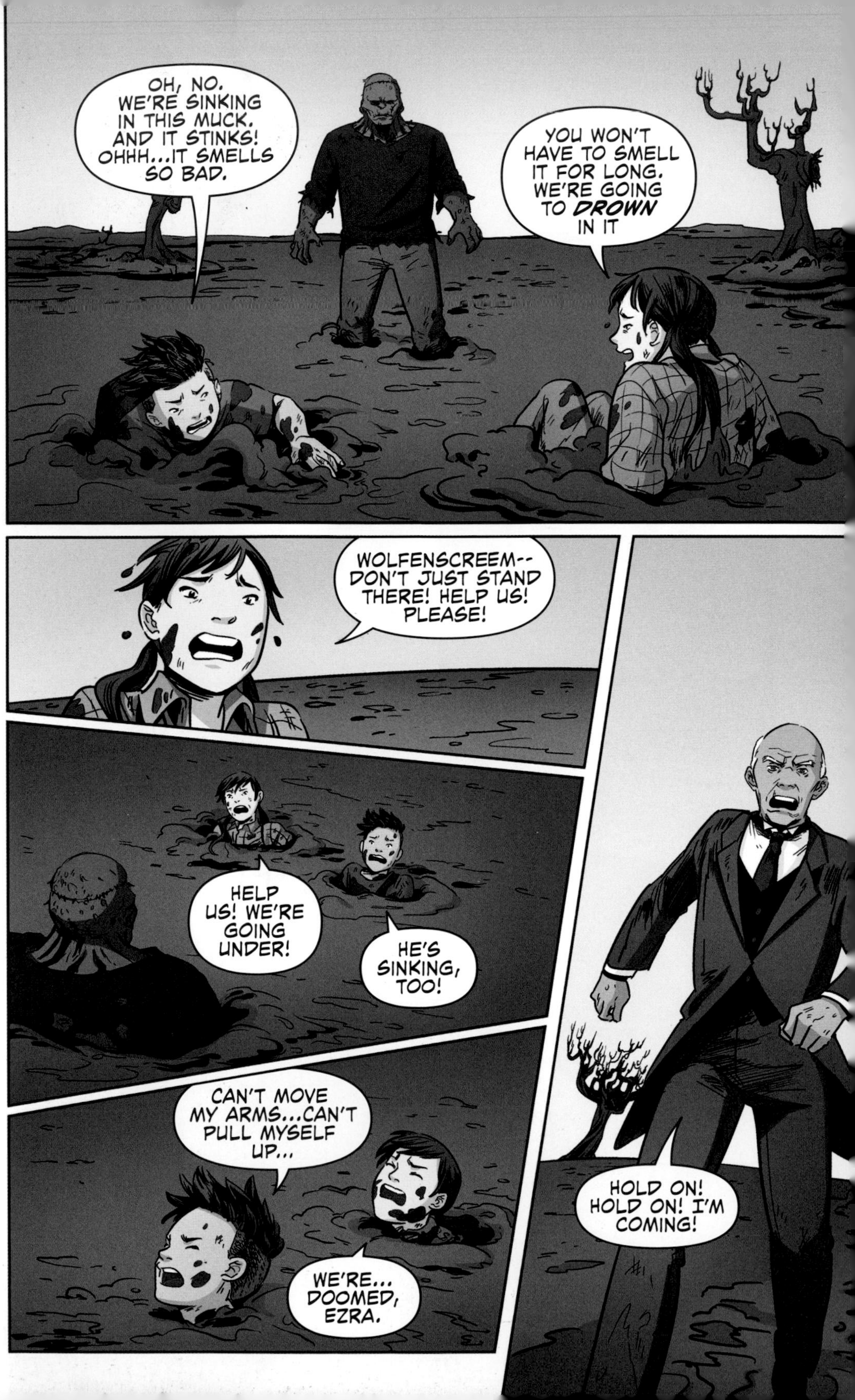
OH, NO. WE'RE SINKING IN THIS MUCK. AND IT STINKS! OHHH...IT SMELLS SO BAD.
YOU WON'T HAVE TO SMELL IT FOR LONG. WE'RE GOING TO DROWN IN IT
WOLFENSCREEM-- DON'T JUST STAND THERE! HELP US! PLEASE!
HELP US! WE'RE GOING UNDER!
HE'S SINKING, TOO!
CAN'T MOVE MY ARMS...CAN'T PULL MYSELF UP...
WE'RE... DOOMED, EZRA.
HOLD ON! HOLD ON! I'M COMING!

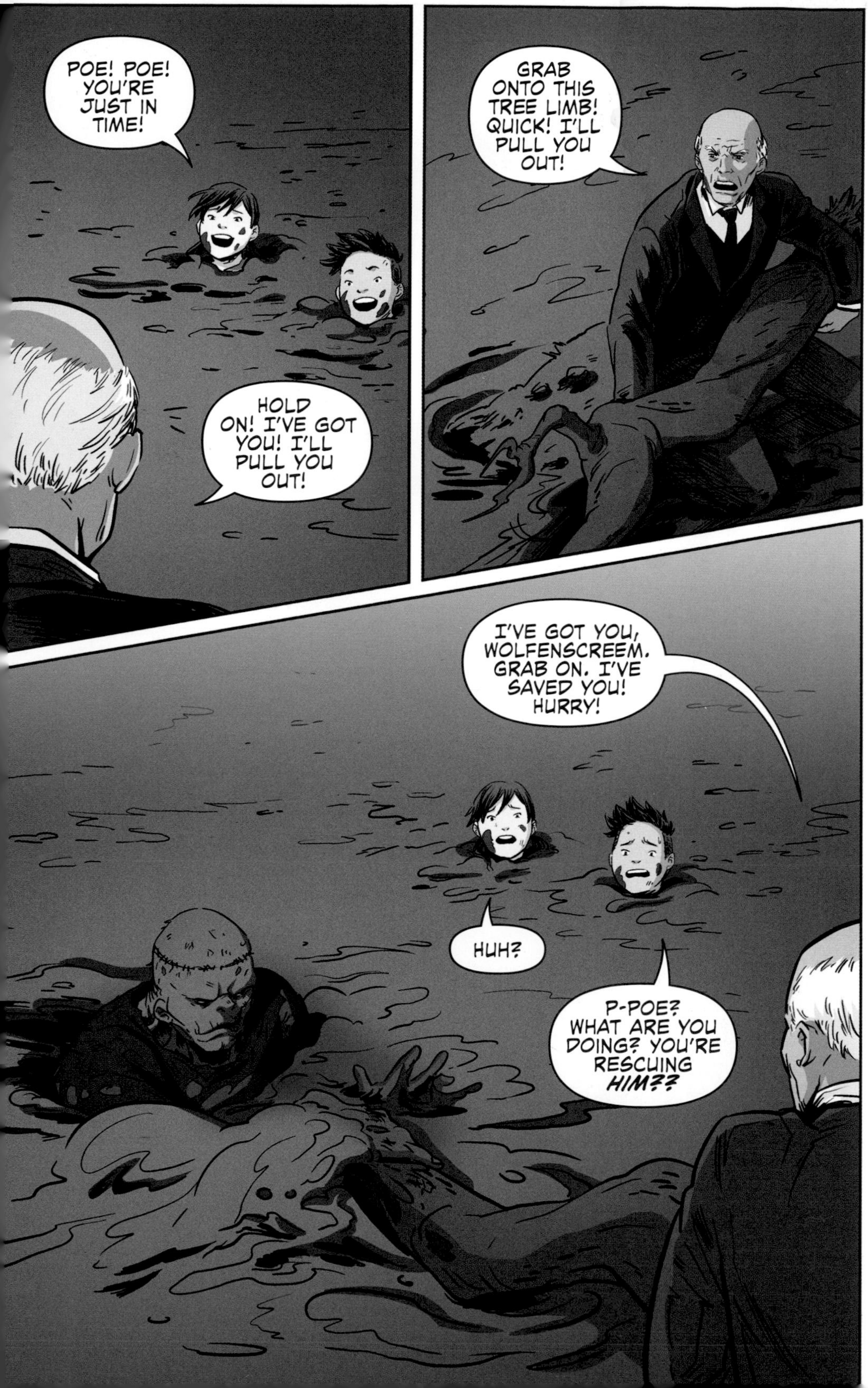
POE! POE! YOU'RE JUST IN TIME!
HOLD ON! I'VE GOT YOU! I'LL PULL YOU OUT!
GRAB ONTO THIS TREE LIMB! QUICK! I'LL PULL YOU OUT!
I'VE GOT YOU, WOLFENSCREEM. GRAB ON. I'VE SAVED YOU! HURRY!
HUH?
P-POE? WHAT ARE YOU DOING? YOU'RE RESCUING *HIM??*

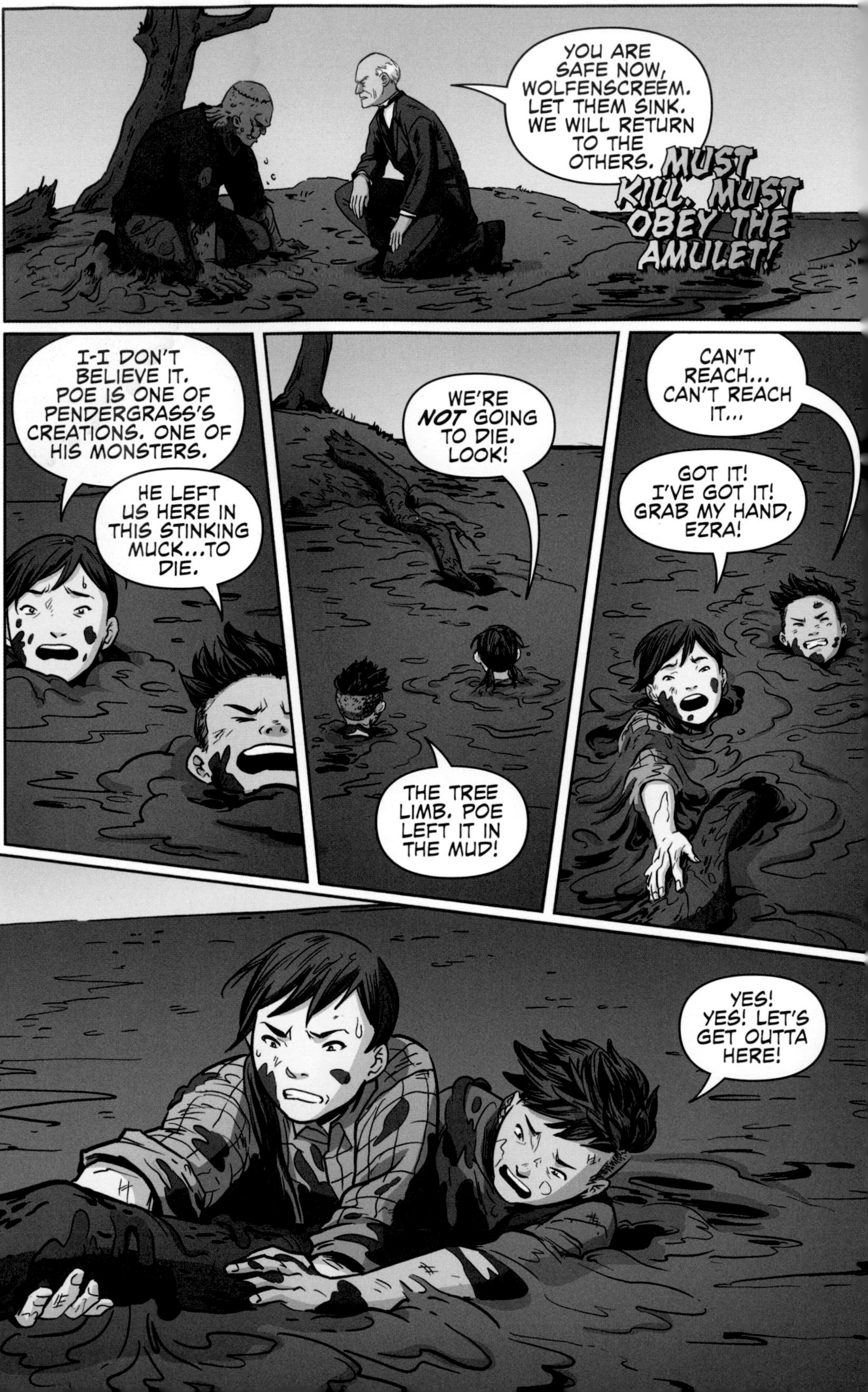
YOU ARE SAFE NOW, WOLFENSCREEM. LET THEM SINK. WE WILL RETURN TO THE OTHERS.
MUST KILL. MUST OBEY THE AMULET!
I-I DON'T BELIEVE IT. POE IS ONE OF PENDERGRASS'S CREATIONS. ONE OF HIS MONSTERS.
HE LEFT US HERE IN THIS STINKING MUCK...TO DIE.
WE'RE NOT GOING TO DIE. LOOK!
THE TREE LIMB. POE LEFT IT IN THE MUD!
CAN'T REACH... CAN'T REACH IT...
GOT IT! I'VE GOT IT! GRAB MY HAND, EZRA!
YES! YES! LET'S GET OUTTA HERE!

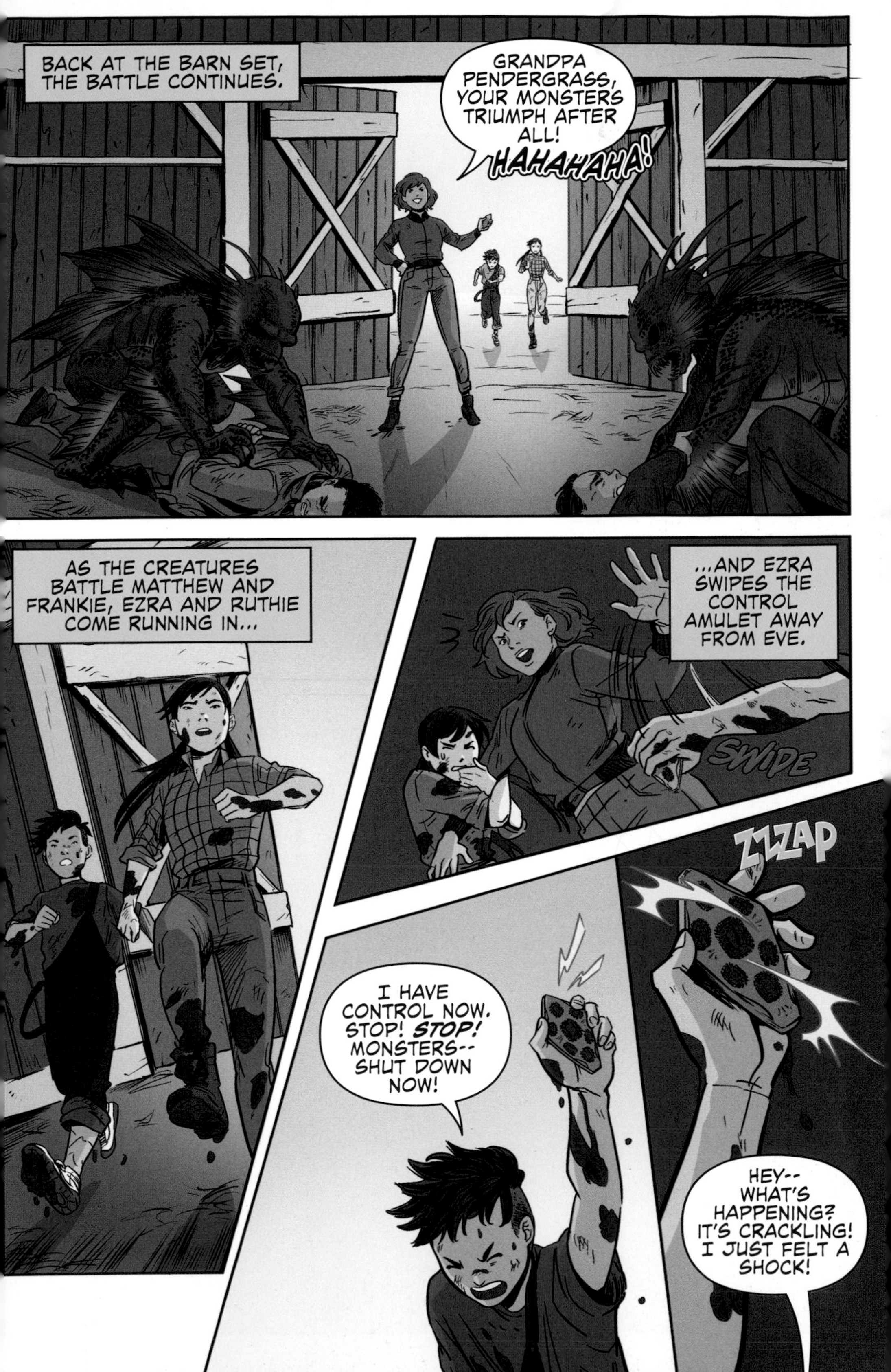
BACK AT THE BARN SET, THE BATTLE CONTINUES.
GRANDPA PENDERGRASS, YOUR MONSTERS TRIUMPH AFTER ALL! HAHAHAHA!
AS THE CREATURES BATTLE MATTHEW AND FRANKIE, EZRA AND RUTHIE COME RUNNING IN...
...AND EZRA SWIPES THE CONTROL AMULET AWAY FROM EVE.
SWIPE
ZZZAP
I HAVE CONTROL NOW. STOP! STOP! MONSTERS-- SHUT DOWN NOW!
HEY-- WHAT'S HAPPENING? IT'S CRACKLING! I JUST FELT A SHOCK!

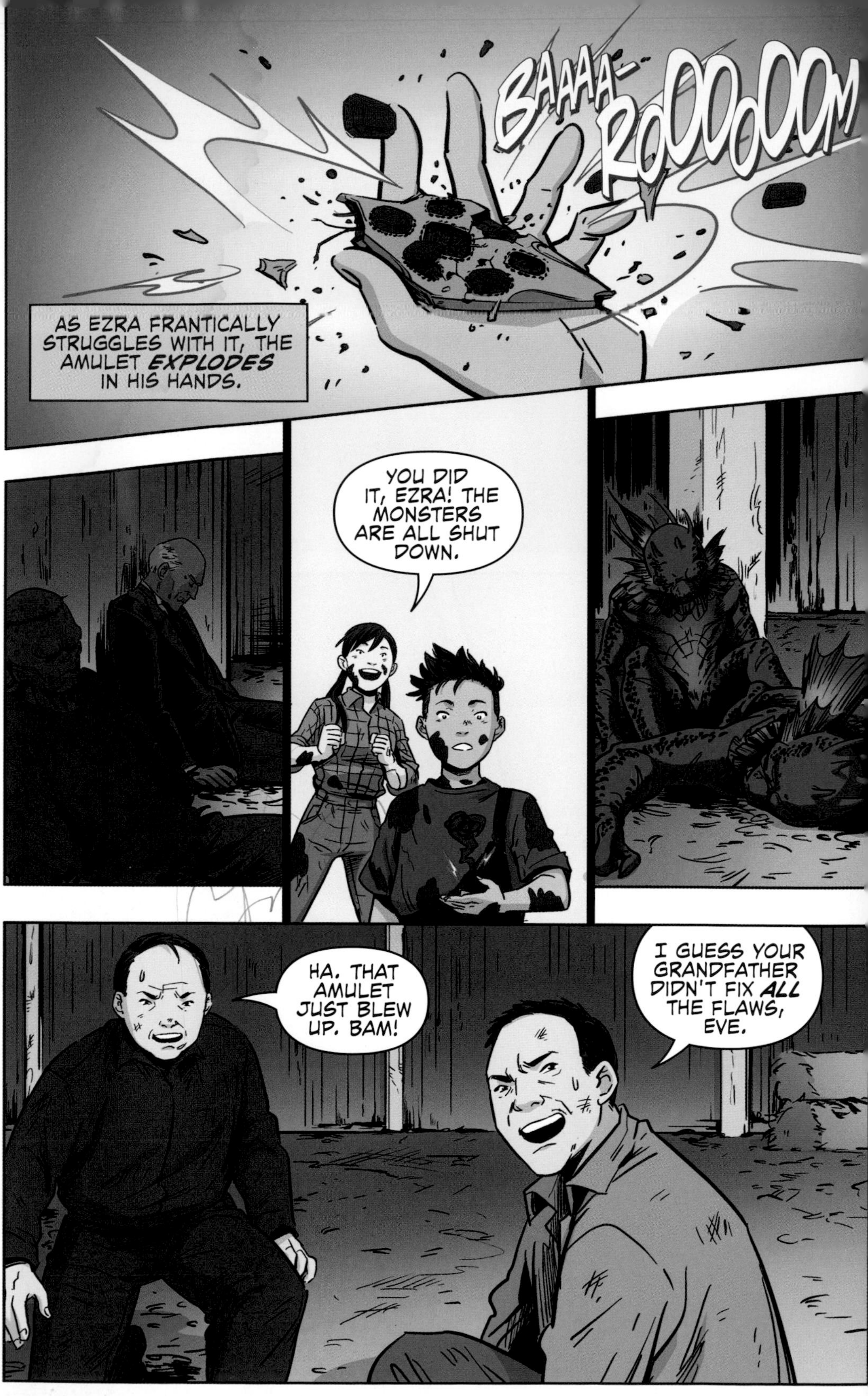
BAAAA-ROOOOOOOM
AS EZRA FRANTICALLY STRUGGLES WITH IT, THE AMULET EXPLODES IN HIS HANDS.
YOU DID IT, EZRA! THE MONSTERS ARE ALL SHUT DOWN.
HA. THAT AMULET JUST BLEW UP. BAM!
I GUESS YOUR GRANDFATHER DIDN'T FIX ALL THE FLAWS, EVE.

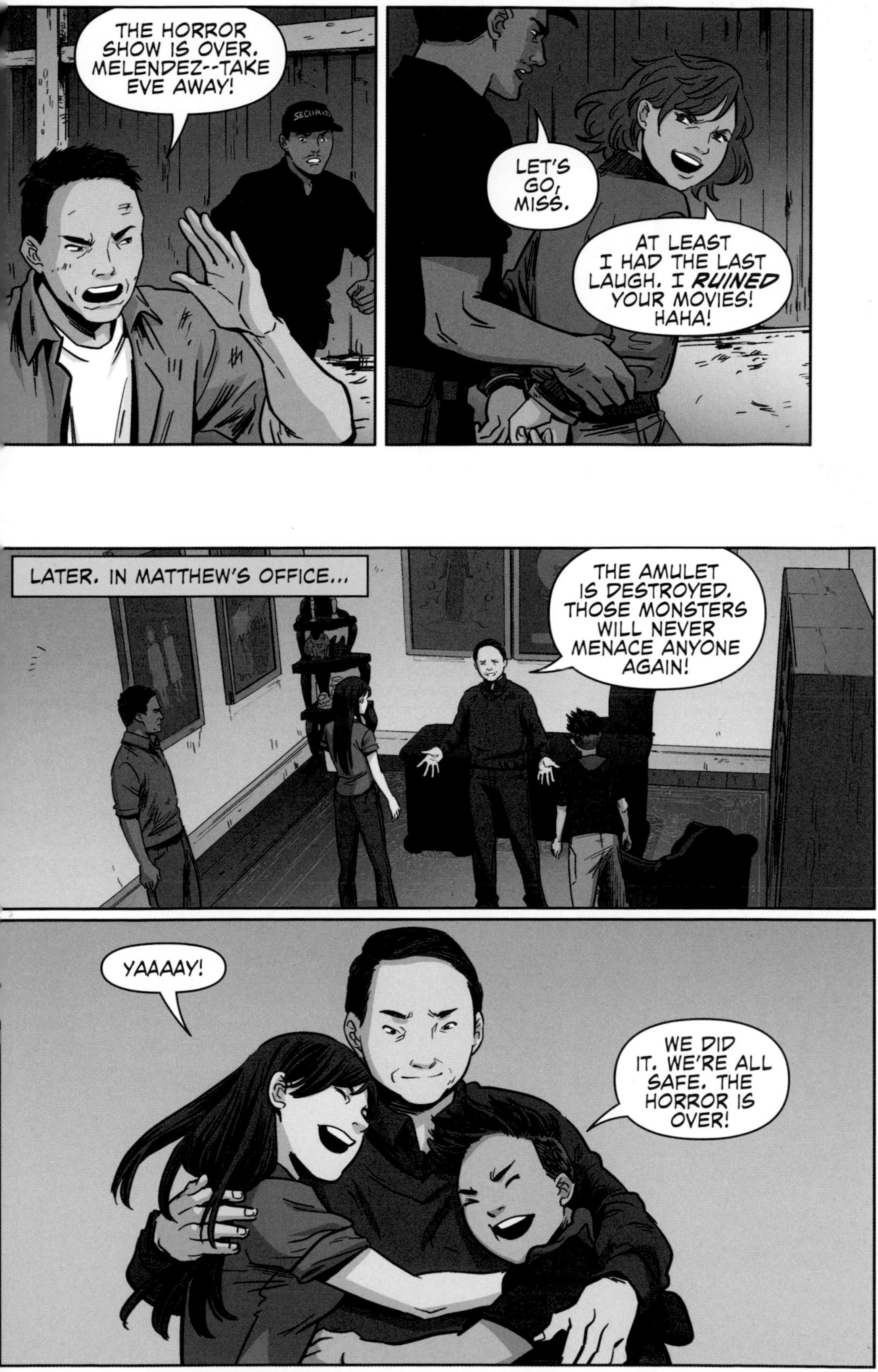

THE HORROR SHOW IS OVER. MELENDEZ--TAKE EVE AWAY!
SECURITY
LET'S GO, MISS.
AT LEAST I HAD THE LAST LAUGH. I *RUINED* YOUR MOVIES! HAHA!
LATER. IN MATTHEW'S OFFICE...
THE AMULET IS DESTROYED. THOSE MONSTERS WILL NEVER MENACE ANYONE AGAIN!
YAAAAY!
WE DID IT. WE'RE ALL SAFE. THE HORROR IS OVER!

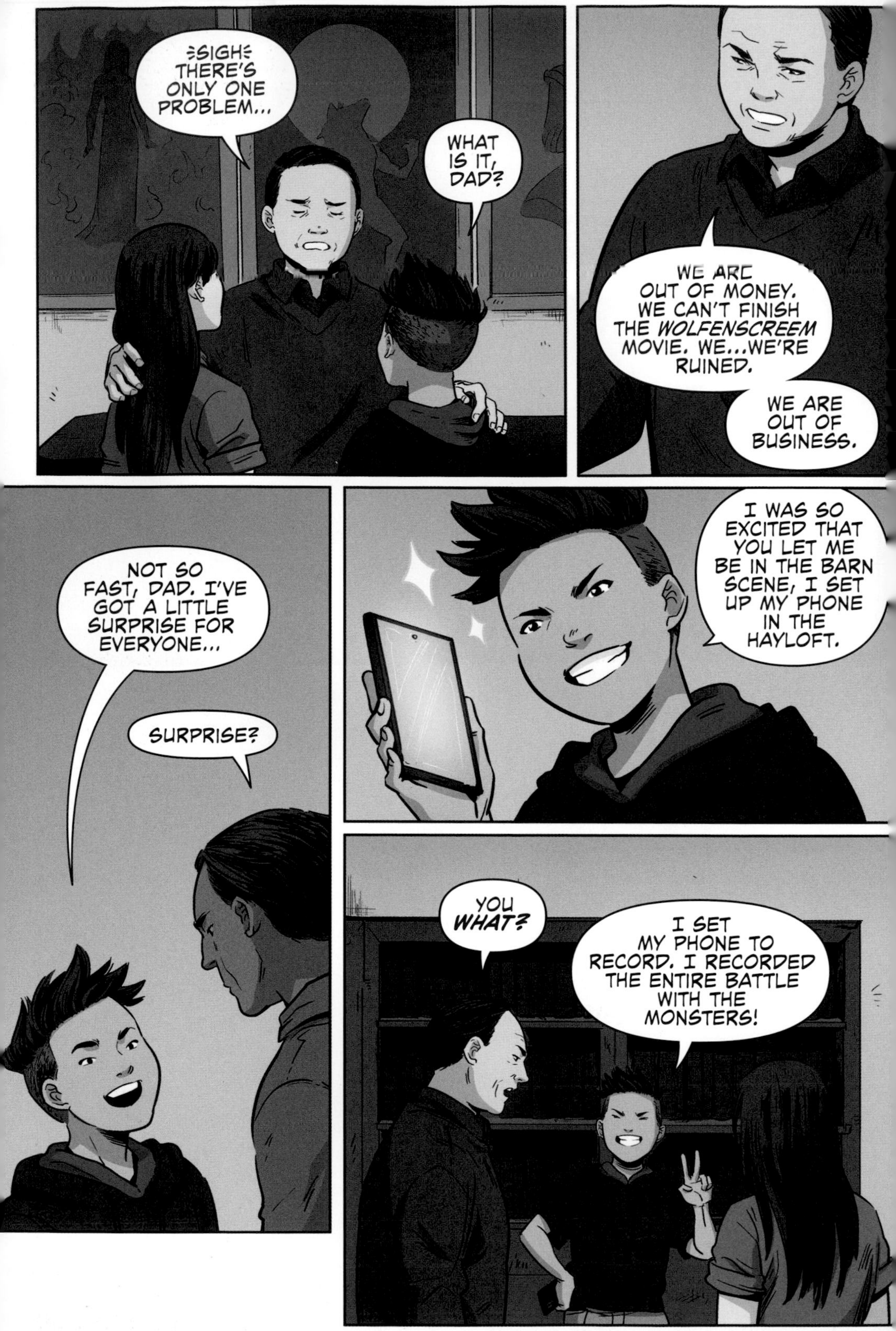

≡SIGH≡ THERE'S ONLY ONE PROBLEM...
WHAT IS IT, DAD?
WE ARE OUT OF MONEY. WE CAN'T FINISH THE *WOLFENSCREEM* MOVIE. WE...WE'RE RUINED.
WE ARE OUT OF BUSINESS.
NOT SO FAST, DAD. I'VE GOT A LITTLE SURPRISE FOR EVERYONE...
SURPRISE?
I WAS SO EXCITED THAT YOU LET ME BE IN THE BARN SCENE, I SET UP MY PHONE IN THE HAYLOFT.
YOU *WHAT?*
I SET MY PHONE TO RECORD. I RECORDED THE ENTIRE BATTLE WITH THE MONSTERS!

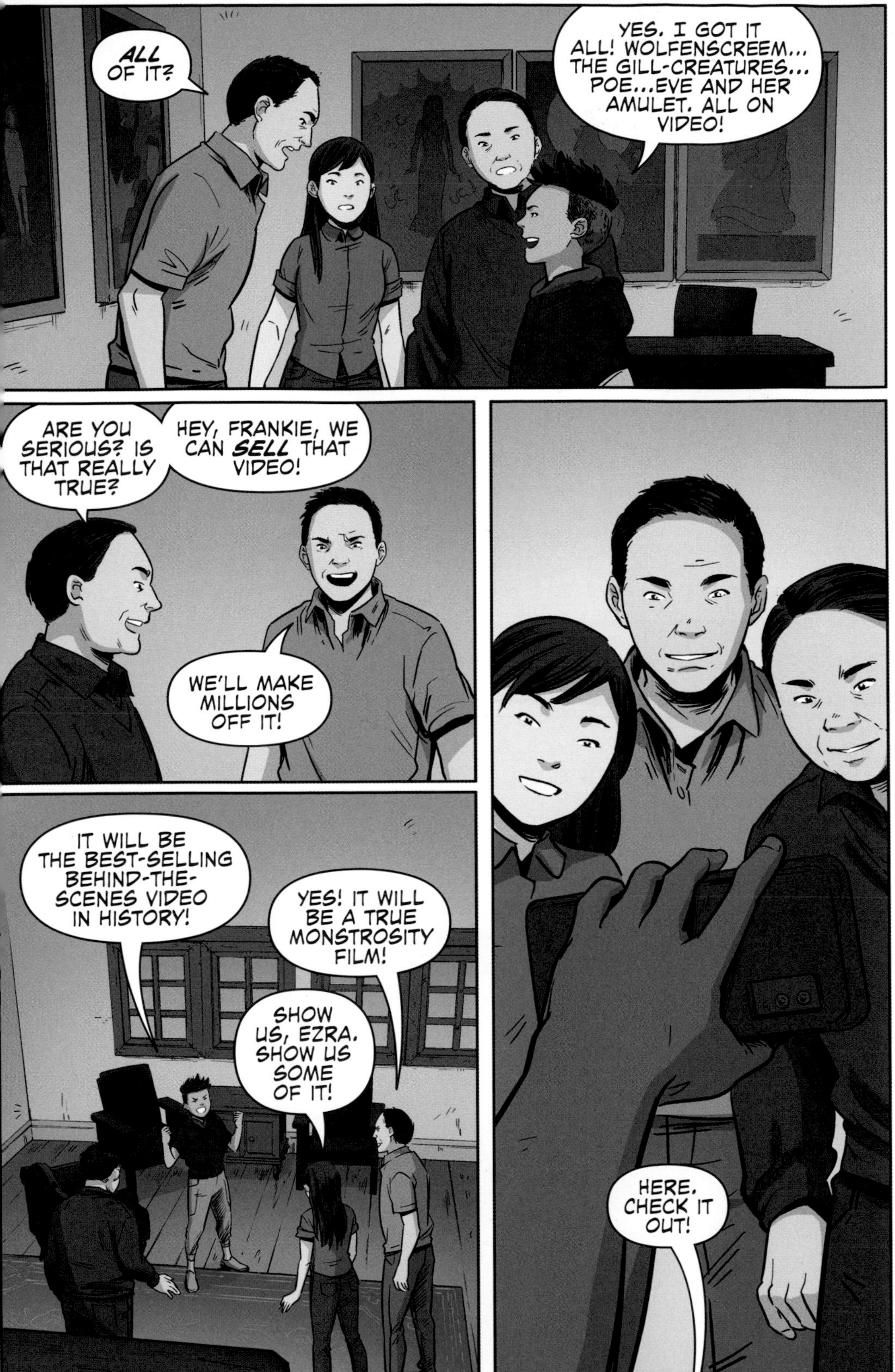
ALL OF IT?
YES. I GOT IT ALL! WOLFENSCREEM... THE GILL-CREATURES... POE...EVE AND HER AMULET. ALL ON VIDEO!
ARE YOU SERIOUS? IS THAT REALLY TRUE?
HEY, FRANKIE, WE CAN SELL THAT VIDEO!
WE'LL MAKE MILLIONS OFF IT!
IT WILL BE THE BEST-SELLING BEHIND-THE-SCENES VIDEO IN HISTORY!
YES! IT WILL BE A TRUE MONSTROSITY FILM!
SHOW US, EZRA. SHOW US SOME OF IT!
HERE. CHECK IT OUT!

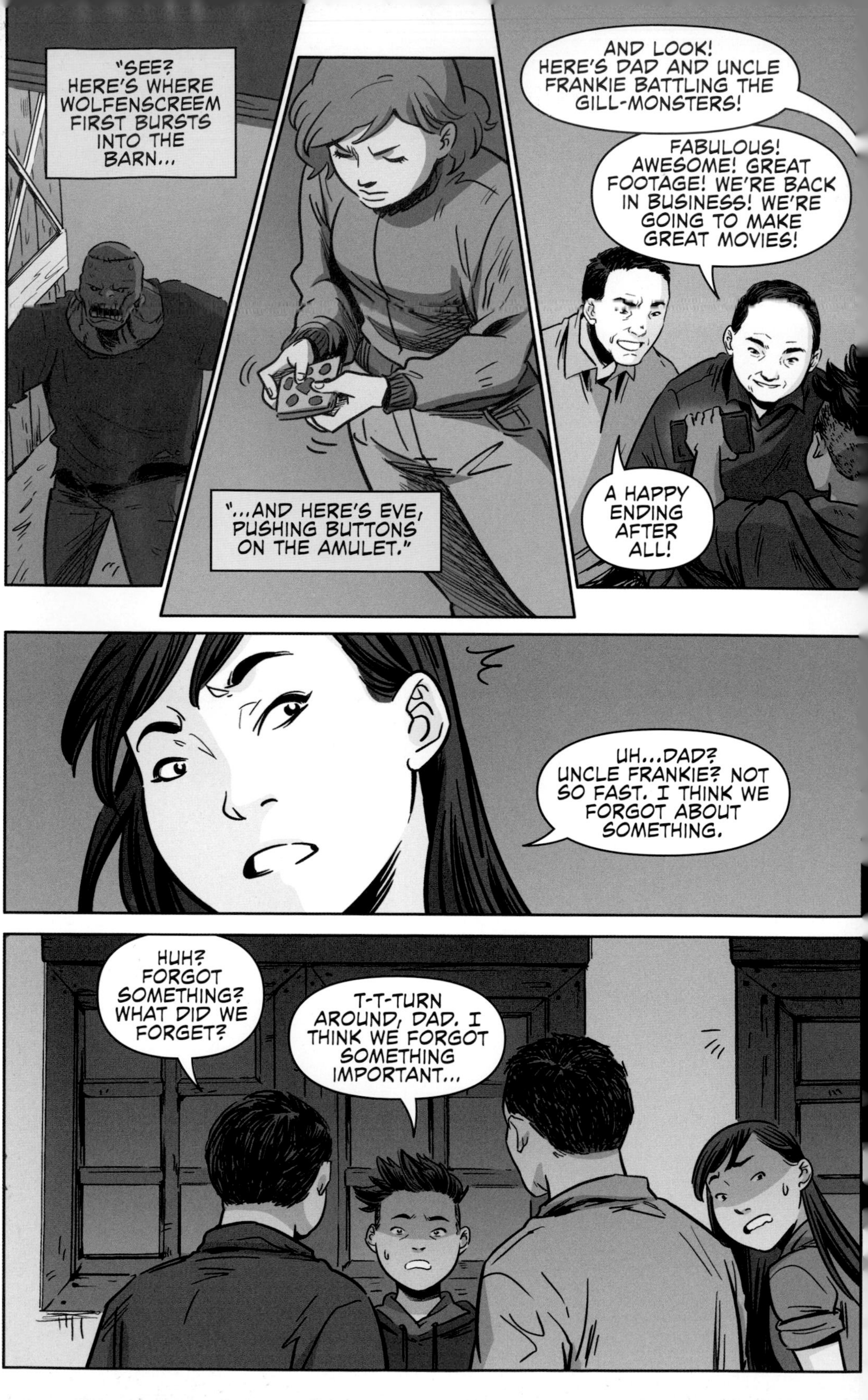
"SEE? HERE'S WHERE WOLFENSCREEM FIRST BURSTS INTO THE BARN...
"...AND HERE'S EVE, PUSHING BUTTONS ON THE AMULET."
AND LOOK! HERE'S DAD AND UNCLE FRANKIE BATTLING THE GILL-MONSTERS!
FABULOUS! AWESOME! GREAT FOOTAGE! WE'RE BACK IN BUSINESS! WE'RE GOING TO MAKE GREAT MOVIES!
A HAPPY ENDING AFTER ALL!
UH...DAD? UNCLE FRANKIE? NOT SO FAST. I THINK WE FORGOT ABOUT SOMETHING.
HUH? FORGOT SOMETHING? WHAT DID WE FORGET?
T-T-TURN AROUND, DAD. I THINK WE FORGOT SOMETHING IMPORTANT...

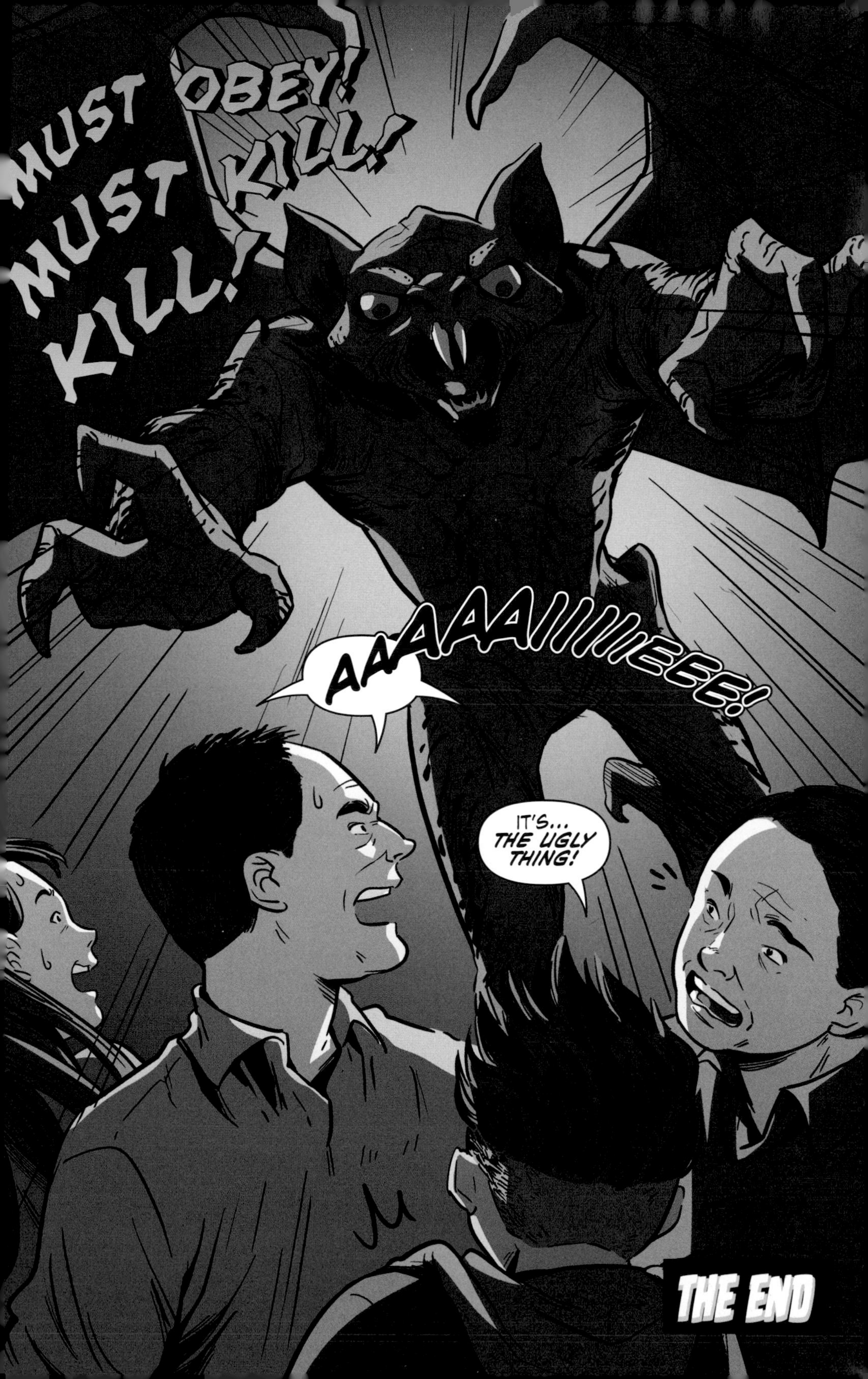
MUST OBEY! MUST KILL! KILL!
AAAAAIIIIIIEEEE!
IT'S... THE UGLY THING!
THE END

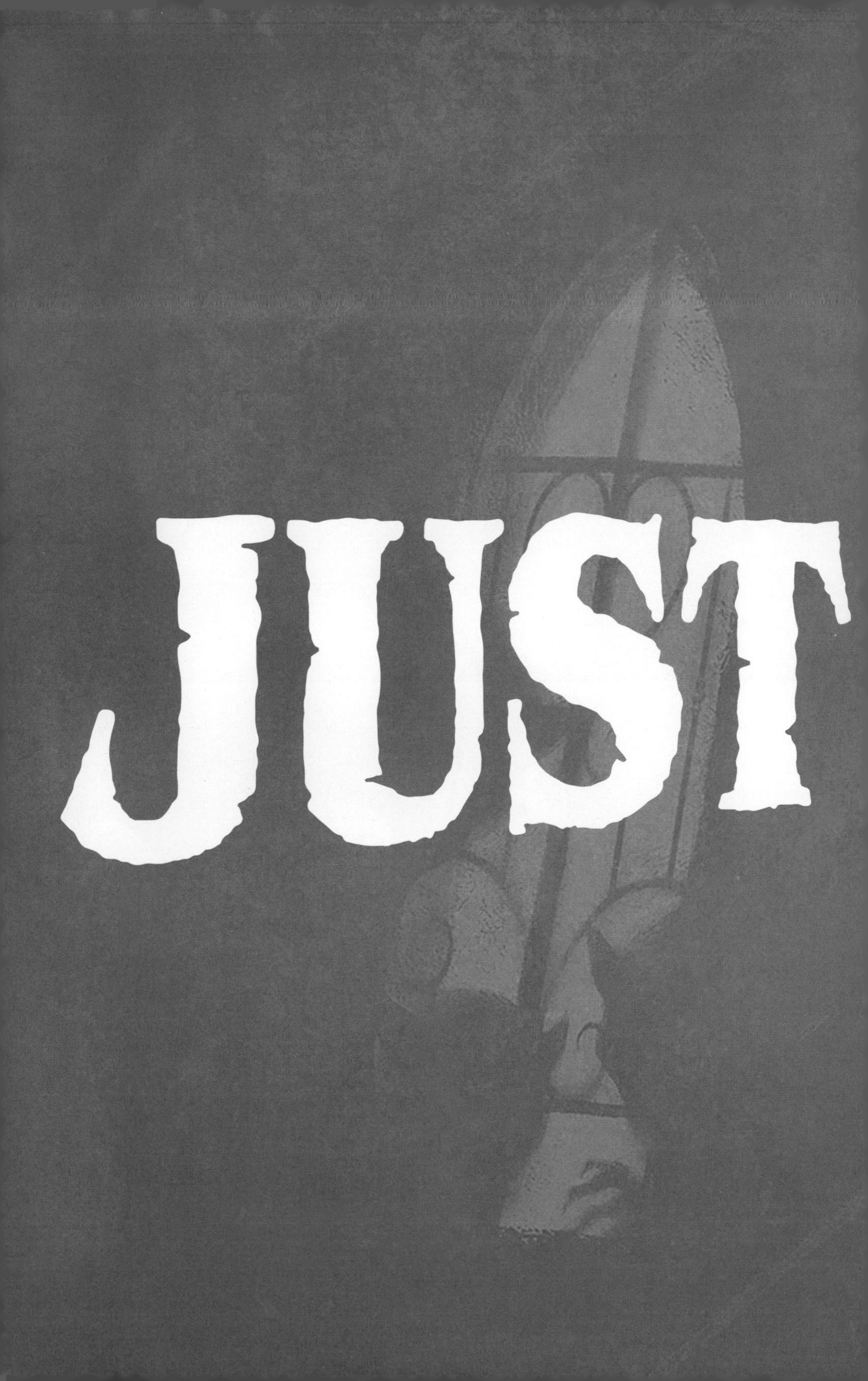
JUST

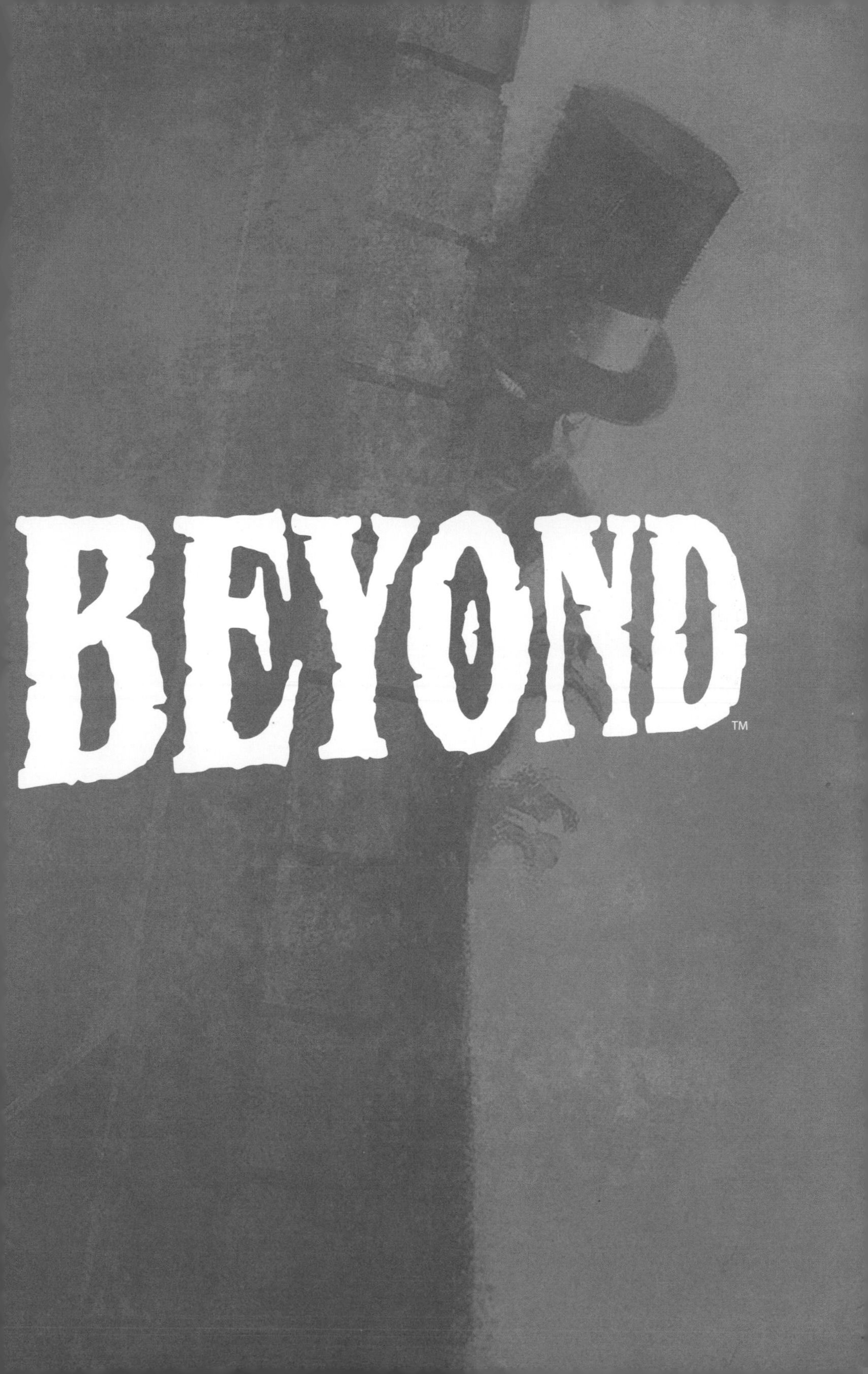
BEYOND™

ABOUT THE
AUTHORS

R.L. Stine

R.L. Stine is one of the best-selling children's authors in history. His *Goosebumps* and *Fear Street* series have sold more than 400 million copies around the world and have been translated into 32 languages. He has had several TV series based on his work, and two feature films, *Goosebumps* (2015) and *Goosebumps 2: Haunted Halloween* (2018) starring Jack Black as R.L. Stine. *Just Beyond* is Stine's first-ever series of original graphic novels. He lives in New York City with his wife Jane, an editor and publisher.

Irene Flores

Irene Flores is an illustrator, occasional author, karaoke aficionado, and full-time coffee drinker. Growing up in the Philippines, she was heavily influenced by both Japanese animation and American comics. She currently lives and works in California, and her goals for the future include more drawing, participating in an escape room, and eating a Monte Cristo sandwich.

Joana Lafuente

Based in Portugal with over 10 years of experience, Joana provides works on illustration, comics, story-boarding and concept art for entertainment and advertising purposes. She has worked on famous pop culture titles such as *Steven Universe*, *Mighty Morphin Power Rangers*, *Adventure Time*, among many more.

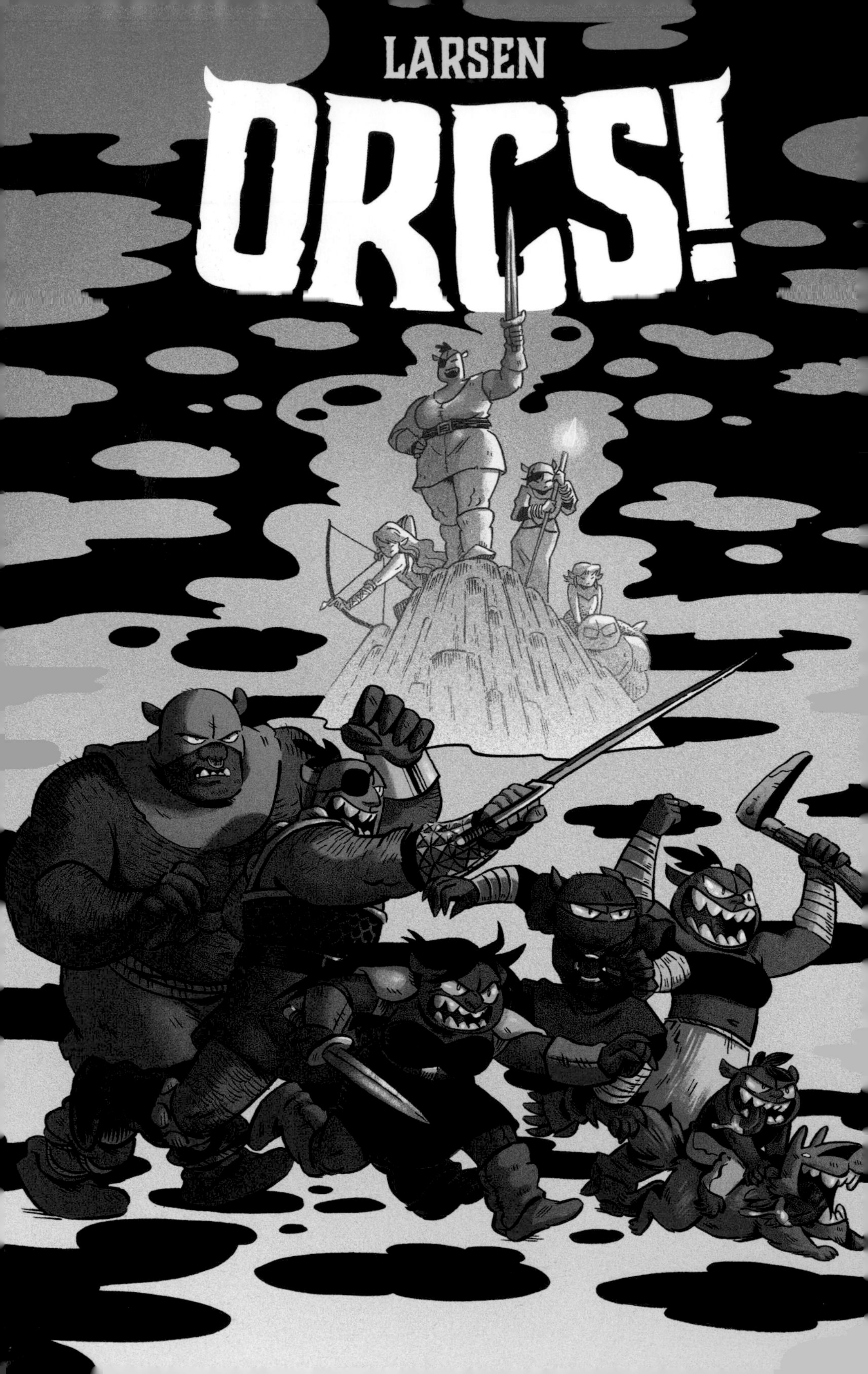
LARSEN
ORCS!

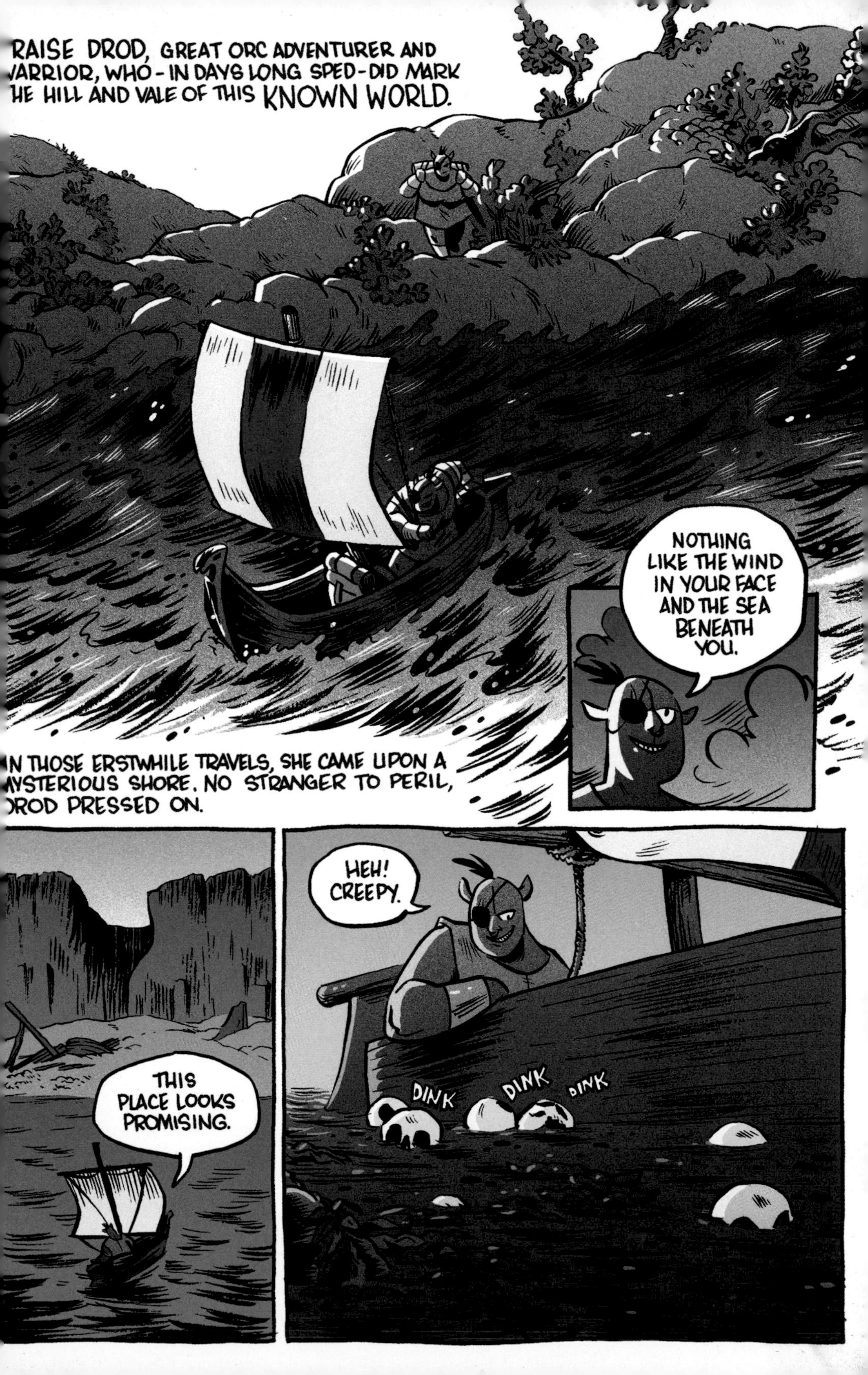
RAISE DROD, GREAT ORC ADVENTURER AND
WARRIOR, WHO - IN DAYS LONG SPED - DID MARK
THE HILL AND VALE OF THIS KNOWN WORLD.
NOTHING LIKE THE WIND IN YOUR FACE AND THE SEA BENEATH YOU.
IN THOSE ERSTWHILE TRAVELS, SHE CAME UPON A
MYSTERIOUS SHORE. NO STRANGER TO PERIL,
DROD PRESSED ON.
THIS PLACE LOOKS PROMISING.
HEH! CREEPY.
DINK
DINK
DINK

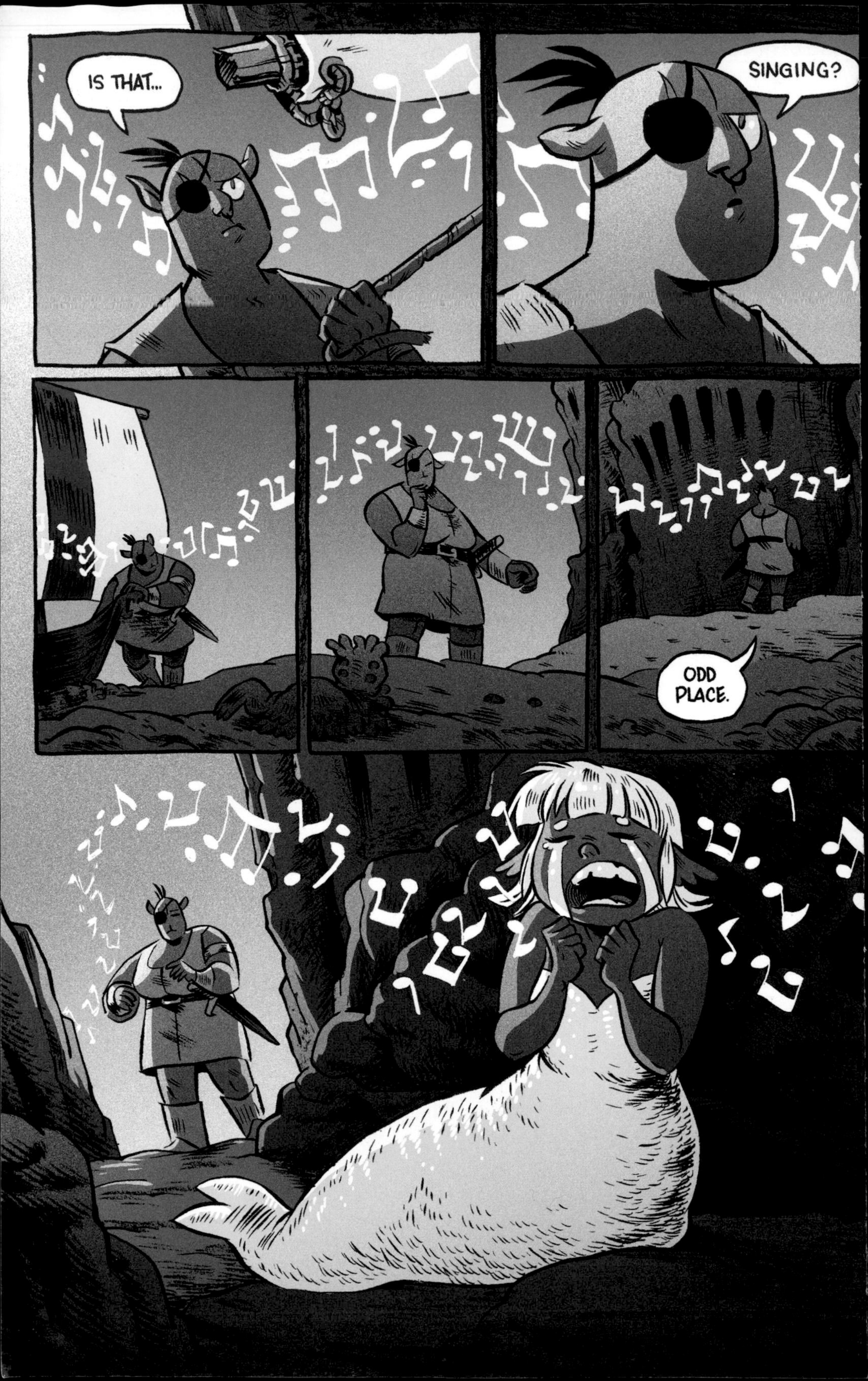
IS THAT...
SINGING?
ODD PLACE.

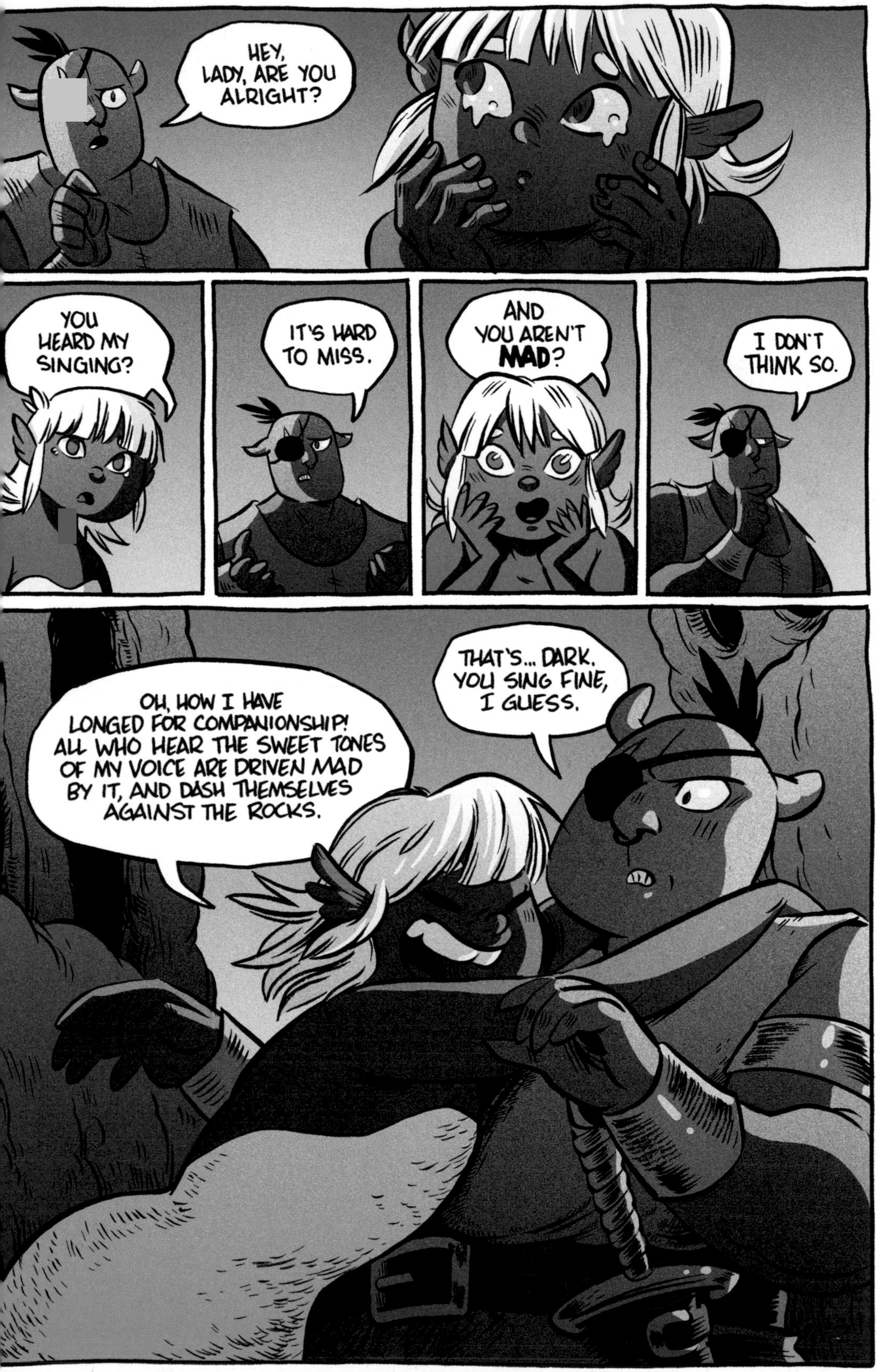
HEY, LADY, ARE YOU ALRIGHT?
YOU HEARD MY SINGING?
IT'S HARD TO MISS.
AND YOU AREN'T MAD?
I DON'T THINK SO.
OH, HOW I HAVE LONGED FOR COMPANIONSHIP! ALL WHO HEAR THE SWEET TONES OF MY VOICE ARE DRIVEN MAD BY IT, AND DASH THEMSELVES AGAINST THE ROCKS.
THAT'S... DARK. YOU SING FINE, I GUESS.

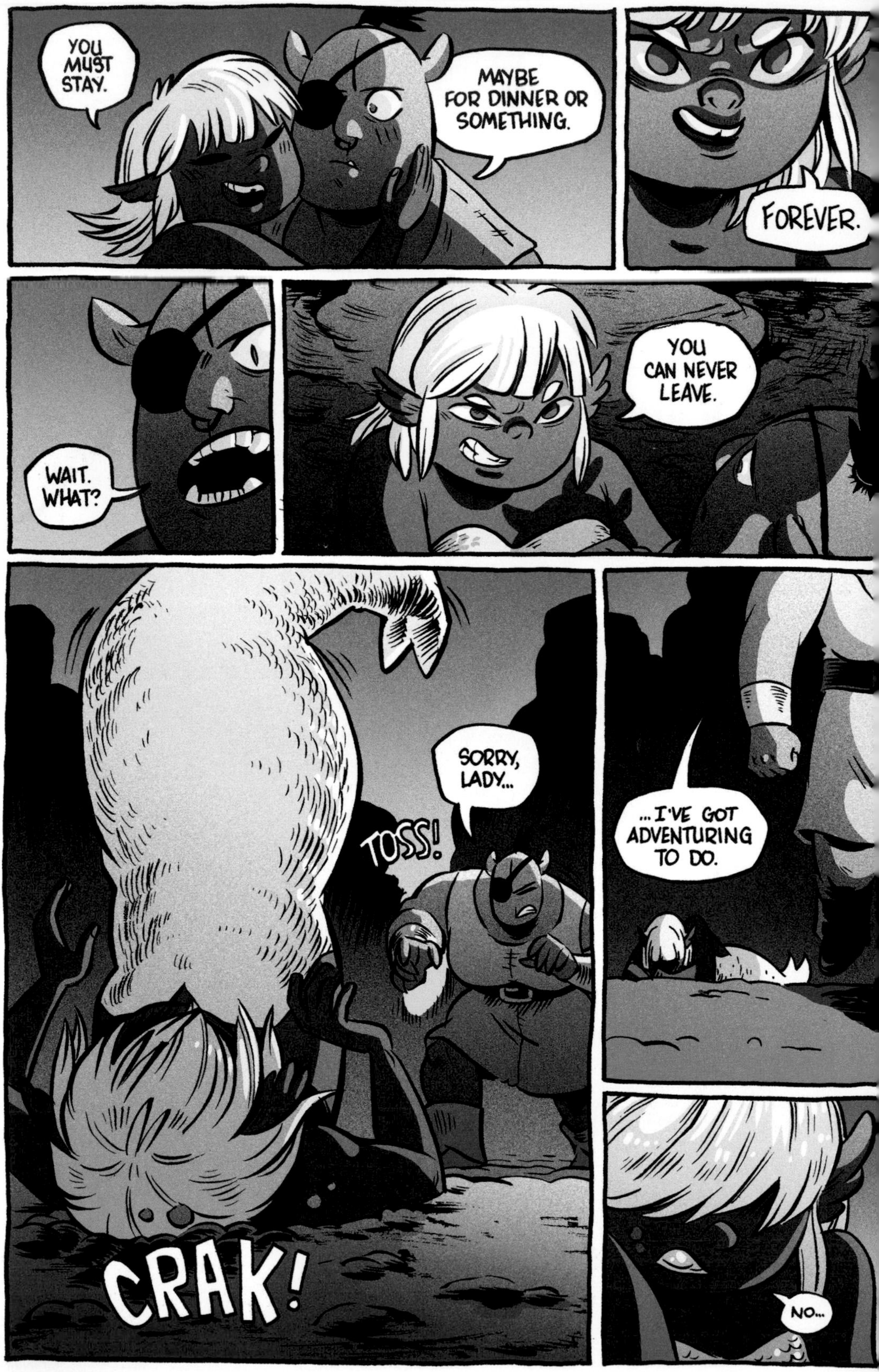
YOU MUST STAY.
MAYBE FOR DINNER OR SOMETHING.
FOREVER.
WAIT. WHAT?
YOU CAN NEVER LEAVE.
SORRY, LADY...
TOSS!
...I'VE GOT ADVENTURING TO DO.
CRAK!
NO...

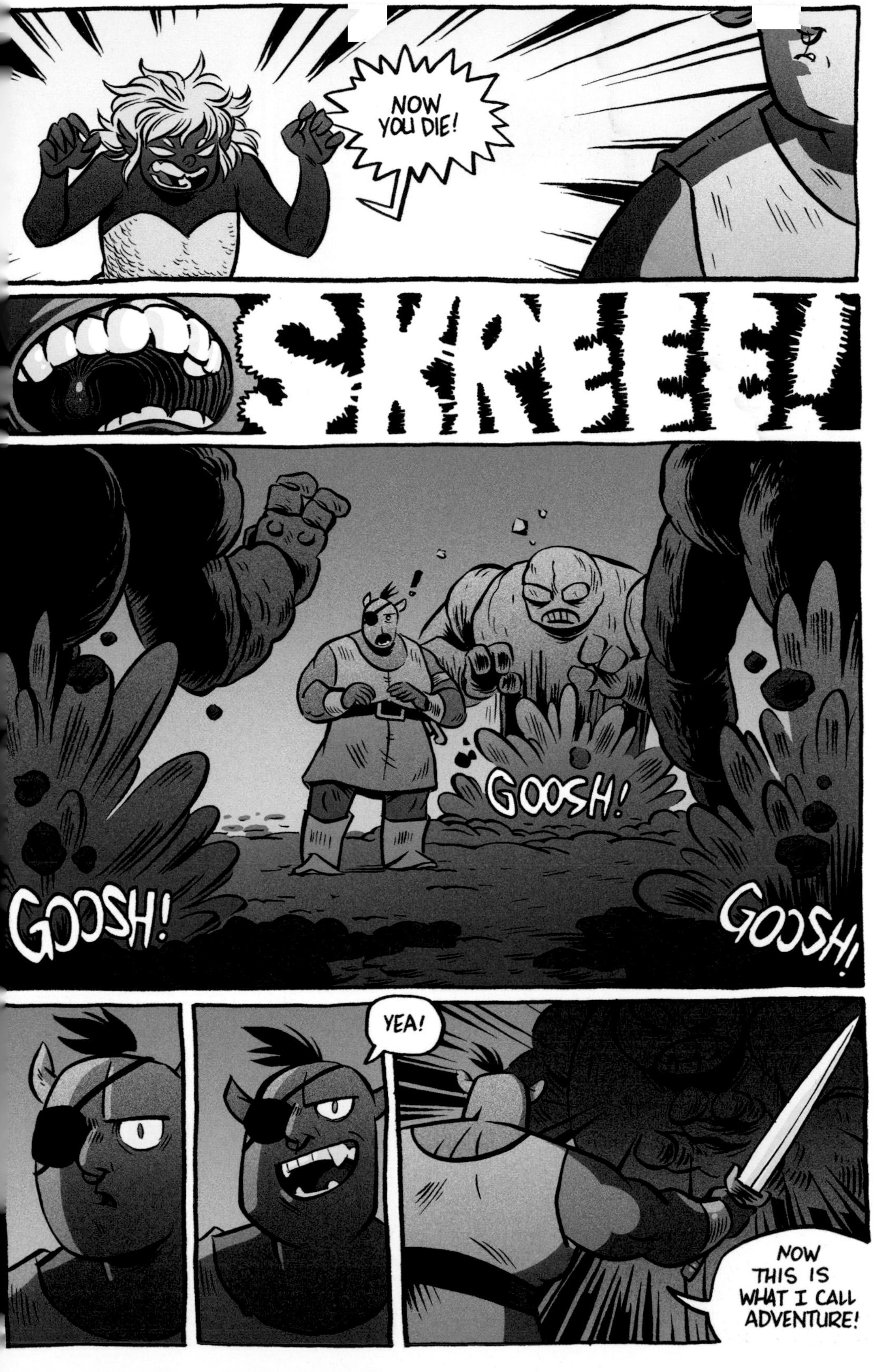
NOW YOU DIE!
SKREEEH
GOOSH!
GOOSH!
GOOSH!
YEA!
NOW THIS IS WHAT I CALL ADVENTURE!

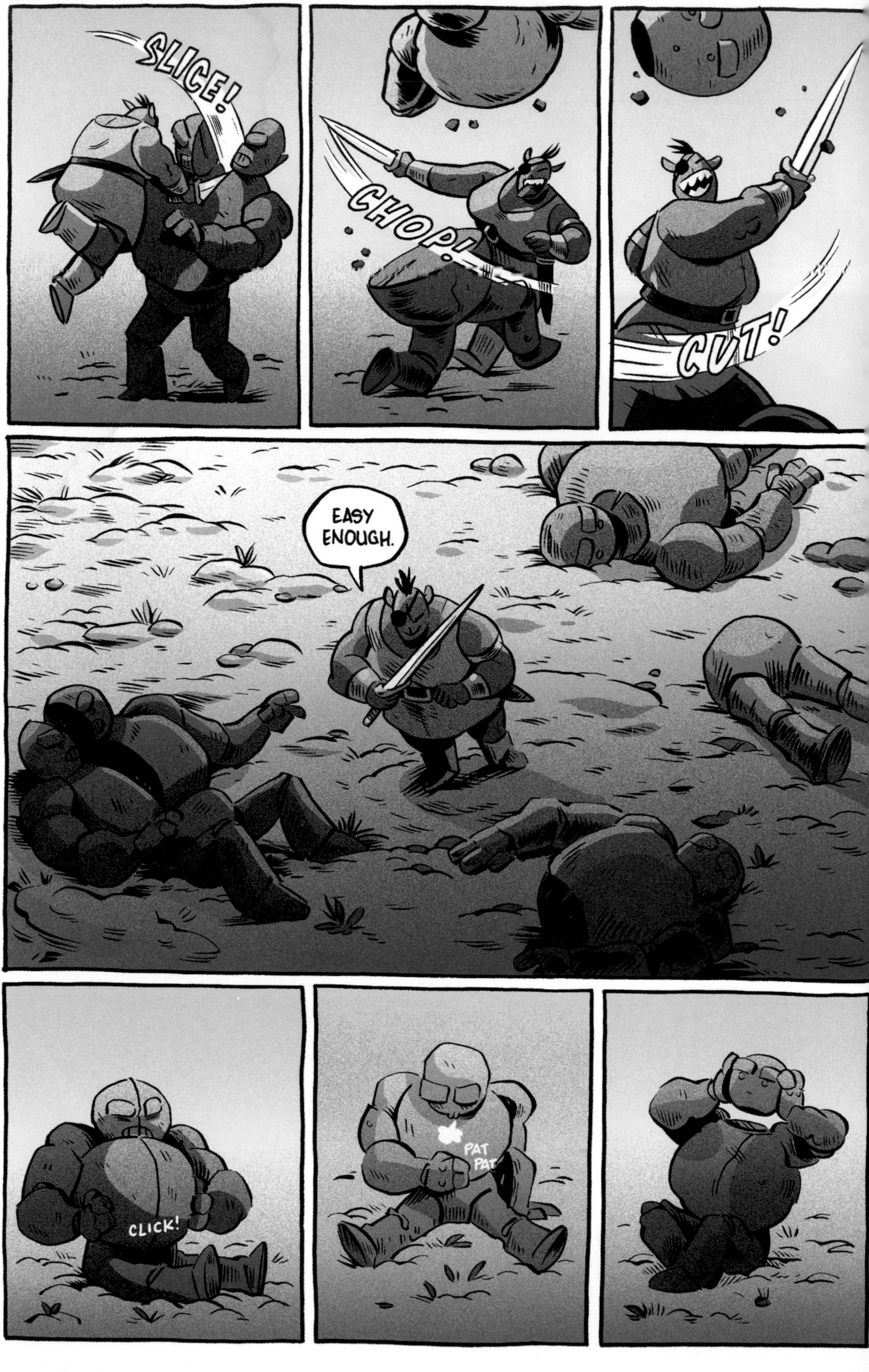
SLICE!
CHOP!
CUT!
EASY ENOUGH.
CLICK!
PAT PAT

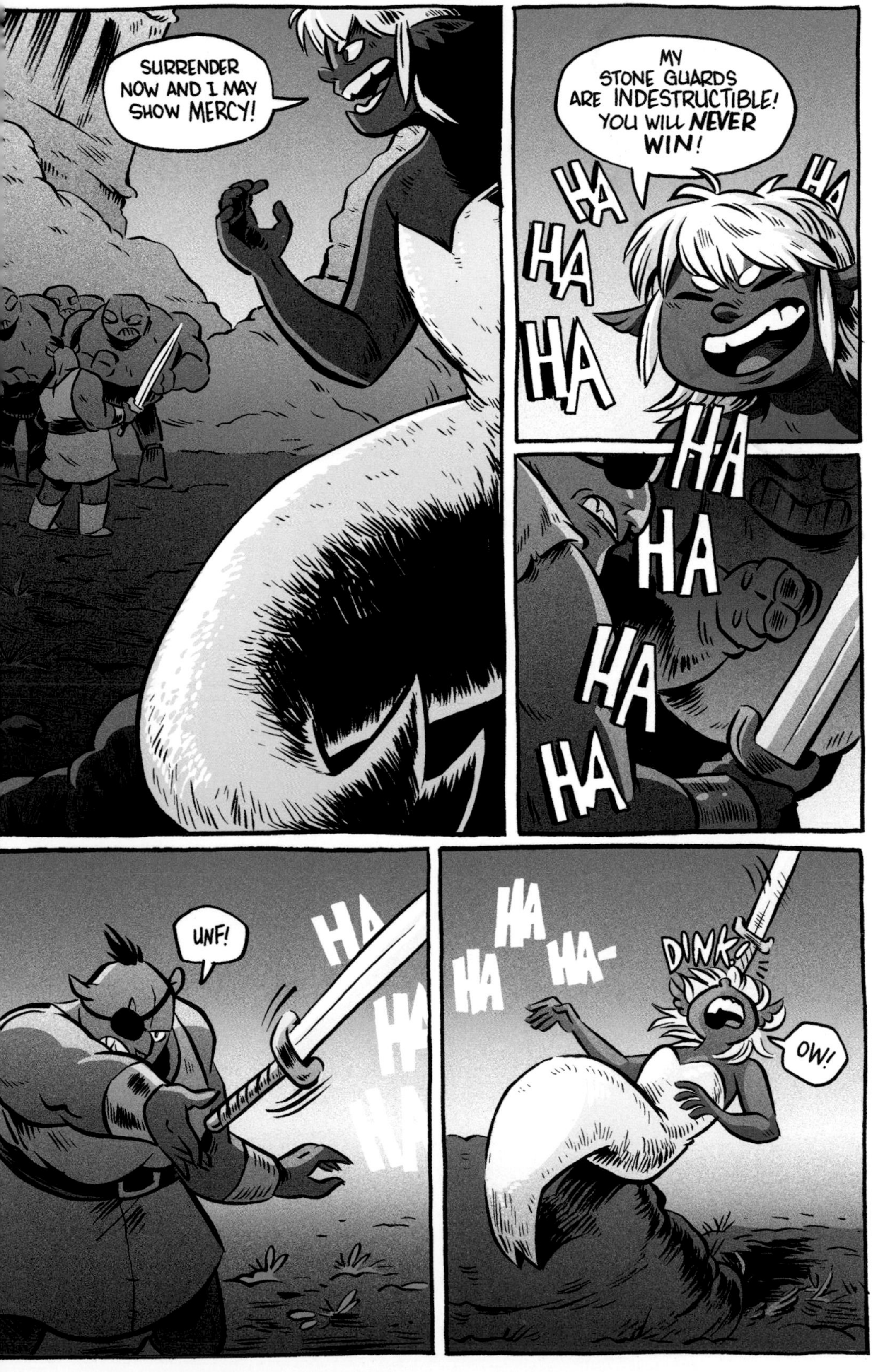
SURRENDER NOW AND I MAY SHOW MERCY!
MY STONE GUARDS ARE INDESTRUCTIBLE! YOU WILL NEVER WIN!
HA HA HA HA HA
HA HA HA HA
UNF!
HA HA HA
HA HA HA-
DINK!
OW!

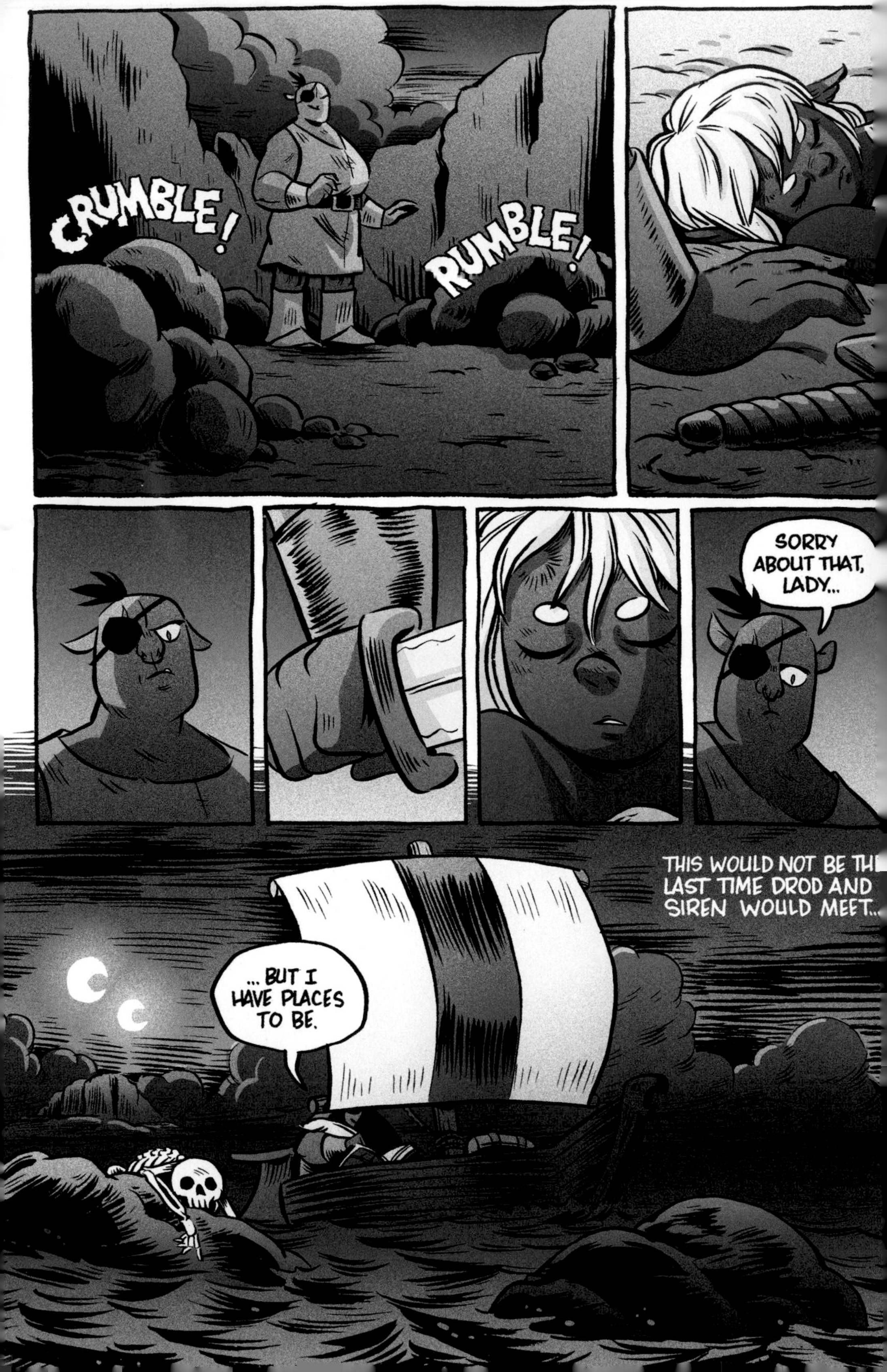
CRUMBLE!
RUMBLE!
SORRY ABOUT THAT, LADY...
THIS WOULD NOT BE TH
LAST TIME DROD AND
SIREN WOULD MEET...
... BUT I HAVE PLACES TO BE.

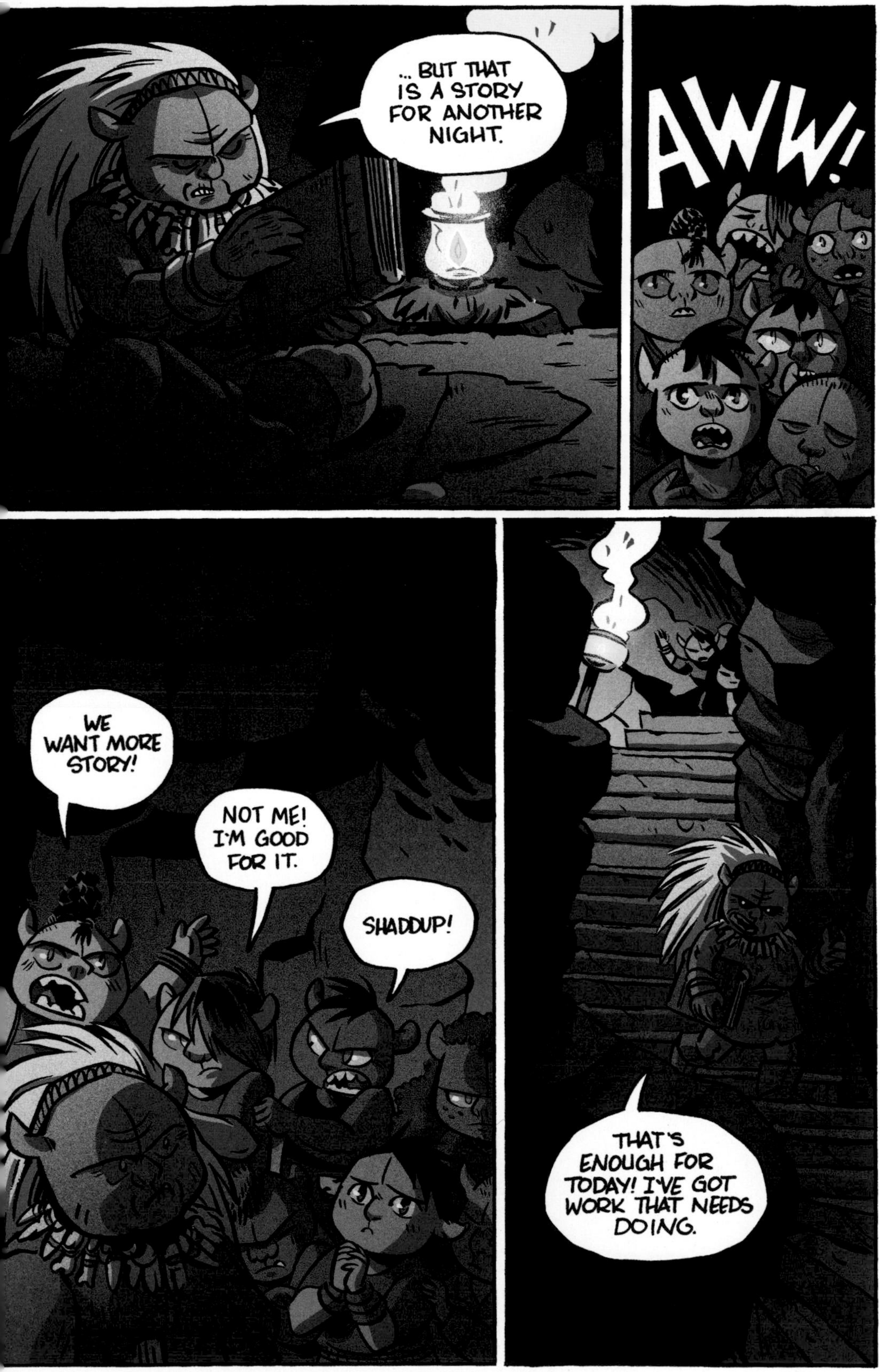

... BUT THAT IS A STORY FOR ANOTHER NIGHT.
AWW!
WE WANT MORE STORY!
NOT ME! I'M GOOD FOR IT.
SHADDUP!
THAT'S ENOUGH FOR TODAY! I'VE GOT WORK THAT NEEDS DOING.

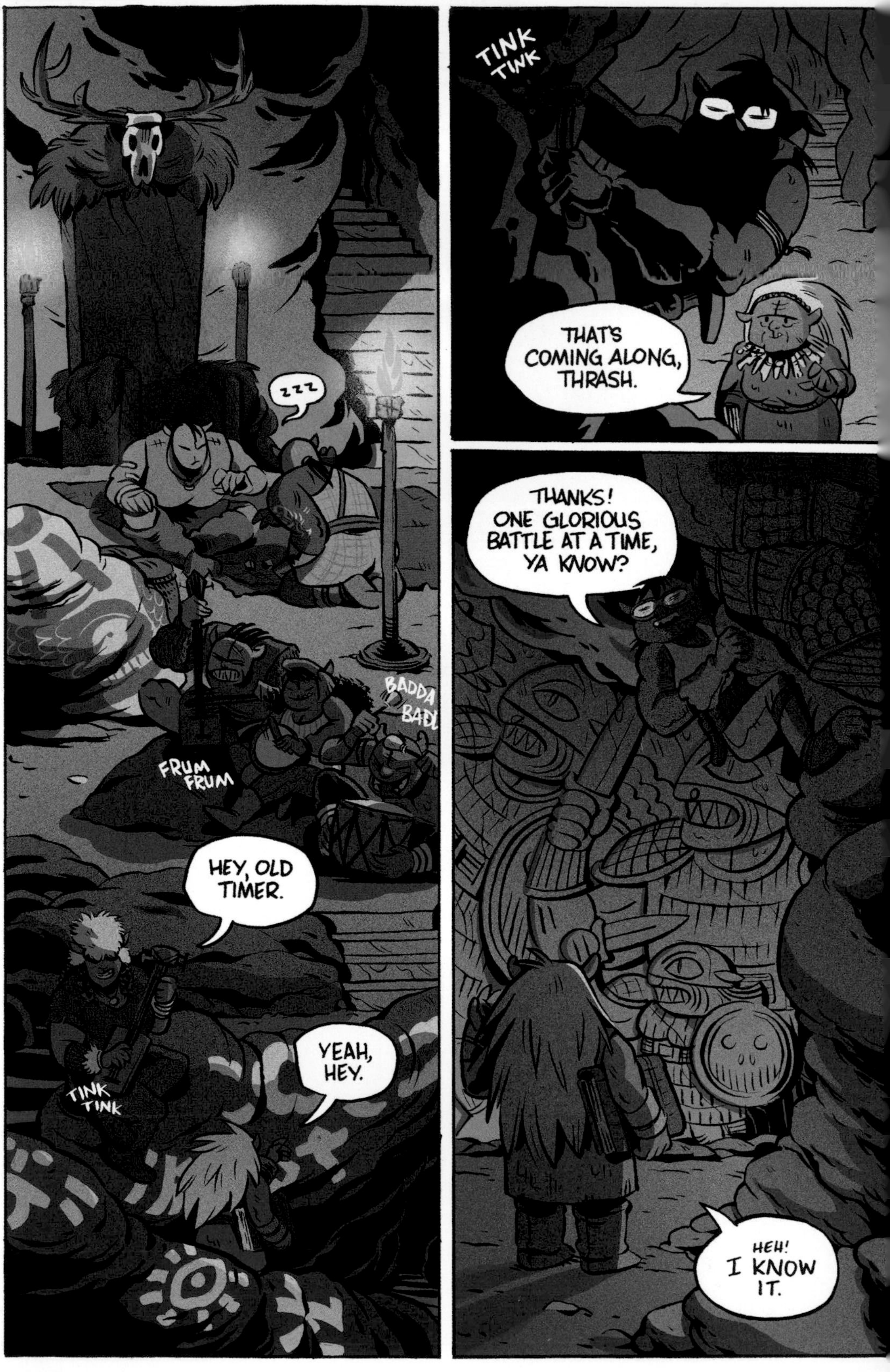
Z Z Z
BADDA
BADD
FRUM
FRUM
HEY, OLD TIMER.
TINK
TINK
YEAH, HEY.
TINK
TINK
THAT'S COMING ALONG, THRASH.
THANKS! ONE GLORIOUS BATTLE AT A TIME, YA KNOW?
HEH! I KNOW IT.

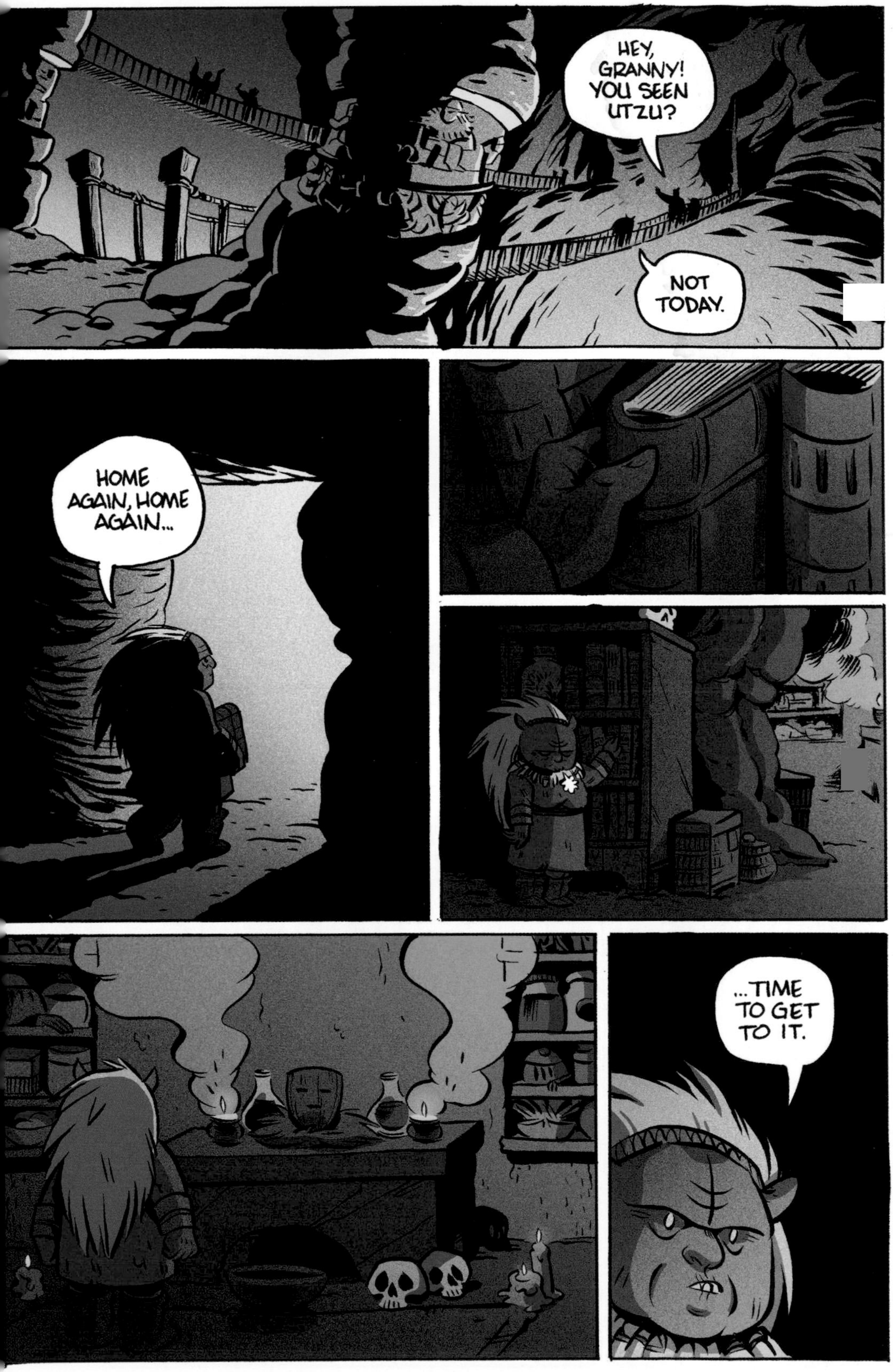
HEY, GRANNY! YOU SEEN UTZU?
NOT TODAY.
HOME AGAIN, HOME AGAIN...
...TIME TO GET TO IT.

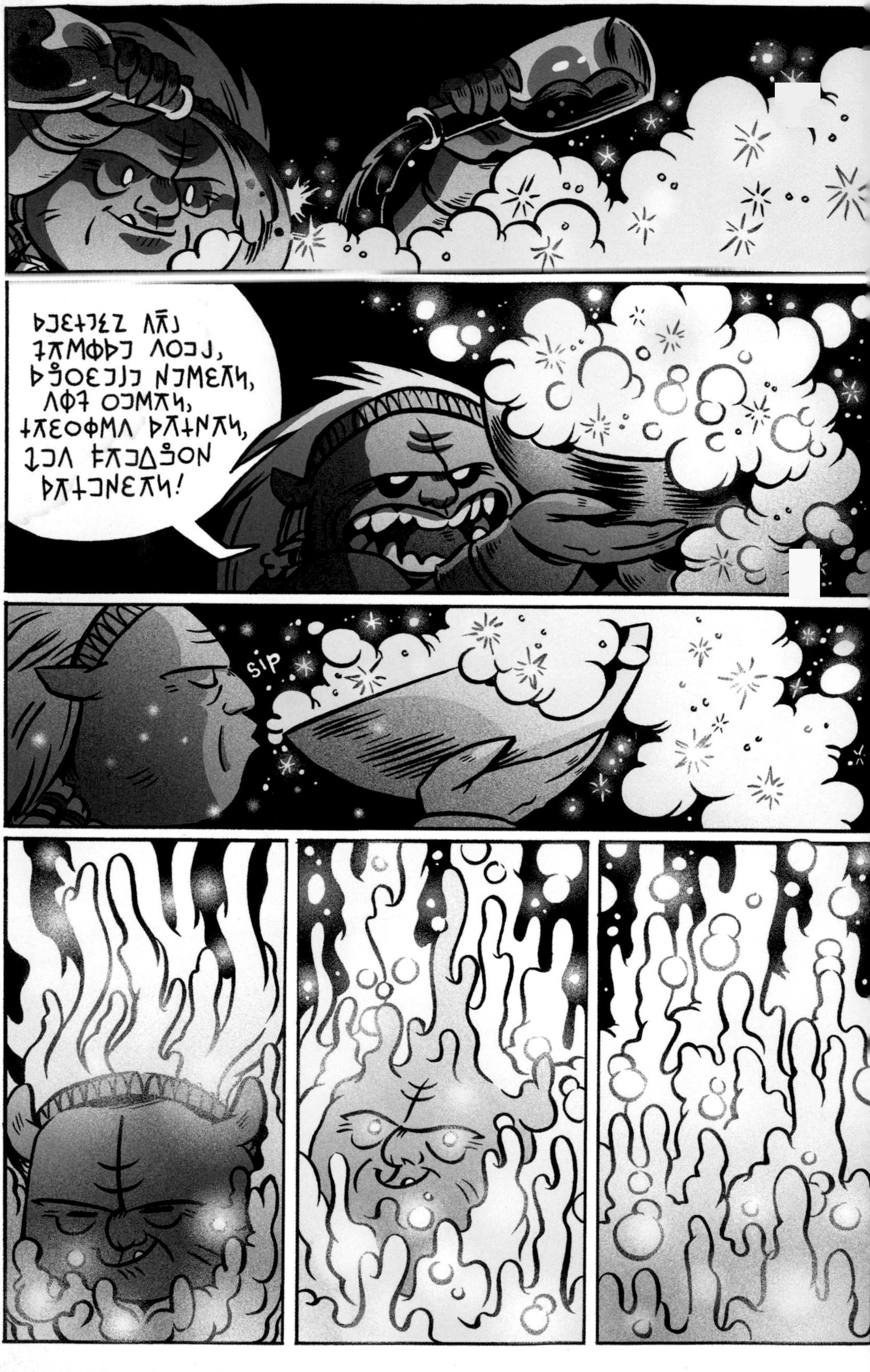
sip

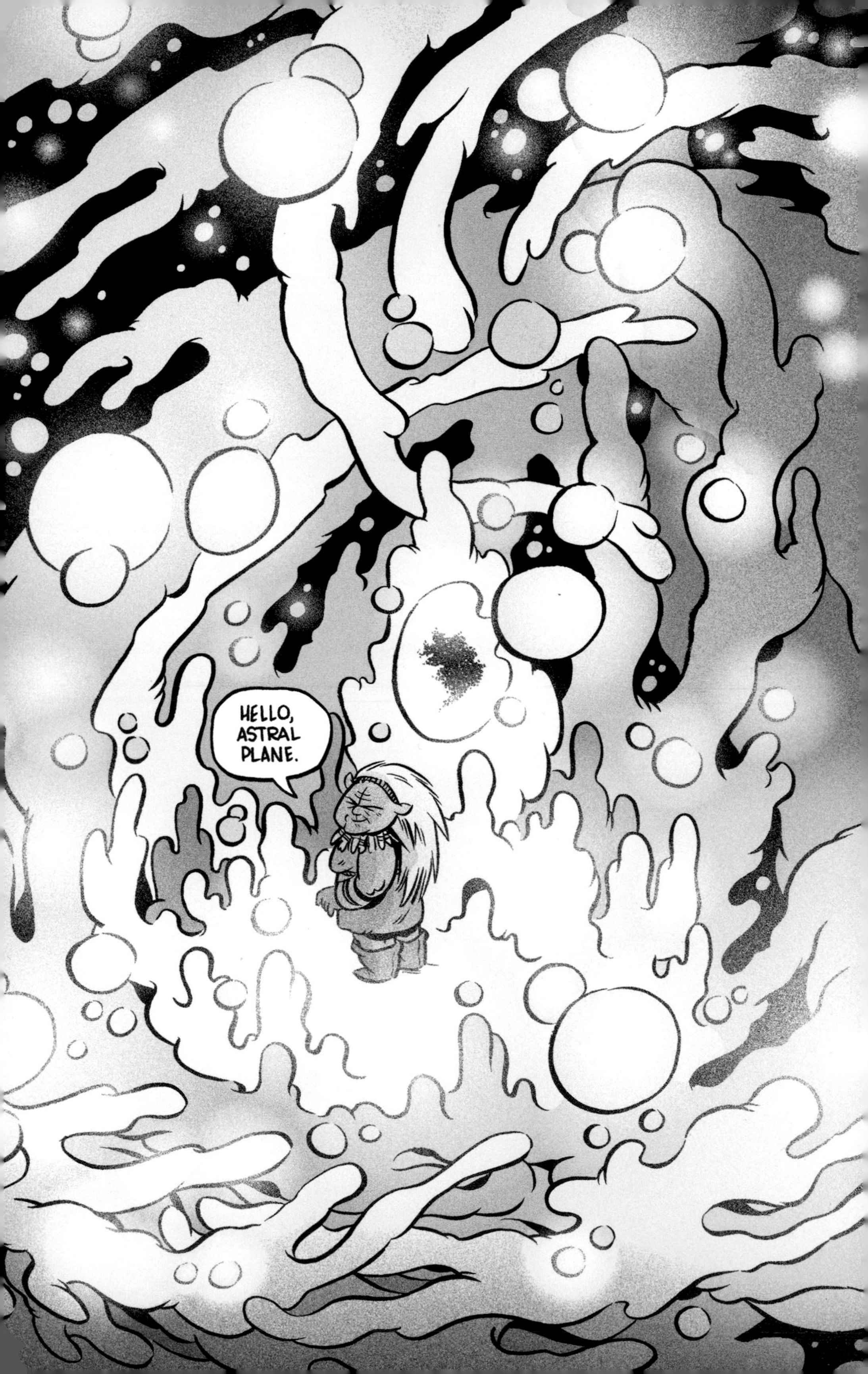
HELLO, ASTRAL PLANE.

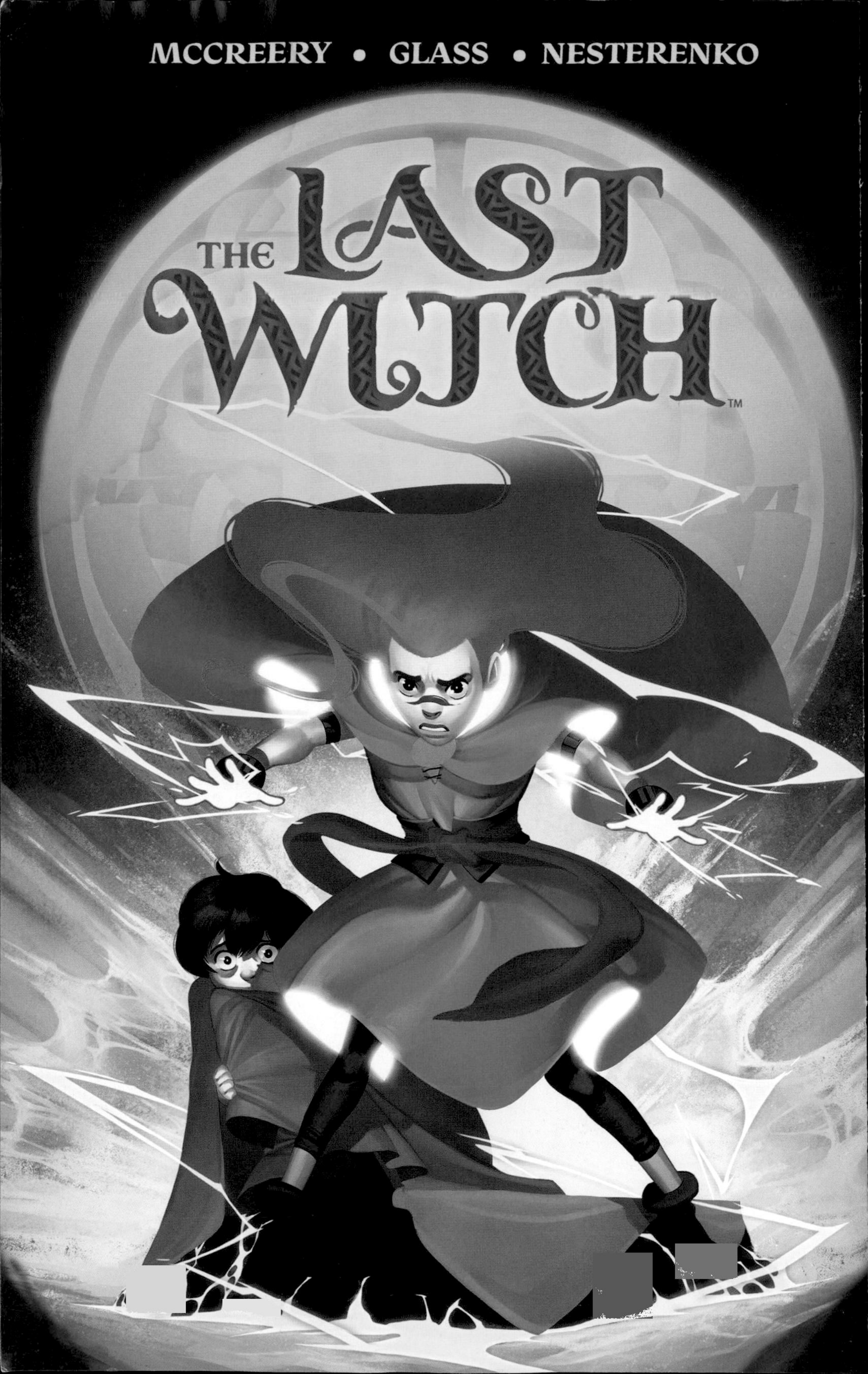
MCCREERY • GLASS • NESTERENKO
THE LAST WITCH™

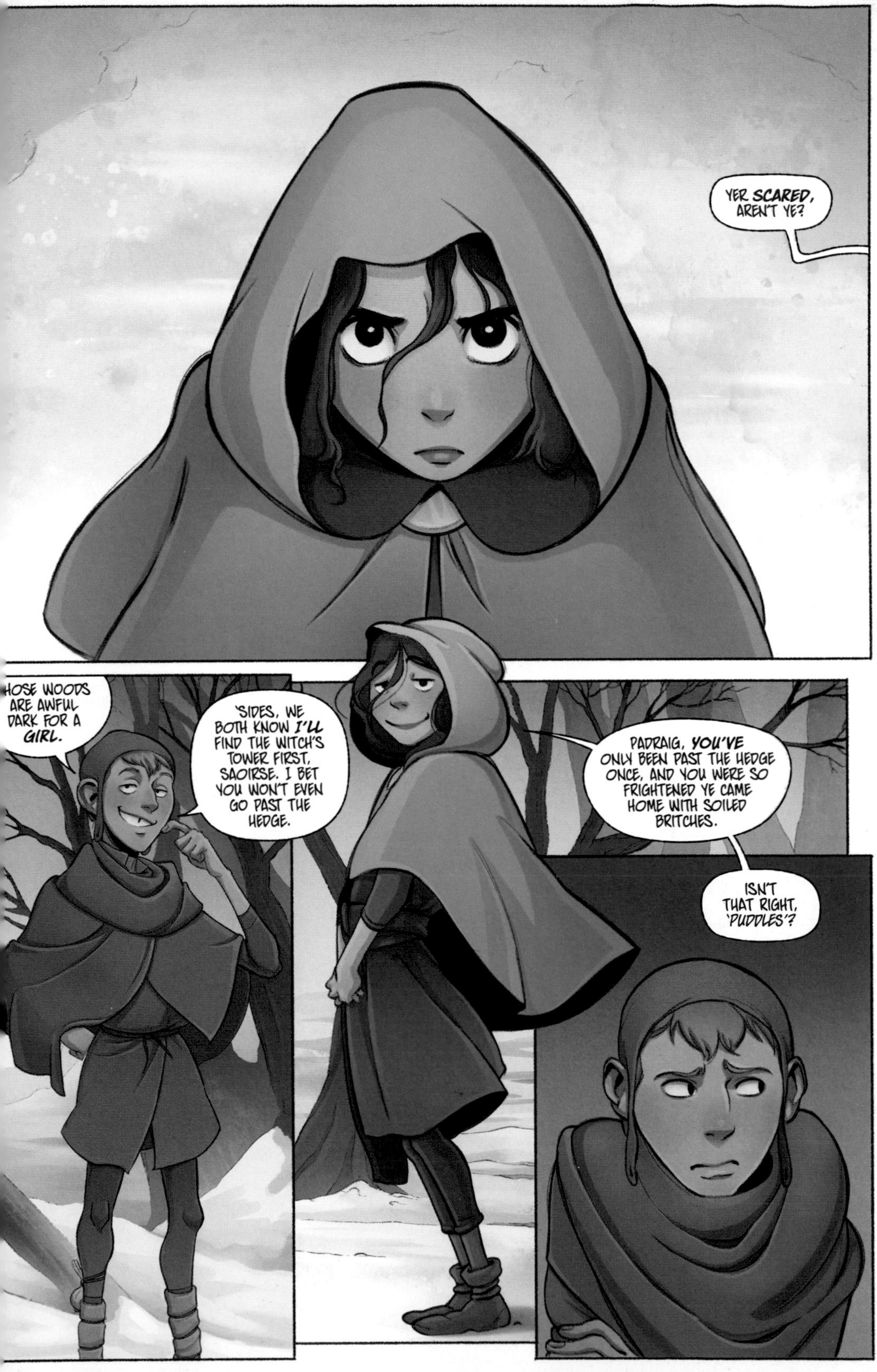
YER SCARED, AREN'T YE?
HOSE WOODS ARE AWFUL DARK FOR A GIRL.
'SIDES, WE BOTH KNOW I'LL FIND THE WITCH'S TOWER FIRST, SAOIRSE. I BET YOU WON'T EVEN GO PAST THE HEDGE.
PADRAIG, YOU'VE ONLY BEEN PAST THE HEDGE ONCE, AND YOU WERE SO FRIGHTENED YE CAME HOME WITH SOILED BRITCHES.
ISN'T THAT RIGHT, 'PUDDLES'?

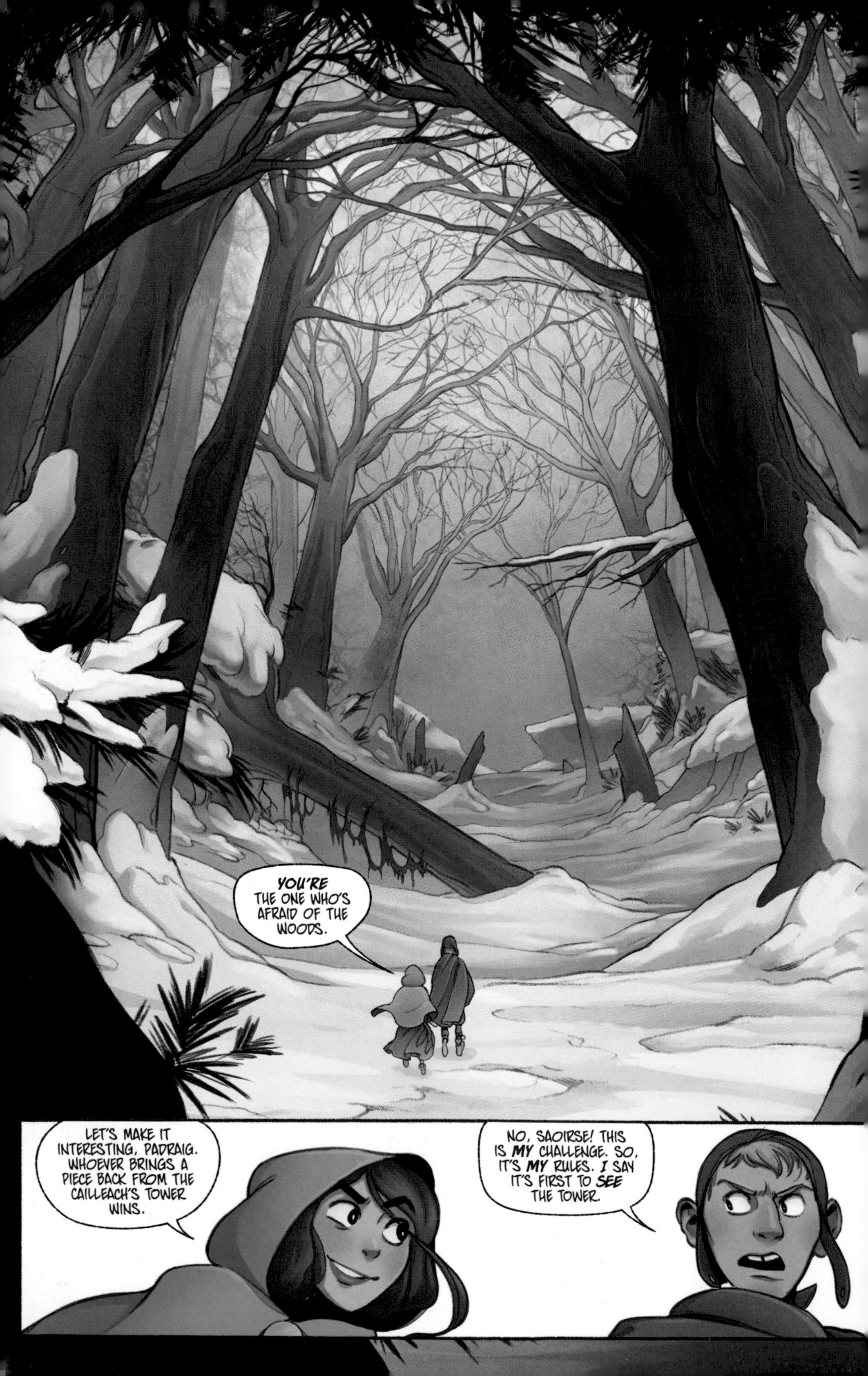
YOU'RE THE ONE WHO'S AFRAID OF THE WOODS.
LET'S MAKE IT INTERESTING, PADRAIG. WHOEVER BRINGS A PIECE BACK FROM THE CAILLEACH'S TOWER WINS.
NO, SAOIRSE! THIS IS MY CHALLENGE. SO, IT'S MY RULES. I SAY IT'S FIRST TO SEE THE TOWER.

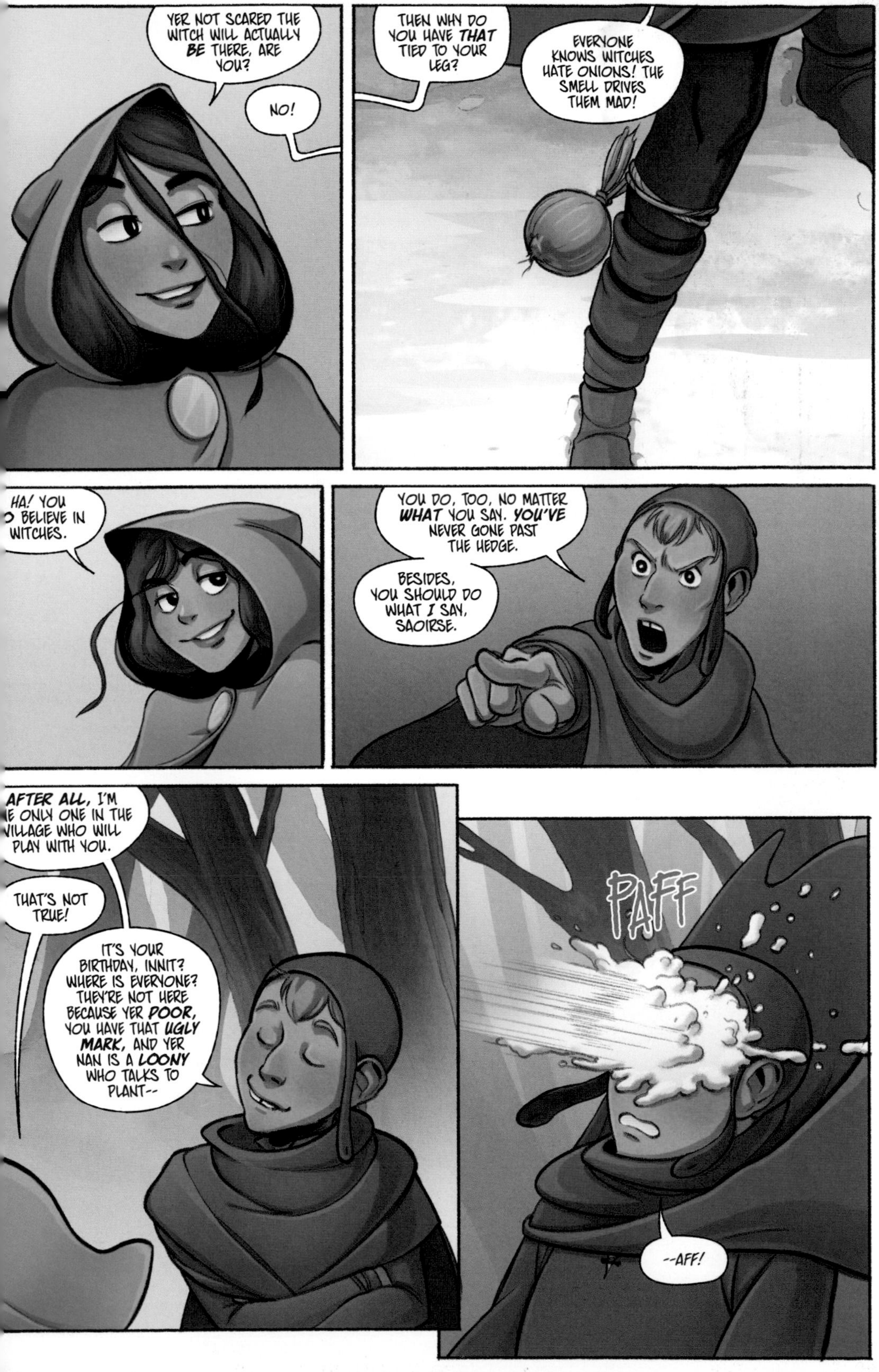

YER NOT SCARED THE WITCH WILL ACTUALLY BE THERE, ARE YOU?
NO!
THEN WHY DO YOU HAVE THAT TIED TO YOUR LEG?
EVERYONE KNOWS WITCHES HATE ONIONS! THE SMELL DRIVES THEM MAD!
HA! YOU O BELIEVE IN WITCHES.
YOU DO, TOO, NO MATTER WHAT YOU SAY. YOU'VE NEVER GONE PAST THE HEDGE.
BESIDES, YOU SHOULD DO WHAT I SAY, SAOIRSE.
AFTER ALL, I'M E ONLY ONE IN THE VILLAGE WHO WILL PLAY WITH YOU.
THAT'S NOT TRUE!
IT'S YOUR BIRTHDAY, INNIT? WHERE IS EVERYONE? THEY'RE NOT HERE BECAUSE YER POOR, YOU HAVE THAT UGLY MARK, AND YER NAN IS A LOONY WHO TALKS TO PLANT--
PAFF
--AFF!

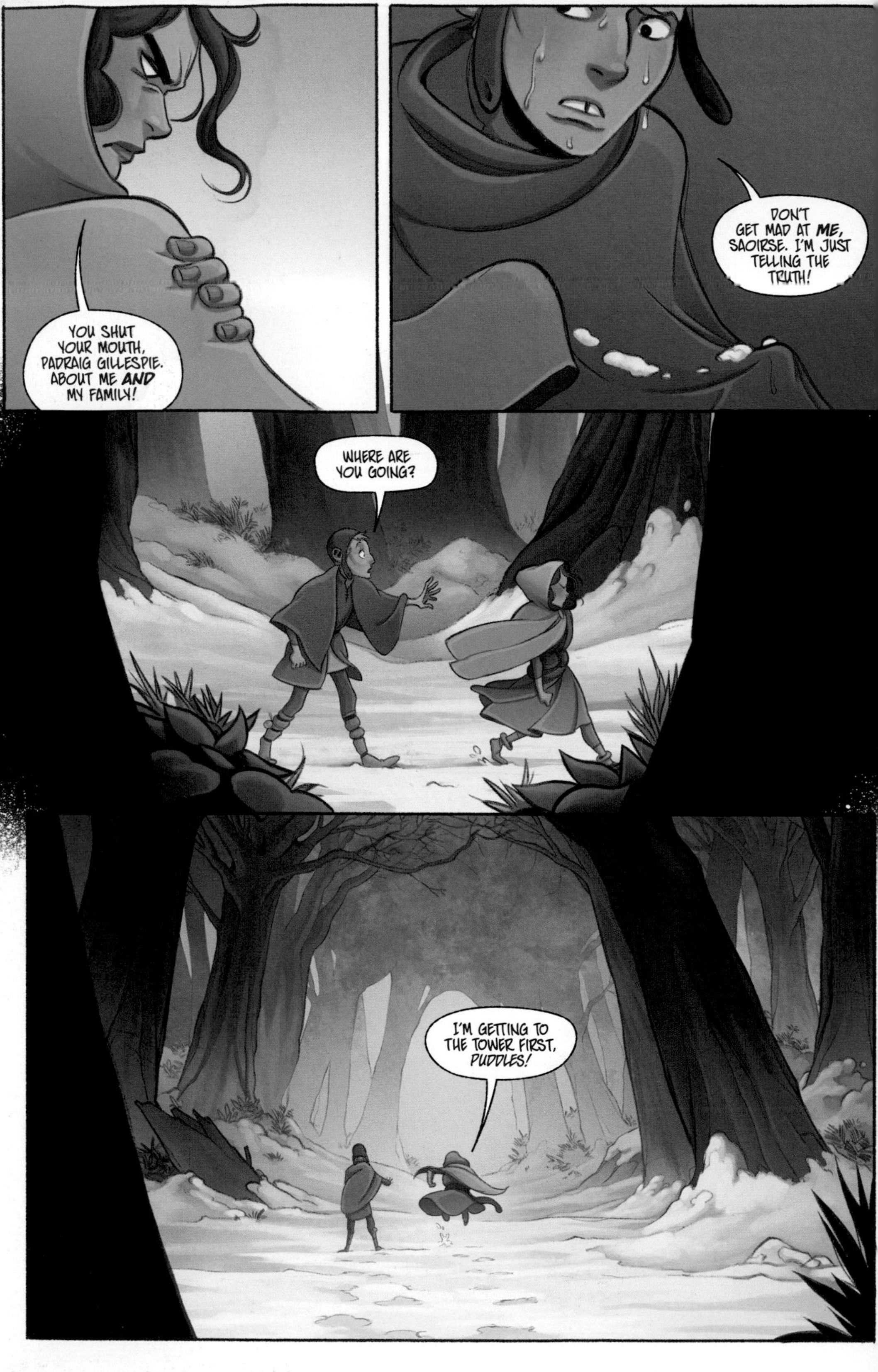
YOU SHUT YOUR MOUTH, PADRAIG GILLESPIE. ABOUT ME **AND** MY FAMILY!
DON'T GET MAD AT **ME**, SAOIRSE. I'M JUST TELLING THE TRUTH!
WHERE ARE YOU GOING?
I'M GETTING TO THE TOWER FIRST, *PUDDLES!*

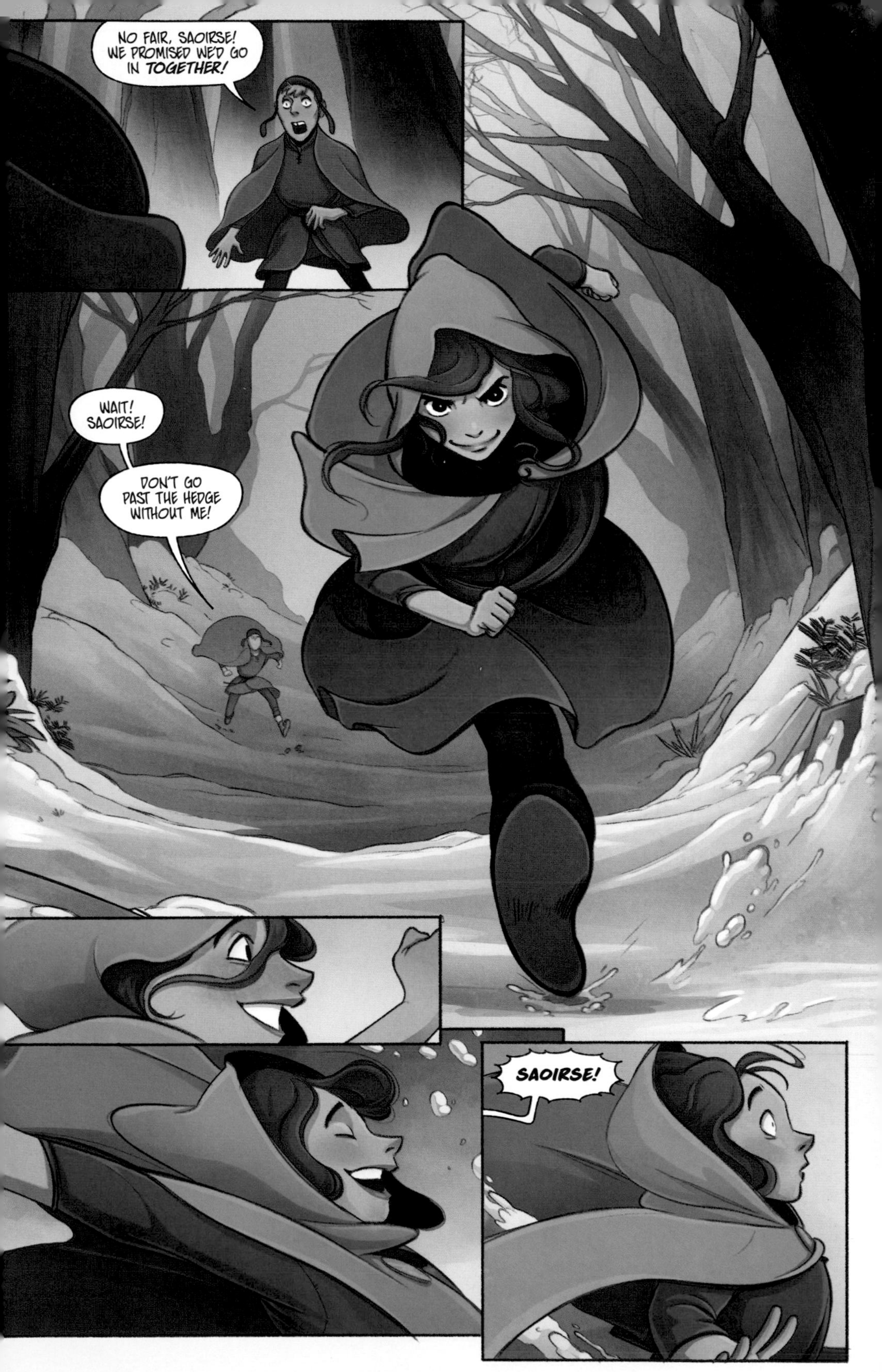
NO FAIR, SAOIRSE! WE PROMISED WE'D GO IN *TOGETHER!*
WAIT! SAOIRSE!
DON'T GO PAST THE HEDGE WITHOUT ME!
SAOIRSE!

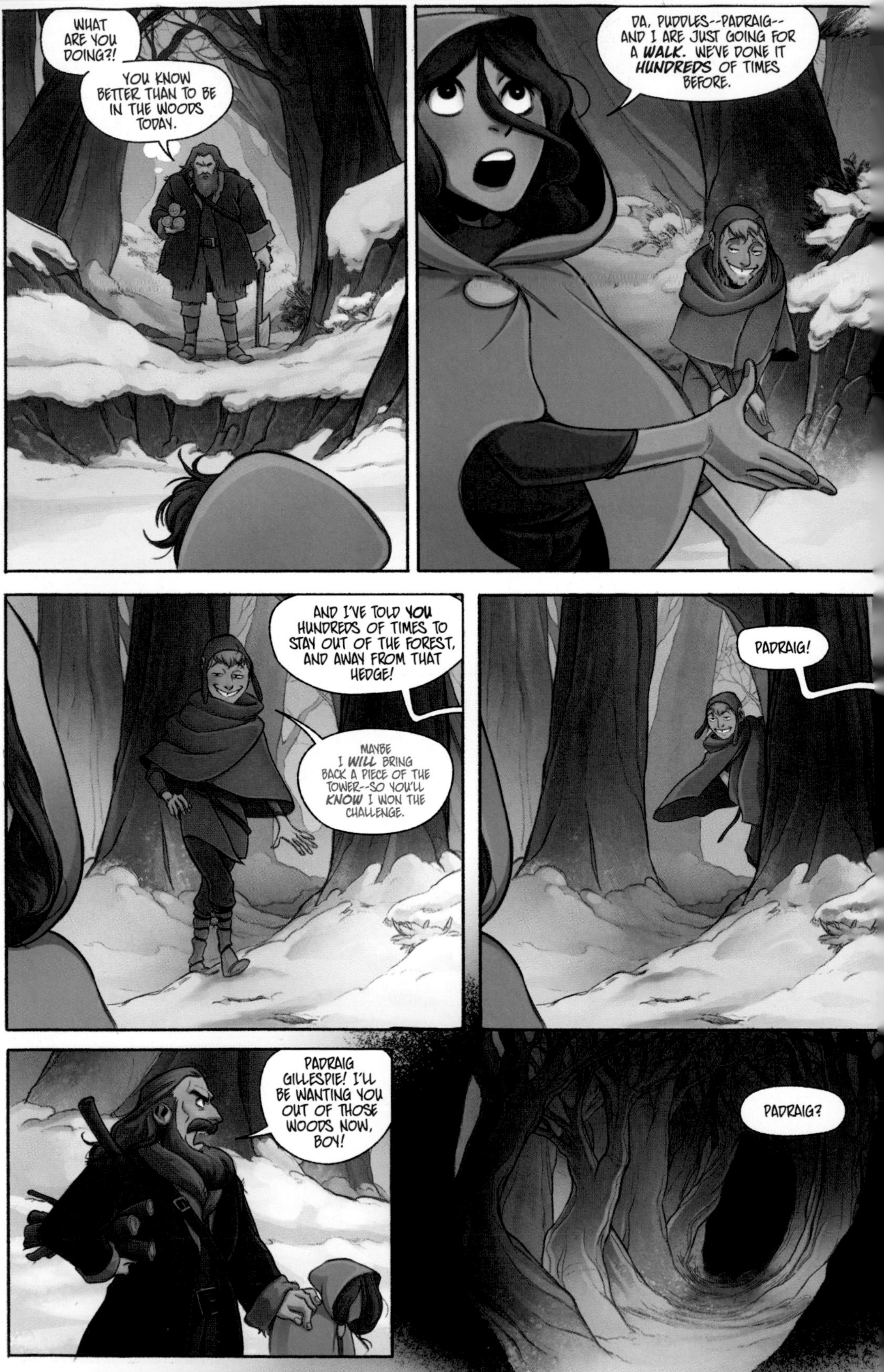
WHAT ARE YOU DOING?!
YOU KNOW BETTER THAN TO BE IN THE WOODS TODAY.
DA, PUDDLES--PADRAIG--AND I ARE JUST GOING FOR A **WALK**. WE'VE DONE IT **HUNDREDS** OF TIMES BEFORE.
AND I'VE TOLD **YOU** HUNDREDS OF TIMES TO STAY OUT OF THE FOREST, AND AWAY FROM THAT HEDGE!
MAYBE I **WILL** BRING BACK A PIECE OF THE TOWER--SO YOU'LL **KNOW** I WON THE CHALLENGE.
PADRAIG!
PADRAIG GILLESPIE! I'LL BE WANTING YOU OUT OF THOSE WOODS NOW, BOY!
PADRAIG?

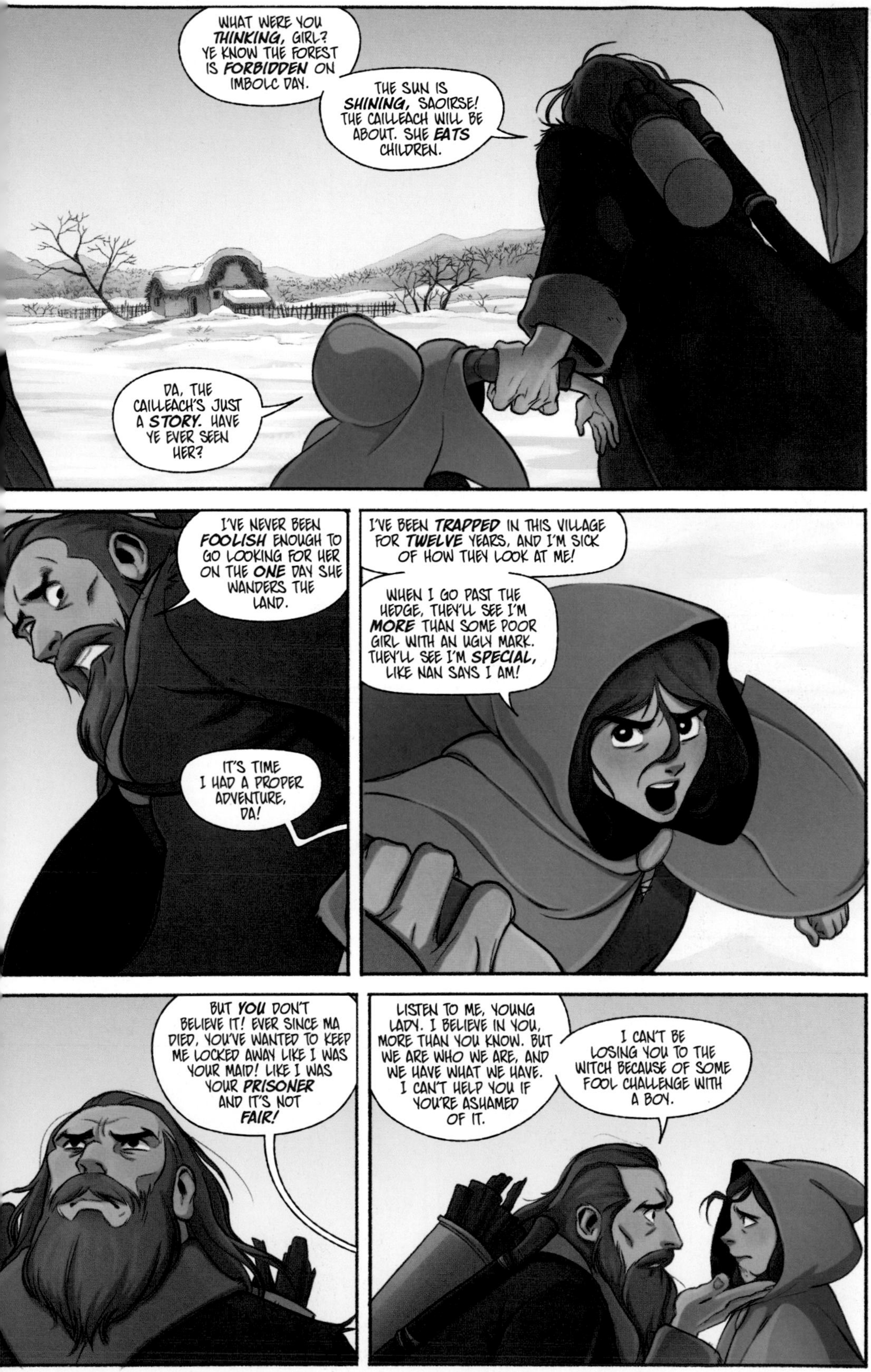
WHAT WERE YOU THINKING, GIRL? YE KNOW THE FOREST IS FORBIDDEN ON IMBOLC DAY.
THE SUN IS SHINING, SAOIRSE! THE CAILLEACH WILL BE ABOUT. SHE EATS CHILDREN.
DA, THE CAILLEACH'S JUST A STORY. HAVE YE EVER SEEN HER?
I'VE NEVER BEEN FOOLISH ENOUGH TO GO LOOKING FOR HER ON THE ONE DAY SHE WANDERS THE LAND.
IT'S TIME I HAD A PROPER ADVENTURE, DA!
I'VE BEEN TRAPPED IN THIS VILLAGE FOR TWELVE YEARS, AND I'M SICK OF HOW THEY LOOK AT ME!
WHEN I GO PAST THE HEDGE, THEY'LL SEE I'M MORE THAN SOME POOR GIRL WITH AN UGLY MARK. THEY'LL SEE I'M SPECIAL, LIKE NAN SAYS I AM!
BUT YOU DON'T BELIEVE IT! EVER SINCE MA DIED, YOU'VE WANTED TO KEEP ME LOCKED AWAY LIKE I WAS YOUR MAID! LIKE I WAS YOUR PRISONER AND IT'S NOT FAIR!
LISTEN TO ME, YOUNG LADY. I BELIEVE IN YOU, MORE THAN YOU KNOW. BUT WE ARE WHO WE ARE, AND WE HAVE WHAT WE HAVE. I CAN'T HELP YOU IF YOU'RE ASHAMED OF IT.
I CAN'T BE LOSING YOU TO THE WITCH BECAUSE OF SOME FOOL CHALLENGE WITH A BOY.

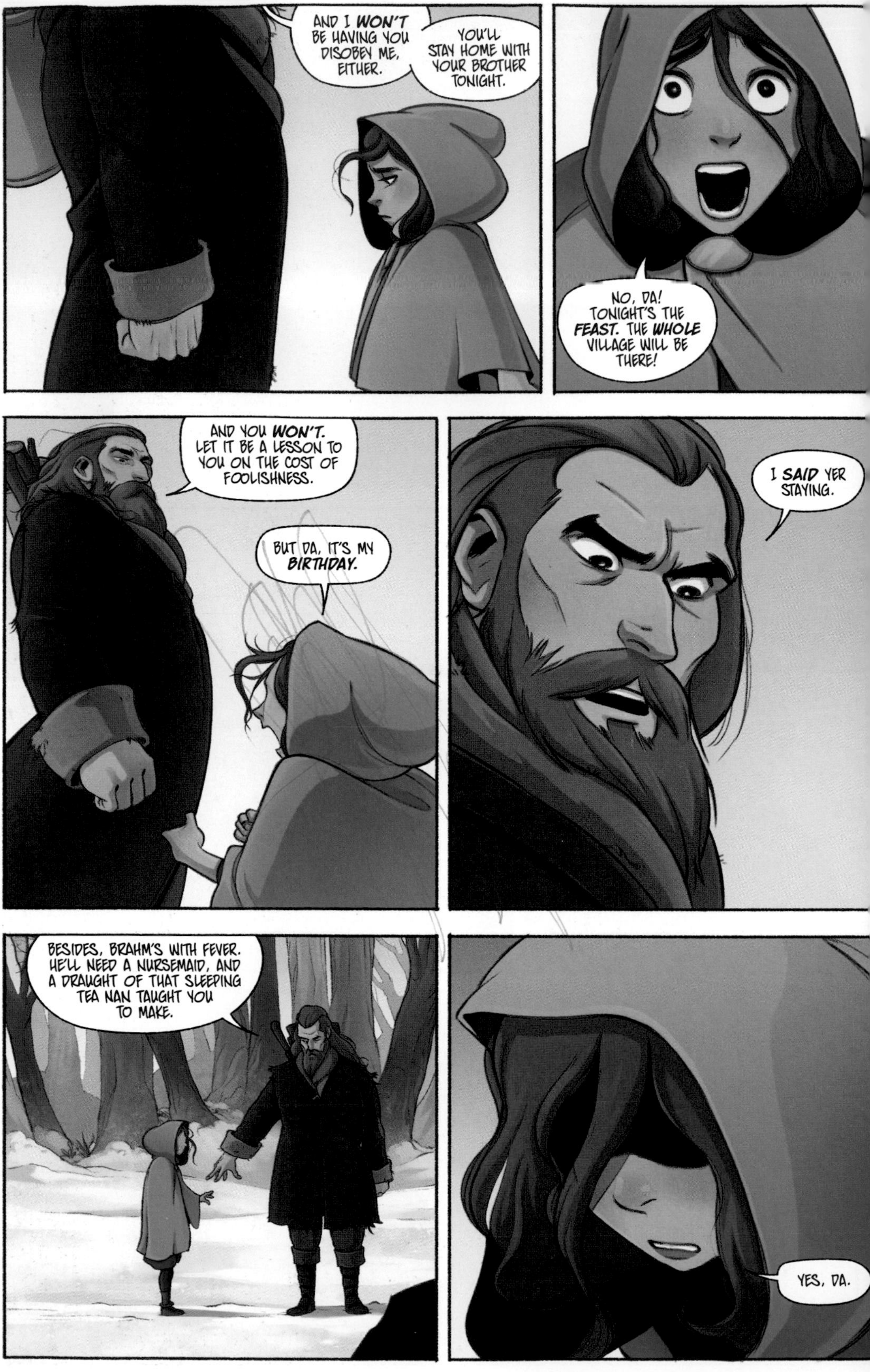

AND I **WON'T** BE HAVING YOU DISOBEY ME, EITHER.
YOU'LL STAY HOME WITH YOUR BROTHER TONIGHT.
NO, DA! TONIGHT'S THE **FEAST**. THE **WHOLE** VILLAGE WILL BE THERE!
AND YOU **WON'T**. LET IT BE A LESSON TO YOU ON THE COST OF FOOLISHNESS.
BUT DA, IT'S MY **BIRTHDAY**.
I **SAID** YER STAYING.
BESIDES, BRAHM'S WITH FEVER. HE'LL NEED A NURSEMAID, AND A DRAUGHT OF THAT SLEEPING TEA NAN TAUGHT YOU TO MAKE.
YES, DA.

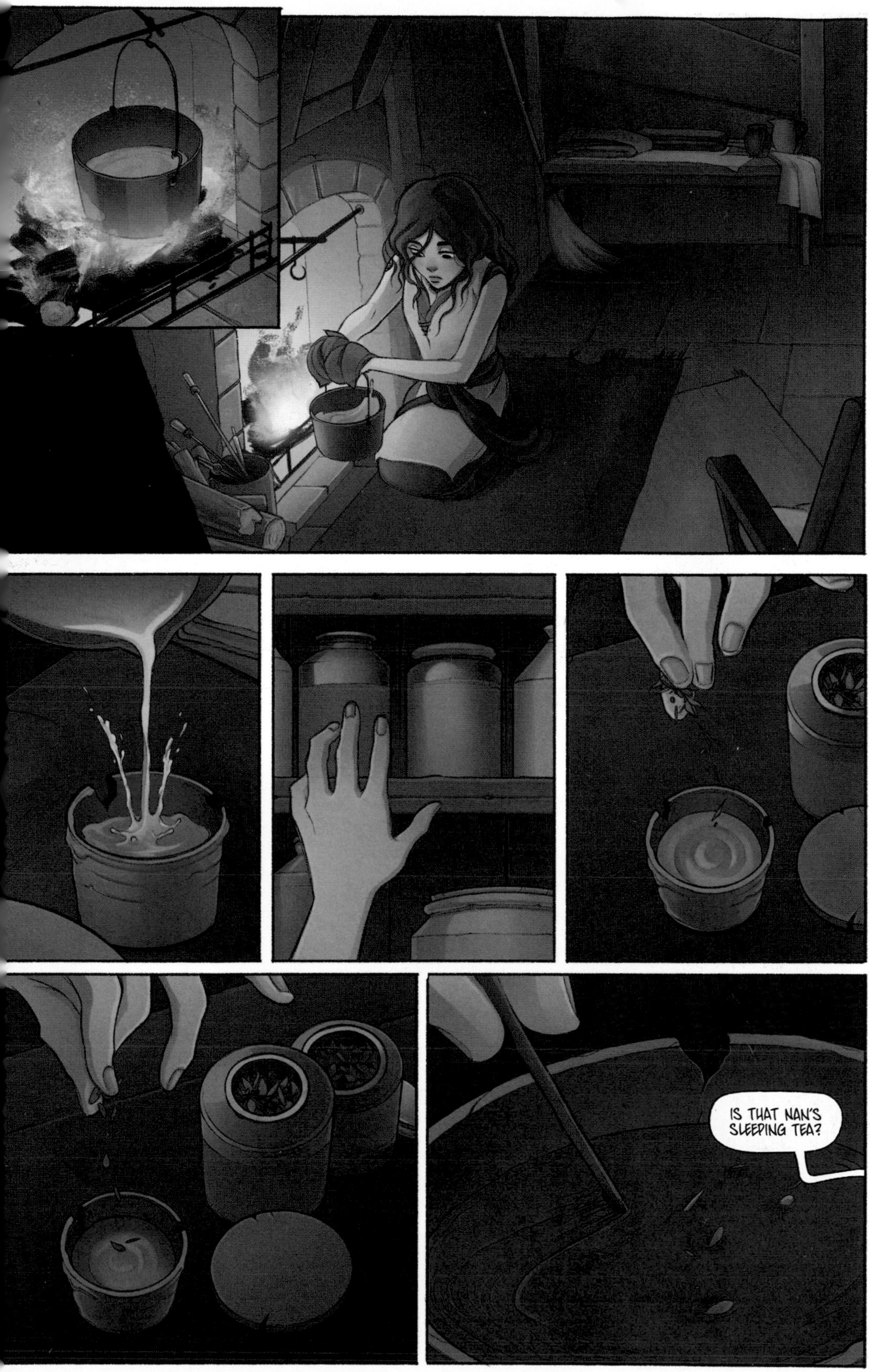
IS THAT NAN'S SLEEPING TEA?

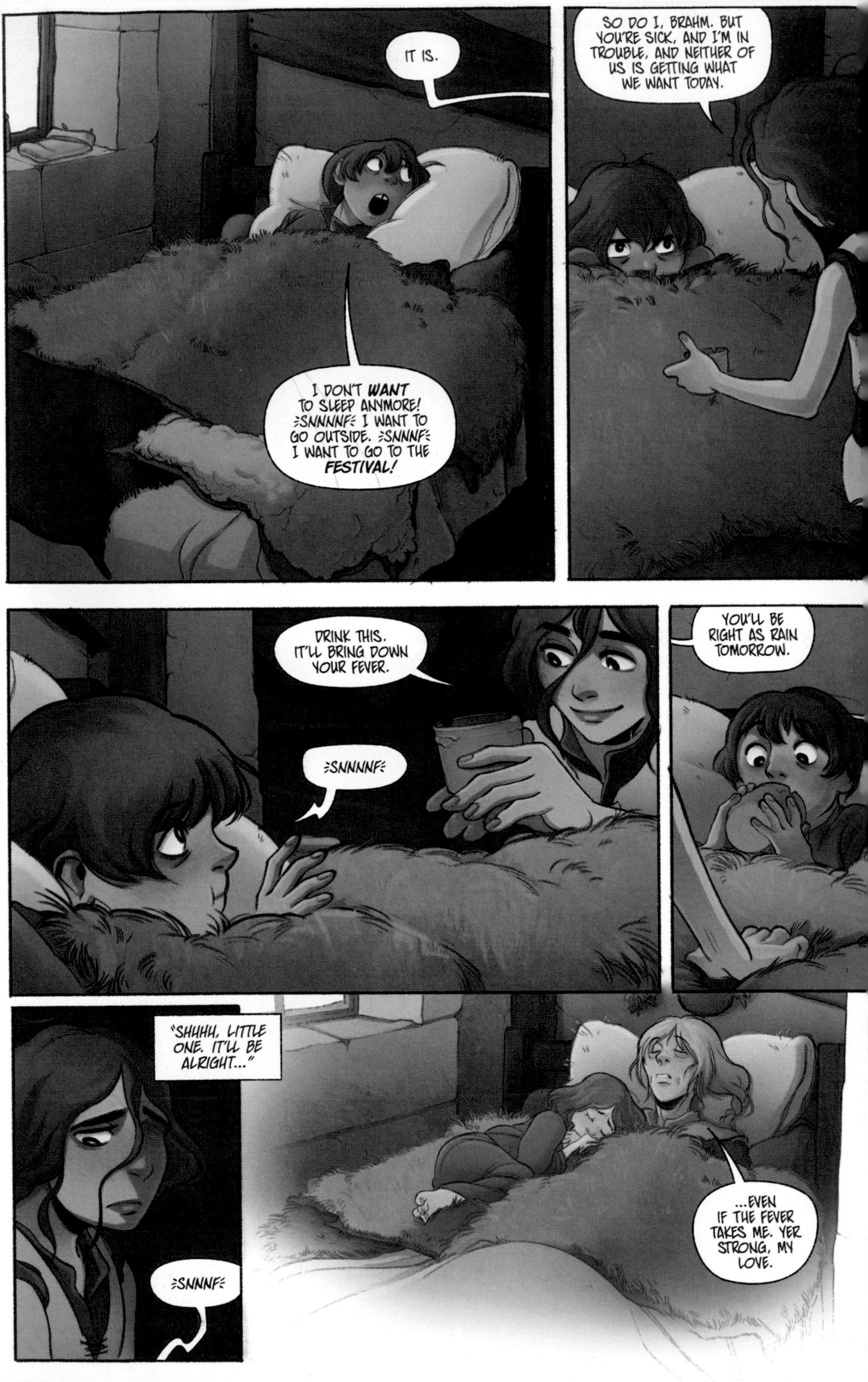
IT IS.
I DON'T **WANT** TO SLEEP ANYMORE! ≡SNNNNF≡ I WANT TO GO OUTSIDE. ≡SNNNF≡ I WANT TO GO TO THE ***FESTIVAL!***
SO DO I, BRAHM. BUT YOU'RE SICK, AND I'M IN TROUBLE, AND NEITHER OF US IS GETTING WHAT WE WANT TODAY.
DRINK THIS. IT'LL BRING DOWN YOUR FEVER.
≡SNNNNF≡
YOU'LL BE RIGHT AS RAIN TOMORROW.
"SHUHH, LITTLE ONE. IT'LL BE ALRIGHT..."
...EVEN IF THE FEVER TAKES ME. YER STRONG, MY LOVE.
≡SNNNF≡

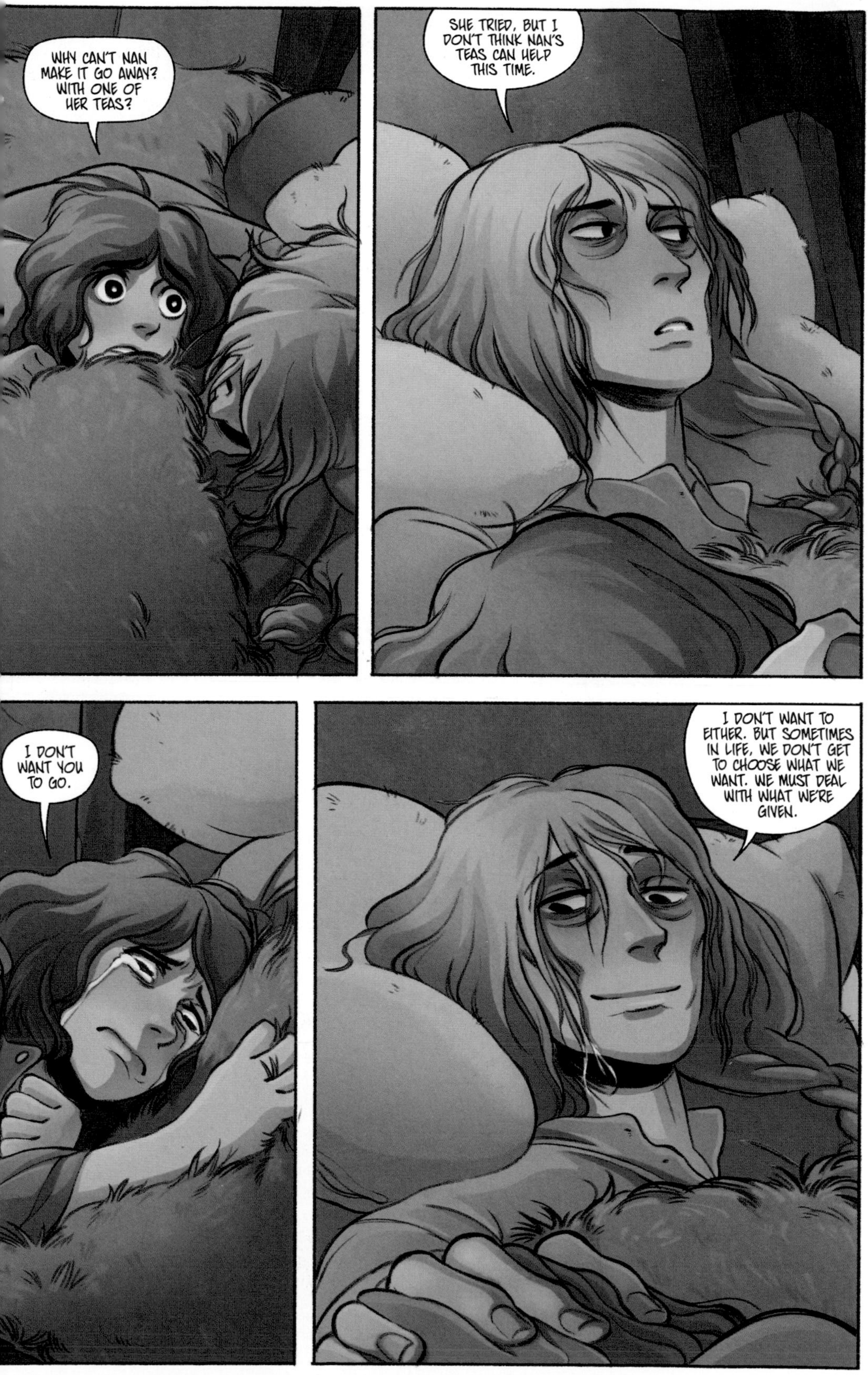
WHY CAN'T NAN MAKE IT GO AWAY? WITH ONE OF HER TEAS?
SHE TRIED, BUT I DON'T THINK NAN'S TEAS CAN HELP THIS TIME.
I DON'T WANT YOU TO GO.
I DON'T WANT TO EITHER. BUT SOMETIMES IN LIFE, WE DON'T GET TO CHOOSE WHAT WE WANT. WE MUST DEAL WITH WHAT WE'RE GIVEN.

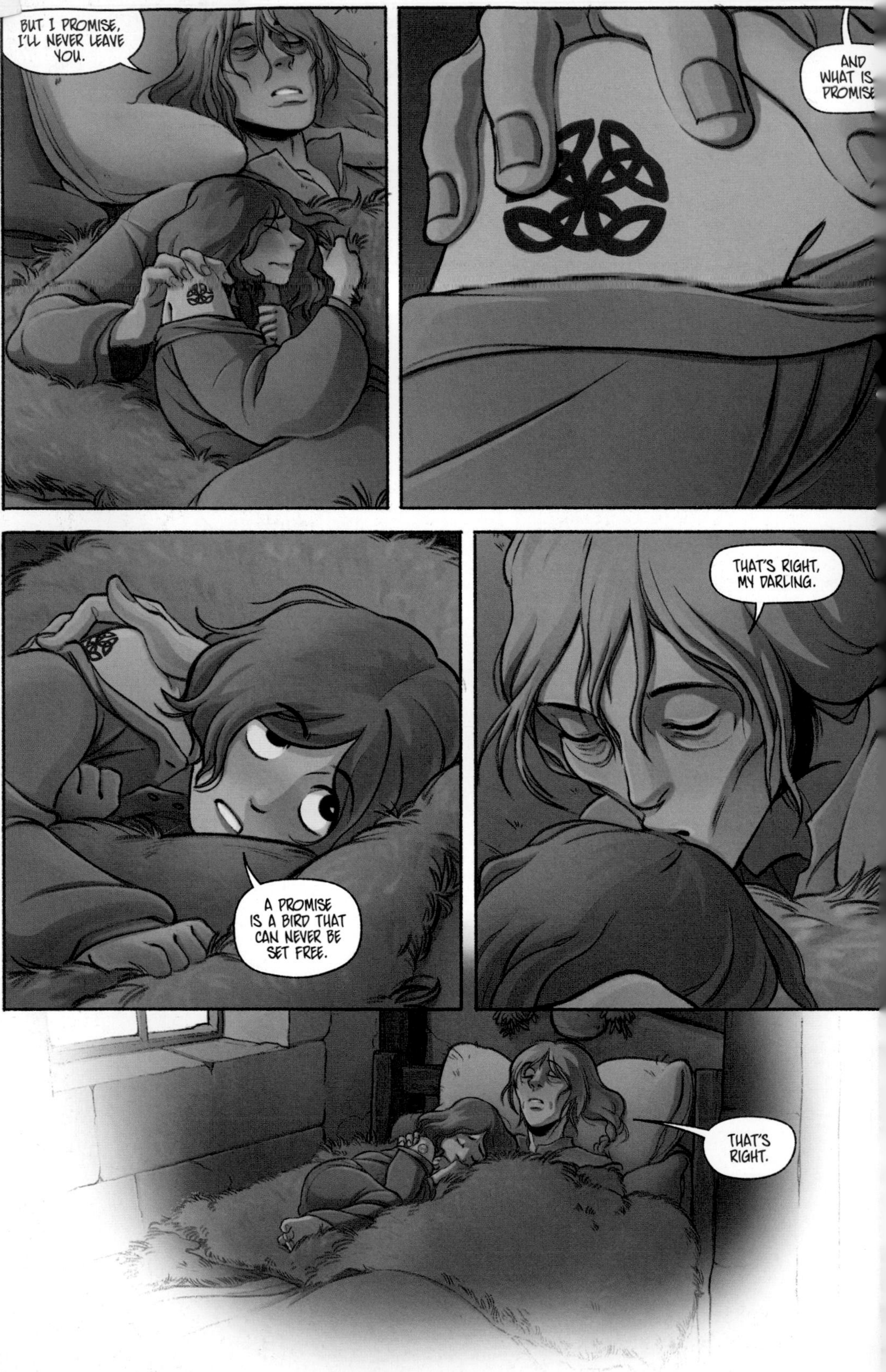
BUT I PROMISE, I'LL NEVER LEAVE YOU.
AND WHAT IS A PROMISE
A PROMISE IS A BIRD THAT CAN NEVER BE SET FREE.
THAT'S RIGHT, MY DARLING.
THAT'S RIGHT.

DISCOVER
EXCITING NEW WORLDS

Just Beyond
R.L. Stine, Kelly & Nichole Matthews
Just Beyond: The Scare School
ISBN: 9781684154166 | $9.99 US
Just Beyond:
The Horror at Happy Landings
ISBN: 9781684155477 | $9.99 US
Just Beyond:
Welcome to Beast Island
ISBN: 978-1-68415-612-2 | $9.99 US

Hex Vet
Sam Davies
Hex Vet: Witches in Training
ISBN: 978-1-68415-288-9 | $8.99 US
Hex Vet: The Flying Surgery
ISBN: 978-1-68415-478-4 | $9.99 US

All My Friends Are Ghosts
S.M. Vidaurri, Hannah Krieger
ISBN: 978-1-68415-498-2 | $14.99 US

Drew and Jot
Art Baltazar
Drew and Jot: Dueling Doodles
ISBN: 9781684154302 | $14.99 US
Drew and Jot: Making a Mark
ISBN: 978-1-68415-598-9 | $14.99 US

Space Bear
Ethan Young
ISBN: 978-1-68415-559-0 | $14.99 US

Wonder Pony
Marie Spénale
ISBN: 978-1-68415-508-8 | $9.99 US

The Last Witch: Fear and Fire
Conor McCreery, V.V. Glass
ISBN: 978-1-68415-621-4 | $14.99 US

Forever Home
Jenna Ayoub
ISBN: 978-1-68415-603-0 | $12.99 US

Jo & Rus
Audra Winslow
ISBN: 978-1-68415-610-8 | $12.99 US

Hotel Dare
Terry Blas, Claudia Aguirre
ISBN: 978-1-68415-205-6 | $9.99 US

AVAILABLE AT YOUR LOCAL
COMICS SHOP AND BOOKSTORE
To find a comics shop in your area, visit www.comicshoplocator.com

WWW.**BOOM-STUDIOS**.COM